ISBN: 978-15336095.

Cover design by Alyson Aversa

Moon Above, Moon Below is a work of historical fiction. Events that are common historical knowledge may not occur at their actual point in time or may not occur at all. Apart from the well-known actual people, events, and locales that figure in the narrative, all names, characters, places, and incidents are products of the author's imagination and are used fictitiously. Any resemblance to current events or locales or to living persons is purely coincidental.

Dedication

To all those GIs (like my father) who served in WW2 not because they wanted to but because they felt it was their duty to do so. They were truly "The Greatest Generation."

Author's Note

This is a work of alternative historical fiction. The story begins by mirroring actual events in France during August 1944 leading up to the imperfect encirclement of German forces in the Falaise Pocket. Taking cues from the personalities of the various Allied commanders, the storyline then diverges from actual history, evolving into a very different telling of that encirclement and its effects on bringing WW2 in Europe to an end.

The designation of military units may be actual or fictitious.

In no way are the fictional accounts intended to denigrate the hardships, suffering, and courage of those who served.

Contact the Author Online:
Email: *wpgrasso@cox.net*

Connect with the Author on Facebook:
https://www.facebook.com/AuthorWilliamPeterGrasso

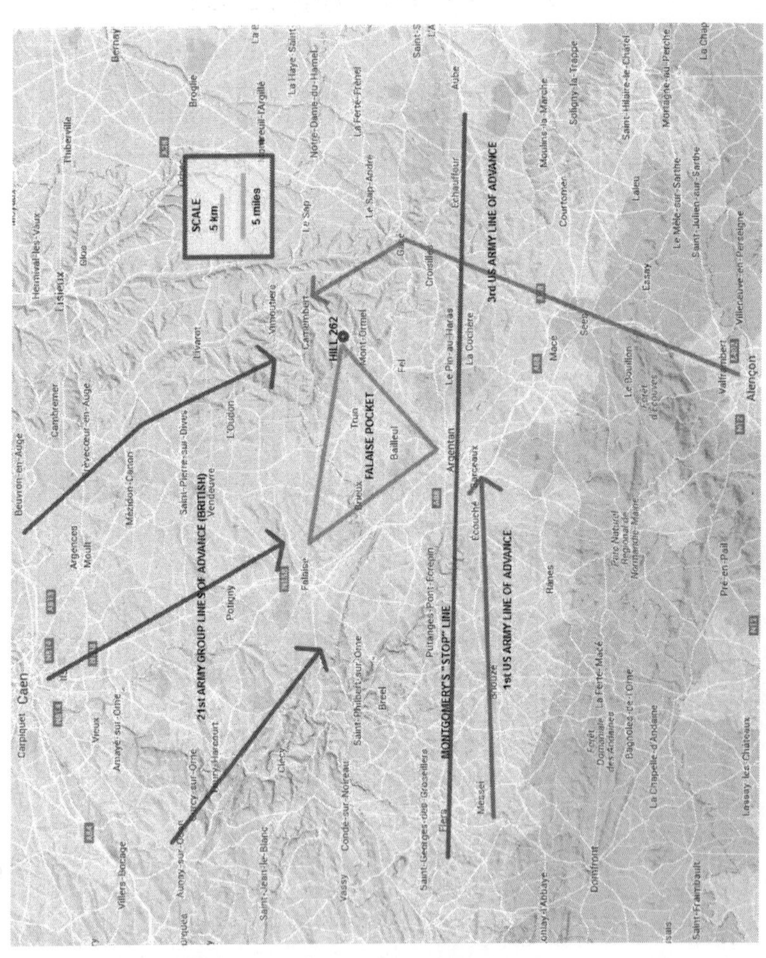

**FALAISE POCKET, FRANCE, 1944:
AN ALTERNATIVE PROPOSITION**

"The remarkable resurgence of the German Army in autumn (1944) owes something forever unquantifiable to the imperfect victory of Falaise."
Raymond Callahan
Historian

Chapter One

Some lucky Kraut might've just taken a piece out of her.

There's a fine stream of oil coming out from under her cowling, painting thin black skeleton fingers up the windshield.

Oil pressure's holding, though...oil temp is okay, too.

No excuse to abort. At least not yet.

Gotta keep my damn eyes outside her cockpit before I hit a tree like Mason did the other day. Wasn't enough left of him after the fireball to put in a bucket, they said. Mostly ashes. Flying this low—and this fast—will get you dead, and real quick. Without any help from the Krauts, either. Just one little slip-up...

God, I don't want to burn.

Shit! Did that oil pressure gauge just spike down? And is that temp starting to creep up?

No. I'm imagining it. They're steady. It's nothing. Probably nothing. Just a little leak. These engines always leak somewhere.

An excited voice in my headphones says, "Blue Leader to Blue Two, we got Krauts in the open on the yellow smoke. My right wing, on three, Tommy." Then he counts one-two-three in less than a heartbeat.

I push her throttle forward and begin a slip to get next to Wilson, my flight leader. The ground—only two hundred feet below—is just a blurry treadmill of green and brown. Everything in France looks like patches of green and brown from up here, even when you're flying much higher and it's not racing past you so quickly.

But I don't see any yellow smoke marker. Just the usual clouds of black and gray boiling up to the late summer sky from the madhouse below. Some of the smoke is tinged red. First time I saw that I thought it was from blood. Turns out it's pulverized brick from buildings blown to smithereens.

No more than a second has ticked off the clock. Wilson's voice screams in my ears, "I got it!" He opens up with his fifty cals, pumping out API rounds—armor piercing incendiaries. Their tracers bounce off the ground only a hundred yards ahead of us like fireworks gone berserk. I still don't see the yellow smoke, so I kick my rudder to align my guns with his and squeeze the trigger.

I stop firing as soon as he does. I have no idea who or what we just shot at.

No time to dwell on it. The town of Mortain looms through the smoke ahead of us—higher than us, actually, perched on the side of that big hill like it is. A north-south line running through the hill marks the operational boundary between us and the RAF. Except for a coastline or river, that damn hill is the clearest boundary marker we've had since coming to France. Clear boundaries between armed forces are real important—matters of life and death, in fact. Especially to pilots. Without them, we might get confused and start bombing the crap out of friendlies all over again. The Brits shrug and call it "own goals." I call it a shitty sports analogy for fratricide. I can only pray I'm not guilty of it. But mostly, it's out of your control. Those imaginary lines the generals draw on maps? Nobody paints them on the ground for the pilots.

We swing our P-47s hard left to get back into the racetrack pattern we've been flying west of Mortain. A whole mess of panzers broke through yesterday north and south of the town—two divisions' worth, the briefing officer said—and started driving west, trying to split the US forces breaking out of Normandy in half. I don't think we're slowing the Krauts down much. Not yet, anyway. But the weather's been good for our flight ops, and whatever Luftwaffe is left in this area has been knocked out of action. In fact, in the month since the squadron moved to France from England, the few German planes I've seen were parked on the ground and centered in someone's gunsight. I wouldn't mind it staying that way for the rest of this damn war.

So around and around we go again in this two-mile-wide circle, praying that making two-fifty down on the deck keeps us untrackable for the Kraut gunners, until we're low on fuel, ammo, or both. I tuck back behind Wilson, covering his tail from the Luftwaffe we've never met in the air...

And I watch my oil pressure gauge start its jittery dance toward zero as the oil temp needle starts its unmistakable climb. She's gonna crap out any second...and I'll be flying something that glides like a brick.

I tell Wilson, "Blue Two to Blue Leader, I'm heading back to A-6. Oil pressure's gone."

I hear the click of his microphone key in my headset, like he's about to reply...and then his plane explodes in a brilliant orange flash, flinging aluminum and steel in every direction like a seven-ton grenade. He manages to get out only one syllable, spoken in the voice of a frightened child: "Ma!"

Chapter Two

As he pulled the rattled Tommy Moon from the cockpit of *Blue Two*, Sergeant Harry McNulty said, "Geez, Lieutenant, not to cast no *dispersions* on your fine piloting abilities or nothing, but couldn't a good Brooklyn *mick* like you keep her in the air another hundred feet?"

Another hundred feet meant the wheels of the dead-stick P-47 would have touched down on the Marston Mat runway instead of the soft muck just short of it. She could've then rolled majestically to an unpowered stop before being quickly towed clear of the other planes stacked up to land.

Struggling to regain his composure, Moon replied, "*Aspersions,* Sergeant. The word you're looking for is *aspersions.*"

"Hey, close enough, Lieutenant. I didn't get to go to no Fordham or nothing like you officer types."

Blue Two's current position was anything but majestic. She was pranged, with the lower lip of her nose cowl buried two feet deep in the mud. That made her tail stick up in the air like a capital "T" canted backward, posing an obstacle to the other planes waiting their turn to land at forward airfield A-6. The runway was short to begin with; having to clear the vertical monument now decorating its threshold made its available length significantly shorter. Already, another aircraft had landed long after clearing *Blue Two's* tail and rolled into the mud at the runway's far end. At least this ship had been going slow enough not to prang when she ran off, but her wheels had promptly sunk to the axles. She'd have to be pulled out, too. "That's all we fucking need," McNulty muttered just loud enough to be sure Moon heard him. "Me and my boys'll be digging these mud ducks out half the night."

He wiped a thin streak of oil off the windshield with his fingertip and studied the dark drop of fluid for a moment. Then he wiped it away in disgust on his coveralls. "So why the hell did you shut her down and go for the dead stick, anyway, Lieutenant?"

"Losing oil pressure. Didn't want to blow the engine."

McNulty exhaled through his mouth, making that motorboat sound with his lips that meant *bullshit.* "We ain't like the Limeys, Lieutenant. We got spare parts up the *recticulum.* Ain't no sweat to swap an engine out."

Tommy Moon was pretty sure the sergeant meant *rectum*, not *recticulum.*

"Looks like she's gonna be out of action a while," McNulty said as he scanned the damage. "What the hell chewed up all these leading edges, Lieutenant? Wings, stabilizers, prop…they're all fucked up."

"Captain Wilson's ship blew up right in front of me. There was shrapnel flying everywhere."

"You think he got out?"

"Not a chance," Moon replied.

"Tough break. So what got him, Lieutenant?"

McNulty's questions were getting painful to answer. Worse, Tommy Moon knew he'd have to answer them all over again at the debrief, and his reply wouldn't be any better than the one he was about to give his crew chief: "Beats the shit out of me."

★★★★

The squadron had long since lost any inclination to grieve its losses. The only ceremony marking today's death was performed by a sergeant as he erased Captain Wilson's name from the squadron readiness board on the operations shack wall, just like he'd done when Mason and the two before him went down. It had been different when they were still flying out of England, with solid roofs over their quarters, real plumbing, a village pub in which to drown their sorrows, and the free time to do so. They'd lost three pilots from the squadron scattered across that year prior to Overlord, each dead man receiving one rousing, beer-soaked eulogy after another from his squadron mates as flirty English barmaids kept the pitchers of warm ale coming and the Yanks spending. Now, living in the desolate mud and olive drab tentage of liberated Normandy, with casualties a regular occurrence, the willingness to mourn had long passed.

"He was a good man," Colonel Pruitt mumbled as Wilson vanished from the board as quickly as he'd vanished from their lives. "Damn shame." Then he turned to Tommy Moon and said, "*Half*, I'm giving you Blue Flight."

Half: Tommy's squadron nickname. Everybody had one that suited him to a tee: *Popeye, Lech, Smiley, Grump,* and so on. So what was more fitting than sticking a very short pilot named Moon with the moniker *Half*? It didn't come as any surprise to him; he'd been called *Half Moon* by friends and foes alike most of his 21 years:

I can thank my big brother Sean for that. It was better than Shrimp, Tiny, or PeeWee, at least.

"Me, sir? Flight leader?" Moon asked. "Aren't Goins and Springer senior to me?"

"Oh, probably," Colonel Pruitt replied, "but I don't give a rat's ass. Let's just say I prefer your…well, let's just say your *objectivity*, Tommy." He lifted a stack of debrief forms from his desk. "According to these, I've got more than enough throttle jockeys who can embellish after-action reports as good as any general. Thirtieth Division is thrilled as hell with the support we're giving them, but like me and you, they're just a little skeptical the Three-Oh-First Fighter Squadron has wiped out a panzer division all by itself, like these bullshit debriefs from your buddies would have you believe." He let the stack of papers drop back to the desk with a loud *plop*, and then added, "If you put any stock in those reports, this war's going to be over in a month or two."

The colonel had a point. Just about every swinging dick in the ETO—from Ike on down—seemed to be convinced they'd be home by Christmas.

"Yeah," Moon replied. "Like they say: *Home alive by Forty-Five.*"

Pruitt swept his hand across the big briefing map decorating another wall. "Look at this...it's Seven August and we're nowhere near Paris yet, after two fucking months on the continent! Hell, Monty and his Brits are still nailing down the area around Caen, and that's ground he said they'd capture by *D plus Three*! Home alive by Forty-Five, my sweet ass."

"I'll settle for the *home alive* part, sir."

"Wouldn't we all, Tommy. But can you believe we just made that strutting Limey fraud *Allied Ground*

Commander? Is Ike fighting a war here, or running for Parliament?"

"You've heard the saying *war is just politics by other means,* sir?"

"Yeah. Didn't some Kraut say that?"

The squadron maintenance officer, a major, entered the shack and went straight for the status board. Without saying a word, he took a red grease pencil and drew a long line through the data for Tommy Moon's aircraft. At the end of the line, he wrote the letters *UTR*, which stood for *uneconomical to repair.* The colonel and Moon watched with the same dispassionate emptiness as when Wilson's name had been erased.

"Shit," the colonel whispered. "Scratch another *jug*."

Jug: common nickname for the P-47 fighter. Officially known as the Thunderbolt, it was heavy, but powerful and fast, with a big ordnance-carrying capability. Rumor had it that its thick, oval fuselage cross-section once reminded someone of a jug, and the name stuck.

"What the hell happened, sir?" Moon asked the major. "We thought it was just some sheet metal damage and a new prop."

"Negative, Lieutenant. McNulty found a cracked wing spar. It's got what sure looks like a supercharger vane jammed into it. Nothing we can do. You're lucky it didn't fold up on you."

A supercharger vane, Tommy thought. *Got to be Wilson's.*

Then the major reassured Colonel Pruitt, "We're getting some replacement *jugs* from the depot in a couple of days, sir, so we'll be back to full strength before you know it."

"Well, *Flight Leader* Moon," Pruitt said, "looks like you've got a couple of days to relax and get yourself organized."

Chapter Three

12TH ARMY GROUP COMMUNIQUE

FROM: BRADLEY–COMMANDER, 12TH ARMY GROUP	DATE-TIME OF ORIGIN 8 AUG 44 1800 HRS

TO:
EISENHOWER–SUPREME COMMANDER, SHAEF

COPY (FOR INFO):
HODGES–1ST ARMY; PATTON–3RD ARMY; QUESADA–IX TACTICAL AIR COMMAND; WEYLAND–XIX TACTICAL AIR COMMAND

COUNTERATTACK AT MORTAIN BY ELEMENTS OF AT LEAST 3 PANZER DIVISIONS (2ND PANZER, 1ST SS PANZER, 2ND SS PANZER) HAS BEEN THROWN BACK AFTER PENETRATIONS OF NO MORE THAN TWO MILES. SURVIVING PANZER FORCES ARE IN HEADLONG RETREAT EAST OF MORTAIN AND BEING PURSUED BY 30TH DIVISION. TACTICAL AIR SUPPORT EXTREMELY EFFECTIVE.

POSSIBILITY EXISTS TO TRAP ALL RETREATING REMNANTS OF GERMAN 7TH ARMY, PROBABLY IN THE TRIANGLE FORMED BY FLERS TO WEST, FALAISE TO NORTH, AND ARGENTAN TO SOUTH, PROVIDED MONTY CAN GET OFF HIS "CAEN" AND CLOSE NORTHERN JAW OF THE TRAP.

ANY "ENCOURAGEMENT" YOU CAN OFFER OUR ALLIED GROUND COMMANDER TO GET MOVING ON THE DOUBLE IS GREATLY APPRECIATED.

SIGNED,
BRADLEY

Chapter Four

Tommy Moon tossed his AWOL bag into the back of the jeep and then climbed into the passenger's seat. The driver, another flyer from the 301st named Hank Kirkland, lounged against a fender nursing a cigarette and the last of the breakfast coffee in his canteen cup. He seemed in no hurry to begin the journey.

"C'mon, Lieutenant," Moon called to Kirkland, "we've got about forty miles of crummy French roads ahead of us."

"I ain't in no hurry, Half. You may be going on a social call but I'm going on business. Shitty business at that."

"Hey, that'll teach you to get yourself grounded with an ear infection. Might as well make yourself useful in the meantime."

"Being an ASO with Fourth Armored was not the *being useful* I had in mind, Tommy. Even if General Quesada thinks putting pilots with the tankers to coordinate air support is the greatest thing since flush toilets. You'll see. You'll get your turn."

Probably not, Tommy told himself. *Not as long as I'm a flight leader.*

"And you'd be a natural, too, Tommy, with a brother in Fourth Armored and everything. He know you're burning leave time just to come visit?"

"Hell, no, Hank. I'm not even sure where his unit is, exactly. I'm taking a shot in the dark here." He took a last look at the map board he'd carefully marked up at the intel section and then tucked it under his seat. "At least the weather's good. We should make it to Mayenne by noon."

"You sure of the route? I don't want to take a wrong turn and drive right into Kraut country."

"Knock it off, Hank. I've seen most of these roads from the air already. So have you. We'll be miles behind the front lines the whole way."

"We'd better be, that's all I can say."

Halfway to Mayenne, the town of Fougères seemed as good a place as any for Moon and Kirkland to stop and stretch their legs. They weren't making forward progress at the moment, anyway. A herd of cattle was being slowly marched through the town, completely blocking their path.

Three main highways intersected in Fougères, providing easy identification for the American bombardiers who had plastered the town in the days before Overlord. The bombing had taken a frightful toll of its civilians as well as its German garrison. The rubble of shattered stone buildings—many of them centuries old—was everywhere. It was much too soon for the citizens of the town to forget their hundreds of dead and injured at the hands of American pilots. The eyes of the bartender and his few morning patrons fell on the shiny wings Moon and Kirkland wore on their chests, symbols that seemed badges of guilt to the Frenchmen. They watched in hostile silence as the Americans took a big round table by the door.

A waitress approached, a haggard, middle-aged woman whose face seemed incapable of smiling. She pointed to the three empty chairs around the table and said, "*Pour le cinq, messieurs.*"

"What the hell did she say?" Kirkland asked.

"She says the table's for five, Hank."

"So what? There's nobody in this dump. What's wrong with these fucking frogs?"

"Shut the hell up, Hank. Let me handle this."

In the schoolboy French the nuns had taught him back in Brooklyn, Tommy began to apologize for their *faux pas*. He was halfway through asking where it would be all right for them to sit when the roar of trucks spilled through the open door of the cafe, growing louder until it was clear they had no intention of stopping for the bovine parade still blocking the road. For a sickening second, the *thrum* of motors blended with the soft *thuds* and the shrieks of animals being mowed down. Those inside the cafe watched in shock as the American deuce-and-a-halves lurched over the thrashing bodies of their mortally wounded victims.

Not a truck in the long column bothered to slow down. As the last one raced by, the waitress split the air of silent outrage by answering Tommy's unfinished question:

"S'asseoir dans le caniveau avec les vaches, meurtriers."

Sit in the gutter with the cows, murderers.

As they drove out of Fougères, Hank Kirkland said, "I tell you, Half, you *parlez vous* that stuff pretty good. That was some hot shit back in town, wasn't it?"

"I don't think the frogs thought so."

"Ahh, fuck 'em. They oughta be kissing our asses. That clown hopping around like some looney in the middle of the street…what the hell was he saying to you, anyway?"

"He wanted to know who was going to pay for all his dead cows."

Expelling a burst of laughter, Kirkland said, "Did you tell him to send the bill to Hitler?"

"No, I told him to send it to General Patton. You did notice those were Third Army trucks, didn't you?"

Kirkland shrugged. He couldn't have cared less.

They drove on through the French countryside, down narrow highways lined and crowned with single columns of tall trees on either side. "It's like driving through a damn tunnel," Kirkland said. Beyond the trees were miles of open, gently rolling terrain. "I'd love to catch me a bunch of Krauts out there in the open," he added. "They could run but they couldn't hide." He weaved the jeep left and right, mimicking the s-turns of a strafing aircraft as he bellowed, with great glee, "*BA-DA-DA-DA-DA*."

"Is that supposed to be your fifty cals, Hank?" Tommy Moon asked.

"Of course."

"Pretty crappy imitation, if you ask me."

Tommy peered ahead into the distance, then rechecked his map.

"Something wrong?" Kirkland asked.

"Yeah, slow down. We're coming to a fork in the road…and it's not showing up here."

The jeep rolled to a stop. Unlike most road junctions, there were no signs pointing toward one town or another. Both paths looked like they'd seen lots of military traffic;

the distinctive marks of tank tracks and tactical tires were sketched in mud on their pavement and imprinted into the soft shoulders.

Kirkland said, "I don't like the north fork."

"Why?"

"Because north gets us closer to the Krauts."

Tommy studied the map for a few moments. It wasn't helping him:

It's all just lines, and none of them mean shit, as usual.

"Yeah, you're right, Hank," Tommy said. "Let's take the south fork. Worst we can do is end up in Laval instead of Mayenne, I think...and that's even deeper into friendly territory." He almost added, *or at least it was earlier this morning.*

As Kirkland guided the jeep to the south fork, he laughed and said, "Ain't this hot shit? Put two flyboys in a jeep instead of a plane and watch them fuck up a free lunch."

Chapter Five

The tall trees lining the south fork road abruptly ended. After less than a mile, the smooth pavement ended, too, devolving into a rutted and muddy dirt track. Kirkland slid the jeep to a stop in the slippery muck. Slamming the gearshift into reverse, he said, "No wonder it wasn't on the map…it doesn't fucking go anywhere."

"Yeah," Tommy Moon replied, "and that isn't our only problem." He tapped the engine's temperature gauge. The needle quivered each time his finger struck the glass but didn't budge from the lower end of the warning range. "I think she wants to boil over. Don't tell me you didn't check the Prestone in this thing when you signed her out?"

Kirkland shook his head.

"Shut her down for a minute, Hank. Let her cool off…and get our bearings in the meantime."

He watched as Kirkland switched off the ignition, waiting to hear nothing but pastoral silence. But it never came. There was still the steady rumble of idling engines—lower-pitched than the sound of the jeep's motor and farther away—but with a menacing, bassy timbre their light vehicle could never project.

Oh, shit…

Those engines were revving now as two German tanks emerged from the woods a hundred yards ahead. Overheating radiator or not, the jeep was cranked, thrown into reverse, and racing backward up the muddy trail.

His head and torso twisted to the rear, Kirkland struggled to keep the skidding wheels on track. His frightened voice an octave higher than usual, he said, "We're gonna have to turn around at some damn point."

"Not in this mud," Tommy replied. "Don't want to get stuck. Wait for the pavement."

"What kind of tanks are those, Tommy? Panthers? Tigers?"

"Nah, they're smaller ones. Panzer Fours, I think."

"*Small,* my ass! They still got guns, don't they?"

A burst of machine gun fire from the lead tank answered Kirkland's question. They couldn't tell where the rounds landed. All they knew was they hadn't hit the jeep.

Moon said, "As long as they're moving, they'll never get a good bead on us, bouncing along like they are."

"But what if they stop to aim?"

"That'll be a different story, Hank."

"Are they gaining on us?"

"No. Just drive, dammit."

They'd almost doubled the distance between them and the tanks when the jeep's wheels hugged pavement again. Tommy got a good grip on his seat and said, "OKAY, HANK, SWAP ENDS NOW."

Kirkland performed the feat far more skillfully than Tommy could have imagined. With a deft jerk of the steering wheel while applying the hand brake, the jeep's rear wheels locked and it snapped around in a vehicular pirouette. Now facing away from the tanks, he slammed the accelerator to the floor.

But when he glanced to the passenger's seat, it was empty. Tommy Moon was gone.

Kirkland didn't slow down. The jeep traveled a few hundred yards before he looked back.

There was no sign of Moon, not on the road, not in the tall grass on either side. The lead tank had stopped, its main gun being tweaked into position for a shot at the jeep.

Shit! Gotta get away!

He pushed harder on the accelerator, but it was already firmly on the floor.

Daring one last look back, he saw the lead tank suddenly plunge off the road as a P-47 streaked low over it, its belly nearly scraping the turret's protruding antennas.

The American plane would be on him in a heartbeat. The muzzle flashes from its guns made Kirkland shriek, "DON'T SHOOT AT ME, YOU STUPID SON OF A—".

Like a band saw, .50-caliber rounds ripped the jeep open right down the middle, bathing Hank Kirkland's legs in metal splinters and gasoline from the ruptured tank below his seat. The armor-piercing incendiaries promptly ignited the fuel.

A human torch from the waist down, Kirkland tumbled from the mangled jeep as it juddered to a stop. He never noticed the three other P-47s whizzing by split-seconds later or the second German tank off the road, her crew bailing out and running to get as far from their tank as they could. He was too busy struggling to shed his burning trousers. All he could think of was:

Ain't this some shit? We're all worried about burning in our cockpits...but I get burned up in a Willys jeep.

He got the trousers off in seconds that seemed like hours. Exhausted, he lay in the waist-high grass and examined his legs. Large, crinkled patches of crisp black skin were charred like the pages of a book thrown into a fire, their curled-up edges revealing the raw redness below. The pain he'd felt when wearing the flaming trousers was gone. He lied to himself that that was a good thing. The only sound was the snarl of the loitering P-47s.

Suddenly, the grass next to him ruffled as if being threshed by invisible hands—and Tommy Moon appeared, crawling on all fours.

"Shit, Tommy, I thought you were some fucking Kraut."

"I could've been. Those tankers are running around here somewhere. I guess it really is true some of them bail out at the first sign of planes. Where's your forty-five?"

Kirkland gave a weary shrug. "Maybe it's still on the road somewhere."

"Here, take mine," Moon replied, pressing the pistol into the man's hand. "C'mon, we're gonna get out of here."

"I don't think I can walk, Tommy. Can't feel my legs."

He began to lift Kirkland across his shoulders—a fireman's carry.

"Wait, Tommy…you ain't big enough to—"

But Moon was already walking, struggling to bear his wounded comrade. "Just shut up and cover our asses, Hank."

Not far down the road, they came to their wrecked and smoldering jeep. Tommy stopped to take a good look. The seat he'd been thrown from was a bullet-riddled tangle of twisted metal.

Moon said, "You know, Hank, when that fancy driving of yours sent me flying—and then you didn't come back for me—I was cursing you and your whole family." He glanced back at the carcass of the jeep. "But now, I'm thinking maybe you did me a real big favor."

Tommy Moon was exhausted. He'd carried Kirkland as far as he could, but they still hadn't made it back to the fork in the road. At least they'd reached the welcome safety of some tree cover. Tommy laid his wounded partner down and said, "I'm going back to that main drag and flag down some help. You wait here. I'll be back for you."

Kirkland nodded and tried to hand the .45 to Tommy.

"No, Hank. You keep it."

As Moon set out again, Kirkland called after him, "You are coming back, ain't you, Tommy? I mean, I wouldn't blame you if..."

"Shut up, you idiot, and try to stay out of trouble."

Once Tommy made it back to the fork, it was just a matter of minutes before a platoon of American tanks, four in all, rumbled up. The lieutenant in the lead tank took one look at the wings on Moon's chest and asked, "You get shot down or something?"

Tommy told his story, finishing with, "Those Kraut tanks—I thought around here was supposed to be way behind the lines."

"Yeah, it's supposed to be," the tank lieutenant replied, "but I guess nobody told the Krauts. We've been mopping up infiltrations for days. Hop on—let's go get your burned-up buddy."

Chapter Six

21st ARMY GROUP COMMUNIQUE

FROM: MONTGOMERY—COMMANDER, ALLIED GROUND FORCES	DATE-TIME OF ORIGIN 9 AUG 44 1200 HRS

TO:
SHAEF—EISENHOWER

COPY (FOR INFO):
BRADLEY—COMMANDER, 12TH ARMY GROUP

IN RECEIPT OF YOUR MESSAGE URGING RAPID ACTION RE ENCIRCLEMENT OF GERMAN 7TH ARMY. BE ADVISED THIS COMMAND HAS BEEN AWARE OF THIS POSSIBILITY FOR SOME TIME AND IS MOVING TOWARDS ITS EXECUTION WITH ALL DUE CAUTION. HASTE IS A POOR SUBSTITUTE FOR PROPER TACTICAL PLANNING AND PREPARATION.

SIGNED,
MONTGOMERY

Chapter Seven

The doctor took one look at Hank Kirkland's legs and announced, "Lieutenant, you're a lucky man. Your war is over." For just a brief moment, the months of treatment ahead—complete with frequent, painful debridements, skin grafts, the almost inevitable infections, even the possibility of amputation—seemed like a gift:

My war is over. And I've still got my pecker, at least.

Tommy Moon said goodbye as he was being wheeled off to burn ward quarantine. As they shook hands, Kirkland, his voice weak but earnest, said, "You won't tell anyone what I did, will you?"

Tommy smiled. "Fog of war, pal. Who the hell remembers?"

★★★★

Two hours of hitchhiking and a few misdirections later, Tommy found his brother's outfit: 37th Tank Battalion, 4th Armored Division. As he walked into the battalion CP tent, the crusty master sergeant behind the front desk gave this diminutive flyboy lieutenant a disapproving once-over as he asked, "You lost, Lieutenant?"

"No, I think this might be the place, Sergeant. I'm looking for a guy named Sean Moon."

"*Crunch?* What do you want with ol' Crunch, Lieutenant? You didn't come to arrest him or nothing, did you?"

"No, just visiting. He's my brother. Where can I find him?"

"Let us save you some time. Private Odom here's gotta run some errands for me down that way. He'll take you to him."

In the jeep with Odom at the wheel, Tommy asked, "Private, do you know how Sergeant Moon got the nickname *Crunch*?"

"Yessir, everybody knows that. That's the sound a *Jerry* makes when you run over him with a tank. I heard tell that Sergeant Moon says when you're up close, it's easier than shooting them, and it saves ammo, too."

Odom turned the jeep down a trail of fresh tank tracks cut through a thick stand of trees. Tommy could see the outlines of a dozen or more Shermans parked under camouflage nets, swarmed by crewmen and mechanics servicing them. He saw Sean, too, berating a team of men slathered in grease and grime, struggling to shove a very long ramming staff down the tube of a tank's main gun. It had been seven months since he laid eyes on his big brother back in England. In that time, Sean Moon seemed to have aged 10 years.

"End of the line, sir," Odom said as he braked to a stop.

Sean did an angry double take as he saw his brother walking toward him. "Holy shit, Half. Just what the fuck are you doing out here?"

"You'd better snap to and salute me, Sergeant," Tommy said, a big grin on his face. "You don't want your men to think you're an insubordinate son of a bitch, do you?"

Sean was grinning now, too. "I *am* an insubordinate son of a bitch, you little jerk-off. Now get over here." He wrapped his little brother in a bear hug that left no doubt he really was happy to see him. With an arm still around Tommy's shoulder, he pulled him toward his tank and the team of men working on it.

"All you assholes, listen up," Sean thundered. "This here's my little brother Tommy. He's a big deal fucking pilot, one of them *Thunderbolt* jockeys who keep our asses covered. Don't none of you ever forget he's an officer and all that shit. If you don't respect him all proper-like, you won't have to worry about no court-martial because you'll be answering to me. Is that fucking clear?"

Eight heads nodded and mumbled acceptance.

"Outstanding," Sean said. "Now get your sorry asses back to work. We ain't gonna be pullin' our puds in bivouac forever."

The brothers Moon settled on a stack of wooden ammo boxes. Sean lit up a cigarette from a K ration pack, then offered one to Tommy. He waved it off.

"You still don't smoke, you little pussy?"

"Nope. And I can't believe you guys smoke around ammo."

"It's in a fucking box, Half. It ain't gonna go off." He pointed to the Sherman, adding, "Besides, we fight inside those *Zippo lighters* over there. You don't have to smoke to go up in flames in one of them." He pushed the sleeve of his coveralls up to reveal the mottled, waxy skin of the burn that covered his arm, like lava that had cooled and hardened.

"Remember? My souvenir of North Africa," Sean said.

"Yeah," Tommy replied, a sickening foreboding coming over him. He'd seen that burn before, when they were both in England in the months before Overlord.

"You still worry about fire in that airplane of yours? You know, burning up with nowhere to run?"

"Every damn day, Sean."

"Well, that makes two of us, brother. You in that plane, me in that tank. But enough of this *sad sack* bullshit. What do you hear from Mom?"

The tank battalion's field kitchen was set up in an old barn. As they lined up for the supper meal, Tommy was sure there wouldn't be enough food for some 200 tired, filthy, and hungry men. When he saw the miniscule portions the cook doled into his mess kit, however, he realized how they were making ends meet. He'd never thought his fighter squadron was being overfed, especially not since they'd repositioned to France. But seeing the tankers' rations, he realized he and the other pilots were eating like kings.

Most of all, he could see the lack of calories in his brother's face. Sean, at six feet, was a good seven inches taller than him, with a sturdy, broad-shouldered frame and a ruddy complexion in better times. Now, that face had gone sallow and gaunt, the body wiry but somehow still strong, his temperament still blustering and commanding. Though the close-cropped GI haircut tried to hide it, Tommy was sure he could see traces of gray in the sandy hair around the temples…

And Sean's only twenty-four.

Twenty-four. An old man in *this man's army.*

They picked the base of a tree outside the barn to eat their supper, close enough to the others so Sean could keep an eye on his crew but far enough so they could talk in private. "My gunner over there—Fabiano—he's been getting into some pretty bad fights lately," Sean said. "Now, between you, me, and the lamp post, that *guinea's* off his fucking rocker. But he's a pretty cool customer when the shit's flying. Don't want to lose him."

Tommy replied, "So you're sticking up for him like you stuck up for me all those years?"

"Apples and oranges, Half. You wasn't no fighter. Your little ass needed protection from the goons. He, on the other hand, needs protection so he don't go berserk and kill someone. You get the firing squad for that. There's plenty of ways to die around here without a bunch of brass hats canceling your ticket."

A jeep pulled into the mess area. A major in spotless battle dress jumped out and yelled, "LIEUTENANT MOON. I'M LOOKING FOR A LIEUTENANT MOON."

"Ahh, shit," Sean mumbled. "This can't be good."

"OVER HERE, SIR," Tommy replied. He started toward the jeep but Sean stopped him. "Whoa…go slow, Half. You're gonna take it in the shorts, for sure. He's from Division. How the hell they even know you're here?"

Tommy pulled away. "Relax, *Crunch.* I can take care of myself now."

"Where the fuck you hear that nickname?"

"It seems like everyone knows it. Apparently, you're some kind of legend, Sean."

"Do me a fucking favor, Half. Don't call me that, okay?"

Tommy started to salute but the major batted his hand down. "You trying to get me killed, Moon? This isn't the goddamn Air Force. No saluting outdoors. There could be snipers everywhere."

You could've fooled me, Tommy thought as he looked at all the men sprawled around the field kitchen, relaxed and enjoying their chow.

"No, sir. Sorry, sir."

"Ninth Air Force has—"

The major had stopped in mid-sentence to glare at something over Tommy's shoulder. "Can I help you, Sergeant?" he asked.

"No, sir," Sean replied. "It's just that the lieutenant here is my kid brother. I wanted to hear firsthand what kind of shit he's getting into."

"Hmm. Brother, eh? Well, suit yourself, Sergeant. What I'm going to say isn't exactly *top secret*."

The major turned back to Tommy. "Here's the deal, Moon. You've been assigned as an air support officer to Fourth Armored. The G3 is putting you here with the Thirty-Seventh."

"But I'm on a three-day leave, sir. I don't have any of my field gear."

"Well, I'm here to tell you your leave's been canceled, Lieutenant. I'm sure Battalion can fix you up with whatever you need."

Stepping around Tommy to get face to face with the major, Sean said, "Hang on a minute, sir. Ain't it a rule brothers can't be in the same unit in a combat zone?"

"Sean," Tommy said, "knock it off, will you? That's not—"

"No, really. Ain't it a rule?"

The major shook his head. "You're both volunteers, right?"

Tommy and Sean nodded in unison.

"Then none of that crap applies," the major said. "Lieutenant Moon, report to the battalion CP in three-zero minutes."

As the major drove off, Tommy told himself, *You knew this was coming, you idiot...with Kirkland out of action and all. But I needed to see my brother. And I think he needed to see me.*

Chapter Eight

ALLIED GROUND FORCES DIRECTIVE

FROM:	DATE-TIME OF ORIGIN
MONTGOMERY—COMMANDER, ALLIED GROUND FORCES	9 AUG 44 1700 HRS

TO:
BRADLEY—COMMANDER, 12TH ARMY GROUP

COPY (FOR INFO):
SHAEF (EISENHOWER); HODGES—US 1ST ARMY; PATTON—US 3RD ARMY; DEMPSEY—2ND BRITISH ARMY; CRERAR—1ST CANADIAN ARMY; CONINGHAM—RAF 2ND TAF; QUESADA—IX TAC; WEYLAND—XIX TAC

12TH ARMY GROUP WILL EXECUTE IMMEDIATE TURNING MOVEMENT NORTH TO ENCIRCLE GERMAN FORCES RETREATING EASTWARD THROUGH THE FLERS-FALAISE-ARGENTAN TRIANGLE.

12TH ARMY GROUP FORCES WILL ESTABLISH AND MAINTAIN—REPEAT, MAINTAIN—AN EAST-WEST LINE THROUGH FLERS AND ARGENTAN. 21ST ARMY GROUP FORCES WILL CLOSE FROM THE NORTH ON AN EAST-WEST LINE THROUGH FALAISE TO COMPLETE THE ENCIRCLEMENT. ALL UNITS SHOULD BE IN THE POSITIONS INDICATED ABOVE BY 0600 HOURS, 14 AUG 44.

SIGNED,
MONTGOMERY

Chapter Nine

In the crowded tent, Tommy Moon was beginning to wonder if the tank battalion commander even knew he was there. Watching from the shadows, Tommy stood in a corner not bathed in the harsh glow of the bare electric light bulbs strung between the big tent's poles. The C.O. had just returned from Division. He was explaining the changing tactical situation to his staff and company commanders: the German 7th Army—the defenders of Normandy—were falling back in retreat. It was a tooth-and-nail fighting retreat, for sure, he told them, but a retreat nonetheless.

For 15 minutes, the commander, a light colonel named Abrams, looking older than his 30 years, stood at the large-scale map hung on a side curtain, making sweeping motions with his arms meant to illustrate the movements of the major units in the fight. Tommy had become so engrossed in the map study—trying to add all those details to the broad stroke aerial view already in his head—that, for a moment, he didn't realize the C.O. was talking about him.

"Over in the corner there," Colonel Abrams said, "stands something—excuse me, *someone*—we've waited a long time for. Lieutenant Moon just happened to be in the wrong place at the wrong time, so he's going to be the air support officer we've so sorely needed. Take a bow, Lieutenant."

As Tommy acknowledged the colonel's introduction, he thought, *The wrong place at the wrong time. Ain't that the truth.*

"You're familiar with all the terrain I've just been talking about, Lieutenant Moon?"

"Yes, sir. Been flying over it for months now."

"Very fine. We've gotten some great air support—"

Abrams paused as some grumbling rose from the crowd and then continued, "From you fighter guys, mostly. The bomber boys…well, let's just say they've been less than impressive."

"Impressive, my aching ass," a voice called out. "They've *only* bombed us twice. *Accidentally*, of course."

"All right, knock it off," the colonel commanded, silencing the tent. Then he turned back to Tommy. "What we're trying to say, Lieutenant, is it sure will be good to have someone who *understands* these problems from the flyboys' perspective and can work them out for us. Without any more self-inflicted fiascos. You guys have done a hell of a job keeping the skies clear of the Luftwaffe, so don't try to do the Krauts' job for them."

Tommy knew they were talking about *Operation Cobra*, the Normandy breakout a few weeks ago, where high-flying American bombers killed over 100 GIs: *But that was due to shitty planning by the top brass. With the paths to target they laid out for the bombers, they were damn lucky they didn't kill even more GIs. Not much an ASO could have done to change that.* But then he thought of all the times that he—even at low level—hadn't been 100 percent sure what—or who—he'd been attacking, either.

"I'll do all I can to help, sir," Tommy said.

"Outstanding. Now I'm told our Sergeant Moon is your brother?"

"Affirmative, sir."

"Excellent. Couldn't be better."

Colonel Abrams returned to the map and, taking a grease pencil, sketched a straight line across its acetate overlay. The line linked two towns some 30 miles north of their present position at Mayenne. "This is the line Twelfth Army Group is to establish and hold. Argentan marks its center. First Army covers west of Argentan. Third Army—that means us, gentlemen—covers the east. We're supposed to be there by sun-up, Fourteen August, five days from today."

"Wait a minute, sir," one of the tank company commanders said. "If we're supposed to be encircling the Krauts—and we're holding this straight line—who's going to close the trap?"

"That'll be Twenty-First Army Group's job," the colonel replied.

More grumbling—louder this time—rose from the tankers.

"Really?" a captain said. "Montgomery and his Brits are going to close it? In what year?"

"At ease," the colonel said. "Those are our orders."

"Then those are really dumb orders, sir," the captain replied. "Just where is Montgomery at the moment, anyway? Wait a minute…let's ask our ASO. He's had a bird's eye view of all this. Let's get it straight from the horse's mouth, not some *charlie-charlie* up at SHAEF with a vivid imagination."

All eyes swung to Tommy Moon.

Abrams said, "Care to step up to the map, Lieutenant?"

Tommy knew it was an order, not a request.

"Well, I haven't been up in a couple of days," Tommy said, "but here's about where the Brits were at the time." He sketched in a line on the acetate.

"Oh, fuck," the captain said. "That's it? Just a little south of Caen? So they moved about five fucking miles in the last couple of weeks while we've been making five, maybe ten, *a day*, kicking Kraut ass the whole time?"

"Looks that way," Tommy replied.

The captain flung his helmet to the dirt floor. "Oh, that's just fucking swell," he said. "Tell you what. I'll bet ten bucks right now that the Krauts will be long gone before any of Monty's boys show up to close that trap." Pulling the bill from his wallet, he waved it in the air and asked, "Who's game?"

There were no takers.

The battalion XO, a pipe-smoking major, said, "You know, when I was up at Patton's HQ last week, the Brit liaison there was still singing that same old song about Monty facing the bulk of the German Armor, while we've got it easy."

"With all due respect, sir," the captain replied, "that's a bullshit excuse. They're up against panzers, we're up against panzers. There isn't any fucking difference."

"At ease, gentlemen," Colonel Abrams said. "We all agree the Brits don't go anywhere fast. But as I've already said, we have our orders."

Stumbling through the darkness of the tankers' bivouac with only pale moonlight to guide him, Tommy finally found the tent where Sean and his crew bunked. Throwing open the blackout curtain to enter, he was met with a tirade of curses from Fabiano, Sean's hot-headed gunner. Once Tommy stepped inside, the lieutenant's bar on his collar reflected just enough of the tent's dim lantern light for Fabiano to soften his tune.

"Gee…sorry, Lieutenant," the gunner said. "Nothing personal, but you gotta keep light discipline. Slip in and out through that crack in the curtains, not throw them open like you're waltzing into the five and dime. You can see one little speck of light for miles at night, and the Krauts are looking, believe you me."

"Ain't that the God's honest truth," another voice drawled from a dark corner. "Nothing fucks up sack time like artillery coming down on your ass."

If Tommy felt like debating the point, he might have mentioned their position was about as secret as an airfield. There was nothing stealthy about a battalion of tanks coming into a position such as this one. Those bellowing engines could be heard a mile away, maybe more. From the air, the track marks they left in the ground were like signposts pointing to their location, no matter how well concealed that location was. But this was their house, and they lived on the tip of the spear. Anyone who didn't play by their rules was asking for trouble.

"No, I'm the one who should be sorry," Tommy said. "I should've known better. Can one of you men tell me where my brother is?"

Fabiano shrugged. "No, sir. He keeps an eye on us, not the other way around." As Tommy turned to leave, the gunner added, "Hey, Lieutenant, how many Krauts you shoot down?"

"None. Don't really see a lot of German airplanes in the air these days."

Tommy took great care slipping through the curtains on his way out. Back in the darkness, with his night vision compromised by the tent's lantern, it only took a few steps to realize he'd lost his bearings. He had no idea in which direction the battalion CP—with the cot they'd loaned him—was located.

Like a blind man, he searched for some clue that would get him oriented—and then, as his night vision slowly returned, he thought he'd found one. Ahead was an empty grayness, distinct from the black labyrinth of trees. He remembered passing through a clearing between the CP and the tank park: *I'm pretty sure it looked just like this. Maybe I'll find my bed, at least. But I wish to hell I could have found my brother.*

Plodding ahead, a dot of orange light appeared. It seemed so far away at first, but then Tommy realized what the dot really was: *a cigarette*. It only took a few steps before he was standing next to the smoker, who was seated with his back against a tree. He didn't need to see the man's face to know it was his brother.

"Geez, Sean…I just got my ass reamed by your gunner for poor light discipline, and you're out here lighting up the whole damn world like sniper bait. Do you realize how far you can see a cigarette's glow in the dark? You got a death wish or something?"

Tommy wasn't sure if Sean heard him. He didn't move, just stared into the infinite darkness, the tell-tale cigarette still pressed between his lips, inviting disaster.

"You going to talk to me or what, Sean?"

With a slow, studied motion, his brother stubbed out the cigarette on the heel of his boot. When he finally did speak, his voice wasn't the bellicose trumpet it had always been. Now, it was a low, forlorn monotone.

"You think we'll be home by Christmas, Half?"

Tommy would've done anything to cheer his brother up—except lie to him.

"I seriously doubt it, Sean."

"Yeah, I don't believe that shit, either."

Sean leaned his head back against the tree. His face caught the moonlight just right, showing Tommy a melancholy expression he'd never seen before. To cap it off, a small, glistening spot rolled down his cheek.

Holy shit. He's crying.

Tommy sat down next to his big brother, put his arm around his shoulder, and pulled him close. They remained in silence, all the while Tommy thinking:

Ain't this something? When we were kids, it was always Sean looking out for me, protecting me and Mom and the girls from Pop's drunken rampages, always standing up to the neighborhood tough guys. Hell, he could be more of a hood than the hoods.

But now, all of a sudden, I'm the one doling out the comfort. Me, the little brother.

War is such a shitty deal, isn't it?

They sat that way for a few minutes, brother to brother. Then, in an even softer voice, Sean said, "Just a matter of time, Tommy."

"Until what, Sean?"

He hugged his little brother as if he was saying goodbye.

"Just a matter of time, Tommy. Just a matter of fucking time."

Chapter Ten

Sunrise had barely begun to brighten the eastern sky. Tommy had little appetite for breakfast. He took the scrambled egg sandwich the cook insisted on giving him—"This *delicacy* is a ritual when we're moving out, sir," the cook insisted—but *delicacy* or not, Tommy couldn't eat it. Coffee was all he could stomach. He was too nervous, and he knew why:

I know the drill in the air. But down here on the deck I'm a raw rookie—and rookies make dumb mistakes that get people killed.

Sean came striding up and asked, "You gonna eat that?"

When Tommy shook his head, his brother's hand swooped the sandwich from the mess kit and he downed it in three quick bites. Pointing to the carbine his little brother had been issued, he asked, "You flyboys even know how to use those fucking things?"

"Hey, we're dead shots with fifty cals, rockets, and bombs. I'm pretty sure we can handle little pop guns like this."

"I hope so, Half, because you just might need it where we're going."

Sean gave an amused once-over to the ill-fitting tanker's coveralls Tommy had been issued; the sleeves and trouser legs had to be rolled up to keep from covering his hands and feet. "I know you pilot-types get to go to English tailors and all that shit, but I see you're learning that around here, we only got *too* sizes: *too* large and *too* small."

Tommy couldn't help but smile. The old Sean had returned. Whatever had transpired last night between them receded to some obscure corner of his memory.

Now maybe I can concentrate on not fucking up my first time out.

"You're gonna ride with Baker Company," Sean told him. "That's *my* company…and it'll be leading the battalion column. You know what you'll be riding in?"

"They told me at last night's briefing I'd be in a tank destroyer with the company commander. I thought he'd have his own Sherman, though."

"Ordinarily, he does," Sean replied, "but as low on *Zippos* as we are at the minute, and the fact that our brand new ASO might actually want to see something besides the inside of a hull, we borrowed one of those contraptions just for you." With a sarcastic laugh, he added, "Ahh, don't worry. You'll love it. It's like driving through a shit storm with the top down."

Tommy wasn't sure what his brother meant until he climbed onto the deck of the M10 tank destroyer. From the ground, it looked just like a tank, with tracks, machine guns, armored hull, and the tube of a big gun protruding from its turret. Once on the deck, though, Sean's comment came into focus: *This fucking turret has no top! You're riding in a big bathtub…with absolutely no protection from airbursts except your damn helmet, for all the good it's going to do.*

Baker Company's commander—that same captain who'd disparaged British capabilities at last night's briefing—was already in that *bathtub*. He smiled when he saw the perplexed look on Tommy's face. "What's the matter, Lieutenant Moon?" he asked. "You don't like convertibles?"

"No, sir…I just wasn't expecting—"

"Don't sweat it, Lieutenant. It's a lot better than a jeep. At least you've got armor on the sides, and there's a whole mess of Krauts between here and Argentan just dying to bounce some bullets off it. Now climb in and get yourself organized on the double. We've got to get moving."

Tommy swung himself into the turret. It was a tight squeeze; besides the captain, there were two enlisted men to man the main gun and the bank of radios. The captain offered his hand and said, "By the way, my name's Al Newcomb. I don't believe we got properly introduced last night."

He watched as Tommy scanned the vehicle's radio equipment. "Got it all figured out?" Newcomb asked.

"Yeah, I think so. This one here…this is strictly for air to ground, right?"

"Yep, that one's all yours." Pointing to one of the enlisted men, he added, "DeLuca here is our radio wizard if you need any help."

"What about artillery, sir? I figured one of their observers would be riding with us."

"Negative, Moon. There's an *arty* FO riding with battalion HQ. Plus, there's usually a little spotter plane or two working with Division puttering around up there, weather permitting, of course…and assuming they didn't get shot to shit on their last mission. Down here on point, though, we pretty much call our own artillery when we need it. And if we need any special coordination, we'll go through that FO up at Battalion."

"Special coordination," Tommy said, "like if we don't want to knock down our own planes?"

"Now you're seeing the big picture," Newcomb replied.

There was a roar of engines from the woodline as Shermans emerged. To Tommy Moon, each seemed a fearsome and impregnable rolling fortress, belching clouds of exhaust smoke as it headed for the road.

"EASTWARD HO, BOYS," Newcomb called out. "LAST ONE TO BERLIN'S A ROTTEN EGG."

★★★★

The column of tanks had traveled five miles down the Mayenne-Alençon highway without a hint of opposition. As the narrow pavement emerged from a grove, there was a sickening *SLAM* and blinding flash as the lead Sherman was turned inside out by a round from a German 88-millimeter anti-tank gun. Four vehicles back, Tommy couldn't see much of the carnage. It took him a few seconds to realize the thing he'd seen shooting into the sky like a bottle rocket was the lead tank's commander being blown from his open hatch atop the turret. It took another second to reassure himself it wasn't his brother's flaming death he'd just witnessed. Sean's tank was several vehicles behind Tommy in the M10.

"Fucking Krauts are in that next treeline," Newcomb said, scanning ahead with binoculars. Then, with surprising casualness, he asked Tommy, "Where are the *jugs*?"

"About five minutes out."

"This'll probably be over before they even get here," Newcomb said.

Tommy watched as the company commander issued a string of terse orders over the radio, each so clear even this flyboy newcomer to ground warfare understood exactly what they meant. Using the burning lead tank as cover, the second in the column began to pepper the far treeline—some 400 yards away—with machine gun and 75-millimeter fire from its main gun. The remaining two tanks of the lead platoon left the road, took up hull-down positions amidst the trees, and added their fire.

Two more shots from the German guns streaked toward the Americans. One hit the hull of the already flaming lead tank, showering sparks and metal fragments on the Sherman sheltering behind it but doing no damage.

The second shot cleaved the turret of one of the hull-down tanks in two.

"Fuck," Newcomb mumbled. "Three shots, two of my tanks dead."

The three tank platoons behind Tommy and the M10 had fanned out wide—one north, two south—leading half-tracks full of infantrymen to attempt a double-envelopment of the Germans. Tommy watched as those flanking elements drew and returned fire. He wasn't sure which tank—or even which element—contained his brother.

The smoke of battle had grown thick over the German and American positions. It was getting difficult to see into the distance.

"It's just a couple of eighty-eights," Newcomb said. "Once we flank them, they're finished. They can't fire in three directions at once."

The radio crackled with the voice of the P-47 flight leader. They were two minutes from the reference point Tommy had given them to begin an attack.

"Have them hold off," Newcomb said. "We're going to put some airbursts over those Krauts."

In the 30 seconds that followed, two more Shermans and one half-track were turned into infernos. Airbursts from American artillery a mile back in the column filled the air above the Germans with gray puffs of smoke. Like low-level flak, those bursts rained shell fragments on the ground below.

"Fuck, they're short," Newcomb said. Keying the microphone, he told the artillery, "Add five-zero, up ten. Repeat."

Another shot from the Germans sliced through the line of American vehicles on the northern pincer, hitting none. Its only victim was a shattered stand of trees.

The next volley of GI artillery arrived, splashing its airbursts right on target. There wasn't another shot from the 88s.

Straining to see through the smoke, Newcomb said, "They're either pulling back…or they bought it." Grabbing the microphone again, he urged his two flanking elements to close in quickly. Then he told Tommy, "Call off the jugs, Lieutenant. We don't need our asses riddled by the Air Force today."

The flanking elements rolled into the German gun position. After a few brief bursts of machine gun fire, the radio blared their *all clear.* The M10—along with the two surviving Shermans of what had been the lead platoon—advanced to join the rest of the company. As they passed the smoldering hulks of the last two Shermans to get hit, Tommy was almost too afraid to look at the names and artwork their crews had painted on the turrets. But neither carried the name *Eclipse of the Hun* or the sketch of a cartoon-character Hitler dangling by the seat of his pants from the thin crescent of a nearly full lunar eclipse. That meant Sean's tank, at least, had survived.

Once inside the beaten position, the tankers dismounted to flush out any remaining Germans. Tommy found his brother briefing Captain Newcomb. Sean's Thompson submachine gun was at his hip like some Chicago gangster as he said, "Only two eighty-eights, sir. They were either manned real light or a bunch of them cut and run on foot. Left all their vehicles behind." He pointed toward a stack of enemy bodies; there were only eight. "You'd expect there to be twice that many manning two guns."

Newcomb shook his head. "Ain't that some shit? Eight fucking Krauts…and we've got about thirty killed or wounded, counting those infantry guys…and the company's down another four tanks—four out of the fifteen we set out with today."

He paused, scanning the battered German guns and vehicles. Then he asked, "Get any prisoners, Sergeant?"

Sean shrugged. "Negative, sir. Didn't work out that way."

Tommy thought his brother's answer was a bit too vague. He'd always heard that German troops usually fought until it was hopeless and then surrendered as if it was all just part of the game. They'd come out with their hands up shouting *Kamerad*…as if to say, *We're done fighting. We can all be friends now.*

If Captain Newcomb thought his sergeant's answer was *a bit too vague*, he didn't press the issue. He didn't seem concerned if his men had killed surrendering Germans or not.

Just then, a four-plane flight of P-47s passed overhead and then circled for a better look.

Tommy said, "That's our air cover. You want me to have them scout up the road for us?"

"Great idea," Newcomb replied.

Sean's sullen gaze swept across the open ground to the four destroyed tanks and the infantry half-track. His lips moved silently, as if counting the dead and wounded.

Then it occurred to Tommy his brother wasn't counting at all—he was saying, over and over again, *Just a matter of time.*

★★★★

They'd been back on the highway 10 minutes when the P-47s radioed their scouting report. "There's an armored unit on the road about five miles ahead," Tommy related. "They're either stopped or moving real slow."

"That can't be good," Newcomb replied. "Nobody's supposed to be in front of us but Germans. Are your flyboys going to engage them?"

"Negative, sir. They say they're Shermans."

Newcomb scowled. "Shermans? How the fuck could that be?"

DeLuca, the radioman, had a theory: "Maybe they're *captured* Shermans, sir…and the Krauts are using them to set us a trap?"

Captain Newcomb found that funny. "Why the fuck would Germans want our *Zippos*? Their Panthers and Tigers are five times the tank a Sherman is."

Tommy asked, “What makes you say that, sir?”

“Because every damn time we engage one, it blows up about five Shermans before someone can finally get around the bastard and put one up his ass. That’s about the only way we can kill them.”

“Let me ask you this,” Tommy said. “Ninth Air Force has been telling its squadrons to hang white phosphorous bombs when we know we’ll be going after German armor. The burning stuff sticks to the tank and supposedly screws up their sighting systems. Plus the fumes get sucked inside and force the crew to abandon the tank. You find that to be true, sir?”

“Yeah, it is,” Newcomb replied, “as long as you flyboys actually drop it *on the fucking tanks* in the first place. But that doesn’t seem to happen very much. Stick with putting rockets and APIs up their asses. That seems to be a lot more reliable.” He told DeLuca to radio Battalion. “Maybe they know who the hell that is up the road.”

Captain Newcomb had his answer in less than a minute: Battalion didn’t know anything. But their orders didn’t change: *Continue the advance. Engage as necessary.*

Chapter Eleven

Captain Newcomb figured his column had covered another three miles down the highway toward Alençon. In the sky ahead, he caught glimpses of the P-47s flying high, wide circles. Tommy confirmed everyone's suspicions as he relayed the flight leader's transmission: "Whoever they are, they're stopped right on the road, but they're not in any kind of fight. No sign of Krauts anywhere. The pilots estimate fifty tanks and a slew of support vehicles."

"That's a fucking battalion's worth," Newcomb said.

Soon, his lead tanks crested a rise in the road. It gave the M10—now third in the column—a splendid view of the traffic jam less than a mile ahead. With binoculars, they could now identify the tanks for themselves. They were indeed Shermans, and they bore the Cross of Lorraine on their turrets.

"They're Free French," Newcomb said, as if he didn't believe his own words. "What the hell is the French Second Armored doing all the way over here?" He took another disbelieving look at his map. "They're not even supposed to be on this road…and they've got it clogged up like a stuck drain. They don't even have any security out, like they're on some damn *admin* march."

As they rumbled closer, they were in for another surprise. DeLuca expressed it first: "Holy shit…they're all darkies."

"Get used to that," Captain Newcomb replied. "Most of the Free French troops are African colonials."

DeLuca asked, "How come, sir?"

"Because most of the white guys in France couldn't exactly get to North Africa to enlist," Newcomb replied. "But there's got to be white guys in charge, though." He jumped down from the M10 in search of a white French officer, beckoning Tommy to follow him: "You said you spoke some French, right?"

"Yes, sir."

"Better come along, then. I might need a translator."

They found a French colonel at the head of the column, relaxing in a jeep as he dined on American C rations. He seemed unconcerned his stalled column was blocking the progress of 37th Tank Battalion—and the rest of the US 4th Armored Division behind it.

When Captain Newcomb pulled out his map and asserted the French were not where they were supposed to be, the Frenchman halted Tommy's translation with a casual wave of his hand and said, "I speak English." Then he pulled out his own map with a completely different set of unit boundaries drawn in. "I have been instructed by my general to wait here for further orders."

Newcomb was fast losing his temper. "But you're in our fucking way, Colonel," he said. "You need to clear the road immediately."

"Just go around, Captain," the colonel replied. He made a sweeping motion with his arm that implied the rest of the countryside was at the Americans' disposal.

"Negative, sir," Newcomb said. "The terrain around here is like another one of your damn *bocages*—tough for tracks, impossible for wheeled vehicles." He looked at the line of French vehicles claiming the road—actually *American* vehicles in French markings—and added, "But I guess you've figured that one out already."

The colonel was more interested in the canned fruit from his C ration box.

"Look, sir," Newcomb said, "if you won't clear the road, I'll get my colonel up here. And if that's not good enough for you, we'll get the fucking division commander."

"You can get Eisenhower himself," the Frenchman replied, "and it will make no difference. This is France, and I follow only the orders of General Leclerc. And he follows only the orders of General de Gaulle."

"And whose orders does General de Gaulle follow?"

"Only God's, Captain."

In the best French he could muster, Tommy asked, "But Colonel, are we not allies?"

The colonel replied in English. "Do not patronize me, Lieutenant. We both fight the *Boche*, so yes, we are your allies, as you say. But we are not your servants."

★★★★

It took six hours—with many frantic radio calls by American officers of ascending rank to Corps and Army headquarters—to get the French off the road and the 4th Armored moving again. The Americans covered only 10 more miles before darkness forced them to bivouac in the concealment of a thick forest for the night. They were still five miles from the waypoint of Alençon and 25 miles from their objective, Argentan. "At this rate," Sean Moon fumed, "the Krauts will be back in Paris sipping beers before we get anywhere near this fucking *Falaise pocket*, let alone close the bastard."

"Speaking of *closing the bastard*," Captain Newcomb said, "I saw the intel report from Division. Looks like the Brits are making worse time than we are."

"So what else is new, sir?" Sean replied with disgust. "Maybe they're fighting the Germans *and* the French, too, just like we are?"

"Hell of a way to talk about our *allies*, Sergeant. But it's worse than that: those frogs we passed…they're supposed to be covering our left flank."

"You're kidding, right, sir?"

"Nope. Dead serious."

Sean threw up his hands in frustration and replied, "Well, then…I guess it's *good night, nurse* for this little campaign." He grimaced as he took a bite of the bitter chocolate bar—the D bar—that came with the K ration. "And you say those frogs were dining like kings on C rations, while we get this *subsistence* shit?"

Tommy's voice came out of the darkness, asking, "Something wrong? Let me guess…they just called the whole thing off and we can all go home, right?"

"Not quite, Lieutenant," Newcomb said. "Your brother was just expressing his lack of confidence in our French allies."

"Don't forget I ain't too crazy about the Limeys, either, sir," Sean added.

Newcomb asked Tommy, "Find out anything interesting from the air liaison?"

"Yeah. It sounds like the Ninth Air Force is pasting the shit out of the Germans pulling back from Mortain. They made it sound like a regular turkey shoot."

"Great," Sean said. "Then they won't be needing us ground pounders none."

"Not so fast," Tommy replied. "There are still plenty of Krauts to go around for everyone, apparently." He turned to Newcomb and added, "I need to run something by you, sir. I was thinking about how we could've used the air support in that fight back up the road, and it occurred to me that no matter how I directed them, they had just as good a chance of dumping their stuff on us as the Krauts, close as we all were."

"We'd just do what we always do," Newcomb replied. "We'd have our artillery or mortars mark the targets with smoke and hope for the best."

"That's just it, Captain…once a fight gets going real good, all we see from the cockpit is smoke and dust. It all mixes together and we pilots can't tell one color smoke from another. That stuff obscures the ground, and if there's not some easily recognizable reference point, it's a crap shoot where the ordnance is going to land."

"Hmm…so what do we do about that, Lieutenant?"

"I'd like to try this, if it's okay with you, sir. Let's put the artillery FO right with us in the M10 so he and I can coordinate white phosphorous airbursts—up real high, above all the battlefield smoke—to mark an approach path to the target. They'd have to be tightly time controlled so the smoke from the bursts doesn't drift away in the wind before the pilots can get a good bead on it. Then they'd have a better of chance of being lined up on—and actually seeing—the target when they broke through all that smoke, because at the speed they're going, they'd only get a second or two for target acquisition. If the FO was right there with me it would be so much easier to set up. He can call the fire missions directly, rather than me having to pass all the coordinates for the WP bursts over the radio first."

As Newcomb mulled it over in silence, Tommy added, "I know the turret's going to get a little crowded with an extra guy and all, but we've already got enough radios to handle it. Plus, the FO can bring his battery-operated set as extra insurance."

"Sounds like you've already worked this out with the artillery, Lieutenant."

"Yes, sir, I have."

"Outstanding," Newcomb said as he got up to leave. "Let's give it a try. I'll catch up with you guys later. I've got to see how the fueling's coming along."

As Tommy ripped open his K ration box, his brother asked, "I'll bet hearing about your flyboy buddies ripping the shit out of the Krauts is making you wanna be back in the cockpit, don't it?"

Tommy needed no words to answer. A wistful glance skyward was all it took.

Chapter Twelve

ALLIED GROUND FORCES COMMUNIQUE

FROM:	DATE-TIME OF ORIGIN
MONTGOMERY—COMMANDER, ALLIED GROUND FORCES	11 AUG 44 1100 HRS

TO:
BRADLEY—COMMANDER, 12TH ARMY GROUP

COPY (FOR INFO):
SHAEF (EISENHOWER)

IN RECEIPT OF YOUR ELOQUENT REQUEST DATED 10 AUG. HOWEVER, BE ADVISED THE ORIGINAL DIRECTIVE FROM THIS COMMAND STANDS: ELEMENTS OF 12TH ARMY GROUP WILL ESTABLISH AND MAINTAIN—REPEAT, MAINTAIN—AN EAST-WEST LINE THROUGH FLERS AND ARGENTAN NLT 0600, 14 AUG. NO UNIT OF 12TH ARMY GROUP IS TO ADVANCE NORTH OF THAT LINE, AS IT WOULD BE UNWISE TO ATTEMPT TO BLOCK SEASONED PANZER FORMATIONS WITH UNTESTED AMERICAN UNITS. I PREFER TO RISK A BLOODY NOSE AT ARGENTAN RATHER THAN A BROKEN NECK AT FALAISE.

SIGNED,
MONTGOMERY

Chapter Thirteen

It was midmorning when a radio transmission from an aerial observer in a spotter plane sounded the warning. A German armored force from the west was speeding toward the same wooded road junction Newcomb's tanks were approaching from the south. The Germans would get there first, posing a roadblock far more potent than yesterday's mere inconvenience at the hands of the French 2nd Armored.

"The AO says they're Panthers, sir," DeLuca, the radio operator, reported. "Six of them, with a couple of trucks tagging along."

Captain Newcomb, on another radio with Battalion, replied with an impatient nod. Tommy Moon was already calling for air support from the P-47s.

"We've got to stop them before they block the junction," Newcomb said. "That's going to be some trick, considering we can't even see them yet through all these trees." Then he turned to the latest addition to the M10's crew: Lieutenant Bill Baxter, the artillery forward observer. "Plaster the junction with HE and WP," he told the FO. "Let's make them stop short on the road so we can get a crack at them broadside through the woods, before they can turn toward us."

Baxter objected. "But, sir, I can put WP right on the tanks."

"How are you going to do that, Lieutenant?" Newcomb replied. "They're not going to stand still for you to adjust the rounds on them…and you can't see the fucking Krauts in the first place."

"Yeah…and save a couple of *willy petes* for me," Tommy added. "This fight's going to be close in and down in the trees again. The jugs will have a hell of a time figuring out who's who."

Newcomb asked, "This is just what you were talking about last night, isn't it, Moon? Marking an airborne approach path to the target with *willy pete* airbursts?"

"Yes, sir, it sure is."

"Well, it better fucking work, or we're in real deep shit."

Once again, Newcomb deployed his forces with a hand steadied by hard experience. As his tanks left the open killing field of the road and fanned out into the woods, Lieutenant Baxter had just finished calling in the artillery fire mission on the road junction. He and Tommy settled into plotting the white phosphorous airbursts to guide the flight of four P-47s.

"Let's use the road junction for the near burst," Tommy said as he wrote down the coordinates. "Put it five hundred feet in the air. For the far one, put it off to the east"—he touched his pencil point to the map—"right here, about a mile out, burst height at one thousand feet. What's the time of flight going to be?"

Baxter did a quick calculation. "One gun can shoot both rounds while the rest of the battery hits the road junction. If we shoot the far airburst first, its time of flight will be about eleven seconds. Then, allowing a little time to reload and adjust firing data, the near one's burst should be pretty much simultaneous."

"Simultaneous. Excellent," Tommy said. "What about the time delay getting our *fire* command to the guns?"

"Considering they'll already have the initial firing data set, a few seconds, at most."

"Great," Tommy replied, adding it all up. "With the usual winds from the southwest and the jugs coming out of the sun, this should work like a charm." He radioed the orienting information to the fast-approaching fighters.

For a moment, Tommy Moon almost forgot one of those men charging at the German tanks in those *Zippo lighters* would be his brother.

The first artillery rounds struck the road junction. They had the desired effect; though a few hundred yards from the impacts, the Germans came to a dead stop on the road. But they weren't Panthers.

"They're assault guns," Newcomb said. "*Sturmgeschutz*, or some shit like that. For cryin' out loud, you flyboys think anything with tracks is a fucking tank."

Tommy asked, "So assault guns should be pushovers?"

"Not exactly. They've got the same main weapon but it can't traverse very much. And there's a lot less armor."

No one noticed the airburst of white phosphorous high above the road junction or the much higher one a mile to the east.

"Okay," Tommy said, "the jugs are turning to the markers. Shut off the artillery."

"Yeah, let the jugs in," Newcomb concurred. "Do it now."

The German vehicles were still motionless, engines revving, as if unsure what to do next.

"Come on, boys," Newcomb beseeched his tanks, "they're showing us their flanks! Don't wait until they turn on you. Punch a round right through them! Take your damn shot!"

But he understood why the Shermans hadn't fired yet. They were bouncing and lurching through the woods; the only way to get an accurate shot was to stop, giving the gunner a stable sight picture before firing. But stopping meant death. You were too good a target when you weren't moving, and the Germans' powerful 75-millimeter gun could kill you before it was even in your gun's range. The only chance of a first-round hit on the move was if you were close—200 yards or less—and they weren't there yet.

Hunkered down in the turret of the M10, Tommy told the jugs to attack with machine guns: *Easier to aim, and even if they miss, they'll scare the living shit out of the Krauts, with their heads sticking out like that. Rockets will probably miss.*

Tommy could only visualize the fight through the eyes of an airman. *Turn, dammit,* he urged the German guns. Sitting on the road as they were, their tougher front armor was facing the oncoming P-47s. But when he peered over the edge of the turret, a tanker's perspective smacked him in the face. *If they turn, they're looking straight at my brother. Dammit...somebody make a move...do something!*

All at once, Tommy got his wish. A Sherman fired and shattered a track on the lead assault gun. She was crippled but by no means dead, pivoting with her good track to face the approaching Americans. The five vehicles behind her belched smoke from their racing engines and began to pivot, trying to turn their toughest armor—and their big main guns—to the Shermans.

They never saw the P-47s streaking out of the sun. Four assault guns erupted in flames, struck by API rounds in their flanks. The crewmen who were still alive and able to move clambered off the hulls, frantically trying to shed burning uniforms as they ran to seek cover in the woods.

That left two German vehicles still in the fight: the leader—frozen in place but her main gun very much alive—and the last one in the column, now rumbling toward the Shermans. Her main gun spit a wildly inaccurate round while on the move.

For the moment, the lead gun's immobility gave her an advantage as she took a well-aimed shot through a rock-steady gunsight. The round penetrated a Sherman's front armor, spraying a torrent of hot gasses and razor-sharp metal fragments into the crew compartment. She came to an abrupt stop. The only thing escaping her hull were multiple jets of smoke colored the gray pallor of death.

A Sherman maneuvered for a shot at the lead gun's thin side armor. Firing on the move from 300 yards out, she missed, the round burrowing into the ground yards short. The German gun replied with a shot of her own, knocking the American's turret askew, rendering it useless. The Sherman began to back away; at least her driver was still alive.

"Shit," Captain Newcomb mumbled. "Two *Zippos* down."

Baxter, the artillery FO, said, "If that Kraut isn't going to move, I can burn her with WP."

Newcomb was about to agree when Tommy blurted, "No, wait. I've got the jugs coming back the other way. They can nail her."

"When?" Newcomb asked.

"Thirty seconds. Shifting the arty will take twice that long."

Newcomb swallowed hard and replied, "Okay. We'll hold for the jugs."

Thirty seconds in combat can be an eternity. In the narrow lanes of the woods a hundred yards off the road, the still-mobile assault gun was caught in a deadly game of *ring around the rosie* with two Shermans. Swirling as if caught in a whirlpool—or circling a drain—the three vehicles struggled to get a point-blank shot at their enemy's rear, searching for a path through the dense trees that would yield an intercepting vector without smacking the main gun into a tree. Two more Shermans were trying to position themselves at tangents to that circle, hoping for a clear shot at the German vehicle without offering themselves up to her far more deadly gun.

One of the Shermans seeking a tangent miscalculated; the assault gun blew her apart at 50 yards.

But then she ran out of luck. Maneuvering for another kill, her main gun struck a tree, forcing her to stop and reverse. In that instant, she was turned into a funeral pyre as rounds struck her from three directions at once.

On the road, the lead assault gun exploded as a P-47 shot up her hull with API. In turn, the other three aircraft riddled the burning lead gun and then set ablaze the two German support trucks trying to slip away from the battle.

And then it was over—the pants-wetting terror of combat replaced with that eerie stillness that provided anything but closure to the mortal chaos just lived through.

"I guess that idea of yours sort of worked, Moon," Newcomb said. "Nice job."

But I still lost three more tanks. That's seven gone in two days. I've got eight left—at this rate, this company will be wiped out long before the division reaches Argentan. Shit, if we hit heavier contact than this—and can't get air support when we need it—we may cease to exist before nightfall.

Regrouping his scattered tank company, Newcomb shifted his platoons' order of march. Tommy overheard the terse commands over the radio that would put Sean's tank at the head of the column. He saw the Sherman named *Eclipse of the Hun* moving back toward the road to take its place on point, his brother sitting on the ring of the turret hatch, casually smoking a cigarette. Sean waved with little enthusiasm as his tank drove past the M10. Tommy wished he'd been close enough to see the look in his eyes.

Chapter Fourteen

The highway to Alençon coursed through the woods for another 10 miles. Newcomb's column encountered Germans only twice in that distance, both times meeting details of infantry armed with light weapons and *panzerfaust*—small but powerful anti-armor rockets carried and fired by one man. Similar in concept to the American *bazooka*, but packing a far stronger punch, its only drawback was its short range: about 110 yards, which left its operator terribly vulnerable to the infantry accompanying and protecting the American tanks from just such a threat. If he could manage to get close enough, though, he could kill a Sherman with one shot. But that had rarely happened since the GIs came ashore at Normandy. It wouldn't happen this afternoon, either; Newcomb lost no more tanks in the woods.

"It's going to get worse," he warned. "We'll be back in the open real soon, and I'm betting we'll be up to our asses in panzers again. And the closer we get to this *Falaise pocket* they keep talking about…well, shit—this could turn into another *Kursk*."

He scanned the low-hanging gray clouds gathering in the sky ahead, lit from within by lightning, flickering like Chinese lanterns. "A fucking storm coming, too," Newcomb said, shooting a disparaging look at Tommy. "That'll do it for our air cover. Your Air Force can't hit shit on the ground if they can't see it."

There was nothing Tommy could say to contradict the captain's assessment. Newcomb was right; losing visual contact with the ground not only prevented a pilot from finding a target, it might even prevent him from finding his way home. Thunderstorms presented an even more dangerous problem. More than one aviator had blundered into their towering columns of cloud to watch his aircraft disintegrate around him, torn apart by the sledgehammer blows of the fiercely turbulent air within. If he was lucky, he'd survive the bailout through nature's fury. Usually, it didn't work out that way.

Once Newcomb's column was clear of the woods, a spotter plane they'd heard transmitting over the radio but seen little of touched down in a grassy clearing beside the road. It had barely rolled to a stop when a bulldog of a man wearing two silver stars on his helmet jumped out and walked with great purpose toward the M10.

"Who the hell is that?" Tommy asked.

"It's General Wood," Newcomb replied.

"The division commander?"

"None other, Lieutenant. That's '*P.' Wood* himself."

"What's the *P* stand for, sir?"

"I heard it's for *professor*. Used to teach college, supposedly."

As the spotter plane's pilot busied himself tying down the light aircraft against the punishing winds the storm was sure to bring, General Wood clambered onto the M10. In a booming voice dripping with the flavor of the American South, he said to Newcomb, "Mind if I ride with you, Alvin? That storm's no place for a li'l ol' airplane."

"Sure, sir. Welcome aboard," Newcomb replied as he motioned for the two enlisted men to make room in the turret.

But the general stopped them from climbing out and riding on the hull deck. "That's okay, boys. You stay right where you are and do your jobs. I'll ride the deck."

Newcomb asked, "What does the situation up the highway look like, sir?"

"No Kraut tanks, surprisingly," the general replied. "That doesn't mean there aren't some well-concealed eighty-eights waiting for us, though. But as long as we can flank them like you've been doing all day, my boy, they shouldn't stop us from liberating Alençon by nightfall."

Wood noticed the wings on Tommy Moon's chest. "You must be our ASO, Lieutenant. What's your name, son?"

After Tommy introduced himself, the general continued, "Do we have you to thank for that brilliant air support this morning, Lieutenant Moon?"

"Well…I suppose so, sir. But I had a lot of help."

Wood gave an amused laugh. "Now isn't this something…we've got ourselves a humble flyboy here. Didn't reckon we'd be seeing the likes of you when your General Quesada agreed to put his boys down here in the dirt with us dogfaces. What made you so lucky to be the first one, Lieutenant?"

When Tommy related the story of how he'd become ASO, Wood roared with laughter. "Wrong place at the wrong time, eh, Lieutenant? Well, it's good to have you, anyway. Now why don't you and my *cannon-cocker* here"—he nodded to Lieutenant Baxter, the artillery FO—"fill me in on exactly how you marked those Kraut guns so your P-47s could find them so easy in that damn forest."

Tommy had heard some stories about General Wood in the little time he'd spent with his brother. He knew he was an artilleryman from way back, so there was no need to spoon-feed him the technical details.

When the explanation was done, the general said, "So, when we're talking target acquisition for you high-speed aviators, drawing a line of approach way up in the air beats a li'l ol' pinpoint on the ground any day? Especially a pinpoint you probably can't even see?"

"That's it in a nutshell, sir."

"Well done, gentlemen," the general said. "You know, I saw those *willy peters* popping up high but I didn't know exactly what y'all were up to. Excellent work. We're going to make that method SOP around here right quick. And it's going to need a name. Let's call it *goal posts.*"

Wood told DeLuca, the M10's radio operator, to tune into the division command net. "Gotta pick up my mail, boys. General Patton expects very timely replies."

By the time General Wood was off the radio, a rain cold for August was drenching the column, but it hadn't seemed to dampen the general's spirits a bit. "I tell you," he began, "ol' *Blood and Guts* Patton is fit to be tied right now. He found out why Montgomery refused General Bradley's request that we be allowed to advance beyond Argentan. Turns out he considers us Yanks *untested* in battle. Says he's afraid we'll get our necks broken if we try and push the Germans too hard. Can y'all believe that shit? Like we ain't been kicking Kraut ass left and right since we got off the boat at Normandy. *Untested*, my sweet ass. Hell, the only test that stick-up-his-ass Limey ever passed was the one for *how long you can wait before you get off your ass and actually do something.*"

Barely visible through the murky translucence, a high ridge line loomed a few miles ahead, dominating the road. “I don’t like the looks of that ridge,” General Wood said. “An artillery observer up there could see halfway to Spain on a good day. He can sure as hell see us even in this pea soup.” He asked Baxter, “Lieutenant, do you have that ridge plotted for fires?”

“Affirmative, sir…and the valley behind it, too.”

“Good,” the general replied. “Captain Newcomb, let’s remount the infantry and pick up the pace. Let’s make ourselves as fast-moving a target as we can.”

In the lead tank, Sean Moon had his eyes glued to the ridge line, too. The tense voice of Fabiano, his gunner, blared in his headset: “Hey, Sarge…you think they got eighty-eights up there?”

“No…they don’t want to be shooting down on us. Better odds of a hit if they shoot level.”

Sean’s head and torso were out of the hatch, straining to see through binoculars a tell-tale glimpse of anything that might indicate an observation post: an antenna, a poorly concealed vehicle, a human form; anything that didn’t match the scrub and small, sparse trees of the ridge. It didn’t help that he had to stop and wipe dry the binoculars’ lenses every few seconds.

Where would I be if I were him? I’d try to be on the front face, near the peak, so I wouldn’t get silhouetted against the sky. But gray as everything is right now, the sky’s almost as dark as the ground. Not much to be silhouetted against.

Over the mechanical growls and squeals of the Sherman came a sharp *THUD* nearly masked in a rumble of thunder. And then another, unmasked this time, unmistakable: *Artillery!*

Behind his tank, the field just north of the highway was being churned by geysers of dirt and mud flung upward with each round's impact. Captain Newcomb's voice, taut like steel wire, was in his headphones, ordering, "Keep moving. Keep it moving. Don't stop."

Even on this relatively smooth road, at top speed, the Sherman pitched like a ship in a stormy sea. A crewman who didn't brace himself would be viciously bounced around her cramped interior mercilessly; he'd be bloody and bruised in no time.

The artillery impacts shifted to the south side of the highway. *We're getting bracketed,* Sean told himself. *That fucking observer's got to be up there somewhere...*

But trying to get a steady view through binoculars in a speeding, lurching tank was almost impossible. He'd already smacked himself soundly in the face with the eyepieces twice.

At the Sherman's top speed of 25 miles per hour, they were closing fast on where the ridgeline closely paralleled the highway. A bolt of lightning backlit the ridge, seeming to linger as if a gift from the gods of weather, allowing Sean a glimpse of what he'd been searching for:

Right there! Can't mistake that shape. It's one of them Kübelwagen things.

Kübelwagen: a German "jeep."

Stupid bastard's sitting right on the ridge line. If it hadn't been for that lightning, though, I still wouldn't have seen him.

"Pull off to the left and stop," he commanded his driver.

"Why, Sarge? Ain't we in an artillery ambush?"

"I said stop the fucking tank, numbnuts. Right fucking now."

As the Sherman lurched to a halt, Sean reached down into the turret, grabbed Fabiano by his collar and pulled his head up through the hatch. "What the fuck are you doing, Sarge? You trying to get us all fucking killed?"

"No, asshole. Follow my target line." He held his arm out next to the gunner's head, his finger pointing to the spot on the ridge where the German observation post was. "That's where the fucker's at. Target further identified by the little break in the treeline. Sight in on that and blow his ass up before he brackets us in."

"But that's at least a thousand yards away, Sarge."

Sean pushed Fabiano's head back down into the turret. "So what? We ain't trying to kill a panzer here, just make a few Jerries wet their pants and run away. Hurry the fuck up before the rest of the column runs over us."

The Sherman's gun roared. The round struck the face of the ridge a little more than halfway to the crest.

"All right," Sean told Fabiano, "so maybe it's a little farther. Give it twelve hundred."

Captain Newcomb's voice blared in Sean's headset. "What are you shooting at, Moon?"

"We spotted the Kraut FO up on the ridge, sir."

"Can you handle it alone?"

"Affirmative, sir."

The third volley of German artillery slammed down, very close to the road this time. None of the speeding American vehicles were hit.

Fabiano fired again. This round seemed to hit right at the crest of the ridge. When the smoke and dust cleared, the kübelwagen was nowhere to be seen.

If there was going to be another volley, it would hit in about 20 seconds.

But that time came and passed. Newcomb ordered the M10 to pull off the road. As it did, General Wood stood tall on its deck, waving his arms in emphatic hand signals for the rest of the column to *keep moving*.

Lieutenant Baxter jumped from the M10 and ran to inspect a crater made by a German shell. He was back in the turret in less than a minute with a jagged shell fragment in his hand. "Just like I thought," Baxter said. "The trajectory of those rounds is almost straight down. The impact marks are nearly round. I'm guessing those guns are probably right on the backside of that ridge."

"Sounds like a good bet," Newcomb replied. He pointed to the shell fragment and asked, "Got a piece of the rotating band there?"

"Yeah. I can't tell the exact caliber...but I'm pretty sure it's not from an eighty-eight."

"That's good news," General Wood said. "Let's high-tail it up to the front of your column, Captain. I want to meet that eagle-eyed tanker of yours who spotted that FO. And while we're up there, maybe we locate that Kraut battery and take it out."

The German artillery battery was right where Lieutenant Baxter suspected it would be, on the backslope of the ridge line. With the American tanks blocking the highway—the only escape route—the

Germans had no choice but to stand and fight. It was a losing gamble, over all too quickly. After the tanks destroyed several howitzers with direct hits and airbursts from Baxter's artillery decimated their exposed ranks from above, the survivors threw up their hands, shouting *Kamerad!* as they surrendered.

A dozen or more bewildered dray horses wandered the smoking ground that only a few minutes ago had been a killing field. The GIs had seen such a sight before but still had trouble comprehending it. General Wood summed it up best: "It's mind boggling, boys, that a technologically advanced army like the Wehrmacht is still largely horse-drawn. Those Kraut bastards might've been told they were fighting a delaying action, but it was no more than a suicide mission for them. It's those poor dumb animals I really feel sorry for, though. Oh well…evacuate the healthy ones to the rear with the prisoners. Shoot any horses you find wounded…and make it quick, for their sake."

Wood gathered his battalion commanders from the leading elements. "Gentlemen," he told them, "we're two miles outside of Alençon and we're losing daylight. We're not going to enter the town until sunrise tomorrow. My G2 tells me there may be up to a regiment of Jerries there, with armor. Now I want to keep the house-to-house fighting to a minimum, for our sake and the sake of the townspeople. But I also want to keep that regiment—if they're still there—from escaping our grasp and living to fight another day." He unfurled a map on the hood of a jeep. "I want the Thirty-Seventh Tank to bypass Alençon under cover of darkness and form a cordon here, on the north side of town. A battalion from Fifty-Third Infantry will accompany the tanks. The terrain west of town should be quite suitable for overland movement by tracks, even at night. Any Krauts who try to duck out the back door, you take them out of the fight for good."

General Wood paused, fixated on the map as if it was still hiding some secret he desperately needed to know. Then he shook his head and said, "Dammit. Not even two full days on this road and between a few little delaying actions by the Krauts and the goddamn Free French in our way, we're already a half day behind schedule…plus we're down seven Shermans."

Chapter Fifteen

12TH ARMY GROUP COMMUNIQUE

FROM:	DATE-TIME OF ORIGIN
BRADLEY—COMMANDER, 12TH ARMY GROUP	11 AUG 44 2100 HRS

TO:
MONTGOMERY—COMMANDER, ALLIED GROUND FORCES

COPY (FOR INFO):
SHAEF (EISENHOWER); HODGES—1ST ARMY; PATTON—3RD ARMY; QUESADA—IX TAC; WEYLAND—XIX TAC

ALL UNITS OF THIS COMMAND ARE ADVANCING AHEAD OF SCHEDULE TOWARD FLERS-ARGENTAN "HOLD LINE," DESPITE SIGNIFICANT DELAYING TACTICS BY ELEMENTS OF GERMAN 7TH ARMY. ANTICIPATE ARRIVAL AT "HOLD LINE" WITHIN TWO DAYS (13 AUG). IF 21ST ARMY GROUP NOT IN A POSITION TO MEET US THERE ON THAT DATE, DOES IT NOT MAKE MORE SENSE TO ALLOW 12TH ARMY GROUP TO CONTINUE ADVANCING NORTHWARD UNTIL FALAISE-ARGENTAN "POCKET" IS CLOSED? THIRD ARMY IN PARTICULARLY GOOD POSITION TO SEAL ANY FURTHER GERMAN RETREAT EASTWARD IF ALLOWED TO ADVANCE BEYOND "HOLD LINE."

SIGNED,
BRADLEY

Chapter Sixteen

The storm was long passed, leaving in its wake a night sky clear and ablaze with stars. Lying on the hull of his brother's dormant tank, Tommy Moon had given up trying to count those stars. He'd given up on a few other things, too, since the sun went down, like trying to catch a nap, something the tankers didn't seem to have any problem taking turns doing. Or wondering whether he'd ever get back into a jug's cockpit. He checked his watch; it read 0005—five minutes past midnight. His third day with 4th Armored had just begun:

And only God knows how many days to go. It feels like I've been here for a year already. Did the Air Force forget all about me? It's funny—when I was a kid, being around my big brother made me feel safe. But here...

Sean's head popped from the turret hatch. "Hey, Half," he called out in a muted voice, "you awake?"

"I am now."

"Ahh, don't bullshit a bullshitter. I've been watching. You ain't caught a wink. What's the matter? You nervous or something?"

"Fuck, yeah, I'm nervous. Aren't you?"

He climbed down from the turret and crouched next to his little brother. "No, Half, I ain't nervous. Just alert." He offered a chunk of D bar. "You want some?"

With a *snap* that sounded thunderous in the stillness of night, Tommy broke off a piece and popped it into his mouth. He wasn't expecting the bitterness of the chocolate. His face looked like he was sucking lemons.

Sean chuckled. "Creature comforts got you by the ass, flyboy. But you get used to the taste of this shit. Eventually. And it'll keep you moving."

Tommy sat up and scanned the velvet darkness of moonlit French countryside all around them. He knew where they were supposed to be on the map but had no clue if they were actually there.

"How do you guys know you're in the right place, Sean?"

"You saw how it works. The captain goes off with the infantry and does his little recon, then he sends guides back to lead us into the positions he wants."

"Yeah, I know all that, Sean. I was here, remember? But really, how the hell do you know where you are when you have to go overland in pitch darkness to get there?"

"Just follow the lines on the map, little brother. Just follow the lines."

"I don't know, Sean…I might have been born at night but I wasn't born *last* night. Lines on a map are one thing, but there aren't any damn lines on the ground. Sounds like a big crapshoot to me."

"Ain't everything, Half?"

"Gee, aren't you the fucking philosopher all of a sudden. But tell me—do you guys fight at night a lot?"

"When we have to, Tommy. Only when we have to."

"I'll bet it gets pretty crazy—a night fight, I mean. Seems like the odds of killing friendlies are pretty damn high."

"Brother, you got no fucking idea."

"Actually, I do, Sean. It's pretty easy to accidentally kill friendlies from the air, too. Even in broad daylight."

Sean gave him a surprised look. "You ever done it?"

"Maybe. I'm not really sure."

With a bemused smile on his face, Sean said, "You pilots get away with fucking murder. Like those assholes who bombed the shit out of Thirtieth Division…even killed a general, I hear. I bet they're all swigging Guinness in some English pub right fucking now, with their hands up some barmaid's skirt and not a care in the world. When us ground pounders kill a friendly by accident, though, you better believe somebody's gonna swing for it."

"Oh, bullshit, *Crunch.* How about…"

But he stopped himself. He'd spat the nickname *Crunch* with all the derisiveness he could summon—his *Irish was up*, as they'd say back in Brooklyn when someone was pissed off. But he knew he shouldn't say the words lining up to tumble from his mouth: *How about you standing over those dead Krauts yesterday…and Newcomb asking you if you got any prisoners…and you said, "Negative, sir. Didn't work out that way." What the hell did you mean by that, Sean? Last time I checked, killing POWs was categorized as murder.*

"I asked you not to call me *Crunch*, Tommy…and I fucking meant it."

"Why? I thought you'd like a nickname like that, considering how you got it and all."

Sean didn't reply. The irritated silence they fell into didn't last but a few seconds. Four human shapes were approaching up the gentle slope from the direction of the road. Two were topped with the unmistakable silhouettes of GI helmets. "Get the password from 'em," Sean told Fabiano, who had already leveled his

Thompson in their direction. "Don't shoot 'em first, okay?"

Softly, Fabiano called out, "I hear it's nice in *Omaha* this time of year."

"Bullshit," a male voice replied. "I prefer *Indianapolis* myself."

"Indianapolis," Sean said. "Today's magic word. Let 'em in, Fab."

The GIs were infantrymen. The two with them were French civilians, one a young woman, the other a middle-aged man. "Where's your C.O., Sarge?" one of the GIs asked Sean. "These folks say they've got some real interesting stuff to tell him."

"He's at the M10 right over there…about thirty yards," Sean replied as he jumped to the ground from the tank's deck. "C'mon, I'll bring you over. Hey, *Lieutenant*," he called to his brother, "why don't you join us, too? This oughta be interesting as all hell."

Even in the darkness, there was no doubt the woman was attractive. Despite her youth, she possessed the composure of one used to being in charge. But her shimmering frock seemed far too grand for a night stroll in the fields, as did the high heels on which she tottered across the grassy turf still soft from the rain. Most of the women they'd seen across the French towns and countryside so far looked like weathered, hardscrabble farm wives, pitifully plain, in old clothes mended many times over, the harsh uncertainties of life in a theater of war etched on their faces. But this one was wearing makeup and intoxicating perfume, too.

Kinda like a whore, Sean Moon thought as she brushed by him.

The young woman walked right up to Newcomb. In thickly accented but precise English, she said, "My name is Sylvie Bergerac. You are the commander here?"

"Yeah, I'm Captain Al Newcomb, ma'am."

She seemed decidedly unimpressed. "You are only a captain. We know there are many Americans just outside Alençon. Surely someone of higher rank is in the area, too. A colonel or general, perhaps?"

Newcomb replied, "Maybe you'd better tell me what's on your mind first, lady, before I waste the time of anyone with *higher rank*, okay?"

"As you wish, Captain," she replied.

She launched into her story. By the time she'd finished her third sentence, Newcomb was sending a runner to get the battalion commander *on the double.*

As they waited for Colonel Abrams to arrive, Sylvie and the older man with her exchanged comments in French. "Can you understand what they're saying, Half?" Sean asked. "You knew all that frog shit real good back with the nuns."

"Yeah, of course I understand. You sure you want to know?"

Captain Newcomb pulled Tommy aside and said, "Hell, yeah, we want to know. What're they saying?"

"Well, sir, in a nutshell, they're saying we're all *dumber than sheep.*"

The captain smirked as he asked, "She mean just present company? Or all Americans in general?"

"For the moment, I think it's just us."

Sylvie had overheard. She shot an annoyed look Tommy's way and said, "*Merci pour les petite faveurs.*"

That needed no translation. Even Newcomb and Sean figured out it meant *thanks for the small favors.* She and her companion wouldn't exchange another word.

"Looks like you got yourself a friend, Tommy," Sean said, patting his little brother on the back. "And a real looker, too."

The runner returned with Colonel Abrams and his radio operator in tow. Sylvie began her story all over again.

"The *Boche* will leave Alençon before dawn, *mon colonel*, along this highway before us. They are a weak force, battered from combat with the Americans at Rennes and Laval—"

The colonel interrupted her: "Just how *weak* are we talking here, Mademoiselle Bergerac?"

"It's *madame, mon colonel*…and just how weak are they? No more than two hundred men."

"Okay…maybe two companies, tops. What about vehicles?"

"About a dozen *camions*," she replied.

"You mean *trucks* with motors? Not horse-drawn wagons?"

"Ahh, *oui*…trucks."

"And tanks?" Abrams asked. "Are there any tanks?"

"*Oui*. Five. The *Boche* call them *tigre*."

All the tankers in earshot let out a collective, "Ahh, shit."

"But there are only five," Sylvie protested.

"Ma'am," Abrams said, "we might kill five Tigers…but in the dark, with no air support, we'll probably lose just about every Sherman in this battalion doing it."

"Then perhaps we can come to an arrangement," Sylvie replied. "Allow the *Boche* to escape. You live to fight them on better terms…and Alençon is spared the inevitable destruction."

For a few moments, the tankers found her suggestion quite enticing. But it was Colonel Abrams who finally shattered their wishful thinking. "Unacceptable," he said. "If they come tonight, we're going to take them on, one way or another."

"I was afraid that would be your answer," she replied.

"Let me ask you something, *Madame* Bergerac," the colonel said. "How do you know all this? And why should I believe you?"

"Because the *Oberst* told it to me."

Abrams was more skeptical now than a moment ago. "Why would a Kraut officer be telling you anything?"

"*Mon colonel*, the *Boche*, like all men, tell a woman many things to remain important once they are finished inside her."

Sean whispered in his brother's ear, "See? I told you that jane's a fucking whore."

Whispered or not, Sylvie understood every word.

Abrams' skepticism was faltering fast. "And when did this *Oberst* tell you they were pulling out of Alençon?"

"A few hours ago, *mon colonel.*" Grinning broadly, she added, "And the *imbécile* had no idea he was telling it to the *maquis.*"

A startled Abrams asked, "You're *maquis*? The Underground? "

"*Oui, mon colonel.*" She opened the musette bag slung over her shoulder and showed him the Welrod pistol within—an assassin's weapon supplied by British SOE. "Perhaps now you believe me?"

****

They began to hear the low murmur of truck engines just past 0300. A few minutes later, an infantry listening post close to the highway reported a column of German vehicles on the outskirts of Alençon, heading north. A few minutes more, and the tankers could see the dark silhouettes of slow-moving trucks without lights passing in single file before them.

Colonel Abrams' voice growled from the battalion's radios: "Do not—repeat—do not engage the wheeled vehicles. Wait for my command."

Huddled behind the M10 with her male companion and Tommy Moon, Sylvie Bergerac felt a flicker of hope blossom within her. "Maybe your colonel will let the Germans escape after all."

"No," Tommy replied, "I don't think that's going to happen. He's just trying to set a trap for the Tigers."

"I do not follow, Lieutenant Moon."

"The Tigers are hanging back. If we start shooting up the trucks now, the German tankers will know exactly where we are and cut us to ribbons before we've had a chance to take them out."

"So you are waiting for the Tigers to show themselves on the road?"

"Yeah. That way, the first hint they'll get that we're here is when they start getting broadsided from our guns. If we can get in the first shot, we've got a chance."

She turned to her companion and explained the American tactics in French.

"We can speak *en français* if that would make it easier," Tommy said.

Sylvie smiled, touching his cheek tenderly as she would a child. "*Merci*, Lieutenant, but I have heard a little of your *français americain.* It is better I translate for *mon papa* than you. But should you not be off to fight with your comrades now?"

He explained what his job was and how he had nothing to do at the moment but keep the *maquis* visitors safe and out of the way.

"But if you are a flyer, Lieutenant, what are you doing here without an airplane?"

"I guess you can chalk that up to luck, Madame Bergerac."

"I would say it is quite the opposite, Lieutenant."

The sound of the trucks faded quickly as they made their way north. After a few moments of anxious silence, a fearsome rumble of heavy machinery began to emanate from the town. "The sound of the *tigres*," Sylvie said.

Captain Newcomb called down from the M10's turret: "Lieutenant Moon, take our guests and go find a hidey-hole somewhere, on the double. This is about to get very messy."

"Come," Sylvie said, "we go to the orchard."

Surprised, Tommy asked, "There's an orchard around here?"

"Yes, behind us, a few hundred meters that way," she replied, pointing into the darkness.

As they moved quickly away from the line of armored vehicles, they could hear the mechanical *whir* as gunners cranked the turrets manually, scanning for targets. The sound of the Tigers' engines grew louder as they left Alençon and followed the trucks north up the highway.

Though the edge of the orchard was well behind the tanks, it was farther up the slope and afforded Tommy, Sylvie, and her *papa* a good view of the road. They counted the Tigers' silhouettes until all five were about to pass right in front of 37th Tank's guns. Tommy saw the brief, repeated glimmer on the southern horizon of artillery firing a few seconds before he heard their muted *poom*.

Our guns, he told himself, *putting up illum rounds.*

Then the night was turned to ghostly day as the illumination rounds popped their flares high in the air over the Tigers, bathing them, the American tanks, and the open fields all around in harsh glare and shadows that danced back and forth across the ground as the brilliant balls of light swung in their parachutes.

The 35 guns of 37th Tank fired as one, their 75-millimeter rounds streaking arrow-straight toward the targets, trailing fiery red tails like comets.

The engines of the American tanks roared to life. Once a tank fires a round, its position isn't a secret anymore. And a tank that can't move is a metal shell asking to be turned into a furnace. The running engines—despite the industrial racket they brought to the battlefield—could now spell the difference between life and death.

Some rounds bounced off the turrets of the Tigers in splashes of orange, probably causing their crews screaming ears and splitting headaches but delivering no knockout blow.

A few rounds hit tracks and road wheels. Crippling wounds but not mortal.

A dozen rounds missed completely, plowing the ground short or disappearing long.

The rest struck the weaker side and rear armor. The trailing Tiger was surrounded by a shimmering red glow for a few moments, until flames belched from her engine compartment. Burning crewmen struggled from her hatches, only to die quickly in a hail of American machine gun bullets.

The second Tiger in the column began to turn toward the Americans, trying to show them nothing but her impenetrable front armor. But she stopped halfway. Her hatches flew open, spewing the same red glow as her sister. If any of her crew managed to escape the inferno she had become, the GIs never saw them.

The third Tiger suffered a shattered left track. But that didn't prevent her from slewing her hull about on the good right track toward the Americans so they had nothing to target but that thick front armor. There was nothing wrong with her main gun, either. The Tiger fired, shooting a Charlie Company Sherman right through the lower portion of her front armor, instantly turning her into a crematory for her five crewmen.

The first and fourth Tiger were very much alive and fully mobile. They, too, had turned toward the Americans and were rumbling up the slope. The Shermans directly in their path backed frantically away, firing shots that, even if they'd hit the Tigers, would've probably just bounced off their glacis plates.

The illumination rounds were dropping low, their light fading fast. Approaching point-blank range now, the German tanks killed three more Shermans before they realized their mistake: there were far more American tanks than they realized. Four Shermans from

Baker Company had circled behind them, pumping round after round of 75 millimeter through the Tigers' soft rear ends until all three were quickly ablaze.

Then it was over, only a minute after it started. The illumination rounds had burned out, leaving the battlefield lit only by gutted tanks burning like torches in the night. The sweet fragrance of a late summer's night was replaced by the stench of burning gasoline, expended ordnance, and roasted flesh.

Now came the difficult task of reorganizing in the dark a battalion of armored behemoths scattered over hundreds of acres. Wounded would have to be cared for; the dead would have to be collected. Vigilance against a counterattack by the German infantry—whether in the trucks they'd let pass or still in the town—had to be maintained.

Sean's Sherman—*Eclipse of the Hun*—was stopped 20 yards behind one of the burning Tigers. She'd fired three rounds into the German monster: *Maybe we killed her all by ourselves.*

But *Eclipse* had taken some hits, too; nothing that took her out of action or turned a crewman into a casualty, but the odor of gasoline inside her hull had become overpowering. "Everybody out," Sean ordered when Captain Newcomb radioed the *cease fire and regroup* command. "Shut her down all the way, so maybe she don't blow."

Climbing down from the turret, Sean saw his driver start to slide off the front of the tank to the ground. No sooner had his feet touched down than he recoiled back onto the deck. Sean could hear him murmuring, "Oh, fuck…oh, fuck." He was hunched over like a man about to be sick.

Sean peered over the tank's nose—and then it was his turn to recoil.

The head and shoulders of a German tanker protruded from beneath the left track. The rest of him was crushed beneath the treads. His eyes—bulging, wide with terror, reflecting the glow of his burning Tiger—still blazed with the last flickers of life's fire.

But not for long. When they glanced over the nose again, his eyes were looking to another dimension, one only the dead could see.

"I never saw nothing," the driver said. "Where the fuck did that Kraut came from, anyway?"

"He must've fell down or something when he was running away, that's all," Fabiano, the gunner, offered. "Too fucking bad for the poor bastard."

As the crew put a safe distance between them and their tank, they heard Sean mumbling, "Not again. Oh, God…not again, dammit."

Chapter Seventeen

Alençon was secured by 0930. The troopers of 4th Armored found only citizens eager to welcome them. The *Boche* were gone. Sylvie Bergerac was ecstatic.

"Thank you, *mon colonel*," she said as she kissed Colonel Abrams on both cheeks in the center of town. "Thank you for sparing us the agony of liberation."

Abrams' only response was a smile more solemn than celebratory. Six hours earlier, when the Germans began their exodus, he really hadn't been thinking of sparing the good people of Alençon the death and destruction a house-to-house fight would have entailed. He'd just wanted as much of the element of surprise he could garner against the superior firepower of the Tigers.

For a tank they're not supposed to have a lot of, we sure seem to come up against them often enough, he told himself. *But this time, we only lost four of ours to take out five Tigers. That's the best scorecard we've had yet.*

The colonel wasn't deluding himself that kill ratio would last: *Our only hope is they run out of tanks before we do.*

****

Tommy finally found his brother in the hastily set up maintenance depot on the outskirts of Alençon. Sean was up to his waist in the engine compartment of *Eclipse*, supervising two mechanics who were fixing her ruptured fuel line. "We would've been *zippoed* for sure if this leak lit off," he told his brother. "We're goddamn lucky all we took was a couple of glancing shots."

Tommy walked around the far side of the tank to see what the results of *glancing shots* from a Tiger looked like. He stopped dead in his tracks when he saw them; it looked like some giant can opener had punched through the side armor. The thick steel had been peeled away as easily as bullets and flak tore through the fragile aluminum skin of his P-47. Another mechanic was preparing heavy steel patches to be welded to *Eclipse* as soon as the fuel line repair was complete. Billowing smoke and showers of sparks around several other tanks in the depot signaled their patches were already being welded into place.

Captain Newcomb walked through the depot, checking on the progress of his tanks' repairs. "Take the time to do it right, boys," he grumbled to the mechanics, "because we ain't going anywhere until the fuel trucks show up."

Sean asked, "Any word when the hell that'll be, sir?"

"A couple of hours, maybe."

"They can take their damn sweet time, as far as I'm concerned," Sean said under his breath. He didn't care if his company commander heard it.

In no mood for smart-mouthing, Captain Newcomb asked, "You got something on your mind, Sergeant?"

"No, sir. Not a damn thing."

Newcomb let it drop; there were bigger problems to tackle than a surly attitude from one of his best fighters. He looked to Tommy and said, "Lieutenant. We've got a meeting with General Wood in fifteen minutes at the town hall. Meet you there. Bring all your maps."

Satisfied the engine repair was in good hands, Sean climbed from the tank to join his brother. "You better hurry, Half. Don't keep his fucking highness the general waiting."

"What's with you, Sean? You've got a bug up your ass. You had one last night, too, before the shit started to fly."

"Fuck off, Tommy. You flyboys wouldn't understand."

"I'm your fucking brother, Sean, and flying is fighting, too. Try me."

Sean wandered away from the maintenance in progress to light a cigarette. Tommy was right behind him.

"You going to talk or what, Sean?"

He took a long drag on his cigarette before answering. "Look, Lieutenant…*Tommy*…I don't know…it's just that I keep seeing their faces, that's all."

"Whose faces, Sean? What are you talking about?"

He looked at his little brother like he'd just asked the dumbest question in the world. "That nickname of mine, Tommy…those Krauts I ran over. I saw their faces…and I just keep seeing them, day after day. And fuck me if it didn't happen all over again this morning. Crushed another son of a bitch. Saw his face, too."

"Sean, it's kill or be killed, right? Shitty as it is, that's our job. Does it really matter how you kill them?"

The logic had no impact on Sean Moon. "They're gonna be waiting for me in hell," he said. "It's just a matter of time. Just a matter of fucking time."

Tommy started to put a comforting arm around his brother just like he had that first night he spent with 37th Tank. But Sean pushed him away.

"Knock it the fuck off, little brother. You ain't the fucking padre…and there's a bunch of wise-ass douchebags watching. I don't need no more fucking nicknames."

Maybe this isn't the time to ask him about killing those prisoners, Tommy thought.

Tommy walked the cobblestones of Alençon's *grand-rue* on his way to General Wood's meeting. All around him, joyous townspeople were singing and dancing with GIs keen on enjoying whatever pleasures they could find. In all the reverie, he noticed something odd, though: it looked like a parade of civilian couples—10, he counted—were avoiding the celebration and converging from several directions on a quaint row house tucked away in an alley. As they reached the house, a couple would exchange a tender kiss. Then the woman entered the house as her man offered a wave of goodbye that seemed heavy with resignation before walking away. Every man and woman was wearing a wedding band.

After all the women were inside, a smiling Sylvie Bergerac emerged, now dressed more casually in trousers, oxfords, and a beret the French would instantly recognize as the mark of the *maquis*. She walked toward the *grand-rue* and Tommy Moon.

"Hello, Lieutenant," she said in English. "You are going to the meeting now?"

"Yeah. And where are you off to, Madame Bergerac?"

"I am invited to your meeting, too."

"Really? They invited you?"

"Is it so strange, Lieutenant, that your general might want the continued advice of the *maquis*?"

"I suppose not, ma'am. But can I ask you something?"

"Of course."

"That house you just came out of. Is that what I think it is?"

"If you think it is my father's house, you are correct, Lieutenant."

She knew her evasive answer didn't satisfy him, so she added, "And yes, it is also a house of prostitution, ever since the *Boche* came."

"But those women…they're all married, aren't they? And aren't you?"

His questions amused her. "Does that disqualify us?"

"No, but…" He didn't know what to say next.

"Times have been very difficult, Lieutenant. We all must do what we can to survive."

Tommy looked more confused than ever. "But I've seen what they did to women who took up with the Germans. The shaved heads, the shaming parades…"

"We did not *take up* with the *Boche*, Lieutenant. And we are not collaborators. Spying on the *Boche* is never collaboration, no matter how you do it."

"You really got a lot of information out of your…ahh, *clients*?"

Sylvie rolled her eyes. "Were you not here last night? Was the information I provided not accurate?"

Point taken, he told himself.

"So I guess your *father's house* is open for business with the GIs now?"

"The times are still very difficult, Lieutenant. And will be for quite a while, I'm afraid."

Trying to lighten the conversation, he asked, "Does that mean you'll be spying on us, too?" He meant it as a joke.

She didn't take it that way. "Not as long as we are on the same side, Lieutenant."

"Okay, fair enough. May I ask where your husband is, ma'am?"

"You are about to meet him, Lieutenant," she replied as they stepped into the town hall.

****

General Wood opened the meeting on a somber note. "I've got bad news, gentlemen—" with a nod to Sylvie, he added, "and lady. It looks like our fuel won't arrive until late this afternoon. We'll be fueling most of the night, by the looks of it, so the division as a whole won't move out of Alençon until tomorrow."

"What's the hold-up with the fuel, sir?" Colonel Abrams asked.

The general blew an exasperated sigh before replying. "Some idiot up at Twelfth Army Group thought it would be a good idea to refuel the French Second Armored first. By the time Third Army could point out we were already miles ahead of the French, it was too late to change horses."

It was Colonel Abrams' turn to be exasperated. "So the damn French are holding us up again, and without actually being in our way this time. Unbelievable." As an afterthought, he offered a contrite look to Sylvie and her husband Bernard, the *maquis* commander at Alençon, and added, "No offense meant to present company, of course."

When Sylvie offered Bernard's translated reply to the room, its cordial tone seemed quite the opposite of what he'd spat out in French: "Of course, *mon colonel*. None taken."

Tommy was pretty sure Bernard had actually said, "Tell these buffoons if they insult us again, we are leaving."

"Naturally," General Wood continued, "this blows our schedule all to hell. Twenty-five miles to go to Argentan, against probable stiff resistance the closer we get, and a little less than two days to do it in."

He tapped a pointer on the map hung on the wall. "I don't plan for us to just sit here, twiddling our thumbs, though. By robbing Peter's fuel tank to fill Paul's, we're going to send a recon team—in force—up the highway to Sées and, if possible, beyond. Sées is a little more than halfway to Argentan. G2 thinks the Germans have pulled out of there just like they did here at Alençon. If the recon team finds that to be the case, the rest of the division, once refueled, can barrel up the road at night and make up for some lost time."

General Wood scanned the room, seeking to find a battalion commander eager for the challenge he'd just outlined whose eyes would actually meet his. Only Colonel Abrams did so, if just for the most fleeting of moments.

"It's yours, Creighton," Wood said.

"Very well, sir," Abrams replied. "How big a team are you thinking? We can probably only scrounge up enough gasoline for two tank companies, tops, and a platoon or so of mounted infantry for security."

"Sounds like an excellent start to me, Creighton," Wood replied. "Pick your team and be ready to move out by noon."

Throughout the general's map exercise, Sylvie and Bernard were in animated conversation. Now that Wood seemed to be bringing the meeting to a close, Sylvie begged for his attention.

"*Mon général*, your information about the *Boche* leaving Sées is incorrect. They are not leaving."

Wood replied, "And how do you know that, Madame Bergerac?"

"Because there are *maquis* there, as well. They informed us."

"How'd they manage to do that, ma'am?"

Finding it hard to control the exasperation in her voice, she replied, "Because we have telephones, *mon général*. This country is not as primitive as you suppose."

Now it was Wood's turn to be exasperated. "You mean to tell me they just dialed you up and told you where the Germans are?"

"Yes. Exactly."

"And you aren't afraid, madame, that the Germans might have compromised your communications system? Maybe even used it to spread false information?"

"Again, *mon général*, we are not primitives. We use a code. The *Boche* have never broken it. Bernard and I stand here as living proof."

Wood scowled. He wanted to believe her. But an army is like a boulder rolling down a hill. Once it starts moving, it's impossible to alter its course without begging for disaster. Besides, nobody contradicts a general. Not even a beautiful, gutsy young woman.

"But you won't mind, Madame Bergerac, if we check this intel of yours out for ourselves by running this little mission of mine?"

"If you must, *mon général*. But we have more information to share with you, as well."

"All right, let's have it."

"My husband and I have received much information about the *Boche* retreat through this *Falaise-Argentan pocket*, as you call it. True, they are hounded by your airplanes, but the vanguard of their column will be much farther east than you realize by the time you get to Argentan, and airplanes alone do not stop those they do not kill. And they do not fly at night, when the *Boche* are marching the greatest distances. You are already too late to trap them if you move against Argentan. You will merely bump into their right flank and risk being encircled yourselves. To cut off their retreat, you must go farther east—to Gacé, perhaps. Maybe beyond."

Ain't that hot shit, the general told himself. *Monty says stop at Argentan and wait for the Krauts and his Limeys, but the Resistance says that train's already left the station.*

Wood took a grease pencil and extended eastward the "stop" line that ran through Argentan. The town of Gacé sat about four miles north of that line—into the zone Allied Ground Commander Montgomery had forbidden the Americans to go.

Four fucking miles, Wood schemed. *I'll bet ol' Georgie Patton wouldn't bat an eyelash at a little "going over the line" like that.*

"This is very interesting intelligence, Madame Bergerac," the general said. "I'll discuss this with higher headquarters immediately. Of course, if it turns out you're wrong about Sées, though, it won't be worth spit."

"But Gacé is beyond the stop line, sir," the division G2 said. "Our orders specify—"

"I know where it is, dammit," Wood interrupted. "I'd like to move on now, because I've got some good news to share, too. More than just fuel is coming today. We'll be getting a dozen replacement Shermans and eight M10s to fill our losses. They're coming partially crewed, so we'll have to fill the empty seats from our existing roster. This will be a chance to move up our most promising crewmen to gunners and tank commanders."

Captain Newcomb raised his hand. "Sir, will the Shermans be A1 models with the bigger gun?"

"Afraid not, Captain. But on the bright side, all the tank destroyers will be up-gunned with the higher-velocity seventy-six millimeter."

"Gee, that's great," Newcomb replied. "Too bad they still won't be worth a damn in a maneuvering fight."

"Are you telling me you don't want the extra firepower, Captain?"

"Negative, sir. Negative. We'll try and make good use of them."

As the meeting broke up, the division G3 called Tommy over. "Lieutenant," he said, "I've just gotten word your replacement is coming in with the new vehicles. It looks like you'll be back in a cockpit before you know it."

Chapter Eighteen

Task Force Newcomb was ready to roll at noon, as planned. Since its mission was recon, it was designed for speed and light on firepower. Of the eight Sherman tanks left in Captain Newcomb's Baker Company, six were repaired, refueled, and ready to go, as was the captain's M10. Another four light tanks—M5 Stuarts of Dog Company—and a 40-man infantry platoon crammed into three armored half-tracks rounded out the force.

Sean Moon's tank, *Eclipse of the Hun*, would be the lead vehicle. He wasn't happy to see his brother climbing aboard the captain's M10. "You shouldn't be coming on this mission, Half," he said. "You're getting relieved. You should be packing your bags and heading back to flyboy-land."

"Ahh, you'd miss me if I didn't come along," Tommy replied. "Especially being out of artillery range and all. You just might need a little *flyboy* support."

"Yeah, but it didn't have to be you. Only an idiot volunteers…and you ain't no fucking idiot."

Tommy winked as he replied, "I'm not worried. I've got my big bad brother to protect me." He was expecting at least a smile in reply. But he got nothing.

The 12-mile drive north to Sées across the verdant, rolling countryside would have seemed idyllic if not for the constant, nerve-racking vigilance required. Given an opportunity like this, surrounded by natural beauty unspoiled as yet by the ravages of combat, your soul wanted to forget you were at war. But your nerves wouldn't let it. At any moment, an anti-tank gun could turn your armored cocoon into a white-hot cauldron of death. Your only chance was to kill it before it killed you.

They saw the town from almost two miles away, the twin spires of its ancient cathedral rising like signposts, its old stone buildings varying shades of gray in the early afternoon sun. “Just what I was afraid of,” Captain Newcomb said, binoculars pressed to his eyes. “If there are Krauts up there in those steeples, they can see for miles. Lieutenant Moon, how far away are your fighters?”

“Ten to twelve minutes, sir, once we call for them.”

Newcomb shook his head. “Shit. That’s a long fucking time.”

They rolled a mile closer. If there were any Germans in Sées, they were well concealed. In the lead tank, Sean Moon’s attention was drawn to several low stone buildings on the outskirts, straddling the narrow road. Calling the captain on the radio, he said, “That’d be a hell of a place to stash a couple of guns. How about we spread out a little?”

“Yeah, good plan,” Newcomb replied. “Let’s get off the road.” Then, in a few brief transmissions, he redeployed his force from column into line formation and continued the advance toward the town. “They can’t shoot us all if we’re spread wide.”

But the Germans could easily shoot one or two. Nobody saw where the first anti-tank round came from. It ripped through the engine compartment of a Stuart moving through the open field west of the highway. Tommy Moon counted all four of her crew as they quickly escaped before she started to burn fiercely.

A few seconds later, another round landed on the road just a few yards in front of the M10, pelting the tank destroyer with dirt, paving stones, and shell fragments that caused no damage and injured no one.

"Well," Captain Newcomb said, "if the Krauts are supposed to be pulling out of here, I guess someone forgot to tell them."

The Shermans were approaching those stone structures from the east when they saw the muzzles of the German guns. "Looks like they've got seventy-fives in those bunkers," Sean reported. "At least three. They've got logs piled on top, too, so don't waste any mortar rounds on them. They won't do a damn thing."

"Can you get behind them?" Newcomb asked.

"Negative, not without showing our flanks. Gotta keep our good side facing 'em."

The main guns of three Shermans fired at the bunkers—old farm buildings turned into miniature fortresses—from 500 yards. When the dust of their impact settled, the only damage was cosmetic.

There was no need to tell Tommy to get the P-47s coming. He already had them on the radio.

"I'm gonna send the Stuarts around the back," the captain said, hoping their greater speed and the smaller targets they presented would get the three remaining light tanks safely through the killing zone to envelop the Germans. That order given, Newcomb directed his M10 and the infantry half-tracks to move right—to the east—and support the Shermans.

Churning across the open field at nearly 20 miles per hour, the Stuarts were quickly outside the fields of fire of the bunkers' guns. Taking advantage of harassing fire from the Shermans' main guns and .50-caliber machine guns, they flanked the German position within minutes and started their turn to assault them from the rear.

The lieutenant in charge of the Stuart platoon came up on the radio net: "How far out is the Air Force?"

Tommy replied, "Six minutes."

"Good. Plenty of time."

The lieutenant swung the line of his three tanks around to blast the bunkers. They were only halfway through that maneuver when his Stuart blew apart like a fragile toy.

"Shit," Newcomb growled as he pressed the binoculars to his eyes. "They're taking fire from farther inside the town. Can't tell if it's from a tank or an eighty-eight or what."

The two surviving Stuarts—now without their leader—kept advancing on the bunkers, looking for a soft spot—a door, a window, any opening—where their light 37-millimeter rounds wouldn't just bounce off.

What they saw instead was a German soldier armed with a *panzerfaust* popping up from behind a log barrier right in front of them. He was quickly cut down by a burst of .30-caliber machine gun fire from a Stuart.

But that burst came at the second he'd squeezed the *panzerfaust's* trigger. As bullets knocked him backward, the rocket fired, propelling itself nearly straight up into the air—and out of the buttoned-up tankers' limited field of vision. For all they knew, it would come straight back down on them—and be every bit as deadly as if the weapon had been fired on a level trajectory.

Another soldier with a *panzerfaust* popped up. He fired—and missed—before the Stuarts had a chance to train their machine guns on him.

But where the hell is the one coming straight down?

Both Stuart commanders arrived at the same, instantaneous conclusion: *This is too hairy. We're driving through infantry with no infantry support of our own. There could be Krauts on our deck any second, stuffing grenades into the vents. Shit, they could be there right now...*

And we're in range of that gun that got the lieutenant.

Both tanks turned and fled in the direction they'd come.

Like a gesture of good riddance, the errant rocket completed its vertical trajectory just yards behind them, its blast deeply cratering the ground and sending a geyser of dirt high into the air.

I'm really fucking this one up, Captain Newcomb told himself. *I should have sent some infantry with the Stuarts. Or not sent them at all. And the town is hot, dammit. The division isn't going to be high-balling it through this place day or night, that's for damn sure. At least now we can give Colonel Abrams his answer...if we get our asses out of here alive.*

Who am I kidding? If we don't come back, he gets the same answer.

Tommy was relieved to see how relatively smoke-free this battle scene was. He'd given up trying to get the mortars to mark the target with airbursts just like he and Baxter had done with artillery; their fire direction procedures were just too rudimentary. One smoke round on the ground would have to do. "Just put a *willy peter* on the road in between the bunkers on my command," he told the mortar sergeant.

"Once your planes hit the bunkers," Newcomb told Tommy, "have them hang around and keep our asses covered so we can get the hell out of here. The Krauts won't try a counterattack if your boys are hanging around up there."

"No problem, sir. They can stay with us all the way back to Alençon, if you want."

They could see the P-47s now, four high and fast-moving silver specks to the northwest. "*Topeka Flight*, spiral down right," Tommy told the flight's lead pilot. "Do not overfly Sées at low level. The town's hot. Repeat, the town's hot."

The planes did as they were instructed, dropping in well-spaced pairs to low level in a swirling descent. As they rolled out of the turn on the attack heading Tommy provided, the WP round from the mortar struck the road and began to spew its thick white smoke into the air."

"Got the smoke," *Topeka Leader* reported.

The Shermans had been raking the bunkers with their .50 calibers to deter the Germans from firing on the aircraft. Once the planes began the attack run, though, Tommy ordered the tankers to *cease fire*. "Thanks for the help, guys," he added, "but let's not have any accidents here today."

It wouldn't have been the first time target-fixated gunners accidentally shot down friendly aircraft.

Topeka Leader and *Topeka Two* flashed by, releasing two bombs each along the line of bunkers. The bombs tore the log roofs off all but one of the bunkers, kicking up a storm of dust and smoke. The last two jugs were starting their attack run, 15 seconds out.

"Good drop, *Topeka Leader*," Tommy said. "Okay, *Topeka Three*, on my mark…three, two, one, DROP."

Those bombs struck the remaining bunker, blowing off its log roof as if it was nothing but twigs.

"Outstanding, *Topeka*," Tommy reported, his voice turning giddy, losing the usual radio monotone. "Orbit south, stand by."

He needed a moment to catch his breath. Though he'd dropped them many times, he'd never felt the swift, earth-shaking violence wreaked by 500-pound bombs up close. From the air, they were just all smoke and dust, with perhaps a fleeting glimpse of the circular shock wave coursing outward from the point of impact as your plane sped away. But viewed from the ground, they were enough to scare you shitless. All the tank, artillery, and mortar shells he'd seen impact in the last few days paled in comparison.

The bunkers might have been pummeled and the Germans within dead or dazed, but the walls of those ancient structures had hardly a stone displaced. They provided excellent cover for the Shermans from the guns in the town as they closed in to mop up.

"Are we looking for prisoners, sir?" Tommy asked.

"Only if they're not already bleeding to death," Newcomb replied. "Let the Krauts take care of their own wounded. Mostly, we're looking for intel…maps, documents. That kind of stuff."

"Can I help, sir?"

"Suit yourself, Lieutenant."

As he walked toward his brother's tank, Tommy heard a man screaming in German. Hurrying to the sound, he found Fabiano, Sean's gunner, standing over a kneeling, frantic Wehrmacht soldier with his hands up. The muzzle of the gunner's Thompson was wedged under the man's chin.

"*Kamerad! Kamerad!*"

"Kamerad my fucking ass," Fabiano said and then took a step back. Leveling the Thompson at the German's head, he said, "I don't want to get any of your shit for brains on me when I blow your fucking head off."

Before he could pull the trigger, Tommy jerked the weapon from his hands.

"Better stay out of this, Lieutenant," Fabiano said. "This ain't no concern of you flyboys."

It was only then Tommy realized his brother was leaning casually against his tank just a few yards away, watching. He could tell Sean had no intention of stopping his gunner from murdering their prisoner.

"Captain Newcomb says to take prisoners if they're not too badly wounded," Tommy said. "This guy seems to qualify."

Fabiano kept looking at Sean, waiting for him to set this annoying lieutenant straight. Even if it was his brother. But Sean just stood there, a look of amused contempt on his face.

"We're supposed to be better than that, Sean," Tommy said.

"Better than what? You ain't gonna give me any of that *knights of the sky* bullshit, are you, Tommy? Chivalry and all that crap? Oh wait...you're a virgin at all this. You ain't never even seen the Luftwaffe, right? So how the hell would you know how it really is?"

Sean shook his head and spit on the ground. "Get out of here, Half. Go back to dreamland."

As he grabbed the German by the arm and led him to Captain Newcomb, Tommy knew he'd never need to ask his brother if he'd killed those prisoners two days ago.

He'd just gotten his answer.

Chapter Nineteen

ALLIED GROUND FORCES DIRECTIVE

FROM: MONTGOMERY—COMMANDER, ALLIED GROUND FORCES	DATE-TIME OF ORIGIN 12 AUG 44 1500 HRS

TO:
BRADLEY—COMMANDER, 12TH ARMY GROUP

COPY (FOR INFO):
SHAEF (EISENHOWER); HODGES—US 1ST ARMY; PATTON—US 3RD ARMY; DEMPSEY—2ND BRITISH ARMY; CRERAR—1ST CANADIAN ARMY; CONINGHAM—RAF 2ND TAF; QUESADA—IX TAC; WEYLAND—XIX TAC

RE YOUR COMMUNIQUE OF 2100/11 AUG, DO NOT—REPEAT—DO NOT ALLOW ANY UNIT OF 12TH ARMY GROUP TO VENTURE BEYOND THE DESIGNATED FLERS-ARGENTAN "HOLD LINE." SUCH A MOVE BY ANY UNIT IN YOUR COMMAND IN THE FACE OF MASSED GERMAN ARMOR RISKS THAT UNIT'S DECIMATION AND RENDERS A SERIOUS SETBACK TO THE GREAT ADVANCES THIS COMMAND HAS MADE SO FAR.

IF YOUR UNITS WILL BE IN POSITION FAR AHEAD OF THE 0600/14 AUG SCHEDULED TIME AS YOU CLAIM, THEN USE THAT TIME TO SOLIDIFY YOUR POSITIONS ALONG THE "HOLD LINE."

YOU ARE FURTHER INSTRUCTED TO MAKE NO MORE "SUGGESTIONS" ABOUT HOW BEST TO COORDINATE THIS OR ANY OTHER ALLIED OPERATION.

SIGNED,
MONTGOMERY

Chapter Twenty

Night had fallen in Alençon before Tommy finally found his replacement, Lieutenant Charlie Webster, in the *Café Madeleine*, whooping it up among scores of inebriated 4th Armored GIs. "These tanker boys sure know how to have themselves a fine old time," Webster said as he drained a glass of whiskey and added it to the half-dozen empties stacked in front of him.

"They're celebrating," Tommy replied. "Tonight's a reprieve—they could've been rolling to Sées right now. What are *you* celebrating, by the way?"

"How about I'm glad you got back in one piece, Half? I heard you guys got beat up a little."

"Sure did. Two light tanks lost, four guys dead. Our jugs did a great job, though."

Webster's reply dripped with the blind certainty only alcohol can provide: "Don't we always, Half?"

"Better lighten up on the fire-water, Charlie. Tomorrow's going to be your turn to shine, bright and early."

Webster didn't seem to hear the suggestion. He was fixed in glassy-eyed captivation on something at the other side of the room. Tommy turned to see what—or who—it was and found Sylvie Bergerac walking toward their table. She looked strikingly beautiful in that same shimmering dress from the night before. With unmistakable delight in her voice, she said, "Lieutenant Moon, you are still here! I thought you would have left us by now."

"No, you're stuck with me one more night. My ride home doesn't leave until morning. May I introduce my replacement, Lieutenant Charlie Webster?"

That was as far as the introduction got. As Webster tried to rise for the lady, he didn't quite make it fully upright before keeling over and landing face down on the polished wooden floor. When he tried to scamper to his feet, he slipped and fell flat all over again.

With the help of two tankers from 37th Battalion, Tommy got Webster back on his feet. "Do me a favor, guys," Tommy said, "and take this gentleman to his billet at the S3's shop."

"No problem, sir," a corporal replied. "Will do."

"And tell my brother I'm looking for him."

"Sure thing, Lieutenant."

As they sloppily waltzed the drunken aviator toward the door, the corporal called back, "Kinda wish you were staying around, Lieutenant. Nobody ever had to carry your ass."

Webster out of the way, Tommy asked Sylvie, "Can I buy you a drink?"

"No, Lieutenant, you may not. I will buy *you* a drink instead. I believe you have more than earned it. You Americans prefer whiskey, I believe?"

She returned quickly from the bar and plunked the glass down before him. "What's that you're drinking?" he asked.

She swirled the clear liquid in her glass and laughed. "It is soda water, Lieutenant. I must stay sober."

He thought of his brother's words from last night: *See? I told you that jane's a fucking whore.*

"Oh, are you working or something?"

Instantly, he wished he hadn't said it. The word *working* sounded so demeaning. He could understand French women resorting to prostitution with their conquerors to feed their families. But the whole concept of bedding German officers for the information they might inadvertently divulge—*spying between the sheets*, as Sylvie claimed to be doing—seemed a silly and dangerous game. But his tone didn't perturb her in the least.

"No, Lieutenant. Not tonight. Not any night, in fact. The need has vanished along with the *Boche*."

She settled back in her chair, taking in the panorama of hard-drinking, rowdy GIs all around them. Then she fixed Tommy in a steady, appraising gaze.

In French, she asked him, "Perhaps I can do more than buy you a drink, Lieutenant?"

Tommy took a sip of his whiskey, running her words through his head one more time to ensure he hadn't misheard them. Once convinced of the translation, he basked for just a moment in the flattery of her proposition before rectitude and its flock of inhibitions came roaring back like cops raiding a speakeasy.

"I couldn't, Sylvie. Not with a married woman. Not that it doesn't sound wonderful, mind you…"

Her face settled into a serene smile. "I did not realize some of you Americans are so amusingly Catholic."

"What? You don't have churches here in France?"

"Of course we have churches, and they are very beautiful. But religion is politics, Lieutenant. Nothing more. It was Napoleon who said, *religion is what keeps the poor from murdering the rich*."

He looked genuinely shocked by her words and could only sputter, “Regardless, but…”

She leaned over and kissed him on the cheek. “You certainly are not like the others. But I expected as much, and you have not disappointed me.”

“So that was just some test, Sylvie?”

“All life is a test, Lieutenant.” She stood and took him by the hand. “At least do me the favor of walking me back to Papa’s House.”

They walked at a leisurely pace through the streets of Alençon, crowded with every GI not on security duty. Content on Tommy’s arm, she said, “Your comrades can be quite a nuisance to an unescorted woman. Thank you for your help.”

The line of GIs waiting for their turn in the bordello wound down the alley and around the corner into the *grand-rue*. Tommy and Sylvie got more than a few askance looks from GIs. “They think I’m jumping the line,” he said.

“Nonsense. You are just being a gentleman. They will see that soon enough.”

“Are you going in? I thought you said there was no need for you to work here anymore.”

“That is true, and I am not going to work in that way. But Papa will need some help with—how should I say?—*administration*?”

At the doorway, a towering Frenchman in a *maquis* beret held the door open for her with one hand while effortlessly holding back the queue of eager GIs pushing to get in.

“*Au revoir*, Tommy,” she said, kissing him goodbye—French-style—on both cheeks. “Perhaps we will meet again someday?”

"Yeah, I sure hope so. That would be great."

As he turned and walked away, he had an inkling of what all those French husbands must have felt when they dropped their wives off for another night of servicing their conquerors. But the conquerors were gone; now they'd be servicing their liberators.

And I've got about a snowball's chance in hell of ever crossing paths with that lady again, dammit.

★★★★

Tommy wandered back through the streets of Alençon, in no hurry to catch some sleep or gather his limited kit before he rejoined the fighter squadron tomorrow. He looked inside every bar he passed, expecting to find his brother. He even looped back to the bordello, standing on a dark corner, trying to be inconspicuous—or as inconspicuous as an airman in khakis could be in a sea of olive drab—as he surveyed the line of restless GIs waiting to pay for a brief encounter with a woman. Sean Moon wasn't there, either. There was no place left for Tommy to go but 37th Tank Battalion HQ.

At the S3 section's tent, he blundered into a gathering of General Wood and his subordinates. "Come on in, Lieutenant Moon," the general called to him. "You'll get a kick out of this, too."

Colonel Abrams pointed to an empty camp stool. Tommy settled in, feeling like a very small fish in a very big pond.

"Lieutenant," Wood said, "I was just about to give the boys here some words of wisdom from General Patton. I was asking the general for his permission to deviate to Gacé, based on what our friends in the Underground told us and how they'd been dead right about Sées. Now, this huge map on his wall had that Flers-Argentan hold line drawn in bright red grease pencil, straight as an arrow. Looks like it extended all the way to the damn Rhine. Well, after mulling it over for a few moments, Georgie Patton walks right up to that map, takes a rag, and erases that line. Wipes it clean off. Then he turns around to me and everyone else in the room—we're all standing there open-mouthed, mind you, because we sure as hell weren't expecting that—and he says, 'Fuck Monty and his fucking hold line. We didn't come all this way so we can stand around, waiting on him to get his ass in gear again. I'll embarrass that strutting little clerk just like I did in Sicily. If Brad or Ike don't like it, they can fire my ass.' Then he asks me, 'Wood, you say Gacé?' And I tell him, 'Yes, sir. That's where we want to go.' So he looks at me, real serious, and says, 'So why the hell are you still standing here, General? Get moving!'"

General Wood stood there for a moment, enjoying the same open-mouthed looks of surprise Patton had received. "So listen up, gentlemen," he continued, "because here's what we're going to do." He pointed to Colonel Abrams. "Creighton, you're going to lead a combat team—let's call it *Combat Command Fox*—to Gacé. CCF will be comprised of two armored battalions—yours and Colonel Jeffrey's Forty-Third, plus Major Bowman's Fifty-First Armored Infantry with two batteries of one-oh-fives from the Ninety-Fourth Artillery. I want to see if the situation and terrain will really allow us to block an entire German Army. The rest of us will stay and secure Alençon until Eightieth

Division relieves us in a day or two, and then we'll join you up there. Or, if it's not working out, we'll pull you back and try something else."

"Just one question, sir," Abrams replied. "A *combat command* like the one you've just described—shouldn't someone higher in rank than me be in command?"

"I believe you're up to the job, Creighton. Do you disagree?"

"No sir."

"Well, then, it looks like you're the man," General Wood said. "Now let's go finish off the whole damn German Seventh Army and get our boys home by Christmas."

★★★★

Tommy found it impossible to sleep. He couldn't leave things the way they were with Sean. First, he had to find him, but wandering in the dark through the tank parks on the outskirts of town was a great way to get shot by jumpy sentries. Maybe he'd get one last chance at first light, right before CCF set off for Gacé.

It was just before dawn as the engines of the American tanks rumbled to life, shredding the night's silence with their mechanized arrogance. Stumbling through the grayness from one platoon to another, Tommy finally saw his brother as he was performing some final preparations on the deck of *Eclipse of the Hun.* It was still too dark to make out his face from 50 feet away, but he didn't need the light of day to know it was Sean.

Tommy was right next to the tank before his brother noticed him. He never got a chance to speak; the look on his big brother's face stopped him cold. Sean's expression was a kaleidoscope, changing in split seconds from *shame*, to *annoyance*, to *dismissal*, to *go fuck yourself.* Then he climbed into the turret, spoke commands to his crew Tommy couldn't hear and didn't look back as the Sherman growled, creaked, and clanked into its place on the ready line.

Chapter Twenty-One

The P-47 was poised on a forward airfield every bit as new as she was, her blunt nose angled upward as if craving the sky. She lacked only two things to make her complete: a pilot and a name. Tommy Moon was about to provide both.

"You guys threw me a curve," Tommy said to Sergeant Harry McNulty, his crew chief. "I had no idea the Three-oh-First moved to this place. We were only on the highway from Alençon an hour, and it would have been a whole lot less if it wasn't for all that Third Army traffic going the other way hogging the road. I didn't even know there was such an airfield as A-14."

"A lot happened in the five days you been gone, Lieutenant," McNulty replied. "As soon as you left, we got the word to pack up at A-6 and move up here with *unparalyzed* speed."

Tommy was pretty sure he'd meant *unparalleled.*

"And when we got here, these new birds were waiting for us, like it was all *deranged* ahead of time and nobody told us. You got a name in mind for this bird, sir?"

"Yeah, Sarge. I'm going to call her *Eclipse of the Hun*."

McNulty made a face like he'd just sucked a lemon. "With all due respect, Lieutenant, just what the fuck does that mean?"

Tommy explained the name and its origin. McNulty gave a *what the hell* shrug and said, "Okay, I get it. Keeping it in the family, then. Two Moons driving rigs with the same name."

"Yeah. That's it in a nutshell." He reached into a pocket, pulled out a piece of paper and handed it to McNulty. "Here's a sketch of the nose art that goes with the name."

The sergeant looked at the drawing—the cartoon Hitler hanging by the seat of his pants from the tip of a thin crescent moon—and let out a roaring laugh. "Now that's some good shit, Lieutenant. A lot better than what you named the last one, anyway."

"Oh, yeah? What was wrong with *Belle of Canarsie*?"

McNulty pinched his nostrils like he'd just smelled something awful. "Don't cut no ice outside of Brooklyn, sir." Waving the sketch like a victory flag, he added, "But this one's pretty darn good. I'll get *Vincent Van Goldbrick* to paint it on once you're back for good today."

Tommy began the preflight inspection while McNulty and his crew did their final checks and fuzed the bombs. Three 500 pounders hung from below the jug, one on each wing just outboard of the landing gear, one below the belly between the wheel wells. He paused reverently and laid his hand gently on the bomb below the left wing. He was quite sure the frightening image of what bombs like this had done at Sées yesterday would never leave him.

A mechanic held up a piece of chalk and asked, "You want to write something on that egg, Lieutenant? A little greeting to the Kraut bastards, maybe?"

"Nah," Tommy replied. "No need. They work pretty damn good just as they are."

"Mind if I do, sir?"

"Help yourself, Private."

Tommy noticed something strange farther outboard on the wing's underside. Calling McNulty over, he asked, "Is this the hard point for the rocket tubes?"

"Yeah, but they ain't all wired up yet. Depot's been a little slow getting us the mod kits. Should have it all done in a couple of days, though."

Together they inspected the aft fuselage, with its high, crowned upper skin extending aft from the cockpit to the vertical stabilizer. "I knew you wanted another *razorback,* sir," McNulty said, "and I didn't have no trouble snagging you one. There were just a few bubble-canopy girls to choose from, anyway, and they found themselves a home pretty quick."

"Good. I'd feel like I was in some kind of fishbowl flying a bubble. And I like all that metal behind my head."

They both knew *all that metal behind my head* was false security. Bullets and flak would go through that thin aluminum like butter. It was the armor plate on the seatback that protected the pilot, and the bubble and the razorback were quite similar in that respect.

McNulty asked, "But a bubble gives you a lot better look out your *six*, don't it, sir?"

"Look at what? Haven't seen much of the Luftwaffe lately. Have you?"

"No, sir. Not one damn plane." He looked worried as he asked, "But you still keep an eye in that rear view mirror for 'em, don't you?"

"Yeah, of course."

"Good, because you know what they say, sir: *the guy who gets you is the one you never see coming.*"

When they got back to the nose of the airplane, the mechanic was still writing on the bomb. Tommy asked him, "You writing a novel there, Private?"

The man stepped back to show his work. "There. All done, sir." In neat block letters, he'd spelled out his message to the Germans:

Come Christmas, we'll all be home. And you'll all be dead.

Eclipse of the Hun—radio call sign *Gadget Blue Leader* —lifted off the runway and promptly afforded Tommy a spectacular view of Alençon just 10 miles to the north. Standing beneath the dome of the noonday August sky, it looked more like a storybook village than a place that was nearly a battlefield just a few days ago. His wingman, Lieutenant Jimmy Tuttle, tucked up his jug off *Eclipse's* right wing.

In a few minutes, they passed directly over Alençon. Tommy could see the *grand-rue* running north-south through the town. He even thought he could pick out *Papa's House*, as Sylvie had called it. If there was a line of GIs waiting to be serviced there, he couldn't tell. And somewhere on the road leading east from town was his brother in a Sherman tank, driving toward Gacé with *Combat Command Fox*.

Climbing to 5000 feet, they headed north toward Sées—just four minutes ahead—but gave it a wide berth. Tommy hadn't forgotten the hidden guns in the town yesterday. They'd do the same for Argentan, another five minutes beyond Sées. If all the intel was true, there would be plenty of unconcealed *roadkill* out in the French countryside to keep them busy.

There were many planes in the air over the Flers-Falaise-Argentan triangle, still not in sight but crowding the radio frequencies: P-47s from the US IX Tactical Air Command supporting Hodges's 1st Army west of Argentan; RAF Typhoons and Tempests north of Falaise supporting Montgomery's Brits, Canadians, and Poles; and their outfit—XIX Tactical Air Command supporting Patton's 3rd Army east of Argentan. Lots of aircraft but none of them German; none of the combat reports were of air-to-air action. Tommy and Tuttle skirted Argentan and dropped lower to scout for German columns reported to be on the highway heading east toward Gacé and beyond.

Tommy spotted it first: from a patch of woods rose a wispy column of grayish-white smoke, moving steadily eastward.

A train, Tommy told himself. *The Krauts must be getting real desperate if they're rolling in daylight with all these planes waiting to hit them. Of course, it might be studded with anti-aircraft guns, too, so no more than one pass.*

Tommy led Tuttle through a diving, three-quarter circle to the left. "We'll hit them broadside. I'll take the locomotive," he told his wingman. "You shoot up as many of the cars as you can. We'll take them as soon as they're out of those trees. Guns only—don't waste your bombs."

Like lambs being led to the slaughter, the locomotive began to pull its cars clear of the woods. The P-47s came in low, hugging the flat terrain, the trees hiding their approach; the trainmen and German soldiers on board couldn't see them coming until it was too late. Caught by surprise, the anti-aircraft gunners atop the two middle cars struggled frantically to depress their 20-millimeter cannons enough to engage fighters on the deck but lost the race; Tuttle's eight .50-caliber machine guns demolished one of those cars and caused the gunners on the other to jump for their lives. His plane streaked low over the train and made her escape.

Tommy's attack considerations were different. *Already, I'm too low and too close, with only one direction for escape: left.*

It's got to be left. If the locomotive blows, I'll get caught up in the blast if I go over the top. If I go right, I fly over a train-load of pissed-off Krauts with guns.

He squeezed the trigger, watching the rounds land short at first and then walk right into the side of the locomotive's big boiler. They made tiny red flashes as they struck the curved iron.

But this was no time to hang around and see the results. He jerked the stick left—and she seemed so sluggish with 1500 pounds of bombs hanging under her, 2000 rounds of .50 caliber, and nearly full tanks—that he thought she'd never turn.

Then suddenly she responded, banking so steeply left he thought he'd bury her wingtip in the ground. Slamming the stick right, she seemed to take forever to level off. But once she did, it was time to climb and rejoin Tuttle.

Damn, that was close. Is this new bird a little screwy? Or am I getting rusty?

"Did I get her?" Tommy asked his wingman.

"Oh, yeah. Blew like a volcano. I only got a couple of cars, though. Sure you don't want to have another go?"

"Positive."

With Tuttle back on his right wing, they climbed to 2000 feet and continued eastward. In a few minutes, they were halfway between Sées and Gacé when the call came over the radio. It was unmistakably Charlie Webster's voice but an octave higher. *Combat Command Fox's* ASO was calling for fighter support. He sounded scared out of his mind.

"Halfback One-four, this is *Gadget Blue,*" Tommy replied. "Tell me your troubles, over."

Webster's next transmission was a breathless recitation of CCF's predicament. They were stopped dead on the road five miles south of Gacé, up against a roadblock making a determined stand with massed heavy weapons. No matter how the Americans pummeled their adversaries with tank and artillery fire, they couldn't break through. They didn't even seem to be weakening the defenders, no matter what they tried.

Shit, Tommy thought. *The lead elements must be taking a beating.* He tried to force the image of flaming Shermans from his head.

Taking a quick glance at the map on his kneeboard, he told Webster, "On station in three minutes. Advise *splash* on last rounds, over."

As soon as the P-47s were close enough to view the battle from above, they could see what *Combat Command Fox* couldn't: there was a stream of combat vehicles—tanks, assault guns, half-tracks, and trucks—flowing south on the highway from Gacé. They had to be Germans, ready to join the swirling mass of smoke, dust, and armored vehicles locked in combat.

No wonder they can't seem to make a dent in them, Tommy told himself. *Knock one out and another one takes its place. But we're flak-bait if we hang around up here, just sightseeing...and this new ship's still got me guessing a little.*

He looked farther south and saw a quartet of tanks blazing on the road. From this height—and through all the smoke and haze—it was impossible to tell German *feldgrau* from American *olive drab*. But based on their location and orientation, he guessed they were American…

And one of them could be my brother's.

Blue Flight broke left just as an arcing ribbon of tracers rose to meet them. But a quick turn and steady descent got them quickly out of harm's way. Down to 300 feet, Tommy told Tuttle, "This column is definitely Krauts. We'll hit them from their ass end. You trail and drop first, then break hard right and I'll drop mine."

Tuttle was relieved to hear that plan. At this low altitude, he'd barely be able to outrun his own bomb blasts without having to dodge the explosions in front of him from Tommy's bombs, too. But he was getting more nervous by the second: they were about to begin an attack run which, if the American artillery was still firing, would fly them straight into those incoming rounds.

"*Blue Two to Leader,*" Tuttle called, "we didn't get *splash* yet. Better abort."

"Negative, negative. We've got time."

Time? Half's losing his mind. We've got a couple of seconds, maybe, until—

Before he could finish that thought, Webster's voice was in their earphones: *"Splash,* over." The last American artillery rounds were impacting. Tommy could see their blasts well ahead of him. "Roger," he replied. "Perfect timing."

Over the German column now, Tuttle pickled his bombs in sequence—*One, two, three*—and announced, "*Blue Two*, breaking right."

Tommy released his bombs in the same *one-two-three* sequence as his wingman.

"*Blue Leader*, breaking right." Then he asked Tuttle, "That wasn't so bad, was it, Jimmy?"

"Yes, it was. I don't like betting the farm against artillery rounds."

"Maybe once you do a stint as ASO you'll get to trust the dogfaces a little. Now let's see if we did any good."

From a thousand feet, it seemed a certainty they had. Their six 500-pound bombs had left a chain of craters hundreds of yards long and inflicted horrific damage on the German column.

"Look at that!" Tuttle said. "We ripped the shit out of them."

True, vehicles were ablaze all along the road, perhaps as many as a dozen, but they were mostly trucks, half-tracks, and assault guns—all thinly armored or not at all. Tommy counted seven tanks—he couldn't tell what type they were—but only one was billowing smoke. As best he could tell from this altitude, six German tanks were still on the move and battleworthy.

"Let's do another pass, same direction," Tommy told Tuttle. "Try and keep those panzer bastards out of the fight. At least give them a headache."

"But shouldn't we hit 'em from a different direction this time?"

"Negative. We're down to guns, so let's shoot up those tankers in the ass where we might actually do a little good. If they're buttoned up, they won't even see us coming."

"Hey, Half, maybe we can skip some rounds underneath and up through their bellies."

"You don't really believe that works, do you, Jimmy? Just aim for the damn engine…and pray we knocked out all the flak guns already."

They came in lower this time, barely higher than the tips of the German tanks' antennas, flying *echelon right* to stay clear of the ejected cartridges from each other's guns. Sights locked on the tanks, they both expended a quarter of their .50-caliber ammunition load—about 300 rounds per plane, almost 40 rounds per gun. But it seemed like wasted effort. Tracers just bounced off the tanks' armor, arcing into the air like stars from a Roman candle.

Tommy wondered, *Did any of that API punch its way inside a tank?*

As they climbed and circled back, it looked like only one tank had suffered damage from the strafing; it was being pushed off the road by another tank. That left five. At least none of the assault guns, half-tracks, and trucks seemed to be in the fight anymore. They sat lifeless on the sides of the highway, some burning ferociously. If there were German soldiers around those vehicles, alive or dead, Tommy couldn't see them.

"*Halfback One-four,* this is *Gadget Blue*. We're clear. Let 'em have it."

With their fuel and ammo sufficient, *Blue Flight* could loiter in the area, standing by for any further requests for help. But it would be hard to tell who was winning from the safe perch of a few thousand feet until, like all battles, it reached critical mass: the point at which one side sensed it was inflicting far more damage than it was receiving. Then, and only then, would the winning side be confident enough to steadily advance and overrun their enemy. From the air, it would look like a surge of ants pressing relentlessly forward.

But critical mass still hadn't happened for either side. The only change seemed to be the growing number of burning armored vehicles littering the battlefield. From Tommy Moon's balcony seat, it looked like a stalemate. With each tank knocked out, the odds of one of them being his brother's grew. He took a look at his fuel gauge: *About an hour's worth before we've got to go home and tank up. If only I could tell who was who down there...*

Charlie Webster's agitated voice was back on the air. "*Gadget Blue, Gadget Blue,* this is *Halfback One-four*. Do you identify red smoke, over?"

A thin, barely perceptible plume of red smoke billowed up from the ground, right about where Tommy figured the American line was. It looked like it came from a GI smoke grenade.

"Roger, got red smoke."

"Okay, *Gadget*, red smoke is *Halfback*. Repeat, red smoke is *Halfback.* Now look about a thousand yards east, over."

A thousand yards east marked the edge of a forest. Tommy was already turning and diving in its direction as he asked Webster, "We're looking at the treeline, affirmative?"

"Affirmative. Krauts with big guns hiding in the woods on our flank. Standby for *goal posts*."

Goal posts: the name General Wood had given to Tommy's idea of marking a target line with white phosphorous airbursts.

"*Splash*, over," Webster reported, a warning the bursts were about to happen.

"There they are," Tommy told his wingman. "Have you ever seen *goal posts* before?"

"Negative, Half."

"Those bursts give us the target line. The lower one is over the target area. Do it *echelon left* this time. We'll probably never see the Krauts, so just stay on the line and let her rip."

"If they know where they are, why the hell ain't they hitting them?"

"They've only got so much artillery, Jimmy, so they need a little help. Now are you coming or what?"

"Affirmative, boss."

Tommy banked his ship left and brought her around to the target line, passing just under the floating puff of the high airburst. Then he started a steep dive aimed short of the low burst, hoping to compensate for *probable error* and not overshoot.

"You still with me, Jimmy?" he asked Tuttle.

"Affirmative. Right on your eight o'clock and dropping like a brick."

As their altimeters spun rapidly down, the battlefield was starting to make more sense. Tommy had a much better idea where the Americans were—and where those invisible guns in the forest were menacing them with flanking fire. It was hard enough for the troopers of CCF to engage an enemy dead ahead of them. To have to fight in more than one direction could be a recipe for their destruction.

The jugs' .50-caliber guns worked over the forest like crazed woodsmen, shredding the tall trees—and hopefully the invisible Germans among those trees—with industrial efficiency. Pulling up from the attack run, Tommy told his wingman, "Let's pull a one-eighty and do that again."

"Hey, Half," Tuttle said, "a couple more passes like that and we'll be guns dry."

"That's what ammo's for, Jimmy…to fire it. Breaking hard right."

With the cushion of altitude, Tommy banked his new ship harder than he ever had before. He was relieved when she responded exactly as he expected.

There…that's more like it. I guess she handles differently with external loads than my old ship. Without the bombs, though, she's pretty nimble. Just like she should be.

As they streaked down for another strafing run, Tuttle said, "Pretty easy to see the line we just shot up. Looks like a tornado went through there. Started a few fires and everything."

"*Halfback One-four,*" Tommy called, "are we doing any good?"

"Affirmative, *Gadget Blue.* We think those guns are trying to withdraw. Maybe move your next pass a smidgen or two east."

The two jugs slid left as requested. Halfway down their strafing run, both ships lurched from the shock wave of an explosion beneath them. Tommy said, "I think we found them. Feels like some of their ammo just went up."

"Speaking of ammo," Tuttle replied, "how much you got left?"

"Not much…about a hundred rounds."

"Roger. Me too."

One hundred rounds—12 per gun, give or take a few. Enough for one more pass at something.

Tuttle added, "I ain't too crazy about trying to get home without any bullets, you know."

And I'm not too crazy about leaving my brother in the lurch.

"Just relax, Jimmy," Tommy said. "When's the last time you saw the Luftwaffe, anyway? Those guys down there need our help, bad."

Webster came back on the air. "That looked great, *Gadget Blue*. Looks like the Krauts in the woods are *kaput*. Nice job. Now give us a little *armed recon* of what's between here and Gacé, over."

They climbed to 1000 feet and headed north. There were still tanks on the road—maybe 10 or 12 now—but they were driving with great haste away from the fight, back toward Gacé. Charlie Webster sounded thrilled to hear it.

The jugs began a descending orbit of the road, lining up for one last strafing run. Wings steeply banked gave the pilots a startling panorama of the ground below out their side canopies: like a classroom's sand table exercise come to life, CCF was surging forward on a broad front across the battlefield. This battle's critical mass had finally been reached, decidedly in the Americans' favor.

“Let’s give those Krauts a goodbye present,” Tommy called to Tuttle.

“You mean you want to dump all our rounds?”

“Affirmativc. And make them all count.”

It took only a few seconds of firing before the P-47’s guns were empty. As they turned and streaked back toward CCF, Tommy was pretty sure he’d gotten a glimpse of two German tanks being abandoned by their crews.

A few moments later, as he sped over the American vanguard, he got a fleeting image of a Sherman commander standing in the turret hatch, waving to him. Waggling his wings in reply, he wanted desperately to believe he’d just exchanged greetings with his brother.

Chapter Twenty-Two

By midafternoon, *Combat Command Fox* had bypassed the German strongpoint at Gacé and taken up defensive positions on forested high ground two miles east of the town. From there, they could command three highways the Germans might use to flee the Falaise-Argentan pocket. But whether or not they could exercise that dominance was in doubt. They were low on fuel and nearly out of ammunition. The supply convoy that was supposed to remedy that situation hadn't shown up.

"Division doesn't know what happened to the convoy, sir," the staff logistics officer—the S4—told Colonel Abrams. "There's been no word. But they should have been here two hours ago."

"I know," Abrams replied. "I've been watching the damn clock, too. So what are we doing about it, Major?"

"If the first one doesn't turn up soon," the S4 said, "Division can cobble together another convoy, sir. But it won't be here before tomorrow, when the rest of Fourth Armored moves up to join us."

Abrams walked off to ponder in silence. *Dammit, did I just fuck up? I didn't dare try and take Gacé as low on ammo as we were after that big brawl south of town. So I did the next best thing...just drove around the place and set ourselves up as a roadblock. That's what we're trying to do, right? Block the whole German army from escaping Normandy...but one more big fight without resupply and we're finished.*

★★★★

Back in Alençon, the French Underground already knew what had happened to the supply convoy. Sylvie Bergerac rushed to 4th Armored HQ in the town hall with the bad news.

"They were on the wrong road," she told General Wood. "Then they were captured."

Wood looked at the map in disbelief. "How the hell could they make a wrong turn?" he fumed. "There aren't that many turns to make, for cryin' out loud."

But one thing was certain: *Combat Command Fox* was in deep trouble if it wasn't resupplied with ammo and fuel ASAP.

"There's nothing we can do about their fuel situation tonight," Wood's division logistics officer—the G4—said. "There are just no more tanker trucks to get it there, even if we had the reserve fuel on hand, which we don't. And you don't refuel an armored unit out of *jerry cans*, five gallons at a time. Not unless you've got a week to do it."

"But we've got the ammo, dammit," the general replied. "We just need to scrape together some trucks to carry it."

The G4 seemed shocked at the suggestion. "Sir, if we empty our dump and send it up the road, then *we've* got no reserve."

"*We're* not in contact with the Germans, Colonel," Wood replied. "They need it worse than we do at the moment."

"But there's no way to get it there, sir."

No sooner had the G4 said those words than five empty deuce-and-a-halves rumbled to a halt outside the town hall. Their drivers climbed down from their cabs and began to *smoke and joke* with some GIs on the street.

"Don't tell me we can't find the trucks, Colonel," Wood said, pointing out the window to the idle vehicles. "An armored division is loaded with wheeled transport. If we can't figure out how to help Abrams and his boys—and I mean right fucking now—we should all be busted down to private."

Visibly shaken, the colonel replied, "Very well, General. Just one question—how do we make sure this convoy doesn't get lost, too? By the time they're loaded up and on their way, it'll be dark. And those drivers have never been where they're going."

Sylvie Bergerac provided the answer: "I would be happy to lead them, *mon général*."

★★★★

There was time for one more sortie by *Blue Flight* before sunset. It would mark the first time all four planes in the flight would be in the air together under their new leader, Tommy Moon.

"Glad you're back, Half," *Blue Three's* pilot, Lieutenant Joe Rider, told Tommy. "I was getting sick and tired of getting farmed out to fill slots in other squadrons. How's your new ship?"

"A little squirrelly when she's bombed up, but otherwise, she flies just like a jug."

A mechanic readying Tommy's plane overheard his comment. "Begging your pardon, sir," the mechanic said, "but are you saying she's slow to roll with an external load?"

"Yeah, that's exactly it, Corporal."

Walking over to a bomb on its wing pylon, the corporal, Marv Goldberg—the man Sergeant McNulty had referred to as *Vincent Van Goldbrick*—said, "I've seen this before, when I was with the Fifty-Sixth in England, sir. This is an *RA* bird, not an *RE*, meaning the Republic factory in Indiana built it, not the one in New York." He pointed to the data stencil on the side of the fuselage to prove his point. "Somebody in that factory doesn't know how to shim the wing mounts for these pylons right. Hang a bomb on it and it messes up the airflow under the wing just a little. It's an easy fix, but we need a lot of ground time, just like I'll need that ground time to get your artwork painted on. That's a great cartoon, by the way."

McNulty, the crew chief, was listening to Goldberg's explanation, too. "That's real good poop, *Van Goldbrick*. Why'd you never say anything about it before?"

"Nobody ever asked, Sarge. And it's *Corporal Goldberg*, if you don't mind."

"Yeah, yeah…sure," McNulty replied. "Now let's get the lieutenant and his team up in the air where they can do some good. You going back to Gacé, sir?"

"Yep. Some Fourth Armored guys still need looking after."

"Is that where your brother is?" McNulty asked.

At first, Tommy couldn't put together an answer. He didn't know if his brother was *there* or even of this Earth anymore. Anything he said would be an expression of hope, not knowledge. But there was no point getting into it now—and no time. He simply replied, "Yeah."

As McNulty helped him get strapped into the cockpit, Tommy said, "That Goldberg sounds like he's just as good a mechanic as he is an artist. Maybe you oughta cut him a little slack with the nicknames."

"Ahh, he knows I don't mean nothing by it. But I tell you, he don't swing a wrench near as good as he does a paint brush. But maybe I did *misunderestimate* the lad just a bit."

"They're going to come soon," Captain Newcomb said, his binoculars trained on the outskirts of Gacé. "It's no secret where we are, not with all the noise we made getting here." Since taking up positions in the forest, they'd made it a point to continue making as much noise as possible, or as least as much as they could within the limits of their dwindling fuel supply. Charlie Company had been detailed to drive a platoon of Shermans around their wooden redoubt, hoping to give the impression from the constant sound of engines there was a far larger force nestled in these woods. Once they'd taken careful stock of their fuel situation, *a platoon* of noise-making Shermans had, by necessity, been whittled down to only two.

Newcomb handed the binoculars to Sean Moon, who, after scanning the town, said, "I see five Panzer Fours, plain as day…and one more who thinks he's hidden behind that building, but his gun's sticking out. By the looks of the muzzle brake, it's a Panther."

"Yeah, but we can't see everything we need to from here," Newcomb replied. "We'll get the Air Force to have another look when they get back."

Sean took in the panorama of the empty sky, still bright despite the late afternoon shadows slicing through the forest. "Where the hell are the flyboys, anyway, sir? I ain't seen or heard a plane in a good hour."

"Lieutenant Webster says they're beating up a column headed this way about eight miles west. Those Krauts were headed straight for us, too."

"Ain't that swell," Sean replied. "With a little luck, maybe most of that column will never get here."

★★★★

Tommy Moon couldn't believe his eyes: *Horses! We're shooting goddamn horses again.*

The German column *Blue Flight* was decimating at the moment—even though it was led by a few tanks and had anti-aircraft guns on a half-track at its midpoint—was composed mainly of horse-drawn artillery pieces and supply wagons.

Two of the planes in *Blue Flight—Blue Two* and *Blue Four*—were armed with rockets. It was wise to fire them first, before they used their machine guns. Otherwise, there was a chance the ejected cartridges from the .50 calibers would damage the exposed wiring to the launcher tubes hung beneath the wings. Tommy sent *Blue Two* to use her rockets against the anti-aircraft half-track and *Blue Four* to do the same against the tanks. He and *Blue Three* followed close behind, dumping 500-pound bombs along the length of the column. After two passes, the rockets and bombs were expended, wreaking havoc on everything but the tanks which, despite the pilots' excited claims of *direct hits*, were scattering, apparently unhurt. *Blue Flight* formed into pairs and made two strafing passes.

As the remnants of the German column passed beneath him, Tommy tried to count the horse-drawn conveyances devastated by his jugs. He couldn't; there were too many. *Fifty, at least…and it looks like each one was pulled by at least four horses.*

Horses. Two hundred dead or wounded horses. Transporting what was once considered the most mechanized and deadly army on the planet. The wounded ones thrashed in their harnesses, their agony unmistakable even to a man in a speeding airplane.

"One more pass, guys," Tommy announced.

Jimmy Tuttle, flying *Blue Two*, asked, "What the hell, Half. Didn't we kill those bastards enough?"

"Not the horses, we didn't. I said do it again, dammit. Put the poor bastards out of their misery."

Chapter Twenty-Three

The lead deuce-and-a-half of the ammunition convoy, inching along the road illuminated only by the faint glow of its solitary blackout headlight, shuddered to a stop. Sylvie Bergerac was riding in the cab with the driver and the convoy's lieutenant-in-charge. She jumped out and walked to a signpost, inspecting the arrows pointing to several towns, one of them Gacé.

Just as I thought, she told herself. *This is one of the crossroad signs we tampered with to misdirect the Germans.* She ran her fingers over the gouged wood and bent nailheads, telltale signs those nails had been pulled and hammered back into the post. *Then, after the ambush, we never undid this little mischief...and now an American convoy has paid the price, too.*

The lieutenant was standing beside her now. "So we have to turn right to get to Gacé, Madame Bergerac?"

"No, the sign was changed to deceive the Germans. We must go left."

"Changed? By who?"

"We of the *maquis*, I'm afraid."

The lieutenant studied his map in the dim glow of his blackout flashlight. "Hmm…yeah. We're here, right?" He pointed to an intersection about halfway between Alençon and Gacé.

"That's correct. You see that taking the left road is the correct way to go."

"Yeah. Absolutely." He checked his watch. "So that'll put us to CC Fox by about 2000 hours."

"Yes, in one-half hour," she replied and then began tugging at the errant sign to yank it loose.

The lieutenant pulled her away. "No time for that now, Madame Bergerac. We'll get it on the way back. I've got it marked on the map now. We won't get fooled again."

Their time estimate was right on the money. Just before 2000, as the eight-truck ammunition convoy crept down a narrow trail that bypassed Gacé and led into the forest, an American captain emerged from the darkness. After a brief discussion with the convoy's lieutenant, the captain put his fingers to his lips and blew a sharp whistle. A team of GIs materialized, each jumping on the driver's side running board of a truck to guide it to the various places its cargo was needed. Before the lead truck pulled away, the lieutenant asked Sylvie, "Where do you want your bicycle, Madame Bergerac?"

"Right here would be fine, Lieutenant. Could someone please lead me to Colonel Abrams?"

It was the captain who replied, "My pleasure, ma'am. Right this way."

Colonel Abrams was surprised to see Sylvie. "I figured it would be a Frenchman acting as guide, but a French *woman*? I'm in your debt, ma'am. *Merci.* But what are you planning to do with that bicycle?"

"I'm going to ride it home to Alençon, *mon colonel.*"

"But that's over twenty miles! And it's nighttime! Ride back with the empty trucks."

Sylvie found his concern funny. "My bicycle has a generator and lights, as you can see, *mon colonel.* And twenty miles is not very far at all. I am used to riding much farther. But I'll be traveling a much shorter distance. Tonight, I'll be going directly to Gacé. My grandmother lives there. I want to visit her."

Abrams looked more concerned than ever now. She could sense the words forming in his head: *But the Germans…*

"*Mon colonel*, we have lived with the *Boche* for four long years. Do not worry about me. My papers are in order."

"But you're *maquis*."

"The *Boche* do not know that."

"But are you carrying that British pistol of yours?"

"Of course not. That would make me a combatant, no?"

"Well, if I can't convince you otherwise, let me just say again, *Merci, Madame Bergerac. Bon Voyage.*"

"Just one more thing, *mon colonel*. Could I appeal to you to spare Gacé as you spared Alençon?"

"Alençon was easy—the Germans pulled out. It'll be up to them what happens here in Gacé."

"And it will be up to your Air Force, too, I suppose."

"You suppose correctly, ma'am."

"Well, then, *au revoir, mon colonel. Bonne chance* to all of us."

He detailed a sergeant to escort her through CCF's position and out to the road. On the way, they passed through Baker Company. A GI called down from the turret of a Sherman, "Hey, lady, ain't you the jane from that *house of horizontal refreshment* who helped us out at Alençon?"

She recognized him instantly. "Ahh…the ill-mannered Moon brother. So nice to see you again, Sergeant. Now if you'll excuse me…"

"Speaking of my brother, I hear you and him were getting pretty chummy. You ain't seen him, have you?"

"Not since last night. And I doubt I'll ever see him again." She kept on walking, pushing the bicycle at her side.

"Don't get that pretty little ass of yours all shot up now, toots."

"I'd be more worried about yours, if I were you, Sergeant."

Within 20 minutes, Sylvie was bicycling through the darkened streets of Gacé. It hadn't been difficult getting past the *Boche* checkpoint at the edge of town. The guards were jumpy; they knew the Americans—the *Amis*—were close by and coming soon. *They are so young*, she thought. *It was probably only recently they traded their Hitlerjugend short pants for the feldgrau of the Wehrmacht. Les Boches must be getting very desperate for manpower.* Their trembling hands fumbled her papers as they struggled to read them. An older *unterfeldwebel* finally bellowed at them to stop pulling at their penises and let her pass.

She smiled as she pedaled away: *I've certainly learned quite a lot of German in these last four years. I understood every word they said.*

Her grandmother's old but tidy house was at the end of *Rue de Manet.* Resting her bicycle against the front steps, she knocked—a gentle knock, so no one would mistake it for the imperious pounding of the *Boche* to which they had become accustomed.

"*Mon petit chou!*" her delighted grandmother said as she opened the door. "What are you doing here? Come in, come in."

As they shared some wine, Sylvie explained the reason for her visit. "The fighting will start very soon, *Grand-mère*. I need to take you with me to Alençon."

The old woman kissed her tenderly on the forehead. "Dear sweet Sylvie…I will not leave. Damn the *Boche* and damn the *Amis*, too. They cannot drive me from the home your *grand-père* built…where your mother was born and grew to womanhood, may God rest their souls."

"But *Grand-mère*, it will be very bad when it happens. I need to keep you safe."

Her grandmother smiled but was unmoved. "This is not my first war, Sylvie…and French houses are built with stout basements so the barbarians can kill each other all they like above us. I will be fine."

Sylvie wrapped the old woman in her arms. She knew there would be no changing her mind. Just holding her close made it seem like everything was all right, if only just for a moment.

"You will stay the night, won't you?"

"Of course, *Grand-mère*. But I must leave first thing in the morning."

"You must get back to your little war games with the *maquis*, I suppose…and to that shit of a husband."

Little war games: from anyone else, Sylvie would have taken offense. But she knew she could no more change her grandmother's opinions on life and war than she could grow wings and fly. And there was no denying Bernard was a shit.

★★★★

Tommy had just finished writing the mission report when Sergeant McNulty stuck his head into the operations tent. "Hey, Lieutenant, I just lucked into another kit for the rocket mod. We got a great chance to do it tonight, when we've got those wing pylons off for that re-shim. It should make the job go a whole lot quicker, but if we run into problems it could turn into an *exercise in fertility*, and she won't be ready at the crack of dawn like you want."

It took a few moments to reach his decision: *I want that stand-off punch the rockets give, even if it is hard as hell to actually hit a tank with one. But I don't want to be stuck here on the ground if the shit's hitting the fan in the morning. McNulty and his boys have never let me down before, though.*

"Yeah, Sarge. Go ahead and do it. Give me the rockets."

"You got it, sir. You gonna be around in case we need your opinion on anything?"

"Me and a couple of the other pilots are going into Alençon for a while. We should be back around 2300."

McNulty's face lit up in a crooked smile. "Chasing skirt beats out beauty sleep again, eh, Lieutenant?"

"Something like that."

"Well, be sure and use a *cundrum*. And nail one for me while you're at it, will you?"

Thirty minutes later, Tommy parked the jeep behind the MP post in Alençon. He and the three pilots in his section spilled out: Jimmy Tuttle, Joe Rider, and Herb Clinchmore. Tuttle asked, "Why the hell are we dumping the jeep here, Tommy? All the good bars are blocks away."

"Because if I ask the provost marshal to keep an eye on it, it'll probably still be here when we get back. And if it's not, you can bet some MP *borrowed* it, and it'll magically reappear before you can finish a cup of coffee."

"Is that some New York City wisdom talking?"

"No, just common sense. And hard experience."

While his section mates headed off to the bars, Tommy walked the few blocks to *Papa's House*. There was the usual line of GIs wrapped around the corner and the usual amount of grumbling as he pushed to the head of the line, assuring the annoyed troopers *this fucking officer* was not cutting in; he was just looking for someone.

When he got to the door, that same giant Frenchman was standing guard. In French, Tommy said, "I'm looking for Sylvie Bergerac. I'm a friend, not a customer. Maybe you remember me from last night?"

The guard couldn't be bothered to look down at Tommy as he replied, "I don't know you, soldier, and I don't know any whore by that name."

"She's not a whore, she's—"

Roughly shoving Tommy aside, the giant said, "Clear the way and get out of my sight before I make you wish you had. This is not the *lonely hearts' club*, you little shithead of an American."

The GIs in the line had no idea what was being said, but it looked likely this huge Frenchman was about to kick the living crap out of an officer, and they were dying to watch. It wasn't to be, however. Tommy turned and walked away.

What the hell did that guy mean he doesn't know her? He sure as hell knew her last night.

Making his way to the *Café Madeleine*, he was struck by how normal everything in Alençon seemed, as if everyone—French civilians and GIs alike—was untouched by the war raging just a few miles up the highway.

Everything in the café seemed normal, too: rowdy GIs being endured by the long-suffering French proprietors for the steady flow of *francs* their business provided. Asking the bartender if he knew of Sylvie's whereabouts, he got the same answer as before: "I do not know any woman by that name."

"But she walked around here like she owned the place last night."

Dismissing Tommy with a scowl and a violent shake of his head, the bartender replied, "I own this place. No one but me. Thank you for speaking your almost intelligible French, Lieutenant…but now I'll thank you to leave my café."

"Can I at least get a beer?"

"No. Get out." He looked ready to leap over the bar and throw Tommy out single-handedly.

At his Alençon HQ, General Wood stood before the big tactical map on the wall. His fingers ran lightly over the town of Gacé and then over to the symbol in the green area representing a forest two miles east: a simple line drawing of a flag, representing the headquarters of *Combat Command Fox*. With a ruler, he measured the distance from the Flers-Argentan *stop line* to that symbol: *five damn miles*.

The Division S3—Wood's operations officer—asked, "Having second thoughts about sending them over Monty's line, sir?"

"Hell, no, Colonel," Wood replied. "When I reported their progress to General Patton, all he said was 'Great job.' Then I asked how he was going to report *our little trespass* to the boys upstairs, and he said, 'I'm not going to tell them shit yet.'"

★★★★

Sylvie's head had just hit the pillow when the snarl of tank engines shattered the night's stillness in Gacé. From her grandmother's parlor window, she could see the darkened silhouettes of German soldiers in formation running up *Rue de Manet*. She heard a voice, maybe that of a sergeant or officer, shouting, "*Macht schnell! Macht schnell!*"

Her grandmother was awakened by all the commotion. Walking sleepily into the parlor, she asked Sylvie, "Has the fighting come back to Gacé?"

"I don't know, *Grand-mère*."

"Are they leaving, perhaps?"

"Either that…or they're going to attack the Americans."

"Or it's the Americans who are attacking, Sylvie. Come away from the window. We must go to the basement."

Chapter Twenty-Four

ALLIED GROUND FORCES DIRECTIVE

FROM: MONTGOMERY—COMMANDER, ALLIED GROUND FORCES	DATE-TIME OF ORIGIN 14 AUG 44 0100 HRS

TO:
BRADLEY—COMMANDER, 12TH ARMY GROUP

COPY (FOR INFO):
SHAEF (EISENHOWER); HODGES—US 1ST ARMY; PATTON—US 3RD ARMY; DEMPSEY—2ND BRITISH ARMY; CRERAR—1ST CANADIAN ARMY; CONINGHAM—RAF 2ND TAF; QUESADA—IX TAC; WEYLAND—XIX TAC; BRERETON—9TH AIR FORCE

RE YOUR STATUS REPORT OF 2200/13 AUG, THIS COMMAND IS ALARMED TO LEARN OF THE DEEP GERMAN SALIENT 3RD ARMY HAS ALLOWED TO DEVELOP IN THE AREA NORTH OF SÉES. I MUST REMIND YOU THAT YOUR CURRENT MISSION IS TO TRAP THE GERMAN 7TH ARMY, NOT ALLOW GERMANS TO DRIVE A WEDGE BETWEEN YOUR 1ST AND 3RD ARMIES AND ALLOW BOTH TO BE DESTROYED IN FLANKING MOVEMENTS.

YOU ARE ORDERED TO ELIMINATE THE SALIENT AT SÉES TODAY, 14 AUG, NLT THAN 2359 HOURS. USE ALL ASSETS AVAILABLE, TO INCLUDE TACTICAL AIR POWER, TO ACHIEVE THIS MOST CRUCIAL OBJECTIVE.

SIGNED,
MONTGOMERY

Chapter Twenty-Five

Sean Moon checked his watch: *0300...are the Krauts coming or what?*

The men of CCF had been listening to the murmur of German engines in Gacé for over two hours. In that time, not one vehicle had left the confines of the town to show herself on the moonlit highways or open fields.

I'm sure glad they've got the gas to waste without going nowhere. Maybe we should've hit that fucking town after all and taken that gas for ourselves.

When he'd last checked *Eclipse of the Hun's* fuel gauge, it read less than a quarter of a tank: *Not even enough to get back to Alençon...or get us through one good fight.*

He scanned the darkness with binoculars one more time. *Not a damn thing happening. Maybe the Krauts are just trying to keep us awake.*

If that was the Germans' plan, it was working. Sean's crew was exhausted, but not a man had dozed off. They broke open box after box of K rations, eating just to stay awake. *If we keep chowing down like this,* Sean told himself, *we'll be out of food, too, before you know it. Damn, I gotta take a leak.*

He slid down from the turret to the hull deck and then to the ground behind the Sherman. For a few moments, the physical relief of urination masked the sound of the distant German engines. But once he was finished, something had changed. The murmur had become a snarling mechanical chorus, growing steadily louder. The German tanks were moving, getting closer. All along the treeline, gunners in Shermans and tank destroyers pressed eyes to gunsights, waiting for the dark shapes to grow larger and into range. Farther back, in clearings that afforded them fields of fire, the mortars and artillery pieces were ready to shoot illumination and HE rounds in high-angle fire onto predetermined target zones.

Captain Newcomb's voice spilled from the company radio net. "Nobody get itchy trigger fingers now. They can't see us for a max range shot, so they're going to have to get close…close enough that maybe we can kill them first."

So they waited.

Fabiano, *Eclipse's* gunner, asked Sean, "How far do you think they are?"

"I make them at twelve hundred yards, Fab."

"So why the fuck ain't we shooting? Those up-gunned tank destroyers we got should be able to cook 'em at this range. And with a lot of luck, these *Zippos* could, too."

Sean replied, "We shoot when the captain says so, and not before. You read me?"

"Yeah. Loud and clear. But I don't fucking like it."

"Too damn bad, Fab."

Sean tried to count those dark shapes, advancing toward them in what seemed two ranks. He got to 17 when a blinding beam of light rendered his eyes useless.

"THEY GOT FUCKING SEARCHLIGHTS ON THOSE TANKS. I CAN'T SEE A FUCKING THING."

It would take time to restore his vision, time they didn't have. Those searchlights were illuminating almost every vehicle in the treeline. Within seconds, the German tanks were firing.

Sean wasn't the only one affected. Night-blind GI gunners all along the line—at least those whose vehicles weren't already knocked out in the first salvo—either fired poorly aimed shots at the dazzling lights or didn't fire at all. Inside *Eclipse*, the only crewman who hadn't been looking into the searchlights when they snapped on was the loader, PFC Kowalski.

"*Ski*," Sean said, "you still got your eyes?"

"Yeah, Sarge."

"Then this is your big chance, kid. Take over for Fab. Squint into the sight so you don't go fucking blind, too."

Kowalski slid across the turret and took the gunner's position. He knew what to do; Sean had cross-trained all his crewmen well. But he'd never had to do it when it was a matter of life and death. Trying to pick out a target through the sight, he asked, "What the hell do you want me to shoot at, Sarge?"

"Pick any one of 'em. There's plenty to choose from."

Aligning the gun tube with a shape that seemed so big—and so close it filled his sight picture—he said, "Okay, I pick *him*. On the way!"

Eclipse shuddered with her own recoil. The breech snapped open, and the acrid stench of expended propellant filled the turret.

"Somebody gonna fucking load for me?" Kowalski asked, his voice taking on the tone of a man relishing his first taste of command. "Or do I have to do everything my goddamn self?"

"Easy, *killer*," Sean replied, fumbling for an anti-tank round. "I got you covered. That first shot hit anything?"

"*Fucking A* it did. Hit him right in the turret. Shoved the tube and that goddamn searchlight right down his throat."

Sean rammed the round in and locked the breach. No sooner had he reported "Up!" when Kowalski yelled, "On the way!"

The searchlights were extinguished and shattered now, their few seconds of dominance erased by main guns and .50 calibers up and down the line. Now it was the Germans' turn to be blind. Their line of tanks slowed and then stopped as drivers and gunners struggled to regain orientation on the battlefield. Colonel Abrams told his artillery observer, "Fire for effect, son."

Volley after devastating volley of short-range, high-angle fire from 105-mm howitzers rained almost straight down on the bewildered Germans. Their tanks—a mixture of Mark IVs, Panthers, and a few of the dreaded Tigers—were impervious to being knocked out by most American weapons when shooting at their tough front armor. But rounds plummeting onto their decks and turret roofs were another matter. Those panzers suffering direct hits from above were quickly turned into flaming coffins as their hulls were breached and their ammo and fuel ignited. As this high-angle death continued to fall, the American tankers' vision was returning. They added their direct fire to the chaos the artillery had caused.

Captain Newcomb's voice was on the radio again. "Kraut tanks don't attack by themselves. There's got to be infantry with them somewhere."

As if to prove his point, the *whoosh* and flaming tail of a rocket from within CCF's perimeter struck a Sherman, turning it into a pyre.

"Shit," Sean said, "we got Kraut bastards with *panzerfausts* up our ass." He climbed out of the turret hatch to man the .50 caliber mounted on the roof. He could see the dark outlines of running men, some of them holding short, thin tubes with one bulbous end that could only be *panzerfausts*. No GI carried a weapon shaped like that.

He pivoted the .50 caliber to knock them down. Before he could get off a burst, he saw the silhouette of a *coal scuttle* helmet of the Wehrmacht at *Eclipse's* rear end. The man wearing that distinctive helmet was climbing onto her rear deck. In his raised hand was something that looked like a stick with a tin can stuck on its end. A short, point-blank burst from Sean's machine gun ripped him apart. The stick he'd carried—a "potato masher" grenade—dropped onto the deck. Sean scrambled through the turret hatch. He wasn't all the way inside when the grenade exploded.

He knew he was hit, feeling the searing metal fragments in his arm and shoulder. But he didn't feel *wounded.* Every part of his body seemed to work just fine. He was back out of the turret and on the .50 caliber in seconds, firing at fleeting shadows in strange helmets, shouting into the turret as he identified panzers for his gunner to engage. He could see the battle clearly now, the field bathed in the light of so many burning tanks from both sides. He offered a silent prayer the foot soldiers he was gunning down weren't his own.

Colonel Abrams was on the radio with a terse message: "Do not pursue. Repeat, do not pursue." It took the adrenaline-fueled tankers several moments to process what their colonel meant: *The battle is over. The Germans are withdrawing back toward Gacé.*

Do not pursue: Sean smiled as the full meaning of those words sunk in: *We won't have to fight house to house in the fucking dark tonight. Thank God.*

He checked his watch again: *0312.*

Not even ten fucking minutes, Sean told himself. *That's all it took.*

When the sun came up in a few hours, they'd know what it had cost.

★★★★

At his HQ at Alençon, General Wood cursed when he read the directive from General Patton. Once his entire staff was roused from their sleep and assembled, he told them, "Gentlemen, Georgie says we can't wait for Eightieth Division to take Sées. We've got to do it our damn selves…and we've got to do it *today*."

"What about CC Fox, sir?" his G3 asked. "They've just fought off a major attack. We won't know what their combat condition is for a few hours yet. They're going to need our support. We can't hang them out to dry."

"Tell me something I don't for damn sure know, Colonel," Wood replied. "It sounds like that little Limey clerk chewed Brad's ass but good for not keeping his *hold line* nice and straight. Like this is some fucking parade ground or something."

The G3 asked, "So Monty doesn't have a clue about CC Fox's whereabouts yet, does he, sir?"

"Apparently not. If he did, there'd be a hell of a lot more shit hitting the fan right now than just tidying up his silly little line. But here's the rest of the deal. Brad's told Ninth Air Force to level Sées at sun-up. Then all we've got to do is *mop up* afterwards, he says…like he's forgotten the rubble of shattered towns makes for terrific defensive fortifications that just might hold us up for days."

"But sir," the G3 replied, "there can't be more than a couple of battalions left in Sées. What happened to the directive *not* to indiscriminately flatten whole towns that aren't heavily defended?"

"Directives are made to be ignored sometimes, Colonel. Just ask George Patton. He's a master at the practice."

Chapter Twenty-Six

The men of *Combat Command Fox* needed only the veiled light of predawn to take the toll of what had happened just a few hours before. The burned-out hulks of a dozen German tanks—one Tiger, the rest Mark IVs and Panthers—littered the open field between the forest and Gacé. The GIs were surprised to find none of those beaten tanks were closer than 500 yards; they had seemed so much closer when the fight was on.

The Shermans and tank destroyers on the west side of CCF's perimeter absorbed the brunt of the attack. Nine were knocked out, with most of their crew dead. Armored vehicles on the other sectors of the perimeter were unscathed, as was the artillery. The American infantrymen miraculously suffered only a handful of dead and wounded, but the German infantrymen who infiltrated the perimeter fared far worse; over 50 were dead, a number of them in the area behind *Eclipse of the Hun.* A precise count proved difficult, as they weren't counting whole bodies, only body parts. Fifty-caliber machine gun fire tends to crudely butcher a man rather than just tear neat holes in his flesh. The GIs loading the noxious stew of fragmented Germans into empty ammo trailers—men who had grown hardened to the gore of battle—had all they could do to keep from puking their guts out.

Another dozen American tanks were damaged but capable of fighting. *Eclipse* fell into that category; the grenade explosion on her aft deck had damaged access plates and the engine's air manifolds. She wouldn't be drivable very far until repairs were made, but all her guns and radios still worked. “Don’t look like we’ll be doing much moving until we get gassed up, anyway,” Sean told his crew as the medic pulled metal fragments from his arm and shoulder. “Scrounge some of the dead *Zippos* and see what you can come up with in the way of parts.”

Kowalski asked, “You gonna be okay, Sarge?”

“Yeah, I’ll live. Now didn’t I just tell you to do something? Get your ass moving.”

At his CP, Colonel Abrams was getting bad news from 4th Armored HQ at Alençon. “They’ve got some big change of plans they won’t talk about on the air,” he told his staff. “What it means to us, though, is our resupply convoy is being delayed. Again.”

Dammit, Abrams thought, *armor’s supposed to be able to shoot, move, and communicate. Until I get some gas, I can only do two out of three. Congratulations, Creighton—you’re the proud commander of sixty some-odd steel bunkers that are stuck in place at the moment. On second thought, bunkers my ass...they’re sitting ducks.*

★★★★

It was 20 minutes past sunrise when the American bombers struck Sées. Two squadrons of B-26 Marauders at medium altitude unloaded 90 tons of high explosives on the town. Four miles south on the highway from Alençon to Sées, the lead elements of 4th Armored Division’s column felt the ground shake and watched as clouds of gray smoke and dust rose over the town. They were too far away to actually see the bombs as they fell but were grateful their distance from it all was, at least this time, keeping them safe. They knew those bombs were being dropped by young men every bit as terrified and prone to error as they were. And once released, errant bombs could never be recalled. They answered only to gravity and the wind, caring nothing for who or what might be beneath them.

Even minus the units of *Combat Command Fox*, 4th Armored was a formidable fighting force. Despite their numbers being further depleted by combat casualties, they still numbered nearly 9000 men in tanks, half-tracks, and trucks stretching for miles along the highway, equal in tank strength to CCF but double its strength in infantry and artillery. They were encouraged to see most of the bombs had actually impacted within the town, not the usual off-target scattering ground troops were used to seeing from high-flying bombers. No flak had been hurled at the Marauders, just strings of tracers, representing futile attempts to hit out-of-range targets. None of the planes seemed to be in any sort of trouble as they turned back to the west after dumping their loads.

"That's a good sign," General Wood said. "No flak means probably no eighty-eights left working in the town to tear up our armor. All we have to do now is deal with everything left alive in there." Picking up the microphone of his command radio, he announced, "All units, execute *Ops Order Able*. Let's roll, boys."

There had been no sleep for the citizens of Gacé, not since the brief, percussive discord of battle in the middle of the night had begun. Once the shooting stopped, the German survivors had spilled back into the town with the roar of vehicle engines and the frenzied shouting of men who were convinced their life and death struggle was not over, merely paused. The people of Gacé felt certain that struggle had, at long last, come to them, too. Those few not already in their cellars made their descent with great haste.

In the ensuing hours, however, the guns remained silent. Wehrmacht soldiers and townspeople alike were expecting an attack which never came. Instead, like a cancer in remission, an uneasy stillness settled over the town, lessened not at all by the sunrise.

In her *grand-mère's* kitchen, Sylvie could find only spoiled milk. Determined to prepare the morning coffee as she knew the old woman preferred, she counted out some ration coupons and announced, "I'm going to the market. I'll be back in a few minutes."

Grand-mère replied, "Very well, but be careful, my dear girl. Very careful."

As Sylvie rode away on her bicycle, she didn't notice two men in suits and ties on the street behind her. If she'd seen them, she'd have known one was the mayor of Gacé. She wouldn't have known the other was Gestapo. Or that the mayor was pointing her out and whispering the word *maquis* to the German.

Fifteen minutes later, *Grand-mère* looked out from her parlor window, wondering what was taking Sylvie so long to return. What she saw in the middle of the deserted street provided the answer: a toppled bicycle and a shattered milk bottle.

★★★★

When they removed her blindfold, Sylvie knew exactly where she was: *I'm at the Gacé police station. I was only in that car for a few minutes. We couldn't have gone very far. And now they're going to lock me in a cell.*

As the cell door slammed behind her, she knew two things: someone had betrayed her, and the only reason she wasn't already dead was they intended to torture information about the *maquis* from her.

Tommy Moon looked over the briefing papers and aerial photos for the morning's mission. His flight would be providing general support for *Combat Command Fox* once again. There was a specific mission requirement, too: photo recon had identified the building that housed the German HQ in Gacé. CCF didn't have a clear view of that building from their hide two miles to the east and was under a directive not to shoot artillery into towns indiscriminately. Therefore, it would fall to the Air Force to take out the HQ with as little collateral damage to the town as possible.

"According to our intel," the briefing officer said, "the building functions as the barracks for the *gendarmerie national*."

Tommy asked, "You mean the police?"

"Yeah, that's it. The police station."

"Hmm…all these other buildings around it…are they all the same height?"

"Some of the ones to the east are taller," the briefing officer replied. "I guess that's why CC Fox can't see the three-story police station from where they're at. The ones on the west side of the street, though, should be shorter. Two stories, tops."

Herb Clinchmore, *Blue Flight's* number four, said, "You're dying to try out those new rockets, aren't you, Tommy?"

"Yeah…but I don't think the approach to this target will work for rockets. Too steep. We'll have another look once we're up there, but this looks like a low-level glide bombing job."

"Swell," Clinchmore said, "so every Kraut with a pea-shooter gets a crack at us."

"Keep your shorts on, Herb. I'm going in first. One of you will have to follow up only if I miss."

"Then do us a favor, boss. Don't miss."

Tommy gathered his three pilots at the big map on the wall. "We'll fly direct to Gacé," he told them. "There'll probably be a lot of smoke and haze above Sées left over from the bomber boys. But they're cleared out already and on the way home, so we won't have to dodge them."

★★★★

Handcuffed and blindfolded again, Sylvie was led from the cell to another room and placed in a chair. She knew she was still in the police station's basement; they hadn't climbed any stairs. Once the guards who'd brought her shuffled out, she could tell there were two men remaining in the room from the sound of their shoes scuffing along the concrete floor.

Shoes, not boots, she told herself. *Gestapo.*

In hushed tones, the two men conversed in German. She couldn't understand much of what they were saying; it seemed to be some sort of code. One word she picked out clearly, though: *baumein.* She knew it meant *dangle.*

Then, one on each side, they lifted her upward from the chair, pushing her against the wall, holding her aloft so her manacled hands slipped over what felt like a hook high on the wall. When they released her, she knew her translation had been correct. She was left dangling from her wrists, her feet barely able to touch the floor, the metal of the cuffs cutting painfully into her skin. With a tug that jerked her head roughly forward, the blindfold was removed. The room they were in was little more than a large closet.

Now that she could see them, Sylvie was surprised how small the two Gestapo men were. Most of the other agents she'd seen—like the one she'd once lured into a dark alley to be shot to death in an ambush—were large, sinister-looking men, who looked undoubtedly capable of the treachery they carried out. These two looked like bank clerks.

She remembered the instructions all *maquis* had received: *if captured, act terrified, proclaim your innocence,* and, most importantly, *admit nothing.* Since being snatched off her bicycle, she had performed as told, with one exception: there was no need to pretend being terrified. Her fright was genuine and barely under control.

The blond one held up her identification card and waved it in her face. In French, he said, "Tell us your real name, Madame Bergerac." The Teutonic inflection of his words made his French sound like he was hocking up phlegm from his throat.

Her voice trembling, Sylvie replied, "That is my real name—"

She started to add *messieurs* but stopped herself. They weren't deserving of even the modicum of respect the title implied.

The dark-haired one stepped forward, producing a dagger from beneath his suit jacket. She recognized it immediately by the inscription on its blade: *Mein Ehre Heisst Treue*—My Honor is Loyalty. The motto of the *Waffen-SS*. He made a small ceremony of slicing the humid air in the cramped room with it, and then placed the cold, sharp blade beneath the hem of Sylvie's skirt, sliding it slowly up the inside of her bare thigh. When he spoke, his French sounded no more refined than his partner's.

"It would be such a shame," he said, "if one so young and so lovely should come to such unfortunate ruin." As he spoke, the dagger's slow ascent ended against the crotch of her panties, the flat of its blade sliding back and forth against her like a cold, cruel lover, its edges etching reddening lines on her inner thighs with machine-like precision.

His mouth opened again as if to speak, but suddenly he was gone, lost in a ferocious upheaval she more felt than saw, as if a coarse, smothering blanket had been thrown over her. She was falling, and the world was tumbling down after her.

And then, nothing.

When she came to, she was lying on what must have been the basement floor, in the thick of a choking dust cloud she could taste and feel. An unnatural shaft of murky light streamed in from above, a distant spotlight trained on this netherworld, a beacon to guide her out.

Struggling to her feet, she thought she could hear a siren, but then realized it was just the screaming of her distressed ears. She stumbled over a man's leg protruding from beneath a pillar of concrete. A few feet away, another man's head and torso lay crushed beneath a wooden beam, his arms and legs splayed like a frog pinned to a dissecting pan. Something shiny in the rubble beside him caught the dull light. She seized it, not knowing for sure what it was until she held it in her shackled hands: *A key ring!*

Her lungs seemed ready to burst, like a diver down much too long. She scaled piles of rubble, struggling upward toward the salvation of the light, each step a gamble that its foothold wouldn't crumble beneath her weight and send her tumbling back to the shattered hell below. Each inch of progress was paid for in pain and blood as sharp debris sliced her flesh. The key ring, with the promise of freedom it held, remained clenched between her teeth.

Every upward grasp of her bound hands became more desperate, less agile. Those hands lunged for what she took to be a jagged beam—or perhaps a broken pipe—trying to slip the handcuffs over it to hold her fast. But she misjudged, and in that sickening second felt herself hanging between life and death— or maybe heaven and hell—waiting for gravity to celebrate its inevitable victory, pull her down, and end her battle to live once and for all.

Tommy Moon finished his orbit over Gacé, pushed her throttle forward, and climbed to join the rest of his flight. He'd just done his job with brutal efficiency, dropping two bombs on the police station that served as German headquarters. But there would be no celebrating. The feeling it left him with was bittersweet: *Maybe it's the new name painted on her nose...or maybe I've gotten a whole lot better at low-level bombing. Either way, the odds are good I just killed a lot of Germans, maybe even decapitated one of their commands. But the odds are just as good I killed some French civilians, too. They didn't have it coming.*

"You put 'em right down the ol' pickle barrel, boss," Jimmy Tuttle radioed. "Blew that building to shit. And it looks like there's about *zeeero* collateral damage to the rest of the street."

The other pilots in *Blue Flight* couldn't have agreed more: "Scratch one Kraut HQ," Joe Rider said.

"Yeah," Herb Clinchmore added, "I knew you'd come through, boss."

"All right, guys," Tommy replied. "Let's knock off the chatter and see what else the guys on the ground need doing."

That one phrase Tuttle had used—*collateral damage*—was sticking in Tommy's head like a stain that wouldn't scrub out. He thought of his brother and wished their parting hadn't been so contentious. But he knew he'd made it so: *There I was on my high horse judging Sean for killing prisoners—something I'll never be sure he even did—and here I am, killing God knows who. What a fucking hypocrite.*

He also knew he'd have to shake these distracting thoughts on the double. Combat flying demanded 110 percent of your attention. Sometimes more.

Chapter Twenty-Seven

Sylvie had no idea whose hands it had been that reached down and pulled her those last few feet to safety. By the time she'd coughed her lungs clear and wiped the caked dust from her eyes, the person was gone. Looking through jagged pickets of wood that were once part of the police station's walls, she could see out onto Gacé's *grand-rue.* Looking up, where the roof once was, she could see four fighter planes passing overhead in the bright morning sky.

And then it all made sense: *We were bombed. The Americans bombed us.*

The Americans saved me.

She still had the key ring; it was clenched in one of her hands. Whether it was her doing or that of her disappearing savior, she had no idea. Wasting no time, she found the right key on the ring and opened the handcuffs, flinging them as far as she could once she'd gotten them off. A few cautious steps through the rubble and she was in the street.

There would be no going back to *Grand-mère's* house; those two might not have been the only Gestapo agents in town. *And I have no idea who betrayed me in the first place.* Wild-eyed German soldiers were everywhere, but she must have looked no different than the other dust-encrusted civilians who'd been too close when the bombs fell. The soldiers paid her no attention.

One thing she was sure of: *My only safety will be with the Americans now.*

But first she had to get out of Gacé. Walking south on the *grand-rue*, she saw how she'd do it. Scores of townspeople had decided to take their chances by fleeing the inevitable battle. They'd become refugees—piling their most precious possessions into wagons, prams, anything that rolled—and began to walk slowly south, toward what they hoped would be safety behind the American lines.

I should have no trouble blending in with these people, Sylvie told herself.

★★★★

By 0800 hours, 4th Armored was in control of Sées. There would be pockets of resistance to clear out, even some concealed armor that might not have shown themselves yet, but the *critical mass* of this battle was decidedly in American hands. Even the distraught civilians—so caught by surprise by the early morning air raid they hadn't had a chance to take to their cellars—could feel the Americans were clearly in control.

An old man in the street pleaded with General Wood: "Our dead are your responsibility, *mon général*. Will you not have the decency to bury them?"

"We have no time, sir," Wood replied, his look of sympathy genuine but his refusal to help unbending. "We must mop up here and move on. If we don't, there will be many more of my soldiers and your townspeople dead. It was the Germans who chose to make your town a battleground, not me and—"

Wood's radio operator interrupted. "Pardon me, General, but there's an urgent call for you."

"Dammit, who is it?"

"Sorry, sir, but it's Third Army."

Wood nearly dropped the handset with shock when he heard the voice coming from it. It was not that of some Third Army staff jockey, as he'd expected. It was the unmistakably shrill voice of General George Patton himself.

"Yes, sir," Wood replied, "I wasn't expecting you here. I can meet you in ten minutes."

"Make it nine, General," Patton said.

Wood's driver made it in seven.

Parked in a grove on the edge of town, General Patton had unfurled a tactical map on the hood of his jeep. As Wood leaned in close, Patton said, "I realize we sent you here to Sées on very short notice, John, and it looks like you've done an outstanding job, just like your boys are doing up at Gacé. Now I'm going to tell you what I want you to do next."

Looking at the map, he didn't need Patton's words to know what *next* was. Broad red arrows swept northward, beyond Sées—and even beyond Gacé. The look of surprise on Wood's face must have been obvious.

"That's right, General," Patton continued, "I want your division to regroup at Gacé like we planned all along. Then, you'll press north, all the way to Orville and Vimoutiers."

"But sir, that's a full ten miles beyond Monty's *stop line.*"

"I don't give a rat's ass, John. We're here to kill Germans, not stroke some strutting little Limey's ego."

Wood needed a few moments to catalog all the reasons he considered this a bad idea. Bending the line to Gacé was a minor *adjustment* of Montgomery's order, which—provided it didn't cause a fiasco—would be overlooked in the big picture. But pushing that line still farther north was willful disobedience. Once past the insubordination of it, there were the truckloads of tactical and logistical problems this freelancing would create. But he could sense Patton growing irritated by his silence.

"Are you asking me to stop an entire German army with my *one division*, sir?"

"No, John, of course not," Patton replied. "First off, they're a badly depleted and battered German army. Finish them off and we'll be sipping wine in Berlin before the first snowfall. And you won't be alone. I'm moving the rest of Twelfth Corps to support the new line. And I'll move up my entire goddamn Third Army if that's what it takes."

"And General Bradley's going along with this?"

Wood could tell from the smirk on his face that Bradley had no idea what Patton was doing. "Brad'll get over it," Patton replied, "and so will Ike. Just like they got over Messina and those other times, too. Kicking Kraut ass always beats licking Limey ass…even though that's Ike's favorite pastime."

He could understand Patton's confidence: *He never got in trouble for winning…just for running his fool mouth. So now he's going for all the marbles by sticking my division's neck out farther than it's ever been before.*

"So we're really going to do this all on our own, sir?" Wood asked.

Patton replied, "Isn't any commander worth his salt always on his own, General?"

★★★★

Blue Flight didn't have to wait long for another target. The leader of a P-38 section was asking for help with a large German armored column they'd encountered near the town of Exmes, six miles west of Gacé. "We're down to guns," the P-38 leader reported, "and we can't get close enough to do any good. They've got flak guns out the ass and more tanks than I've ever seen all in one place."

Tommy asked, "Which way are they headed?"

"East, toward Gacé."

Shit. Right toward CC Fox, Tommy told himself.

"We're going home for a refill," the P-38 leader added.

It only took a few minutes for *Blue Flight* to get there. Skirting north around the German column, Tommy could see exactly what the P-38 boys were talking about: he estimated at least 40 vehicles, mostly tanks of various marks. Interspersed were six or more half-tracks—*flakwagens*—with mounted anti-aircraft guns. They spewed bright tracers in breathtaking, treacherous arcs across the sky as they tried to chase the American planes away.

"At least there aren't any horses," Tommy told his pilots. "*Blue Three* and *Four*, fly decoy on top. *Blue Two*, you and me will come out of the sun with rockets. Go for the *flakwagens* first. Don't get too close and let them shoot the shit out of you."

As Rider and Clinchmore in *Blue Three* and *Four* orbited high over the Germans, taunting their gunners, Tommy and Tuttle flew away to the southeast, into the sun. "Okay," Tommy radioed, "that sharp bend in the road—that's the *IP*. *Tally-ho*." *Eclipse of the Hun* heeled over into a diving, 180-degree turn that would put her on a steep attack path. Tuttle's plane would circle the IP—the *initial point*—once, and then follow.

A clarity swept Tommy's mind, clearing it of everything but the task at hand. He was no longer just a pilot. He and his plane had once again become a *weapons system*:

Okay, looking good. Eighteen-degree angle of descent set. Range to target four thousand yards. Thirty inches manifold pressure. Launch rockets at range two thousand yards, two thousand feet altitude. First half-track at outer ring, moving center, dead on the reticle. Fire three rockets, then throttle to the stop, pull up, and turn back into the sun and out of Tuttle's way...and away from the bad guys. Then be ready to do it all over again.

Damn, these Krauts got balls. They aren't even scattering.

His eyes in a steady, cyclic scan over gunsight, altimeter, engine gauges, and airspeed indicator, he teased small corrections from the stick and throttle, coaxing the targeting data toward its solution. A ribbon of tracers sprayed far off her right wingtip: *Target still moving. It's got to stop to shoot accurately. Coming up on release point....FIRE.*

Three rockets raced from their wing-mounted tubes a half-second apart, the glowing orange balls of their motors' exhaust shrinking to pinpoints as they sped away. Tommy felt the urge to stay on the current flight path and watch where those rockets hit. It was almost overpowering. But every second drawing closer to the *flakwagens* made him a better target.

"Rockets away, pulling out," he told Tuttle. "Your turn, Jimmy," he added, those last syllables sounding strained as the g-forces of the tight turn tried to pull everything in Tommy's upper body to his feet.

Halfway through the turn, Joe Rider broadcast his assessment of the rocket attack: "Close, but no cigar, boss. You got 'em a little dirty, though. Give 'em hell, Jimmy."

Tuttle's approach to the target was lower and faster. He released his rockets at a greater range than Tommy.

"Not even close, Jimmy," Rider reported as the rockets splashed into the ground well wide of the German column.

Shit, Tommy thought, *what the fuck good are these rockets if you can't put them where you need them? I think your only chance of a hit is to empty the tubes all at once—fire all six of the sons of bitches and hope for the best.*

The rockets must have had some effect on the gunners, though, even if it was just psychological. Their volume of fire had dropped off quite a bit—maybe even enough to get in close for a strafing run. That was guaranteed to be far more effective than errant rockets.

"*Blue Flight* from *Blue Leader*. I'm going to strafe from the sun. That should keep their heads down while you guys come in behind me and dive-bomb them."

Tuttle replied, "You sure you don't want to do another rocket run, Tommy? They might not work after you fire the guns, remember? The damn wires breaking?"

"Yeah, I'm dead sure. Save the rockets for something standing still. I'll worry about them not working later."

Orbiting over the IP, Tommy asked, "You guys in position?"

"Roger," Rider replied, "about two miles behind you and way up high, boss."

He nosed *Eclipse* over and began the strafing run. The approach path was almost the same as the rocket pass, but a little faster—and she wouldn't be pulling out until she had passed over the entire German column. Aiming for a point ahead of the lead *flakwagen*, he squeezed the trigger at 500 yards. If anyone was firing back at him, he couldn't tell.

I'm hitting them! Look at all those bright flashes as the API tears through those half-tracks!

He saw bright flashes against the forward hulls and turrets of some tanks, too, but he knew from hard experience it was just pyrotechnics, doing no harm to the tanks or their crews.

At least it's keeping those tankers inside and buttoned up, where they can't get a bead on us.

And then there was nothing but empty highway beneath him. Tommy pulled *Eclipse* up and turned hard, hoping to catch a view of the rest of his section as they dive-bombed the column.

The timing was perfect; he had a front-row seat. The other three jugs staggered their bombs—six 500-pounders in all—along the *flakwagens* in the center of the column. Through the smoke and dust of the explosions, only two of the half-tracks emerged, and they weren't firing anymore. All the others had come to a halt; one was overturned on the side of the highway, another was on fire. Tommy could see the ant-like figures of soldiers running from the stricken vehicles.

"Outstanding drop, guys," Tommy told them. "Okay…two-plane teams, now—let's hit the tanks in the ass. Give these rockets another chance to see if they're worth a shit."

But they weren't *worth a shit* this time, either. By now, most of the tanks had scattered off the highway, seeking defilade in dips of the terrain that would shield them from every attack angle except directly overhead. Some found it, some didn't. Herb Clinchmore in *Blue Four* loosed a sheaf of four rockets at one tank still on level ground but scored no hits. Lining up for a broadside shot on another which had achieved imperfect cover in a gulley, Clinchmore fired his last two. One malfunctioned, falling well short. The other missed.

Joe Rider got off two rockets before the rest failed to fire. One of the rockets that had actually fired glanced off the glacis plate of a big tank—Rider swore it was a Tiger—and exploded harmlessly in the air. The other missed.

Tommy noticed something interesting as Jimmy Tuttle bore down on several tanks churning across open ground. They seemed to be slowing as he closed in on them, and then, without the tanks coming to a stop, crewmen jumped off and started running toward the safety of some trees. They would have been better off staying in their tanks. All six of Tuttle's rockets missed completely, but his strafing of the crewmen a few seconds later appeared brutally on target.

Tommy spotted a tank which appeared to be stopped on level ground. In reality, the crew thought they had picked a defilade with good cover. But it was too shallow, appearing flat from the air. He fired his last three rockets at the tank's six o'clock. It was hard to tell how many hit, but at least one obviously did. The tank exploded, launching the commander through his turret hatch as if shot from a cannon.

Tommy didn't think much of the score: *Twenty rockets fired...with four duds still on Rider's wing...all to knock out exactly one tank. And it looks like more crews are abandoning their tanks. God only knows why.*

Blue Flight was down to guns now, and they knew those .50 calibers wouldn't be much use against the tanks. Tommy and Tuttle, the two who had done the strafing, were low on ammo. They all heard the call on their radios: two freshly bombed-up flights were on the way to relieve them and try to beat up this German column some more. That gave *Blue Flight* a few minutes to deal with some unfinished business below.

"*Blue Three* from *Blue Leader*, you and *Four* still got all your .50 cal, right?"

"Affirmative."

"Okay, then you two go finish off those *flakwagens* that are still running...and anybody else on foot down there, too. *Blue Two,* you and I will cover high."

As *Blue Leader* and *Blue Two* climbed for a better view, Tommy watched as Rider and Clinchmore rolled into their attack on the *flakwagens*. It looked like a straightforward run on a fast-moving ground target—about a 70-degree angle between the target's line of motion and the jugs' direction of attack—the two planes in echelon, with Clinchmore trailing off Rider's right wing.

Tommy was climbing in a shallow turn that kept his left wing down and out of the way for a better view below. But if he kept slowly turning left, the action would be below *Eclipse's* nose and out of sight. He focused his attention back inside the cockpit just for a moment as he steepened the turn and then reversed its direction, a move which would yield a view of the attack once again but over her right wingtip instead.

He finished the maneuver just in time to watch the lead jug—Rider's plane—as it appeared to be skimming along the ground, still firing...and then a shriek came over the radio, a garbled syllable that seemed a cry for help, a howl of victory, and a wail of defeat all rolled into one. Rider's plane merged with the *flakwagen* he'd targeted, and both dissolved in the same fireball.

"NO…JOEY!" It was Clinchmore's voice.

Then, nothing but stunned silence over the radio until broken by Jimmy Tuttle: "What the fuck just happened?"

Tommy had a pretty good idea *what the fuck* had just happened: target fixation—the tendency of a shooter to get so focused on his objective he forgets about everything else and flies straight into the ground. Strange but true; he'd seen it once before and heard about it plenty.

Sure, maybe it wasn't that at all. Maybe his plane got shot up and wasn't controllable. Maybe he was already dead...

But that scream, like he realized too late he'd fucked up.

Tommy could hear his brother's voice in his head, and the words seemed terribly correct:

Just a matter of time.

Chapter Twenty-Eight

The tankers of *Combat Command Fox* didn't waste much time licking their wounds. They'd spent every minute since sunrise carting off the German dead, burying their own, and scrounging their unserviceable tanks and tank destroyers for ammo and gasoline that hadn't already been consumed by fire. Now it was midmorning, and they'd managed to collect 350 gallons of gas in five-gallon jerry cans, enough to fill up two Shermans or parcel out one jerry can to each of the 60 surviving tanks. Those five gallons would allow a Sherman to drive only four miles.

"Better than nothing," Sean Moon said as his driver poured their can into *Eclipse's* nearly empty tank. "At least it'll give us a running start when we gotta get the hell out of here."

Captain Newcomb tallied the jerry cans and said, "Make sure you set aside a couple for the ambulances."

Sean asked, "You expecting any of us to actually live through this, Captain?"

"Yeah, I'm hoping we all will, Sergeant Moon. But right now I'm worried about guys dying because we couldn't get them to a field hospital."

Picking through the collection of weapons the German dead left behind, the GI infantrymen hoarded a dozen or so *panzerfausts*. They couldn't wait to see just how much better they were at killing tanks than their less-than-impressive bazookas. The fact that they'd be carrying out this research on German armor brought a certain ironic satisfaction.

Colonel Abrams stuffed the new orders that had just come over the radio into his pocket and went back to scanning the western approaches to CCF's forest enclave. "Somebody's got to come gunning for us again soon," he told his assembled staff officers. "Between what the rest of Fourth Armored just pushed out of Sées, whatever is still left in Gacé, and the horde that's coming east from Argentan, we're going to get hit with the whole shebang smack in the face. It's just a question of when. We'd better all pray that Fourth Armored is already here when it happens."

Miles to the west, they could see the rising smoke of a battle. "That's got to be the Air Force beating up some Krauts," Abrams said. Turning to his ASO Charlie Webster, he asked, "What's going on over there, Lieutenant?"

"There's a couple of flights of jugs plus some P-38s beating up a German column near Exmes, sir," Webster replied. "That's probably what we're seeing. It's only about six miles as the crow flies."

"I know where the hell Exmes is, Lieutenant," Abrams said. "But what are those planes right over there?" He pointed to a flight of four single-engined fighters descending out of the north, crossing in front of CCF's position. Their silhouettes were nothing like the Americans were used to seeing.

"Oh, shit," Captain Newcomb said, "they're Krauts! *Focke-Wulfs*, aren't they? Geez, that's all we fucking need right now."

"No, they're not Krauts," Webster replied. "They're RAF *Typhoons*."

"What the hell is the RAF doing down here?" Newcomb asked, before the answer dawned on him and every other officer standing there: *Airplanes go wherever they want. We're the ones who don't belong here, on the wrong side of Monty's stop line.*

Abrams asked, "Can you raise them on the radio, Lieutenant?"

Charlie Webster began to fumble through the pages of his *signal operating instructions.* "Yeah…but I've got to figure out the Brit frequency, sir."

Watching as the planes began to peel off into steep turns toward CCF's position, Colonel Abrams replied, "Better make it quick, Webster. If they aren't getting into attack position, I'll shit in my steel pot."

Anxious to get back to his company, Newcomb asked, "One question, sir…if they attack, do we engage?"

Without hesitation, Colonel Abrams replied, "Affirmative."

On the dead run, Captain Newcomb made it back to Baker Company. He got there in time to watch his men track the circling Typhoons with their .50-caliber machine guns. The planes were standing off a mile or more away, the glare of the midmorning sun off the dark wings and fuselages making their markings nearly impossible to read.

"Are these clowns Krauts or what?" Sean Moon asked.

"The ASO says they're RAF," Newcomb replied.

"I don't know, Captain. They look like Krauts to me. Do we shoot 'em?"

"If they attack, yeah."

"What do you mean *if*, sir? Why the fuck are we waiting?"

Fabiano popped up through the turret hatch. "Hogan thinks they got invasion stripes on 'em, sir. They gotta be Limeys."

Invasion stripes: the broad black and white bands hastily painted on the wings and aft fuselages of Allied aircraft for Operation Overlord, an attempt to prevent their being shot down accidentally by jumpy Allied gunners. Now more than two months after D-Day, those hastily applied stripes were weathered but still in place.

Newcomb took a look through binoculars as one of the planes flashed the lower side of its wings their way. "I can't tell," he said. "Can't tell if they have stripes, roundels, or anything."

Sean clenched the handles of the .50 cal tighter. "Limeys or not, if those fuckers get any closer, I'm knocking their asses down."

"Hang on a minute, Sergeant," Newcomb said. "Suppose that was your brother up there?"

"They ain't my brother, Captain. I know what a fucking jug looks like, and they ain't no jugs."

The four planes flew a few more orbits, as if they, too, were unsure of what they saw before them. Then they stopped turning, formed into pairs abreast, and dove down on the forest and the waiting gunners of *Combat Command Fox.*

★★★★

Sylvie and the refugees from Gacé plodded slowly south, reaching the village of Nonant-le-Pin by 1100 hours. From the heights of the village, they could see the thick black smoke rising from Sées, some six miles to the south. "The *Amis* and *Boche* are fighting," Sylvie told the others. "It is not safe to go there right now."

The company of German soldiers at Nonant-le-Pin could see the smoke, too. They were mostly old men and young boys, infantrymen left in the village to guard a cache of supplies. All were fully aware that once the American tanks rolled through Sées, they'd be the next ones beneath the tracks of the Shermans. They seemed more terrified than the refugees huddled in the village square, trying to decide which way to run.

"We should turn west," one refugee woman said.

"No," another replied, "that will take us straight into the teeth of the fighting. We must go east."

"No, no, no," an old man said. "There is nothing but the *Boche* to the east."

A group of refugees had already made up their minds. They'd turned back north, toward Gacé, hoping to return to the safety of the basements they'd chosen to forsake just a few hours ago.

They didn't get far. German soldiers blocked their path and herded them to a church, not hesitating to club with rifle butts any civilian who protested or moved too slowly. Sylvie got as close as she dared and stole a peek inside the church. It was already full of French civilians under guard.

They're going to use them as human shields when the Amis come, she told herself, *or lock them inside and set the church ablaze in some sort of reprisal. You'd think these frightened amateur soldiers would run for their lives...or surrender.*

A squad of soldiers stomped down the cobblestone street and began to corral the rest of the dithering refugees. Still separated from that group, Sylvie was able to duck behind a chicken coop and stay out of sight. She worked her way from there to behind a pig pen—and then a German soldier noticed her, yelled *Halt!* and ran toward her. He didn't get far. Trying to round a corner of the pen, he slipped in a runoff of pig excrement and fell hard, cursing as he went down. She heard the *thunk* of his helmet like a dropped pot against a fence post, the muffled clatter of his rifle as it tumbled into the muck. Before he could find his feet again, she was gone. There was nothing the soldier could do but curse some more.

Running through high grass on the village outskirts, Sylvie rejoiced in her luck: *That's twice today I've been saved by fortune—once by an American bomb, once by pig shit.*

Avoiding the roads for now, she headed northeast across open fields. *My only safety is with the Americans now, and the closest ones must be Colonel Abrams and his men in the forest near Gacé.*

Not before a dozen air-to-ground rockets had smashed into CCF's position, a score of .50-caliber machine guns had flung long bursts at the intruding aircraft, seven GIs lay wounded, and one of the Typhoons crashed into the forest just beyond CCF's perimeter did the other three RAF planes fly away to the northwest.

"I don't think they believed we're an American unit," Charlie Webster said, microphone still in his hand and on the verge of tears after trying to convince the

RAF to break off their attack. "I think they're just out of ammo."

The damage assessment was surprising short: only one vehicle destroyed, an empty deuce-and-a-half blown up by a lucky British rocket; of the seven GIs wounded, only one required evacuation for a chest wound—and that was from a spear-like shard of a shattered tree.

Even more surprising, the pilot of the crashed RAF Typhoon suffered only a broken arm and a collection of bruises. A team of GI infantrymen freed him from his smashed cockpit and brought him to Colonel Abrams' CP. As a medic set his arm, Abrams asked the young pilot, "Just what made you boys decide we were fair game?"

He replied with only his name, rank, and service number, as the assembled Americans shook their heads in amused disbelief.

"Son, you're not a POW," Abrams said. "We're Americans—your allies. We're on the same side. Now tell just why the hell you decided to attack us."

The young Englishman repeated his name, rank, and service number.

"Look, *Pilot Officer Darby*," Abrams said, "you're obviously a little shook up. We'll take good care of you while you come to your senses." Then he told the medic, "Put this man in the doc's care until he comes out of it."

As the pilot was led away, Abrams asked the infantry lieutenant who'd brought him in, "Did we shoot that lad down, or did he just crash?"

"From the looks of his plane, sir, it's hard to tell. But we didn't see a bullet hole anywhere." Hesitantly, he added, "I did have to stop my men from beating the shit out of him, though."

"Well done, Lieutenant. Believe me, they're not the only guys who want to kick some Limey ass right now. But we're not going to do that. I'm assigning you to make sure no one else tries to attack that pilot."

"Yes, sir…but permission to speak freely?"

"Granted."

"Why are we being so nice to the guy, sir? He did try to kill us."

"And we were trying to kill him, Lieutenant. I'm not sure how, but he and his buddies fucked up, plain and simple. It isn't the first time and it won't be the last. You know your Bible, son?"

"Yes, sir. A little."

"Then maybe you remember this verse: *Let he who is without sin cast the first stone.*"

Abrams then turned to Charlie Webster and said, "And speaking of sinners, Lieutenant, I'm assigning you, my ASO, to make sure an air attack on us by friendlies never fucking happens again. Is that clear?"

The colonel went back to studying the latest orders just in from 4th Armored. "They've cleared Sées," he said, "and they'll start coming up the highway to Gacé in the next hour or two. If they don't get hung up too badly around this pissant little town called *Nonant-le-Pin*, they'll be here before nightfall. Now here's the thing…they want us to stage a coordinated attack with them on Gacé. We strike from the north while they hit it from the south."

The operations officer looked confused. "But we're already blocking any Germans trying to escape the town, sir, even with our hands tied the way they are. Can't we explain to General Wood that—"

"It won't cut any ice. He's got different ideas, apparently."

"But, sir, if we come out in the open and then have to fight our way into the town and our tanks start running out of gas…"

"Tell me something I don't already know, Major. Let's stop feeling sorry for ourselves and think of something clever to keep General Wood happy without getting our asses cooked."

The operations officer looked no less confused.

"Remember," Abrams added, "Fourth Armored's got our fuel. Let's make it as easy as possible for them to reach us. We've already been stuck in one place too damn long."

★★★★

It was 1400 hours and CCF still didn't have a viable plan to attack Gacé. "The only thing that makes sense," the operations officer said, "is for us to execute a double envelopment of the town. Otherwise, we just squirt Krauts out of the place like a tube of toothpaste. Maybe even get ourselves enveloped in a counterattack."

His brow furrowed, Colonel Abrams replied, "Maybe…but I just can't believe there are all that many Germans left in Gacé. I wish we could prove that, though. Those aerial photos from this morning don't give us much to go on. What's the latest on Fourth Armored's position?"

"The lead elements are just leaving Sées now, sir," the operations officer said. "Even if they met no resistance at all, it'd be almost dark by the time the bulk of the division got here."

That was the worst news Abrams had heard all day. “And we’ve got a German armored column of unknown strength still bearing down on us, retreating from the west. I don’t reckon our Air Force or the RAF is going to kill anywhere near all of them before they get here. And if they don’t show up until dark, either…well, shit, I don’t even want to think of the chaos that’s going to happen when all these forces collide in the night.”

Charlie Webster had information he thought might help. “Actually, sir, all reports are that our air power is tearing the hell out of that German column near Exmes.”

Without enthusiasm, Abrams replied, “I’ll believe that when I see it, Lieutenant. You flyboys have a bad habit of grossly exaggerating your kills. The fact is, your planes put on a great show against Kraut armor, but they don’t kill all that many tanks, despite what you think you see from the air. But while we’re on the subject, can you shed any light on why the RAF attacked us?”

Webster swallowed hard before answering. “Well, sir, everything points to them just being lost. As I figure it, they were farther east than they thought. Once they caught sight of us—or at least caught sight of those dead tanks out there and all the tank tracks into these woods—they just assumed there had to be Krauts lying low here.”

A voice with an English accent added, “I believe I can confirm that, Colonel.”

Pilot Officer Darby had returned to lucidity. He stood before them, his broken arm set and in a sling, ready to come clean. Pointing westward with his good arm, he said, “I’m told that town over there is Gacé. We…well, we thought it was Exmes.”

"I see," Abrams replied. "Were you the flight leader, son?"

"Oh, no, sir. I'm quite junior."

No shit, every one of the Americans thought. *You look about twelve years old, kid.*

"We really didn't see how there could be any cock-up, sir," Darby added. "You Yanks aren't supposed to be here."

Abrams asked, "How do you know that?"

Darby pulled a map from his flight suit and handed it to the colonel. A thick red line, straight as an arrow—Montgomery's *stop line*—had been drawn from west to east across the map. Where they stood at the moment was a good six miles beyond that line.

"You're well north of Monty's line, sir," Darby said. "Like I said, you aren't supposed to be here."

"But dammit, Darby," Abrams replied, "we had panel markers out, clearly marking us as an Allied unit. Didn't you see them?"

"Yes, sir, we did. But the Krauts have used our panel markers to mislead us before. We've been instructed to ignore them."

"You're kidding me."

"No, sir. Those are our instructions."

"Well, ain't that fucking great?" Abrams said, studying the map. Then he asked, "These markings for the British, Canadian, and Polish positions—are they current?"

"As of this morning, sir."

Abrams whistled in disbelief. "That's as far as they've gotten? They're not even past Falaise yet? You could drive the entire Wehrmacht through the gap between us and them."

Darby shrugged. “They’re doing their best, sir. We all are.”

“I’ll tell you what, Pilot Officer Darby…we’ll get you out of here just as soon as we can, okay?”

“Take your time, sir,” the young Englishman replied, rocking the broken arm in its sling that made him useless as a pilot. “I’m in no bloody hurry.”

Chapter Twenty-Nine

Blue Flight, minus the fallen Joe Rider, was back in the air again, covering 4th Armored's right, or eastern, flank as they rolled north up the highway from Sées. There were intelligence reports of a German infantry division on the move from L'Aigle toward Gacé on a roughly parallel highway along that flank. Several flights of P-47s and P-38s had mauled it already. Now it was *Blue Flight's* turn to join the fray.

Tommy played *Eclipse's* throttle and prop lever, trying to coax a little more speed from her. *Lots of drag with all these bombs and rockets hanging off the wing. I should've had them take the fucking rocket tubes off. You can't hit a tank with them worth a damn, anyway. But this mission's supposed to be against soft targets—no armor to speak of—so I'll give them another try. Especially since the last guys in reported the Krauts were loaded with flakwagens. Nobody's said anything about eighty-eights, though, thank God.*

They were over the highway now, and dispersed groups of German trucks and horse-drawn artillery were clearly visible. But a little farther to the east, Tommy noticed something even more interesting: *Holy shit! Am I seeing things? There must be half a dozen Ju-52s on the ground, with trucks backed up to their loading doors. Are they flying in supplies or pulling troops out?*

"*Blue Flight* from *Blue Leader*, how about we shoot up some *Iron Annies* on that makeshift airfield over yonder?"

"Count me in," Jimmy Tuttle replied, "but don't forget the cardinal rule, boss."

"Yeah, I remember: *make only one pass at an airfield.* Okay…Jimmy, you're with me. Herb, give us top cover."

"Roger," Clinchmore replied, "but if any Kraut fighters pop up, I'm sounding the alarm and diving straight for the deck. I'm dead meat without a wingman covering my ass."

Tommy replied, "Sounds like a plan, Herb."

Together, Tommy and Tuttle dropped lower, lining up to attack the landing field from the east. "They're parked in such a nice, straight line," Tommy said. "I'll go for the far three. Jimmy, you take the near three."

"Roger, boss. *Tally ho.*"

"Okay," Tommy replied, shoving her throttle forward, "let's pour the coals on and be bad targets."

"Hey," Tuttle said, "*flakwagen* at two o'clock."

"Good eyes, Jimmy. I'll get him. You stay on the planes."

The German gunner spit a line of tracers in his direction as he struggled to find the range. That gave Tommy an idea: *No point getting too close. Seems like rockets might be perfect for this job.* He swung *Eclipse's* nose dead onto the target, and squeezed off two rockets. Rolling hard right and diving for the treetops, Tommy couldn't see the ribbon of tracers chasing his tail, failing to keep up with him. He couldn't see if the rockets had done any damage, either, until he'd turned almost 180 degrees and gained some altitude again.

Once *Eclipse* came around, Tommy saw the billowing black smoke of a burning vehicle. Through the smoke came the rapid sequence of flashes from ammunition cooking off in the blaze.

Damn, I guess I did hit it. No time to pat myself on the back, though. Where the hell are the rest of my guys?

Clinchmore was just a voice on the radio, unseen but still in position high above as top cover. Tommy found Tuttle's plane, just a speck to the south after finishing his attack on the Ju-52s. All six of the German planes were still on the ground, two of them consumed in flames. Tiny figures of men were scurrying to get away from them.

Looks like Jimmy had a great pass—two destroyed, three damaged, maybe.

But one of the planes—the first in the parking line—was moving, taxiing to the edge of the broad clearing serving as an airfield.

She's trying to take off.

By the time Tommy had wheeled his ship around and dove on the Ju-52, she was off the ground, struggling for altitude, and flying so slowly *Eclipse* would streak past her in a matter of seconds. But the big, cumbersome Junkers was filling *Eclipse's* gunsight. He squeezed the trigger.

Bullet strikes twinkled along the top of the Ju-52's wings and fuselage. Big chunks of her corrugated metal skin flew off. With Tommy's second burst, the left wing folded at its root and the Junkers plunged to the ground. She became a ball of fire on impact.

Holy crap! I just got an air-to-air kill! Those gun cameras better be working.

He was so wrapped up in the adrenaline rush he didn't hear Jimmy Tuttle's first *mayday* call. But the second call, in the high-pitched screech of a man scared half to death, was impossible to miss.

"I'm losing her," Tuttle wailed. "Prop's running away…too low to bail out."

Tommy replied, "I'm coming, Jimmy. Try switching tanks."

There was no reply for a moment, and then Tuttle's voice—sounding embarrassed and relieved—said, "Ahh, shit…I didn't switch tanks before we went hot. Rear one's reading about *zip* now. Forgot how long we've been up."

"So everything's okay now?"

"Roger, boss. Back to normal."

"Great. Hate to have you pack it in now, after you just chalked up two destroyed and three probables damaged."

"Really? I did that good?"

"Affirmative. You did a great job."

"That only adds up to five, Tommy. What about the other one?"

"I got him in the air."

"No shit! Looks like ol' *Vincent Van Goldbrick's* gonna be busy tonight. He'd better have a stencil for those German crosses."

"He does. Now let's show some radio discipline and get back to work."

Tommy and Tuttle climbed to 8000 feet to rejoin Clinchmore. With *Blue Flight* re-formed, they turned their attention back to the German column moving north on the road to Gacé.

"You see that thunderstorm coming?" Clinchmore said. "Been getting bumpy up here for a while. Maybe we ought to abort and get behind it."

"Negative," Tommy replied. "We'll finish up here first. We've got time."

Tuttle added his two cents: "T-storm'll kill us as quick as the Germans, boss."

"Both of you, keep your drawers on, dammit. The guys on the ground don't get to take weather breaks."

Tommy took another look at the approaching storm. The towering column of cloud, lit from within by flashes of lightning, suddenly seemed so much closer.

We've got time, he told himself, not quite as sure as when he'd said it out loud a few moments ago. Then he said, "I'll do the *drop*, you guys do the *sweep*. Break…*now*."

Tuttle and Clinchmore banked hard and pulled away, reversing direction while diving lower to get into attack position. Tommy orbited as he prepared to dive-bomb the highway, targeting what appeared to be the command element of the German column: a collection of small vehicles—probably *kübelwagens*—and larger trucks. Since experienced troops and vehicle drivers scattered when they were about to be bombed, Tuttle and Clinchmore would sweep in right behind his bombs, one over each shoulder of the highway, making a low strafing or rocket pass as needed. There would be no safe haven on or off the road for the Germans.

"*Blue Team* in position," Tuttle reported.

Tommy throttled back, nosed *Eclipse* over, and began the downhill run. He was focused on only two things: keeping the gunsight's pipper on the truck he'd picked as the aiming point and the altimeter as it wound down like a clock running rapidly backward.

Seven thousand…six thousand…five thousand…four thousand…three—

"Bombs away."

He pulled the stick back with gentle urgency and shoved the throttle forward. A prime target in level flight now at 1500 feet, it was time to make good his escape. Somebody *had* to be shooting at him, even if he couldn't see it. He banked hard right, away from the highway and the coming storm.

There was a sharp *thump*…and then another, like the sound of snowballs hitting a car. Or large-caliber bullets hitting an airplane. Gingerly, Tommy moved the control stick, first left and right, feeling *Eclipse* respond with gentle banks, and then back and forth, feeling the nose rise and fall. All perfectly normal. Her instruments reported normal readings, too. He checked for the tell-tale whiff of smoke in the cockpit. Nothing.

Sounded like they hit the tail, or maybe the aft fuselage. Everything feels okay—probably just tin damage.

Tuttle and Clinchmore were about half a mile ahead. They slowed to let Tommy catch up. As he did, he could see both planes still had their bombs underwing, as he expected. But the coming storm left them little time to climb back to altitude for another dive-bombing run. "You guys got enough fifty cal for another low-level pass?" he asked.

"Just barely," Tuttle replied.

"Then let's do it. Jettison the bombs in the general direction of the Krauts first."

The bombs dumped, they turned back for one more attack on the German column. The low sky to the southwest had turned almost black from shafts of torrential rain. The low-hanging base of the thundercloud was a deathly gray, morphing slowly to sun-bleached white at a top so high no airman could reach it. Within and below the cloud, lightning flashed like the handiwork of vengeful gods.

Darkness at ground level made the Germans almost impossible to see from their cockpits. The wind blew fiercely from right to left across their path of attack, constantly trying to blow the jugs off their target lines.

But they pressed the attack in a ragged line abreast, firing burst after burst until their guns were empty. When they reached the head of the German column, driving rain turned their windshields and canopies practically opaque.

Breaking right at five-second intervals so as not to crash blindly into each other, they turned away from the blinding storm. Within moments, the slipstream had wiped their cockpit glazing clean. It was time to head for home.

Tommy could see Tuttle's plane ahead to the left, but there was no sign of Clinchmore. Radio calls to him received no reply, only the crashes of static. They were in clear air now, the storm an ominous sideshow off their right wingtips, flying a circuitous path around it to get back to A-14. Climbing higher, Tommy could see for miles. But there was no sign of Herb Clinchmore.

★★★★

Sylvie waited out the storm in a farmhouse, the unexpected but nonetheless welcome guest of the elderly farmer and his wife. They offered her a bite to eat and a chance to wash up; the reddish-gray grime from the bombed-out police headquarters earlier this morning still clung to her skin and clothes. By the time the heavy rains and vicious lightning of the thunderstorm had swept through, she was as refreshed as the day's ordeal allowed and ready to complete her walk to *Combat Command Fox*. It was two hours until nightfall. She felt sure she could make the journey in one.

From the crest of a small hill, she could see one of the roads on which she'd led the ammunition convoy to CCF. Surprisingly, no troops—*Boche* or American—were on it, so she took it.

I'll make better time on the road than plodding through these thickets.

Soon she was at the crossroad with the sabotaged signpost, the one the *maquis* had altered to ambush the *Boche* but had brought an American convoy to ruin as well. The switched signs still hadn't been put right, despite that American lieutenant's assurances he'd get it done.

Americans…they have such short memories, if any at all.

She was still a few hundred yards from the edge of the forest when a GI popped up from the high grass as if out of nowhere, pointing a rifle in her face while demanding the password.

"I have no idea what your silly password is," Sylvie replied. "I am here to see Colonel Abrams. I was here just last night, in fact, guiding your trucks to you. Please, take me to your colonel."

A sergeant materialized from a well-camouflaged hide. "I remember her," he told the rifleman. "She was the jane with the bicycle. What brings you back to these parts, lady?"

"I have information for Colonel Abrams."

"What's your name, miss?"

"My name is Sylvie Bergerac. *Madame* Sylvie Bergerac."

"Keep her here a minute," the sergeant told his trooper. Then he vanished back into their hide. She could hear the *whir* of a field telephone being cranked and then his muffled voice in conversation.

In a few moments, the sergeant reappeared. "Go ahead, Bickerman," he said. "Take the lady to the CP. Then get your sorry ass right back here on the double."

As Sylvie and her escort walked past the outpost, she was startled to see it contained two more GIs manning a machine gun. Although this spot had been in her field of view the last few minutes, she'd been oblivious to the outpost's presence.

They're learning, she told herself. *Flawless concealment*.

Inside CCF's perimeter now, they walked through Baker Company's position. Sylvie came face to face with Sean Moon. "If it ain't our favorite little French lady," he said. "You just can't stay away, can you? Seen my brother?"

"I haven't seen much of anything since yesterday."

"Well, if you do, tell him I said to go fuck himself."

Sylvie replied, "I think not, Sergeant Moon. It would sound so much better coming from you."

At the CP, Colonel Abrams was surprised and delighted to see her. "Have you been inside Gacé, madame?" he asked.

She told him of her odyssey. He was amazed at how matter-of-fact her manner was as she listed the details.

Abrams asked, "Can you tell us the German strength and disposition inside the town?"

"Of course. There can't be more than two or three companies of infantry left. Tanks number no more than six."

"Maybe that's why the aerial photos showed so little," Abrams said. "There's just not much to show."

"I can also tell you of the *Boche* at Nonant-le-Pin, if that will help."

When she told him that village contained nothing but a company of third-rate infantry, Abrams sent a staff officer running to the radio to relay that intel to 4th Armored.

"Not sure why, but they've been poking around Nonant for hours," the colonel said. "Now maybe they can just steamroll the place and get their tails up here. Once again, Madame Bergerac, your help has been invaluable. What are your plans now?"

"I'd like to get back to Alençon, if I could, *mon colonel.*

"Consider it done. We've got an ambulance headed down there within the hour. You're welcome to ride along."

"Thank you, *mon colonel*. But if I may—and I know I've asked this before—may I ask you again to be merciful with the town of Gacé?"

"Your grandmother?"

"Yes…among others."

"I give you my word, Madame Bergerac. My men will be as merciful as the Germans permit."

"That is all I ask, *mon colonel.*"

★★★★

At an RAF airfield just south of Caen, the senior officers had just sat down to supper in their elegant

chateau when an agitated intelligence officer burst into the dining room. "Sir," he addressed the group captain, "excuse the intrusion, but *Taffy Flight* reports attacking an armored unit in the vicinity of Gacé that identified itself on the wireless as a Yank unit."

"And what is your assessment of that claim, *Leftenant*?" the group captain asked before taking another sip of wine.

"We feel it's just another German ruse, sir, especially considering how far it is beyond Monty's *stop line*. A very well-executed one, though."

"Was *Taffy's* attack a success?"

"A brilliant success, sir. Numerous armored vehicles destroyed. One Typhoon was lost, unfortunately, shot down by vicious flak."

"Ahh, bad luck," the group captain said. As he sliced into his steak, the product of freshly butchered cattle his officers' mess had appropriated from a nearby farm, he added, "Well-executed ruse or not, *Leftenant*, it wasn't good enough to fool this command. Tell your shop to keep up the good work." He then told *Taffy Flight's* squadron leader, "And give your boys a hearty *good show*, as well, Oliver."

When the intelligence officer was almost to the door, the group captain called after him. "We are planning to hit those *faux Yanks* again, are we not, *Leftenant*?"

"Yes, sir. As soon as possible."

Chapter Thirty

ALLIED GROUND FORCES DIRECTIVE

FROM:
MONTGOMERY—COMMANDER, ALLIED GROUND FORCES

DATE-TIME OF ORIGIN
14 AUG 44
1900 HRS

TO:
BRADLEY—COMMANDER, 12TH ARMY GROUP

COPY (FOR INFO):
SHAEF (EISENHOWER); HODGES—US 1ST ARMY; PATTON—US 3RD ARMY; DEMPSEY—2ND BRITISH ARMY; CRERAR—1ST CANADIAN ARMY; CONINGHAM—RAF 2ND TAF; QUESADA—IX TAC; WEYLAND—XIX TAC; BRERTON—9TH AIR FORCE

RE YOUR STATUS REPORT OF 1800/14 AUG, YOU ARE AGAIN REMINDED TO HOLD YOUR UNITS ALONG THE DESIGNATED FLERS-ARGENTAN LINE. 21ST ARMY GROUP CONTINUES ITS APPROACH TO THAT LINE FROM THE NORTH AND WILL BE IN POSITION WITHIN 48 HOURS TO COMPLETE THE ENCIRCLEMENT OF GERMAN 7th ARMY.

DO NOT—REPEAT, DO NOT—MOVE NORTH OF THE LINE DESIGNATED FOR YOU. THE CHANCES FOR FRATRICIDE COMMITTED BY YOUR LESS BATTLE-HARDENED TROOPS WHEN EXECUTING A PINCER MOVEMENT REMAINS A GREAT RISK WITHIN THIS COMMAND.

SIGNED,
MONTGOMERY

****

General Omar Bradley, 12th Army Group Commander, threw down the directive from Montgomery in disgust. “Bullshit,” he said to his chief of staff. “Patton’s just told us Monty’s boys aren’t even past Falaise yet, so *forty-eight hours*, my sweet ass. The Germans will be long gone by then, and we’re sitting here with our thumbs up our asses on this damn line of his, waiting for him to play the big hero.”

He tried to say out loud that last sentence in Monty’s directive with all the mocking inflection of a British accent he could muster, but as he got to *fratricide by your less battle-hardened troops*, the words dissolved on his tongue like a bitter pill.

“Bullshit,” Bradley repeated. “Absolute bullshit. Who the hell does he think he is? If Ike wasn’t so scared shitless of Winston Churchill, none of this would be happening.”

Chapter Thirty-One

The thunderstorm had slowed 4th Armored to a crawl on the highway to Nonant-le-Pin, delaying their arrival on its outskirts until twilight. Armed with the intelligence Sylvie had provided Colonel Abrams, though, taking the village was breathtakingly easy. A single Sherman rolled down the deserted and still rain-slicked main street, only to be confronted by a *kübelwagen* that had raced up in front of a church. When they saw the tank before them, the three German soldiers in the vehicle hesitated for a moment, as if not quite sure what to do next, and then lit the crude gasoline bomb they'd made from a wine bottle. The GIs in the tank were far more certain what to do: they riddled the *kübelwagen* with the bow-mounted .30-caliber machine gun until the three occupants were dead and their vehicle turned into a mighty bonfire.

When the squad of GI infantrymen accompanying the Sherman found the doors of the church barred from the outside, they broke those doors open, liberating the townspeople inside who'd been seconds from incineration. It didn't take much deduction to know the flaming wine bottle full of gasoline was meant to torch the church and its occupants.

In short order, the lead element of 4th Armored rounded up the rest of the hundred-odd Germans in the village, who were all too eager to surrender. The German commander—a *hauptmann* whose attempts to sneer at his captors were foiled by the facial tremors of one scared for his life—was asked by an American major why his men were trying to burn civilians alive.

His reply: "They must be made to pay for dishonoring my brave soldiers."

The American major looked at the sorry collection of terrified teenagers and old men in Wehrmacht uniforms being herded away to a POW collection pen. "Your men aren't brave," he told the *hauptmann*, "they're just lost sheep being led around by murdering pieces of shit like you."

By the time General Wood's jeep made it to the village center, it was nearly dark. "We'll stay here for the night," he told his staff. "Tell CC Fox to hang on until morning."

****

Tommy felt nothing but defeat as he and Tuttle touched down at A-14. Skirting the thunderstorm to get home had given him too much time to dwell on the day's events: *I've lost two of my guys in one day. Do I even know what the hell I'm doing as a flight leader?*

Still, a voice in his head was telling him, *It's not your fault. It wasn't you who got target fixated and flew Rider's plane into the ground. He did that all by himself. And Clinchmore...well, you've got no idea what happened to him yet.*

I don't think the storm got him, though. Me and Jimmy came through it okay. Still, how'd he go down without us knowing?

His dejection turned to elation and then puzzlement as he and Tuttle taxied past Clinchmore's plane, safe and perfectly intact on the ramp. *Eclipse's* prop had barely stopped spinning when Tommy asked Sergeant McNulty, "Lieutenant Clinchmore…how long has he been back?"

McNulty, his eagle eyes scanning Tommy's airplane, didn't answer the question. Instead, he puffed up with mock indignation and asked, "Why the hell has my airplane got holes in its tail, Lieutenant? Big ones, too, dammit. You're gonna have my *tin-peckers* up all night again, ain't you?"

"Yeah, real sorry about that. Now how about answering my question about Lieutenant Clinchmore?"

"He's been back about twenty minutes, give or take, sir."

"Is he okay?"

"He walked away on his own two shaky legs. I guess that makes him okay."

McNulty called to the mechanic working in the cockpit of Clinchmore's ship. "What do you think, *Sparky*…anything wrong over there?"

Sparky—the nickname given to all the squadron's radio technicians—replied, "Ain't a damn thing wrong with this set, Sarge. It's working perfectly. I'm talking to ground stations five miles from here, for cryin' out loud. Airborne, he could've worked stations fifty or sixty miles away, easy."

"Wait a minute," Tommy said. "Clinchmore said there was something wrong with his radio?"

"I don't know none of the *perpendiculars*, Lieutenant…I mean, I ain't *his* crew chief, am I?—but he did *collude* that his radio wasn't working up to *speculation.*

That's a record, even for McNulty, Tommy told himself. *Three abuses of the King's English in one sentence*. But malaprops aside, what his crew chief had just divulged was interesting fare.

Colonel Pruitt, the squadron C.O., thought it interesting, too. He told Tommy, "I think you'd better remind your pilots that there are SOPs you follow when your radio craps out. Cutting and running isn't one of them. Get to the bottom of what happened and advise me."

"Will do, sir," Tommy replied, "as soon as I find him."

Herb Clinchmore hadn't even bothered to debrief once back at A-14. Tommy retraced his movements from Operations to his quarters, a tent Clinchmore shared with three other pilots. Only one of them was there. He said his tentmates had left for Alençon in a jeep five minutes before.

That's convenient, Tommy thought, *because that's where I'm headed, too.*

★★★★

The streets of Alençon were crowded with GIs looking for alcohol and women. The ambulance driver followed Sylvie's directions, snaking through the milling throngs until she told him to halt in front of *Papa's House*. He knew the place well. He'd frequented it himself.

"You *live* here, ma'am?" he asked.

"That's not so surprising, is it, Private? Considering the man everyone calls *Papa* is my actual father."

"Well…it's just…just that—"

"Just what, Private? That it's a whorehouse?"

Even in the darkness she could tell he was blushing. She said goodbye with a chaste kiss on his cheek and stepped from the ambulance. The line of GIs awaiting admittance parted like the Red Sea for her entrance.

She went first to the back room that was *Papa's* office. After kisses of welcome, her father wrapped her in his arms and said, "Well, my prodigal daughter returns once again, praise God. You look a bit tattered, little girl, like you've been off *playing war* again. Did you win it single-handedly this time, too?"

"Not quite, Papa." She decided to spare him the details of her brief imprisonment and lucky escapes for now. Instead, she asked, "Have you seen my husband?"

Papa rummaged through a desk drawer. When he found what he was looking for, he handed it to her, saying, "Here…he left you a note."

Some women would have burst into tears reading what Bernard had written. Sylvie just smiled, breathed a sigh of relief, and stuffed the note in the pocket of her skirt.

"My husband, along with all the other young men of the *maquis*, has been called into the French Army," she said. "We knew that was coming from the day de Gaulle started referring to the Resistance as the *French Forces of the Interior*. He'll be leaving in the morning for induction at Le Mans."

"Should you not go to him, child? Show him some tenderness and mercy on his last night?"

"I'm sure he's quite busy saying goodbye to his many lovers. I think it's better I wish him good riddance, at least for now."

"I can't say I blame you, little girl. I never did understand why you married that communist scumbag."

"For the thousandth time, Papa, Bernard is not a communist."

"A man is who he associates with, my child."

"I'm so tired of arguing about this. Let's just call my marriage a romantic mistake in the confusion of war, Papa. To hell with him. Right now, what I need most is a bath and some clean clothes."

★★★★

Tommy found Herb Clinchmore at *Café Madeleine*, already under the influence of the alcohol he'd slugged down. When asked why he returned to base without so much as a wing waggle, Clinchmore replied with a slurred, "I don't think I like your tone, Moon."

"Just answer the damn question, Herb. You work for me, remember?"

Clinchmore began to mumble something about *the radio*.

"There was nothing wrong with your radio, Herb. I was there when the radio tech checked it out."

"I'm the goddamn pilot, not some little greaseball wrench bender. If I say the radio didn't work, it didn't fucking work."

"Radios don't fix themselves, Herb. And did you forget the procedures for flying with a radio out?"

Clinchmore was getting loud and attracting attention. "You know, *Half*, I don't have to take this shit from you, you little pipsqueak. If you want to have me court-martialed, go right ahead. I'm betting no court in *this man's army* is gonna convict a pilot for bringing his fucked-up plane home safe and sound."

"You want a court-martial, Herb? That can be arranged. I'd say you're racking up a pretty impressive list of charges right now."

"You don't have the balls, Tommy," Clinchmore replied, still louder. "And everyone knows you're all sweet on those fucking ground pounders and how you're all fucked up because you got a brother down there and how that's been affecting your judgment and all. Well, I'm here to tell you, if you don't fly, you ain't shit. I don't give a fuck about any of them ground pounders. The only ass I care about is—"

Clinchmore's words were cut off by the beefy hand of an infantry lieutenant clamped around his throat. That hand jerked him from the chair, spun him around, and was now cocked to deliver a killer jab to the drunken pilot's startled face. Behind the infantryman, a crowd of fellow *ground pounders* had gathered, eager to join in and do a little *pounding* of a different kind.

"Hang on there, buddy," Tommy said to Clinchmore's assailant. "This isn't your fight."

"Him and his big fucking mouth just made it my fight, pal."

Everyone knew Herb Clinchmore was a split second away from being beaten to within an inch of his life. The bar owner and his bouncers were already moving in to break up the imminent mauling. They liked the whopping increase in business the Americans brought. Too much fighting on premises would cause the Army's Provost Marshall to designate *Café Madeleine* off limits to GIs.

But it was a woman's voice which provided the antidote to the poisoned atmosphere. "*Mes amies*," Sylvie Bergerac pleaded, "isn't it enough that you have to fight the *Boche*? Can't you see this is not the time for fighting? It is the time for drink, for fellowship…and to spend some time around the corner at *Papa's House* in the warm comfort of a woman."

Her words worked like a soothing salve. They gave Tommy the second he needed to get Clinchmore out of the bar alive. His two tentmates were already out in the street, having fled the moment they saw the odds stacked badly against anyone wearing aviator's wings.

"Get him the fuck out of here," Tommy told them. "If anybody's going to kill him, I've got first dibs." There was no argument from Clinchmore's tentmates as they scuttled him off down the street.

Tommy walked back inside the pacified café. Sylvie was sitting at the bar, chatting with the owner. She beckoned him to join them.

"Lieutenant Tommy Moon, I'd like to introduce the proprietor, my uncle Honoré," she said in English.

Tommy shook his hand, wondering if there'd be any glimmer of recognition from the night before, when this same man had claimed not to know her and thrown him out of the bar, to boot. But there was none.

In French, Tommy asked, "Don't you recognize me? I was in here last night, looking for Sylvie."

The uncle smirked as he replied, "Americans all think they are so unforgettable. But at least he speaks almost intelligible French."

"Be nice, Uncle. This one is a gentleman."

His smirk turned to a smile. "Ahh, she likes you, airman. Be careful, before she steals your wallet as well as your heart. Now, if you two will excuse me, I have a business to look after."

"What did he mean by that, Sylvie?"

She smiled and said, "Uncle Honoré is always teasing me about how I drum up business. He says I have a *nose for money.*"

"Yeah, I noticed when you broke up that fight, you managed to hawk the bar and *Papa's House* all in the same sentence."

"*Hawk*?" she asked. "What does that mean?"

"Promote…build up."

"*Voilà*," she replied, smiling triumphantly.

"And by the way, thanks a lot for doing that."

"Doing what, Tommy?"

"Breaking up the fight."

She shrugged, like it was something she did 10 times a day. "Come, Tommy. Let's get you another drink and find a quiet place to talk."

Tucked at a table for two in a dark corner of the bar, she said, "I saw your brother this afternoon—"

"You saw Sean? Where? Is he okay?"

"Near Gacé. And yes, he is well."

"Wow, that's great! My brother's okay! But what the hell were you doing in Gacé?"

She told him of leading the ammunition convoy to CCF, of visiting her grandmother, her capture by the Gestapo…and her liberation courtesy of an American bomb.

For a moment, Tommy was stunned into silence. He finally managed to ask, "The place you were being held…you said it was the police station?"

"Yes."

"On the *grand-rue*?"

"It's not a large town, Tommy. There is only one police station."

He fell back into silence again. She watched the expression on his face change from surprise, to guilt, to horror, and back to guilt again.

"It was your plane, then?"

"It...it must've been." He felt—and looked—like he'd just confessed to breaking every one of the Ten Commandments. The feeling lasted the few seconds it took her to lean across the table and kiss him full on the mouth, a deep, open-mouth kiss that felt wonderful and deliciously guilty. In the back of his mind, a chorus of priests and nuns from his school days in Brooklyn ranted on and on about the first step on the path straight to hell being the *French kiss*.

Like they'd ever know.

She pulled him to his feet and said, "Come with me, my savior."

As they stepped from the *Café Madeleine*, they came face to face with Sylvie's husband, Bernard, his arm wrapped around another woman. Both couples seemed to freeze in place as husband and wife exchanged looks of contrition without any hint of apology. Their marriage dissolved in one final glance of dismissal. And then both pairs made off in opposite directions, just as their lives were doing.

★★★★

Tommy knew Sylvie was leading him to *Papa's House*. He tugged her to a halt and said, "Nothing's changed, you know. You're still married." It sounded less a statement of fact than an attempt to convince himself.

She pulled him close and replied, “You’ve used that excuse already, Tommy. You’ll have to think of another one.”

But as their mouths melded into another exquisite kiss and their bodies pressed tightly together, she could feel he’d already stopped thinking.

Chapter Thirty-Two

The field telephone from *Listening Post One-Eight* clattered its muted ring as the call came in to CCF's CP. "We've got company coming," the sergeant at the LP reported in a hushed voice. "No idea how many. Not enough moonlight to see good."

The captain at the CP asked, "Which road are they on?"

"I'm not real sure. They may not even be on a road. They're going slow. I'm guessing they're moving at the pace of foot traffic."

The captain told his runner. "Get Colonel Abrams, on the double."

Abrams was at the CP within a minute. "Which LP is reporting?" he asked.

"One-Eight, sir."

"Hmm…the south side," Abrams said, his eyes glued to the dimly lit map. "How much you want to bet this is the remnants of that infantry division our flyboys beat up right before the storm?"

"I'd say it's a real good bet, sir," the captain replied. "But *remnants* or not, I'm worried if they're not on either road they could be walking right into us."

"Yeah," Abrams replied. "I see your point. Take an artillery FO with you and get out to the LP. We may have to light them up." Then he told the operations sergeant, "Tell every unit the shit's about to hit the fan."

His words couldn't have been more prophetic. No sooner were they spoken than another phone in the CP began to ring. It was Captain Newcomb on the line from the west side of the perimeter. He reported, "We've got heavy engine noise from Gacé. Sounds like the Krauts might be on the move."

The phone from the tankers on the north side rang, too. "We hear vehicles...sounds like a lot of them. Can't tell yet if they're moving across our front or toward us."

Only the infantry and artillery on the east side of the perimeter had nothing to report.

Colonel Abrams said, "We're either about to get hit on three sides, or there's a mass exodus of Germans passing us by."

"Should we fire the illum now, sir?" the operations sergeant asked.

"Negative, negative," Abrams replied. "Let's let the darkness be our friend a little bit longer."

It only took a few minutes for the darkness to change from friend to enemy. "I can hear them breathing," the sergeant at LP 1-8 whispered into his field phone. "I think they're going to pass just west of the LP. A hundred yards away, more or less. They sound like they're on an *admin* stroll or something. I can hear 'em yakking, like they don't have a clue we're here."

"That'll put them right smack in front of our west sector," Abrams said, "in an open field with no cover or concealment, except for those few tank carcasses. Ask him if he can tell *how many* there are now."

The LP sergeant's reply: "I have no fucking idea. I'm seeing a lot of silhouettes and hearing a lot of boots shuffling along. Could be fifty…could be five hundred. I don't know. Permission to pull back?"

"Permission granted."

"So what's the plan, sir?" the operations officer asked Abrams.

"We're going to let them march right in front of us and then cut them down."

The colonel could tell that wasn't what the operations officer was expecting to hear. "What would you propose instead, Major? Let them pass? Maybe try and capture them?"

"No, no…of course not, sir. But what about the tanks in Gacé…and whatever it is we're hearing on the north side?"

"What about them, Major? If they come out to fight, we fight them. If they try to break out, we try and kill them. Get the preplanned fire missions laid in on the artillery and mortars. Just make damn sure nobody starts shooting until I say so."

Midway down the western side of CCF's perimeter, Sean Moon was poised on *Eclipse's* .50 caliber as the rest of his crew stood ready on her .30 calibers and main gun. The leading element of the German infantry had just ambled across their field of fire, looking more like phantoms in the darkness than human forms. Sean offered a silent plea: *Let's not wait too damn long now and let them get away. Just a couple minutes more and we'll have a maximum kill zone. They won't know what hit them. This is gonna be fucking slaughter.*

Seconds seemed like minutes, minutes like hours, as the unsuspecting Germans trooped past. Yet, with the enemy practically close enough to hit with a rock, the GIs waited as ordered.

Yeah, keep 'em coming, Sean thought. *I can hear the vehicles crawling along in the column now, too. Nothing but light trucks, thank God.*

A whispered command over the radio: "Stand by for illum. Hold your fire. Repeat—hold your fire."

Sean could hear the dull *ploompf* of the mortars firing the illumination rounds. *Let's see what the Krauts do when they hear that. Do they freeze in place or do they run?*

The Germans did neither; they kept walking. No sooner had the flares begun to pop high over their heads, bathing the startled Germans in their pale, surreal light, than the command spilled from CCF's radios: "COMMENCE FIRE."

Whether they froze or ran made little difference now. A hail of machine gun bullets from two companies of tanks sliced them down in the open field like wheat at harvest. The only direction for them to run was west, toward Gacé. But there was no outrunning the grazing fire of all those machine guns. Some threw up their hands; it was a futile gesture. There would be no mercy in the vagaries of night. Bullets accepted no surrender.

In less than a minute, it was over. As the killing zone fell dark again and the American machine guns fell silent, the only sounds on the still night air were the wails of dying Germans lying in the field and the distant growl of tank engines coming from Gacé.

"I think those tanks are moving out," Captain Newcomb reported over the field telephone to Abrams' CP. "Can't tell which way they're going, though. Request we light them up."

Colonel Abrams agreed. In less than 30 seconds, the artillery fired a spread of illumination rounds to light the highways running north and east out of Gacé, some two miles from CCF's position. Binoculars pressed to their eyes, both the colonel and Newcomb watched five tanks assemble on the north side of town. They appeared to have no interest in engaging CCF.

"They're running," Abrams said. "If Madame Bergerac's info is right—and when hasn't she been right?—that's all the armor they have in Gacé."

"Shall we engage them with artillery, sir?" the operations officer asked.

"I'd like to, Major. I really would. But I don't think we'll do much damage to them at this distance. They're sure as hell not going to stand still while we shoot them."

Sean Moon entered the CP. "Begging your pardon, sir, but Captain Newcomb told me to come talk to you. I've got an idea how to take out those tanks leaving Gacé."

"Go ahead, Sergeant," Abrams replied. "Let's hear it."

"I think I can take them by surprise, sir," Sean began. "I've got two jeeps already lined up with enough gas in 'em to cover about ten miles, plus five GIs and all those *panzerfausts* we picked up last night. We can intercept them here"—he poked the map at a point on the north highway a few miles down the road—"and set up an ambush. If these Kraut rockets are as good as everyone thinks they are, we can knock out all those tanks before they know what hit them."

Abrams wasn't convinced. "How are you going to find that spot in the dark, Sergeant?"

"There's a trail out of these woods that heads that way, sir. It's *got* to go to the highway…and if it doesn't, we'll take the jeeps overland. It's pretty easy terrain around here, and I can sure as hell read a compass. We'll be moving faster than the tanks over a more direct route, so we've got a little bit of time to play with. And they'll never hear the jeeps over the noise of their own engines."

"All right," Abrams said, "let's assume you get where you want to be. Have any of you ever used a *panzerfaust* before?"

"Yes, sir. Me and Sergeant Algood fired a couple of captured ones for practice when we were back in the Cotentin. It's pretty simple, sir. Simpler than a bazooka, even. No wires to screw with. Just point, shoot, and then chuck the launch tube away."

"And you're actually *volunteering* to lead this ambush, Sergeant Moon?"

"I never volunteer for shit, sir. But it's my idea, so I guess I'm the guy to lead it. And I figure us tankers know where to hit Kraut armor better than some infantry-types, anyway."

Colonel Abrams looked around to gauge the reaction of his staff. Only the operations officer looked skeptical. "If you've got something to say, Major, say it fast. We're running out of time."

"I'm worried about those vehicles we heard to the north, sir. We don't know what they are or where they're going. If they're coming to reinforce the ones leaving Gacé, our men just might end up caught between them."

Sean replied, "I like my chances in the dark all the same, Major." Then he checked his wristwatch and asked Abrams, "What's it going to be, sir? I've got to get moving if I'm going at all."

Abrams patted Sean on the shoulder and said, "Do it, Sergeant. And good luck to you. Just do me one favor…take some bazookas for backup."

"With all due respect, sir, we'll be carrying enough as it is. So if it's all the same to you, I'll leave those stovepipes behind."

★★★★

Just as Sean suspected, the forest trail led them straight to the highway. The narrow ribbon of pavement—a darker shade of gray than the surrounding fields in the colorless night— meandered like a calm river across the rolling countryside. The GIs stashed the two jeeps behind a patch of scrawny trees which wouldn't have provided much in the way of concealment in daylight. But this was the middle of the night; though only 50 yards from the highway, the jeeps were as good as invisible.

Once they shut off the jeeps' engines, they could hear the rumble of the tanks moving slowly up the highway, still hundreds of yards to the south. "Looks like we got here just in time," Sean said. "Now listen up…me and my guys will take the other side of the road and spread out good. When the lead tank gets even with this trail here, my guys'll knock out the first and last tank. As soon as we do that, Sergeant Algood's team will take out the three in the middle from this side of the road. Got that?"

The five men nodded.

"Remember what I said about where to hit them bastards," Sean continued. "No matter what type they are—and you may not be able to tell that for sure in the dark—hit 'em high on the hull just aft of the turret. If you happen to end up behind one, put it right up her ass. Do not waste rounds shooting at the front. If they've got shit hanging off the sides and turret for extra armor, hit it *twice*. The first one will knock all that shit off. Then you'll have a clean target for the second shot. We've got a dozen of these *panzerfausts*—that's two per tank with two in reserve if we need 'em. We'll be too fucking close to miss, so don't waste them. And for God's sake, don't shoot them in the sprockets or road wheels. That'll stop them from moving but all their guns'll still work. Go for the quick, clean kill. Those crews'll be driving with the hatches open, for sure, so blow them right out of them fucking hatches like Fourth of July fireworks. Any questions?"

There were none.

"Oh, yeah…one more thing. Don't fuck up, okay?"

Once satisfied Algood's team was positioned properly on the near side of the road, Sean led his men across the pavement. Still unseen in the darkness, the blacked-out German tanks lumbered closer, the clanking and squeaking of their tracks now as plain as the thrumming of their engines. *Slow going with no headlights*, Sean told himself. *Take your time, Adolph…we got all fucking night.*

But it didn't take quite that long. In a few minutes, the Germans rolled into the gauntlet. The GIs held their fire—just like they'd been told. As soon as the leader—a Panther tank—was even with the trail, Sean let his rocket fly.

The tank commander, standing steadfast and imperious in his turret hatch, began screaming to his crew when he saw the glow of the rocket streaking toward him. But there was no time for the Germans to convert commands into action; the trap was sprung. The sound of the rocket's explosion on impact with the aft hull was surprisingly weak, but its effect was surprisingly deadly.

The rest of the GIs let loose with their *panzerfausts*. In an instant, the first four tanks brewed up and spit their flaming crews through the hatches just like the fireworks display Sean had envisioned.

But the last tank in the column—another Panther, obvious from its close silhouette—caught a break. It was lagging behind the one before it, and that gave PFC Farley a longer shot with a poor angle, more head-on than lateral. Still trying to target the vulnerable spot on the aft quarter of the hull Sean had dictated, his first rocket missed, skimming over the tank and flying harmlessly into the night.

The glowing trail of the rocket motor painted a line in the air that pointed back to Farley like an accusing finger. The tank turned toward him; the crew ducked into their hatches and buttoned up. His second rocket struck the front armor, exploded, but hurt nothing other than the tankers' eardrums. Their machine gun fire raked the tall grass, hitting Farley in the legs without their even knowing it.

They'd seen the rocket trails that killed the four tanks in front of them, too, so they knew they faced a team of killers lurking invisibly in the darkness. And they had no infantry support of their own to keep those killers off their back. The tank lurched to a halt and then reversed, backing away from the killing zone. She kept spitting machine gun fire blindly to cover her escape.

"RAKOFSKY," Sean called to his remaining team member, "GIMME THAT FUCKING ROCKET AND GET FARLEY BACK TO THE JEEP! I'M GONNA GET BEHIND THAT BASTARD."

Sean sprinted through the waist-high grass, his Thompson in hand, two *panzerfausts* slung over his shoulder. He heard the staccato bursts of Thompsons from Algood's team behind him and thought: *Maybe every crewman in those brew-ups didn't get roasted after all.*

As he ran, he'd watch the turret traverse and then dodge left or right to avoid its next burst of blind machine gun fire. *Forget the bow gun*, he told himself. *It can't get me. Just keep watching that fucking turret.*

Running through a field in the dark is always a risky game. Sean stumbled and fell several times, each one sending his weapons clattering along the ground. With each tumble the tank's lead on him increased.

Gotta stop him...but it's a bow shot. All I can do from this angle is knock off a track.

Dropping to one knee, he fired a *panzerfaust*. It hit and shattered the right track's drive sprocket. The tank began to pivot as the severed track fell off its road wheels. The pivoting stopped with its right side facing Sean.

He fired his second—and last—rocket. He was too close to miss that vulnerable aft quarter.

But even with its hull breached, the tank refused to brew up. Someone was trying to crawl out of the commander's hatch. Sean sprayed the turret with Thompson fire. The crewman dropped back inside.

Did I hit that son of a bitch...or does he want to play hide and seek?

The turret began to swing Sean's way, but he had no trouble scrambling out of its field of fire.

I've got to smoke these bastards out.

He climbed onto the rear deck, pulled a thermite grenade from his belt, and stuffed it against a vent grille.

That oughta do it. Now we'd better get our asses clear.

Sean caught up with Rakofsky, who hadn't made it far with the wounded and wailing Farley draped across his shoulders. They watched as the thermite grenade began to do its job, its intensely hot fireball melting its way through the tank's ventilation system. "Anybody still alive in there will be trying to get out in a second or two," Sean said, readying his Thompson.

The thermite grenade's fire was bathing the dying tank in light as bright as a welder's torch. "No matter which way they try to get out, we'll see 'em, for sure," Sean said.

They waited 10 seconds, 15, 20—and then a man slithered from the driver's hatch on the bow, slid down the glacis plate on his belly, and hit the ground face first. He was trying to get to his feet but not succeeding. At least not at first.

Sean leveled his Thompson at the tanker. But then he jerked its barrel skyward.

"What the hell are you doing, Sarge?" Rakofsky asked. "He's dead meat."

Sean didn't reply. There was something about this tanker. He couldn't say what it was, precisely. Maybe it was the fact the young man was short—very short. Like his brother. Maybe it was because he'd been fighting to escape a fiery hell—just like a tanker would or a pilot trapped in his burning cockpit would, too. Maybe it was the earnestness in his face when, once on his knees, he raised his hands over his head and pleaded *Kamerad!*

Or maybe Sean Moon had had enough killing for one night.

Flames were now licking from all the Panther's hatches. There couldn't be anyone left alive inside. Slowly, Sean approached the surrendering tanker.

"Careful, Sarge," Rakofsky said, "it could be some Kraut trick."

"It ain't no trick, Rak. This poor fucker's finished."

He pulled the tanker to his feet and led him away.

"I'll bet this night didn't go like you planned," Sean said to his prisoner as he prodded him toward the jeeps, not knowing or caring whether he understood. "You watched your buddies get cooked by your own weapons, and you—the sole survivor of this little fight—end up a guest of Uncle Sam for the duration. Congratulations, pal, you just beat the odds. But for the rest of us bastards, it's just a matter of time."

"Hey, Sarge," Rakofsky called, "speaking of *a matter of time*, you hear those engines?"

"Yeah, Rak, I hear them. That's why we're getting the hell away from this road, on the fucking double. We need to get Farley here to the doc but quick, too."

★★★★

They were halfway back to CC Fox when Sean brought the jeep to a halt. Algood, driving the jeep behind, couldn't understand why.

"What the fuck's the deal, Sean?" Algood asked. "Ain't we done enough for one night?"

"I want to see who's making all that noise. You take Farley and your guys back to *Fox*. And make sure you loosen his tourniquet in five minutes. Don't lose the Kraut, either."

"Yeah, sure…but Sean, you're going to be out of gas before you know it. This ain't no time to play recon. Let's all just go the fuck home."

"No can do. Home could turn into a pretty shitty place if we let some Krauts waltz right in on us. Now load up Farley and the Kraut in your jeep and get the hell out of here. That's an order."

"That jeep's gonna be pretty damn full, Sean. Too damn full."

"We've done worse. Get a move on."

"Suppose the Kraut makes a run for it?"

"He ain't going nowhere, Algood. Look at him…he's happier than a pig in shit. He knows his war's over."

"I don't know, Sean…he may have a little *accident* or something on the way back."

"Don't you fucking dare, Algood. He's my catch, and we're gonna turn him over to the S2 upright and breathing, so keep your hands off. Now why are you still here?"

★★★★

It didn't take much driving to find out what all the racket was. Sean parked the jeep behind a small hill, and then he and Rakofsky climbed to its top. Half a mile to the north they could see the shadowy outlines of at least two dozen German tracked vehicles, with long guns mounted on their hulls. They weren't tanks; they were tank *destroyers*. Despite having to overcome the disorder of the darkness, the *destroyers* were being noisily positioned as a defensive stronghold.

"Fuck," Sean mumbled, "I think they're *Ferdinands*."

"What the hell is that, Sarge?"

"A Tiger chassis with an eighty-eight mounted on it. Never seen one before, just heard stories. They can turn a *Zippo* inside out from way off."

"But they've got no turret," Rakofsky said.

"Right," Sean replied, "that's their weakness, just like our M10s. The crew's got armored shields on the front and a little on the sides, but they're wide open on top to airbursts. Come on…we gotta get to the radio."

Back at the jeep, Sean unfurled his map across the hood. "Okay, we're here," he said, marking the spot with a pencil, "and they're *there*." Jotting down the coordinates, he went to the jeep's radio and called in the fire mission to CCF's artillery. That call ended with the following: "Tank destroyers with exposed crew. Shell HE, Fuze Time, Adjust fire, over."

"Stay with the radio, Rak," Sean said. "I'm going back up to the top. I'll yell the corrections down to you."

"How the hell are you gonna see anything without illum rounds, Sarge?"

"I'll do it by sound. Maybe if they start running we'll light 'em up. But for now, let's not ruin the surprise."

The first adjustment round seemed at the perfect burst height—about 40 yards high—but a little long.

"Drop one hundred," Sean said.

The next airburst was a little short, just as Sean hoped it would be.

"Rak, tell 'em add five-zero, fire for effect."

For the next few minutes, the Germans' disorderly attempt to establish a position collapsed in the relentless steel rain as Sean raked the artillery fire back and forth across their position. A few crews abandoned their guns and ran. Some tried to drive their vehicles away. A few made it; most didn't.

After the last rounds fell, the only sound was the murmur of idling engines from a few abandoned *Ferdinands*. Sean thought about calling for some illumination rounds now and trying to finish off those crewless vehicles with direct hits from HE rounds with Fuze Quick, but he let the idea go.

There's gotta be a few of them Krauts still around who ain't dead or dying. And I've been in one place too damn long already.

Chapter Thirty-Three

Tommy awoke with a start and checked his watch. *Ahh, shit! It's almost 0500. I've got to get back to A-14.*

Sylvie was still asleep beside him, her naked form half-covered by the rumpled bedclothes. She stirred as he rolled out of bed.

"Wait, Tommy," she whispered. "I'll make you breakfast."

Stepping into his trousers, he replied, "I don't have a lot of time."

"That's okay. We don't have a lot of breakfast, either." She pulled on a robe and shuffled from the tiny bedroom.

In a few minutes, she returned, a cup of bitter ersatz coffee in each hand. Handing one cup to him, she retrieved a hunk of bread from the crook of her arm and handed that to him, too. Then she sat on the bed, patting the mattress beside her in invitation. "Come back to bed, lover," she said with an inviting smile. "Talk to me before you run off. Will you be flying today?"

"Yeah, probably."

She waited for him to say more, but he'd filled his mouth with bread.

"You don't speak much in the morning, do you, Tommy?"

He held up a finger as if to say *wait* as his teeth worked on the chewy crust. When he finally got it all down, he said, "Actually, there are a few things we need to talk about."

"Like what?" she asked, hoping the quaint Catholic morality he'd dismissed last night was not about to make a comeback.

She breathed a sigh of relief when his first question was, "Why'd your uncle deny knowing you the other night?"

"Perhaps you would prefer every stranger inquiring about a member of the *maquis* be given detailed instructions where to find her?"

Tommy felt silly for asking. "No, I suppose not," he replied. "I should have figured that was the case."

She tousled his hair and said, "I think you are afraid that maybe I am a woman of great mystery—a prostitute, a spy, an assassin—with many false names." She threw her head back and cackled with gusto. "I'm laughing at myself, Tommy, not you."

He wouldn't have cared if it was directed at him. He'd never heard her laugh like that before. It sounded so wonderful, so carefree.

With what she'd been through in these years at war, he admired—no, he was *jealous*—that she could still laugh at all. And he still knew so little about her. She may have been through so much more he didn't know about. Not yet, anyway.

He had another question. "With your husband and all the others getting pulled into the Free French Army now, where does that leave the *maquis*?"

"We knew this was coming for a while, Tommy, ever since you Americans and British managed to not get thrown back into the sea. True, now the *maquis* will more and more be nothing but old men and young women, but we'll still have our job to do behind the *Boche* lines."

"But you're not behind the *Boche* lines anymore, Sylvie."

She smiled wistfully and replied, "Today, perhaps. I cannot speak for tomorrow."

Time was too short. He gulped the rest of his coffee and said, "You're safe now. Stay here in Alençon. Don't go doing anything stupid."

Kissing him, she replied, "I never do anything stupid, Tommy."

She'd meant it to be comforting. He found it anything but.

At the door, he told her, "If you happen to see my brother again, tell him I'm going to kick his ass all the way back to Canarsie."

"I don't understand, Tommy. Is that a joke?"

"Not really. But don't worry. He'll understand."

★★★★

"That little POW of yours is singing like a canary," Colonel Abrams said to Sean Moon. "According to him, the Krauts got one hell of a *FUBAR* circus going on. They're trying to pull back and consolidate to keep us from closing off this gap, but we're creaming them every time they make a move—like bringing up those *Ferdinands* you knocked out."

"That's the thing, sir," Sean replied. "We didn't knock out the Ferdinands, just took out a lot of their crews. I think we oughta go back there right now with a crate of thermite grenades and put them all to the torch before more gunners show up and make them operational again. I was just lining up some—"

"Whoa, Sergeant! Take it easy. You've done enough for one night. Get yourself some chow and let someone else do the demolition work. The infantry boys will handle it. And grab a little sack time while you can."

"Sleep, sir? I don't think I'll be getting much of that. Why should today be different from any other? Anyway, I want to check on my guy who got wounded."

"Better hurry, Sergeant. I just got the morning casualty report. Your man is Farley, right?"

"Yes, sir."

"Well, I believe PFC Farley's war is over. He's being evacuated. Probably all the way back to the States. The doc says he's trying like crazy to save his legs, but…"

"Farley's a fighter, sir. All us *micks* are. He'll make it."

"Let's hope so. By the way, Sergeant…how do you rate the *panzerfausts*?"

"If I was an infantryman, sir, I'd grab every last one I could and ditch the bazookas."

★★★★

The sun was up, and the few German troops left in Gacé—little more than a company or two of infantry with no heavy weapons support—capitulated quickly to the overwhelming force as CCF moved in from the north and the rest of 4th Armored approached from the south.

With 4th Armored came the fuel tenders, a long-awaited blessing as dozens of CCF's Shermans ran out of gas as they swept the town's streets clear of surrendering Germans. Colonel Abrams' rolling stock would finally get their gas tanks filled, but slowly; the process would take all morning as the scant fleet of tenders worked their way through the thirsty tanks and trucks.

General Wood gathered his commanders alongside the highway just north of Gacé. Spreading a map on the hood of his jeep, he began, "Colonel Abrams, you've done one hell of a job up here, despite your hands being tied for lack of fuel. Besides the forces you've fought and destroyed around Gacé, your presence has forced the Germans pulling back from the west to swing their retreat to the north. So, as Patton says, we're doing Monty a big favor by pushing the Krauts to him, instead of him having to move his forces rapidly south to engage them."

"Yeah, *rapidly* is the key word there, sir," Abrams added. "You know what they say: if you want something done quickly, don't give it to Monty."

After the chuckling died down, Wood continued, "But here's the problem: General Bradley's just had himself a fit when Patton finally told him what we've been doing here. He went running to Ike, and as usual, Ike's hemming and hawing, trying to find a way to politic his way out of the fact that we all just stepped on Monty's toes in a big way and Churchill's going to climb up his ass. But Ike knows full well if he or Brad orders us back to that silly *stop line*, we might as well kiss goodbye our chance to finish off an entire German Army right here and now. And of course, that means we'll just have to fight them somewhere else—a whole lot closer to their homeland, if not actually *in* their homeland, and for God knows how long."

An infantry colonel asked, "But, sir, how is it possible Monty and the Brits *don't* know we're here? They've been flying recon, haven't they?"

Wood replied, "I think I'll let Colonel Abrams answer that one. Creighton?"

"My boys got attacked by the RAF yesterday," Abrams said. "We might've even shot one of them down. We rescued that pilot, and he said they thought we couldn't possibly be *Yanks*, as though no one would have the balls to cross Monty's line. I'll bet they still don't think we're Yanks."

Wood added, "That's probably very true. In fact, Patton said Monty's communique from last night was bragging about *a devastating RAF strike on a German armored unit just east of Gacé*. Gentlemen, they could only be talking about CC Fox. They were the only sons of bitches there."

"Where's that pilot, anyway?" the infantry colonel asked. "He knows better now. He could spill the beans on us."

"Don't worry," Abrams replied. "He's *convalescing* in Alençon, at the field hospital there. And we'll keep him there as long as necessary."

"So, gentlemen," General Wood said, "you're probably wondering what all this means for our future plans. Well, I'm here to tell you it don't mean jackshit. While the politicians play their silly games, Patton wants us to keep moving north until we meet up with some Brits—wherever the hell they are—and close this trap. Then maybe we can end this fucking war. After all his foot-dragging at Caen, we can't afford another *Montgomery victory*."

★★★★

Tommy made it to the flight line just as Jimmy Tuttle was climbing into the cockpit of *Blue Two.* Sergeant McNulty had *Eclipse of the Hun* armed, preflighted, and ready. Staring down from his perch on her wing, the crew chief patted the freshly painted *swastika*—a "kill" symbol—below the canopy rail. Then he said, "Don't rush yourself none, Lieutenant. The war's gonna wait for certified *knights of the sky* like you." His voice dropped a few decibels before he added, "*Irregardless* that it was just a li'l ol' *Junkers* you knocked down."

As he hoisted Tommy's flight kit into the cockpit, he added, "I figured you'd be a little late and all, busy as you were with celebrating your kill and all that *cherchez the femmes* jazz. Not to mention the drumming out of Lieutenant Clinchmore." He pointed to Clinchmore's plane, sitting idle in its parking spot, as evidence. "It's a shame. A perfectly good airplane going to waste."

"Wait a minute, Sergeant. Nobody's *drumming out* Lieutenant Clinchmore. Colonel Pruitt decided he might benefit from some time with the ground pounders as an ASO—maybe get a little better appreciation for what the guys he's supposed to be helping are up against."

McNulty gave him a sly smile and replied, "I don't suppose you made that *preposition* to the good colonel, did you, Lieutenant?"

"You mean *proposition*?"

"That's what I said, ain't it?"

"Well then, Sergeant—maybe I did, maybe I didn't. And I'm depending on you to dispel any rumors among the enlisted men about Lieutenant Clinchmore getting *drummed out*, is that clear?"

"Absolutely, sir. Now let's get you airborne before them other squadrons steal all the good pickings."

★★★★

A note for Sylvie had arrived at *Papa's House* right after sunrise. She read it, burned it, and then began to pack her musette bag.

Her father, passing in the hallway, asked, "Taking a trip, little girl?"

She smiled, said nothing, and then took her Welrod pistol from its hiding place in the wall. Placing it in the bag, she said, "Papa, I need to borrow a bicycle."

"Of course. Take Claude's. May I ask where you're headed?"

He expected her answer: "No, Papa. You may not."

Chapter Thirty-Four

The morning sky was a crystal dome of brilliant blue. It had seemed empty and tranquil when they first left the ground, but once *Blue Flight* climbed above 3000 feet, it looked like every aircraft in the American and British inventory was in the air, darting about like the specks in a shaken snow globe.

Just so none of those planes are Krauts, Tommy told himself.

The radio frequencies were buzzing with constant exchanges between airmen and ground liaisons coordinating their fires. On the receiving end of those bombs and shells, the retreating columns of the German 7th Army—sandwiched in that 12-mile gap between Falaise and Argentan—were being hammered by Allied artillery and air power. From the air, it seemed the perfect representation of how this morning's briefing had summarized the grand strategy: *bottle them up and let the artillery and Air Force finish them off.*

Except the Germans weren't *bottled up* quite yet. Despite enormous casualties and destruction of combat equipment, they were still flowing slowly but steadily eastward, trying to reach the River Seine and become part of a coherent defense which would deny the Allies Paris and beyond.

For Tommy, Tuttle, and the other pilots of the 301st, their business was some 16 miles farther east, providing recon and flank protection for 4th Armored. The division's long, slender column poked north like a probing finger reaching for the British, who were still too far away to touch.

The voice of Charlie Webster, ASO with Colonel Abrams' 37th Tank Battalion, was on the radio, directing elements of the 301st—including *Blue Flight*—to an area northeast of Gacé. German armored units were heading west—*toward* the exodus of their comrades fleeing east—in an attempt to ensure their breakout from the Allied trap.

This must be part of the Kraut counterattack the brass have been worried about, Tommy thought. He had to push the thought of last night with Sylvie from his head. But as he did, though, another thought tried to take its place, a far less pleasant one: *If Webster's calling the shots on Fourth Armored's line of advance, that means Sean's outfit is in the lead again.*

Webster transmitted, "Heavy armor reported on the Gacé-Bernay highway. Repeat, heavy armor."

That puts them on Fourth Armored's right flank, Tommy told himself as he glanced at the map on the clipboard strapped to his thigh. *Our guys are pushing straight north, up the Gacé-Vimoutiers highway. That's all they need—Kraut tanks hitting them broadside, trying to slice their column to pieces.*

They passed over Gacé and started to descend, looking for the German armor Webster had called out. It didn't take long to find a column of tanks, half-tracks, and trucks stretching along the arrow-straight Gacé-Bernay highway like an ominous dotted line, with one end aimed straight at 4th Armored.

"*Halfback One-four,* this is *Gadget Blue*," Tommy called to Webster. "We got 'em, about two miles east of you. Got to be at least fifty vehicles. Vector a couple of more flights this way. We're going to need some help."

They flew abreast of the column to its rear before reversing direction to attack. "Some of those half-tracks look like they might be *flakwagens*," Tommy said to Tuttle. "We'll hit them first. Looks like four or so in the front half of the line. I'll take them, you take the back half. Any trucks we take out in between will be a bonus."

"Roger. You gonna use guns or rockets, boss?"

"I think I'm going to save the rockets for the tanks. Give them one more chance to see if they're worth a shit."

They swept in low and fast, just a hundred feet above the treetops, zigzagging up the highway to keep the flak gunners' sight pictures constantly shifting. Tuttle hung well back to give himself a split second to dodge any explosions Tommy's shooting might leave directly in his path:

It'd be a crying shame to get knocked down by flying chunks of the thing your buddy just blew up.

Attacking at such high speed, the ground below was just a blur. Tommy did his best to align his gunsight with his targeted halftrack, still hundreds of yards ahead. He squeezed the trigger on his stick, tapping his rudder pedals left and right to sweep the road with .50 caliber. The scene before him dissolved into a blurry canvas of dirt and pavement being hurled into the air, bright flashes of bullets striking metal, licks of flame, and moving shapes that could only be men running away from the vehicles being ripped apart by API rounds.

He counted the four half-tracks he'd assigned himself as they slipped beneath *Eclipse's* belly and then pulled hard left, clinging to the treetops to escape the German column's fire. *Am I too low?* he wondered. *I don't want to have to bring her home like Dunphy did that time, with his prop tips all green and mangled from skimming trees. That beat-up prop damn near shook the engine off her mounts.*

But *Eclipse's* big radial was still snarling with her usual smoothness, all 18 cylinders working in perfect harmony. Far enough away from the German guns now, Tommy climbed to get a good look at what *Blue Flight's* attack had done so far. He expected to see Tuttle's plane over his left shoulder, but there was nothing there.

"*Blue Two* from *Leader*, where the hell are you?"

"I'm on your *six*, boss."

Tommy checked the rear view mirror on top of the windshield frame but could see nothing but a dull sheen. The mirror had frosted over. Again.

"Get on my wingtip where I can see you, Jimmy. Damn mirror's fogged up again."

"Yeah, what else is new? Coming up on your right side. Looks like we've wreaked a little havoc down there, boss."

Jimmy Tuttle's last remark was something of an understatement. Tall flames and thick black smoke were billowing from the middle of the German column, a sure sign of burning fuel. "One of us must've set a gas truck on fire or something," Tuttle added.

"Yeah, great," Tommy replied, "but with the wind the way it is, that smoke's going to ruin visibility if we attack from the north or east. You see any flak?"

"Too busy to notice. I don't think anything hit me, though."

"Me either. How about we go high and do a little dive-bombing on the tanks up front? The smoke won't bother us then."

"Tally-ho," Tuttle replied.

It took a few minutes to climb to 8000 feet, where they'd start the dive-bombing run. From that altitude, the war below seemed an abstract, nothing but plumes of wind-whipped smoke in a palette of grays and black hugging the rolling hills, now flattened by the perspective of height. The German column was almost invisible. The highway they drove on was just a pencil line sketched through fields of brown and green.

"Hey, boss," Tuttle transmitted, "let me go first this time."

"Sure. Have at it."

"Okay, then. Meet you downstairs."

Banking *Eclipse* left, Tommy set up an orbit that would give him a clear view of Tuttle's downhill run while allowing himself to keep an eye on his own tail. *That's all I'd need: to get jumped while I'm fat with bombs and rockets...and all alone.*

By the time *Eclipse* completed one circle, Tuttle had released his bombs, pulled out of the dive, and was making his escape to the south. From Tommy's perspective, the bomb strikes were almost imperceptible: *But they look damn close to the lead tanks. Maybe he even hit one? Or at least came close enough to scare the crap out of its crew?*

"All yours, boss," Tuttle reported.

Tommy rolled out of the orbit and throttled back, ready to start his dive. There was something he always found so unnerving—almost sacrilegious—about nosing over and starting down, as if he was turning this magnificent flying machine into nothing more than a brick. But it was the best way for a single-seat fighter to accurately deliver a bomb—provided the plane and its pilot could withstand the merciless aerodynamic forces involved in diving and pulling out. *You know what they say,* Tommy reminded himself, *if there's one thing a jug can do, it's dive. It had better—because it certainly won't climb.* He swallowed hard and pushed the stick forward, like he'd done so many times before.

Halfway down this roller-coaster ride, Tommy was locked on his target: two tanks pulled up next to each other, moving slowly if at all. *Hell, if I can't hit at least one of them, I'd better turn in my wings.*

He caught a quick glimpse of what Tuttle's bombs had done; a tank hull spewing smoke and flames was straddling the road, its turret blown off and laying upside down on the roadside.

But this was no time to sightsee. His own targets were rapidly filling his gunsight reticle. The wildly spinning altimeter would pass through 3000 feet in a brief moment. He punched off the bombs and began the pull-out, straining against the g-forces pushing him hard into his seat.

Level at 1500 feet, he found his wingman orbiting a few miles to the south. "Did you hear *Halfback* calling us?" Tuttle asked.

"No, I was a little busy. What's up?"

"Don't know. Something strange going on. They're calling for air-to-air help."

"Any of the P-38s responding? They've got top cover today."

"Negative. They're tied up."

"Then let's get over there."

They picked up the Gacé-Vimoutiers highway and flew north along 4th Armored's column at 4000 feet, low enough to give nervous GI gunners a clear view of the P-

47's distinctive silhouette; high enough that those gunners probably couldn't hit them. Not at the speed they were traveling.

"Shit, we've got company," Tuttle said. "Check your three o'clock low."

It took a few moments for Tommy to fully grasp what he was seeing. There were what looked like a dozen fighter aircraft—maybe more—below them, their mottled green wings and fuselages difficult to see against the backdrop of the terrain. They seemed to be swarming to attack the spearhead of 4th Armored.

"I think they're *FWs*," Tuttle said, meaning the planes were *Focke-Wulf 190s*, the Luftwaffe's formidable multi-role fighter.

"No," Tommy replied, "I don't think so. The noses aren't right for *FWs*—too long. They're Typhoons. It's the RAF."

"Then they're fucking lost, boss. The bad guys are east of here."

"*Halfback One Four*, this is *Gadget Blue.* You got those Brits on the horn?"

"Negative. They don't respond."

"Swell," Tommy replied. "Let me try."

He thumbed frantically through his signals booklet to find the RAF's frequencies. Tuning to one, the voices of British pilots began to spill from his earphones, all sharing a common *Taffy* call sign.

"*Taffy Leader*, this is *Gadget Blue Leader.* We're the P-47s just to your west. Do you copy? Over."

"Hello, *Gadget Blue*," came the cheery reply. "Care to join us while we bash the Jerries down below?"

"Negative, negative, *Taffy Leader*. Those are not Jerries. Repeat—they are not Jerries. The Krauts you want to bash are a couple of miles east, on the Gacé-Bernay highway."

"*Gadget Blue*...if they're not Jerries then who the bloody hell are they? There are no Yanks or frogs this far north."

"And there are no Krauts who speak English like they do, either. Did you ask them to authenticate?"

"Negative. We don't ask the enemy for permission to attack."

"Look, friend," Tommy pleaded, "we're all wasting gas like crazy up here for nothing. Try authenticating with them. Is that too much to ask? Or are you big fans of *own goals*?"

"Perhaps I should ask *you* to authenticate, *friend.*" All the cheer was gone from his voice.

"Go ahead. Lay it on me."

The frequency fell silent. *I guess they switched over for a private chat*, Tommy told himself.

Two of the RAF planes had climbed to *Blue Flight's* altitude and formed a *Lufberry*—a defensive circle that made it difficult for any plane outside the circle to attack those within.

Okay, Tommy thought, *if that's the way they want to play it.* He signaled Tuttle to form a *Lufberry* of their own.

Taffy Leader was back on the frequency. "*Gadget Blue*, authenticate *mike victor*."

After a few more flips through the pages of the signals booklet to find the day's code sheet, Tommy had the answer: "I authenticate *queen.*"

The cheerfulness returned to *Taffy Leader's* voice as he said, "Very good, *Gadget Blue*. I suppose that makes us officially mates."

"Damn right it does. Now how about doing the same for those boys down there?"

"Negative, *Gadget Blue.* We'll take your word for it. But this is highly irregular. Some Yank down there's asking for a good hiding from Monty."

"How about we save the *hidings* for the Krauts? Like I said, there's that armored column a couple of miles east that could stand another dose."

"We'll see what we can do. Cheers."

All but two aircraft of *Taffy Flight* turned and headed east. The two that didn't flew away to the northwest.

"Where do you think those two are going?" Tuttle asked.

"I'm betting they're heading home," Tommy replied. "Maybe they can't wait to spill the beans on this *highly irregular* situation they found."

Webster was back on the frequency. "Thanks for the help, *Gadget Blue*," he said. "You guys still loaded for bear?"

"Affirmative."

He read Tommy the coordinates of German tanks attempting to block the highway in front of 4th Armored. "We don't have a good line of sight on them. They keep ducking behind a rise."

"Mark the target line with *willy petes*," Tommy replied.

"Will do. Stand by."

The radio fell silent for almost a minute until Webster reported, "Shot, over."

Tommy dropped her left wing to get an unobstructed view of the target area. Fifteen seconds later, Webster said, "Splash."

Five seconds after that, two white puffs appeared in the sky to the north, about a thousand feet below *Blue Flight's* altitude.

"Got it," Tommy said. "Shut off the artillery. We're going in."

"Time for some rockets, boss?" Tuttle asked.

"Afraid so."

Circling behind the target line in the sky, Tommy counted eight tanks.

Where the hell did they come from? Were they supposed to be the roadblock while those other guys we hit sprung the ambush? Looks like the Krauts are throwing in the kitchen sink to stop this trap from closing.

"Let's work the line from both ends," Tommy said. "I'll take left, you take right."

"Roger, boss. How many you gonna salvo?"

"Two at a time."

In a shallow descent for the rocket attack, Tommy lined up the left-most tank in his gunsight. *I've got a clean shot right up his ass, but he's moving, dammit. Just so he doesn't turn.*

A little closer...a little closer...Now!

Two rockets streaked from their launcher tubes, one from each wing. He pulled *Eclipse* up and rolled her left. As near as he could tell, no one was firing at him. With the target hidden beneath the belly of his turning aircraft, all he could do now was pray the rockets were on the mark.

Once *Eclipse* had come around full circle, he could see they'd missed. The tank looked perfectly intact. And it was still moving.

Tuttle's luck wasn't much better. "Well, maybe I got it dirty a little," he said. "Gonna try again."

They made two more passes apiece until the six launcher tubes on each plane were empty.

Not one of the German tanks was hit by a rocket. What *Blue Flight* did accomplish, though, was to force those tanks into 4th Armored's field of fire, where rounds from artillery and tank destroyers proceeded to chew them to pieces. But not before the Germans had knocked out three Shermans.

"Close but no cigar with those damn rockets," Tommy reported to Webster. "Got something that needs strafing? That's all we've got left."

"Negative. But maybe you could do a little recon up north? See what else is in our way?"

"Roger. We can do that."

Chapter Thirty-Five

Blue Flight climbed to 5000 feet and headed north up the highway toward Vimoutiers. They'd have about 30 minutes for the recon Webster had requested before needing to return to A-14 and refuel. But they could cover a lot of ground in those 30 minutes.

And as soon as I land, Tommy vowed, *they're taking these fucking rocket launchers off this airplane. I'd rather carry an extra bomb than those useless stovepipes. At least I can hit something with that.*

There wasn't much to see at first. As they flew farther north, the gently rolling terrain was becoming hillier, almost mountainous in spots. *If it looks craggy to me from way up here*, Tommy thought, *the ground pounders are going to feel like they're going up and down Mount Everest...*

And there'll be more good hiding places—on high ground—for the Germans to defend from. This won't be getting any easier for us or the Brits, wherever the hell they are.

Something caught his eye down below: a cloud of dust hugging the ground. Beneath it, a small convoy—Tommy counted five vehicles—was moving along a dirt road that wound its way to the peak of the highest hill in the area. His first impression was they were Germans; he dropped lower for a better look, with Tuttle wide off his right wing.

Once down to a thousand feet, the convoy looked anything but German. The lead vehicle was an American-made jeep with mounted machine gun. The next in line was an armored car—*a British Humber, I think*—and the rest were light trucks, also British. The vehicles' occupants were waving enthusiastically at the P-47s.

Tommy marked the spot on his map: a place labeled *Hill 262*.

"You really think they're Brits?" Tuttle asked.

"Maybe...but based on how far east we all are, they're probably Canadians. Or maybe Polish. But it's all the same British Army. Looks like some kind of recon party."

"Yeah, just like us," Tuttle replied with laughter in his voice. But that voice tensed and raised in pitch with his next words: "We got company again, Tommy...and it ain't the RAF this time."

Tommy's head swiveled to find the threat, but he could see nothing. Tuttle's next shriek told him why: "One on your tail!"

A look in *Eclipse's* rear view mirror did no good: *Damn thing's fogged up again! Happens every time you descend, dammit!*

There weren't many options what to do next. Their lack of altitude was hemming the jugs in, forcing them to fly into narrow channels between the hills.

And the guy on your tail always has the advantage.

"Can you get him off me, Jimmy?"

"I'm trying, boss. Can't maneuver much in these damn hills, though."

And there was the problem: they'd have to climb—the one thing any German fighter could do better than a jug. Especially one with six rocket launcher tubes hanging below its wings, creating loads of drag.

Tommy had no choice but to stay low. He told Tuttle, "Just keep turning with me. How many others are there?"

"At least two more, waiting up high."

Waiting to pounce as soon as we do something stupid, in other words.

Tommy pulled a tight left turn around a hill and stole a quick glance over his shoulder. The plane on his tail was an *Me-109*, its long, square nose, fat prop spinner, and slab-sided canopy impossible to mistake.

I haven't seen any tracers whizzing past me, so if he's fired already, he missed by a mile.

Or maybe he's just biding his time while he lines me up.

Close as he is, if he gets me in his sight I'm in big trouble.

Another peek over his shoulder: the *109* wasn't in the same position now. The warmer air at low level had cleared Tommy's rear view mirror and he could see the German behind him, struggling to match *Eclipse's* steep turn. But he still didn't have a good shot—he fired, but the tracers sailed over the jug's right wing.

Tommy throttled back a little and tightened his turn. The *109* tried to match the move but swung wider to the outside.

I don't think this guy's much of a low-level flyer, Tommy thought. *Maybe I'll give him a little test.*

He rolled *Eclipse* level, dove to the treetops, and aimed her at a narrow notch between two hills.

Tuttle's anxious voice was in his earphones immediately: "What the hell are you doing, Tommy?"

"Just follow me, Jimmy."

Tommy ignored the green blur of trees just feet below him as he focused on the notch. They hadn't even reached it yet when Tuttle screamed, "Holy shit! The Kraut just went in! He bought the farm!"

Tommy's first thought: *One down, two to go.*

His second thought: *Or maybe we let sleeping dogs lie and get the hell out of here. We're not configured for dogfighting with these damn launchers hanging out.*

Blue Flight stayed down on the deck and headed south with throttles to the stops. The German fighters followed, but stayed high. After a few minutes, they were nowhere to be seen.

Tommy radioed in what they'd seen on the recon to 4th Armored: little evidence of Germans on the ground but an apparent British Army recon party on Hill 262. His elation over besting a foe—without even firing a shot—didn't last long: *It was just luck I was up against a rookie who couldn't handle his airplane very well. A veteran pilot on my tail like that would've made mincemeat out of me. Maybe the brass are right when they insist the Luftwaffe is running out of experienced pilots. They sure seem to be running out of airplanes, few as we've seen.*

There was a call for air support. Another P-47 squadron had caught a retreating German column near the crossroads town of Chambois, eight miles west of Gacé. "It's a turkey shoot, boys," the flight leader reported. "Nothing but soft-sided vehicles. We're empty now, so come on over and help yourselves."

Tommy checked his fuel gauge and then told Tuttle, "I'm getting low, but I've got enough for a pass or two. And it's only about eight minutes back to base from there. How're you looking?"

"I'm good. I figure we could do it."

Two highways and a number of smaller roads crisscrossed at Chambois. Every one of them was packed with slow-moving traffic: German soldiers on foot, horse-drawn wagons, trucks that would be traveling much faster if not engulfed in this sluggish parade.

The jugs that preceded *Blue Flight* had made it a point not to shoot up the town; if a German soldier made it there, he'd be safe for a little while. But he had to make it there first, and many hadn't been able to do that.

The roadways just west of town were a slaughterhouse. Bodies of soldiers by the hundreds lined the roadsides, intermixed with scores of dead horses, shattered wagons, and burned-out trucks.

Those guys weren't fighting anymore. They were just running.

The stench of death had risen high into the sky. It filled their cockpits; Tommy struggled to hold down the vomit rising in his throat. Even his oxygen mask didn't protect him from the damning odor. He pulled it off, more afraid he'd puke into it and choke.

More Germans kept coming down those roads. How they were able to make their way through all that carnage, Tommy couldn't imagine.

They've got to be running on pure fear.

The urge to just leave them alone—to fly on home without firing a shot—was almost overpowering. But he knew they had to be stopped. Otherwise, he—and his brother—would just have to fight them someplace else.

And maybe then the odds wouldn't be in our favor. Not like they are now.

He forced down the nausea once more—and with it, swallowed any hint of mercy.

"We'll do it two-abreast," he told Tuttle. "Keep our rounds spread wide so when they try and run off the road…"

He didn't need to finish the sentence. Tuttle knew he was going for the maximum kill zone.

Minutes later, out of bullets, fuel, and any sense of remorse, Tommy turned *Eclipse* to final approach at A-14. His only thought:

I hope and pray I can forget all this once it's finally over.

But as her wheels touched safely home, he knew that could never happen.

Chapter Thirty-Six

ALLIED GROUND FORCES DIRECTIVE

FROM: MONTGOMERY—COMMANDER, ALLIED GROUND FORCES	DATE-TIME OF ORIGIN 15 AUG 44 1800 HRS

TO:
BRADLEY—COMMANDER, 12TH ARMY GROUP

COPY (FOR INFO):
SHAEF (EISENHOWER); HODGES—US 1ST ARMY; PATTON—US 3RD ARMY; DEMPSEY—2ND BRITISH ARMY; CRERAR—1ST CANADIAN ARMY; CONINGHAM—RAF 2ND TAF; QUESADA—IX TAC; WEYLAND—XIX TAC; BRERETON—9TH AIR FORCE

THIS COMMAND POSSESSES IRREFUTABLE AERIAL RECON EVIDENCE THAT ELEMENTS OF YOUR 12TH ARMY GROUP HAVE CREATED A DANGEROUS AMERICAN SALIENT IN THE AREA OF THE GACÉ-VIMOUTIERS HIGHWAY PROJECTING SOME 12 MILES NORTH OF YOUR ASSIGNED POSITION.

THESE FORCES OF YOURS ARE DANGEROUSLY EXPOSED TO SUPERIOR GERMAN FORCES FROM THREE DIFFERENT DIRECTIONS SIMULTANEOUSLY. WHATEVER FOOLHARDY VENTURE YOU ARE UNDERTAKING RISKS THEIR ENCIRCLEMENT AND COMPLETE DESTRUCTION AS WELL AS EXHIBITING AN INSUBORDINATE DISREGARD FOR THIS COMMAND'S ORDERS. WE CAN ONLY PRAY IT HAS NOT ALREADY COME TO CATASTROPHE.

YOU ARE HEREBY ORDERED TO IMMEDIATELY WITHDRAW THESE FORCES TO THE FLERS-ARGENTAN LINE.

THIS COMMAND WILL EXPECT A COMPLETE ACCOUNTING IN WRITING OF THE ACTIONS THAT CREATED THIS RECKLESSLY UNWISE SITUATION, WITH THE NAMES OF THOSE RESPONSIBLE, NLT 1200 HOURS OF 16 AUG 44.

SIGNED,
MONTGOMERY

Omar Bradley read Montgomery's directive in a state of furious silence. When he was finished, he ripped it into little pieces and told his chief of staff, "Well, the cat's definitely out of the bag now. Get Ike on the landline right this damn second."

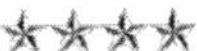

It wasn't Bradley's phone call that set Dwight Eisenhower stewing. It was the cable he'd received from Washington earlier that afternoon. Its author was General Marshall, the Army Chief of Staff. The words in its closing paragraphs had stung like sand flung in his eyes:

You would be wise to remember, General, that political talent can be a great asset to a soldier, but not when politics interferes with his soldierly duties. Churchill only leans on you because he realizes he can expect no further favors from the President and reckons you are more easily bent to his wishes. But never forget it is the President and not the British Prime Minister who is your commander-in-chief. Political expediency must never be portrayed as a substitute for the strategic initiative your commander-in-chief demands. Such expediency is what you've succumbed to, I believe, by placing Montgomery as overall commander of your ground troops.

Now his proven sluggishness is once again threatening to let a golden opportunity slip through our fingers, something your American subordinates have had no difficulty recognizing and are taking the initiative to correct. It is no surprise that Patton has once again "interpreted" an order in a way more to his liking. I suggest you should choose not to punish his success, even if that choice means ruffling some British feathers.

You've successfully dealt with conflicts between the personalities involved several times before in the past two years. It has never been more important that you do so once again, without delay.

Chapter Thirty-Seven

SHAEF DIRECTIVE

FROM:	DATE-TIME OF ORIGIN
EISENHOWER–SUPREME COMMANDER, SHAEF	16 AUG 44 0001 HRS

TO:
MONTGOMERY–COMMANDER, 21ST ARMY GROUP

COPY (FOR INFO):
BRADLEY–12TH ARMY GROUP; HODGES–US 1ST ARMY; PATTON–US 3RD ARMY; DEMPSEY–2ND BRITISH ARMY; CRERAR–1ST CANADIAN ARMY; CONINGHAM–RAF 2ND TAF; QUESADA–IX TAC; WEYLAND–XIX TAC; BRERETON–9TH AIR FORCE

EFFECTIVE THE DATE AND TIME OF THIS DIRECTIVE, THE DUTIES AND RESPONSIBILITIES YOU EXERCISED AS COMMANDER, ALLIED GROUND FORCES, REVERT TO SUPREME COMMANDER, SHAEF. YOU WILL RETAIN THE DUTIES AND RESPONSIBILITIES OF COMMANDER, 21ST ARMY GROUP, UNTIL OTHERWISE ADVISED.

SIGNED,
EISENHOWER

★★★★

SHAEF DIRECTIVE

FROM:
EISENHOWER—SUPREME COMMANDER, SHAEF

DATE-TIME OF ORIGIN
16 AUG 44
0100 HRS

TO:
BRADLEY—COMMANDER, 12TH ARMY GROUP; MONTGOMERY—COMMANDER, 21ST ARMY GROUP

COPY (FOR INFO):
HODGES—US 1ST ARMY; PATTON—US 3RD ARMY; DEMPSEY—2ND BRITISH ARMY; CRERAR—1ST CANADIAN ARMY; CONINGHAM—RAF 2ND TAF; QUESADA—IX TAC; WEYLAND—XIX TAC; BRERETON—9TH AIR FORCE

THE DIRECTIVE FROM COMMANDER, ALLIED GROUND FORCES, DATED 15 AUG 44, 1800 HRS, IS RESCINDED. 12TH ARMY GROUP WILL CONTINUE ALL EFFORTS TO CLOSE THE FALAISE GAP. THE FLERS-ARGENTAN "HOLD LINE" PREVIOUSLY ESTABLISHED IS NO LONGER IN EFFECT.

21ST ARMY GROUP IS DIRECTED TO CLOSE WITH 12TH ARMY GROUP FORCES IN THE VICINITY OF VIMOUTIERS WITH ALL DELIBERATE SPEED. ANY FURTHER DELAY IN OBTAINING THIS OBJECTIVE WILL RESULT IN SIGNIFICANT PORTIONS OF THE GERMAN 7TH ARMY ELUDING THE TRAP WE ARE ATTEMPTING TO SET.

SIGNED,
EISENHOWER

★★★★

George Patton seemed ready to bite off the head of the aide who woke him. "Another of Ike's goddamn directives? *That's* what you woke me for?" After he read it, though, a relieved smile settled on his face. It was the look of a man who knew he'd just escaped the hangman's noose. Again.

"Well, I'll be a son of a bitch," Patton said. "Looks like Ike's little love affair with the Brits just might be hitting a rough patch. Or maybe he finally decided to stop playing diplomat and grow some balls."

★★★★

Bernard Law Montgomery had made it a standing order never—*repeat, never*—to wake him with administrative details. Eisenhower's directives, arriving in the dead of night as they did, fell into the strictest definition of that category, despite the fact one relieved him of a command and the other countermanded an order he'd given. So instead of immediate delivery, the directives arrived at his caravan on the breakfast tray. They destroyed far more than his morning meal.

His aide had never seen the usually self-satisfied general so upset. He paced the caravan like a petulant schoolboy for a few minutes, shaking his head in bewilderment, muttering things like *bloody Yank idiots* and *clueless amateurs playing at soldiering*. Finally, in a sputtering voice, he told the aide, "Get Field Marshall Brooke on the line. No, no…wait. Make it the Prime Minister."

Chapter Thirty-Eight

Even though it arrived in the dead of night, the welcome news they no longer worked for Montgomery spread through the American ranks like wildfire. For the next 36 hours, 4th Armored continued its plod north toward Vimoutiers, slowed by frequent but brief skirmishes with exhausted German troops fleeing eastward. Having little ammunition and even less will to fight, the shouts of *Kamerad!* usually came fairly quickly after contact was made. Wehrmacht prisoners by the thousands clogged the highway as they were marshaled south, further slowing the American advance.

"Our success is our own worst enemy right now," Colonel Abrams reported to 3rd Army HQ on his command's sluggish progress.

The afternoon of 17 August brought a new, more dangerous enemy: the 2nd SS Panzer division, moving swiftly westward with heavy armor to open a path for the German breakout, collided with 4th Armored's right flank. Sean Moon and the rest of 37th Tank Battalion, at the leading edge of the American advance, found themselves fighting very different foes on two fronts simultaneously.

As his tank was off the line being refueled and rearmed, Sean fumed over the contrast. "The Krauts on the left can't wait to surrender, the ones on the right want to slug it out like it's the end of the fucking world."

Captain Newcomb replied, "It'll get better once Fifth Division moves in on our right flank later today."

"Yeah, if we're still alive by then."

An hour later, Sean's tank was back with Baker Company as they advanced toward Hill 262. Elements of the Polish 1st Armored Division—part of 1st Canadian Army and the eastern flank of Montgomery's 21st Army Group—held the hill and its commanding view of the French countryside and the Germans hell-bent on retreat. But they were an isolated force, unsupported by any other British or Canadian troops.

For the Poles, just getting to the hill had been difficult, slowed by fighting the same brief but frequent struggles with fleeing Germans just like the Americans were doing to the south. But holding the hill, with its spectacular vantage point for artillery observers and air support officers, was proving far more difficult. The same 2nd Panzer Division that was trying to drive a wedge through 4th Armored wanted that high ground, too.

If the Americans from the south and British from the north could link up with the beleaguered Polish outpost on Hill 262, the Falaise Gap would be closed. Tens of thousands of German troops—maybe as many as a hundred thousand or more—would be caught in the trap and, whether killed or captured, out of the war for good.

Sean Moon felt a flicker of hope rekindle in his war-weary soul: *Maybe if we bag all these Krauts we've got a chance to wrap this up by Christmas after all?*

That hope blazed for only a second. A round from a German gun struck the tank to his left, the unspeakable violence of the impact like the blow of a gigantic hammer. The Sherman's front armor peeled open as if made of paper; her interior became a crematory's oven for the five men within. Sean's flame of hope died just as quickly as the men in that tank.

And they were still three long miles from Hill 262. Through that three-mile gap, the Germans kept flowing like a raging river.

Captain Newcomb's M10 pulled up behind Sean's tank. "We've got to get behind these Krauts coming to rescue their buddies," the captain yelled. "Sergeant Moon, take your platoon and find a way."

"My platoon?" Sean said. "What platoon? I'm down to two fucking tanks, Captain. Didn't you just see Hammond get blown to shit?"

"Two's all you need, Sergeant. It'll be easier for you to move faster that way."

Easier, my ass, Sean told himself. *It's just a matter of time...and I can feel mine running out real quick.*

"Get moving before it gets dark, Sergeant," Newcomb said. "Everybody's got weak spots in a free-for-all like this one. I'll plug up ours. You go find theirs."

★★★★

Sean led his platoon eastward, probing for that elusive weak point in the German lines along the hilly terrain. *Some fucking platoon,* he thought, because it was down to just his tank—*Eclipse of the Hun*—and Sergeant Iggy Sposato's *Anytime, Baby.*

Sometimes, they dashed quickly along open ridge lines, dropping into defilade when German guns looked within killing range. Other times, they were forced by the terrain to crawl single-file down winding trails barely wide enough for the Shermans, where an enemy tank or gun—or even an infantryman with a *panzerfaust*—could be around the next twist at point-blank range. It had taken them over an hour to travel two miles, and in that time Sean still hadn't found an avenue of attack the Germans couldn't easily counter. He brought his two tanks to a halt in the little village of Survie, which was occupied by a company of American infantry. The *red diamond* insignia on their shoulders marked them as members of 5th Infantry Division.

"Nice you guys from the Fifth could stop looting long enough to give us a hand, sir," Sean said to a lieutenant as he climbed down from *Eclipse's* hull. "I'm Moon from 37th Tank."

"Wasn't much to loot, Sergeant Moon. Looks like you Fourth Armored guys got to it all way ahead of us."

Sean laughed. "So what's the story, sir?"

"Don't really know yet," the lieutenant replied. "We just got here ourselves. I'm Peterson, C.O. of Easy Company, First of the Tenth Infantry. Are you the tank support they've been promising?"

"If I am, that's news to me, sir. I'm running recon, looking for the back door into these Krauts trying to throw the Brits or Poles or whoever the hell they are off Hill Two-Six-Two."

"Hell, we're recon, too," Lieutenant Peterson said. "I guess we ought to compare notes."

"Sure, just let me get my guys positioned. Any place special you think we should be, sir?"

"There's only one paved road running through here. How about a tank at each end?"

"That'll work." Shouting to Sposato in the turret hatch of *Anytime, Baby*, Sean said, "Iggy, spin around and go cover the southern approach."

"Hook up with Sergeant Bostick," the lieutenant told Sposato. "I'm sure he's got a good place picked out for you already."

With a roar of her engine and the clatter of tracks on cobblestones, *Anytime, Baby* about-faced and headed off down the street.

"There's an alley by the church on the north end, Sergeant Moon," the lieutenant said. "That would be a great place for your tank, I think."

"Yeah, I see it," Sean replied. He yelled to Fabiano to *make it happen.*

As *Eclipse* rumbled away, Sean and the lieutenant entered a *bar-tabac* and spread a map across a small table. The barman looked nervously on, apparently convinced the presence of the Americans would bring death and destruction down on the people of Survie.

Trying to soothe the barman, Lieutenant Peterson said, "*Ça va.* It's okay. You'll be all right."

The barman looked skeptical. So did Sean, who asked, "You sure about that, sir?"

"No. But what do you want me to tell the guy? That five minutes from now his town could be a pile of rubble?"

"That might be a little more honest, Lieutenant."

"Let's not get ahead of ourselves here, Sergeant Moon." Peterson traced a finger across the map and asked, "Now where'd you guys come from?"

Sean sketched the route they'd already reconned. "There's no good way around there to flank the Krauts. We'll either get the shit blown out of us in a big slugfest on one of these ridges or we'll get trapped in some gully, all lined up like cattle at the slaughterhouse."

"What about the Air Force?" Peterson asked. "You tankers have direct radio links to the jugs, don't you?"

"Yeah, we do, sir. And they've been blowing the shit out of the Krauts around this Hill Two-Six-Two all damn day, but it's been like *the loaves and the fishes*: the more you eat, the more there are. And it'll be dark soon. Them pilots will be boozed up and shacked up until morning. And a lot of shit can happen out here in the dark."

They hadn't realized the barman was standing over them with another Frenchman at his side. "What kind of *shit* do you have in mind?" the barman asked, in near-perfect English.

"You speak English," a surprised Peterson replied. "Sorry, but I never thought to ask."

"Ça va," the barman replied. He pointed to the man beside him and said, "Marcel has information that might be of great use to you gentlemen."

Sean pointed to the lieutenant and said, "Hey, he's the only *gentleman* here. I'm a sergeant. I work for a living."

"Forgive me, Sergeant. I didn't mean to insult the working class."

"No offense taken, pal. And I didn't mean that you wasn't—"

"All right, knock it off," Peterson said. "You can work on your *Alphonse and Gaston* act some other time. Can we get back to what Marcel has to say?"

"Of course, Lieutenant," the barman replied. "Allow me to translate."

Marcel wove a detailed description of 2nd SS Panzer's headquarters, which was concealed in a wooded area two miles to the north, near the village of

Champosoult. He carefully prepared a drawing of the camp's layout, right down to the defensive positions and the van in which the *brigadeführer* commanding the division lived. He even outlined the latrine's location. The barman translated Marcel's final sentence: "Cut off the head and the snake dies, no?"

"Damn right," Lieutenant Peterson said. "Now, Sergeant Moon, couldn't we get the Air Force to blow this place to holy hell at first light? That'll throw the Krauts into a tizzy, and then you tankers should be able to roll right through Champosoult and right up their asses."

"Yeah, sure," Sean replied, without optimism. "All we gotta do is get our tanks over to here"—he pointed on the map to the highway near Champosoult—"in the middle of the fucking night. Half of 'em will get lost. The other half just might end up shooting it out with each other."

Peterson grimaced; he knew exactly what Sean meant. He'd blundered through night moves, too.

"One more thing," Sean said. "We'd have to make sure that fucking HQ itself don't move in the middle of the night."

"I think that's something me and my boys can handle," Peterson replied. "You can even help, if you like, Sergeant Moon. How good are the radios in your tank?"

"This village is down in a valley, sir. We can get maybe five miles out of our set right now, enough to get this intel back to my unit. Range should get a little better after dark."

"That's better than what I've got," Peterson replied, "so I'm going to have to lean on you for the commo."

He rolled up the map. “Come on, let’s get up on the high ground outside of town and take a look where we’re going…before we lose the daylight.”

Sean radioed the intel back to 37th Battalion. Then he, Lieutenant Peterson, Marcel, and the barman scaled the ridge just east of Survie. At the top, they found the artillery lieutenant who was Peterson’s forward observer. He had the boxy batteries from his radio spread out on a broad, flat rock open to the sky, as if baking in the waning sunlight.

“Best I can do for a recharge,” the FO said. “Warming them up gives them a little more juice, keeps them going a little longer. Got to try and make them last until the next resupply, whenever the hell that’s going to be.”

Marcel pointed to the woods concealing 2nd SS Panzer’s HQ. Peterson asked his FO, “Those woods…are they in range of any of our guns?”

The FO checked his map, and then replied, “Nope. It’s about a mile too far.”

Peterson asked Sean, “What about Fourth Armored’s artillery?”

The answer: “No, I don’t think so. They can barely reach Hill Two-Six-Two.”

“How come they didn’t move up with you tankers?”

“Because they ain’t got the gas to do it yet, sir.”

“Well, then,” Peterson said, “it’s the Air Force or nothing. Do you think the rest of your tanks will be joining us tonight, Sergeant?”

“If the colonel says so, they’ll sure as hell try,” Sean replied. “They’ll let us know what they’re gonna do real soon.”

Lieutenant Peterson began to draw his plan on the map. "Okay…if we're going to do this, I'll infiltrate my men around the Kraut's HQ at sunset. Our friends here say there are only a couple of roads heavy vehicles can use to get in and out. It won't be too tough in the dark to slow them down if they try and make a move. We can make it sound like we're a whole damn regiment if we have to."

Looking down into Survie, they could see Fabiano standing on *Eclipse's* turret, waving his arms to catch their attention.

"Maybe that's the news we've been waiting for," Sean said as he started down the hill toward the village.

"We'll be right behind you," Peterson replied. "I'm almost done up here."

When he got back to *Eclipse*, he found his crew chowing down on food supplied by the people of Survie. The meal came with a bottle of wine, too.

"No drinking," Sean said, "not even wine. We're gonna get real busy one way or the other real soon. I don't need any of you assholes seeing double."

Fabiano shrugged and handed over the wine bottle, still without a drop missing.

"You did save me some of that grub, though, didn't you?"

"Of course," Fabiano replied. "Nothing's too good for our fearless leader," he added, pointing to a satchel full of bread, fruit, and cheese. "But maybe you want to look at this message from battalion first. We just finished decoding it."

The message was short and simple: his recon party was to meet *Combat Command Baker—CCB*—at a highway intersection two miles south of Survie. Sean was then to guide CCB to the jump-off point for the assault of 2nd SS Panzer's rear. All this was to be accomplished in the dark of night, exercising total blackout discipline.

Sean stuffed the message in his pocket. "Well, at least they didn't tell us to take the Krauts on all by ourselves." He asked Hogan, his driver, "How's our gas holding out?"

"Three-quarters of a tank, Sarge."

"Okay. Should be enough. Give me a couple of minutes to fill the lieutenant in on the plan, and then we hit the road again. Fire the old girl up."

In the fading light of day, Sean could see Peterson and the others still descending the ridge. He was walking down the street to meet them when three women on bicycles approached. The youngest and prettiest of the trio was staring at him with a big smile on her face.

Holy shit! It's that Sylvie what's-her-name.

"Hello, Sergeant Moon," Sylvie called out as she rode in a circle around him. "Fancy meeting you here."

"How about that! You seen my brother?"

"As a matter of fact, I have. Two days ago."

"So he's okay?"

"Oh, he's fine. *Quite* fine, in fact. He gave me a message for you. Isn't this strange I can deliver it now?"

"What'd he say?"

"He said he was going to *kick your ass all the way back to Canarsie*, whatever that means."

Sean laughed gleefully, and then stopped suddenly. His face turned serious as he asked, "You didn't tell him what I said, did you? You know, about him fucking himself and all."

"Of course not."

He smiled again, breathing a sigh of relief. "Oh, good. Thanks. But let me ask you… just what the hell are you ladies doing in this hellhole, anyway?"

She stopped and dismounted, calling to the other women in French to go rest for a few minutes. Then she told Sean, "We are riding north, to Vimoutiers."

"Ain't this a little out of your way?"

"Yes, a bit. But we thought it might be less"—she searched for the right word—"less *turbulent* on this highway. But I see we may have misjudged."

"Yeah, this ain't a good place to be right now."

"Sergeant, *no* place beyond the American lines is a good place right now."

"You weren't planning on riding at night, were you?"

"Why not? Our bicycles have lights."

"But…but you might not want to go *this* way. Not *this* night."

Sylvie regarded him thoughtfully—kindly—before saying, "I understand. Thank you for the warning."

He leaned closer and whispered, "You ladies ain't up to any of that *maquis* stuff, are you?"

She gave him a withering look that answered his question yet implored him to *shut up.*

"Oh, I get it. Just between you and me then, right?"

She nodded. The withering look hadn't faded.

"Hey, I gotta go," he said. "Good seeing you again, Sylvie."

"Yes, we must go, as well." Her face softened to a smile, and she kissed him on both cheeks. "It was good seeing you, too, Sean. Good luck to you."

****

Sean got his two tanks to the intersection south of Survie as the sun set, giving him just enough light to find good places to conceal them. Once the Shermans were tucked among the trees well off the highways, they shut down their engines so they could listen for the approaching *Combat Command Baker*.

"When they get here," Sean told Iggy Sposato, "I'll take the lead element north to the staging area past Survie. You stay at this intersection and make sure every last vehicle in the column doesn't miss the turn."

"So I'm the road guard?"

"Gee, you catch on fast, Iggy. Now don't fuck this up. We're gonna need every swinging dick in the right place when the sun comes up."

Three hours later—2200 by their watches—there was still no sign of Combat Command Baker. Sposato said, "They should've been here a fucking hour ago."

Sean replied, "No shit, Iggy."

"What do we do if they don't show?"

"What do you think? We find a way to get our asses back home…wherever the hell that turns out to be."

It was another hour before the sounds of night—the wind in the trees, the din of insects, and the constant thunder of distant artillery—began to yield to the sounds of motors. Lots of motors.

"Looks like they made it after all," Sposato said as he picked up his red-lensed flashlight to play traffic cop.

"Not so fast, Iggy," Sean replied. "Them engines…they don't sound like something with Uncle Sam's initials on 'em. They're *Maybach* engines, I'm betting."

"Maybachs? You think it's Kraut tanks coming?"

"Yep."

"Fuck, Sean…what the hell are we gonna do?"

"We're going to stay real quiet and out of sight and let them pass."

"But what if they spot our *Zippos*?"

"That'd be some trick in the dark, Iggy. But if they do, we're fucked, ain't we?"

The intersection of the two highways formed a cross like the cardinal points of a compass. CC Baker was expected from the west. The German column was coming from the south.

"How could they be coming that way?" Sposato wondered aloud. "I thought we held everything south of here."

"Apparently not. Or maybe they're part of the big Kraut pullback from the east…and they're lost as shit."

Sean's theory seemed to have some merit. The blacked-out lead vehicle—its silhouette in the moonlight unmistakably a Panther tank—drove halfway through the intersection before juddering noisily to an abrupt stop. In the darkness, the Americans couldn't see the line of vehicles behind it, but the sudden hush of their idling engines made it a certainty they had stopped, too.

Standing on the ground in front of his powered-down tank, Sean could hear the soft mechanical *whir* of its turret as Fabiano manually traversed the main gun onto the German tank, waiting for his commander's order to fire. But everyone knew if they had to fire, they were as good as dead, anyway. That was enough to keep fingers off the triggers and impulses in check.

A *kübelwagen* pulled alongside the Panther. The man in the passenger's seat climbed onto the tank's deck and began arguing with its commander in the turret hatch. Each man unfolded what appeared to be a map. Then they argued some more.

"Come on, come on," Sean whispered, imploring the Germans too far away to hear. "Make up your fucking minds. Just don't go west."

West: right into the face of *Combat Command Baker*.

"Why don't we just call in artillery on them?" Sposato asked. "We're well inside their range here."

"Iggy, has it crossed your mind that the Panther might be the lead vehicle of a *battalion*, maybe? Or even a *division*? Unless we light the place up with illum, we won't know how many we're dealing with. And if we light the place up—"

Sposato finished the sentence for him. "If we light it up, then they'll see us, too."

"Damn right they will."

"Okay, Sean. You win."

"Experience before youth. Wins every time, Iggy."

The German from the *kübelwagen* walked over to the road sign marking the intersection. He lit it with his flashlight, and then yelled something at the Panther commander, who yelled something right back. Their disagreement, apparently, wasn't over yet.

"I guess they don't believe the signpost," Sposato said.

"Or their maps, either. Face it, they're fucking lost, Iggy. Just sit tight and watch what they do."

It took the Germans several minutes more to come to some sort of agreement. Then the Panther revved its engine and continued north. The rest of the column—all driving without lights like their leader—rolled by in what seemed an endless parade. When the last vehicle finally passed Sean's position, they had counted 46 tanks, 10 assault guns, a dozen half-tracks, 21 trucks, and a handful of *kübelwagens*. Whether it was their intention or not, they were all headed straight into the boiling cauldron of Hill 262.

"Where the hell are all these Kraut bastards coming from?" Sean said. "We've got to get the word to battalion what we just saw."

"But ain't we still supposed to be keeping radio silence?"

"Fuck radio silence. They've got to know this."

"Yeah, sure," Sposato replied, not sounding at all convinced. "But I'd still like to know where the hell CC Baker is."

"Wouldn't we all, Iggy?"

★★★★

It was going to be a long night for Sergeant McNulty at airfield A-14. Shaking his head, he asked Tommy Moon, "I'm not sure I see the *necessarity* in all this, Lieutenant. You really want them rocket tubes off?"

"Yep. I can't hit shit with those damn things. Get rid of them."

"Maybe you shouldn't be so *self-defecating*, sir, just because—"

"*Deprecating*, Sergeant. *Self-deprecating*. But I'm not blaming myself—it's the whole design. Those rockets are more wishful thinking than an effective weapons system."

"I could have sworn just the other day you thought them rockets were the answers to a virgin's prayer, Lieutenant."

"Then I guess I'm not a virgin anymore, Sergeant. And I sure as hell stopped praying a long time ago. Even if I did pray, I'm pretty sure no one's listening."

"As you wish, sir," McNulty replied, "but what about the rear view mirror? You really want to lose that, too?"

"Yep. Good riddance to it."

"Look, Lieutenant…the rockets are one thing, but I sure wish you'd *reconnoiter* the mirror."

"You mean *reconsider*, don't you, Sarge?"

"That's what I said, ain't it? And you ain't gonna get much more speed out of her by taking it off."

"I know that," Tommy replied, "but every time I need the damn thing, it's fogged up. They either need to put a heater in it…or just throw it away. I'll take the measly couple of miles per hour extra it'll give me when it's gone."

McNulty shook his head once more and asked, "So you're planning on lugging three bombs and eight guns for the duration?"

"Until something better comes along, you're damn right."

Chapter Thirty-Nine

At his CP a few miles south of Hill 262, General Wood felt like punching the map hanging on the tent wall. It had only been 24 hours since being freed from Montgomery's chains. That freedom had plunged them headlong into a ferocious battle with a German Army that didn't seem to know it was beaten.

Wood still held in his hand the message Sean had sent, the one advising of a battalion-strength panzer force moving north near Survie, probably to add to the formidable forces already facing 4th Armored and the Poles on the hill. The general told Colonel Abrams, "Those boys of yours…they did a great job." He sounded like he was paying tribute to the dead.

"Sergeant Moon's an old hand, sir," Abrams replied. "If there's a way for him to get out, he'll find it."

"All right, gentlemen," Wood continued, "as you've already figured out, *Combat Command Baker* isn't going to happen tonight. We got to hold on to this position, and it's going to take every ounce of strength we've got to do it. It was a good idea in theory, but we can't afford to disengage any of our forces right now to make up an *ad hoc* maneuver unit. The rest of the whole damn Twelfth Corps is trying to get up here and help us out, but the Germans have held them up, too. And there's still no sign of the Brits coming to the rescue, either. By all accounts, they're still ten miles away. Maybe more."

Abrams had a question. "Sir, did we find out why those Poles were in such a damn hurry to sacrifice themselves on that hill?"

Wood shook his head. "We still don't know, Creighton. Maybe they believed Monty's bullshit, too. Damn shame, I'd say. They seem like the only outfit in Twenty-First Army Group showing any initiative at all."

"And they're paying one hell of a price for it," Abrams replied.

General Wood smacked his pointer against the map. It made a sharp, electrifying sound, like the crack of a bullwhip.

"Listen up, gentlemen," he began. "This is what we're going to do. General Patton sees this fight we're in as a grand opportunity. Monty might be slow as molasses coming to meet us, but we can sure as hell push the Germans to him. Once we do that, this thing we call the Falaise Gap will be closed, whether the Brits move another mile closer or not. Now, it's going to take a hell of a lot of artillery and air power to help us do that. Patton's ordered all corps and division artillery units to be on the road tonight."

An infantry commander asked, "You mean they finally got some gas, sir?"

"Affirmative, Colonel. By sun up, our guns will be much closer than they are today and should be able to reach well past Hill Two-Six-Two. That'll be a big help. And the heavy bombers of the Eighth Air Force will be helping out our Ninth Air Force boys by flying multiple sorties against targets we've specified, starting at dawn."

A collective groan rose from his officers. "What's the matter?" Wood asked. "You don't want their help?"

"No, sir," Abrams replied, "it's not that at all. It's just that every time the heavies agree to lend us a hand…well, you remember what happened during *Cobra*. And all those other times, too."

"That's the risk we're going to have to take, gentlemen," Wood said. "We need the firepower, and we need it bad. If we take a few errant bombs in the process, well…"

There was no need to finish the sentence. The assembled officers all knew what those next words would be: *tough shit*.

Wood continued, "Patton said something I think you'll all get a kick out of. He supposes that Monty's dragging his feet at Falaise is just the Brits paying back the favor Hitler did them at Dunkirk."

The general waited a few moments for the smirks and laughter to fade. Then he said, "All right, let's figure out how we're going to save these Polish fellows come morning…and where we're going after we do."

★★★★

Sean wasn't lost; he could tell you the exact coordinates of his two tanks on the map. The trouble was, he couldn't figure out how to retrace his steps in the dark. The roads and trails they'd used in yesterday's late afternoon recon couldn't be found with any certainty in the blackness of night. They'd already had to double back on a dead-end trail taken in error and nearly gotten Sposato's tank mired in a mucky depression in the process. Now, at 0230, he decided the best course of action was to lay low off the highway until dawn and take his chances finding the way back in broad daylight.

"We got about four hours until sunrise," he told both tank crews. "That's two-hour shifts. Half of us on guard, the rest catch some shut-eye. Everyone stay in the vehicles."

"Ahh, come on, Sarge," Fabiano whined. "It's hot as a bitch in there. And you guys all smell something awful. A little fresh night air might be nice."

"Too fucking bad," Sean replied. "I don't need to have to come looking for any of you if things go tits up. And if things get crazy all of a sudden, I don't want to accidentally run over anybody, either. So you're all staying inside the *Zippos*."

Fabiano thought about saying, *Hell, Crunch, you never worried about running over people before.* But he thought the better of it. They were in deep enough shit already. No sense making it worse by antagonizing the man in charge.

And they could hear another parade of armored vehicles rolling down the highway, the sound of their engines decidedly not American.

★★★★

Sylvie hadn't told Sean the whole truth about where she and her companions were going. They weren't headed to Vimoutiers. They'd just arrived in the dead of night at their real destination, a small village called Orville on the main rail line. Cautiously, they cycled past the maquis safe house, looking for the blue light in the upstairs window that meant *all is well*.

"The light…I see it," Sylvie said. Per their instructions, they rode into the courtyard behind the house, hid the bikes in the storage shed, and knocked on the back door. A man in late middle age opened it just a crack, allowing the women to see the long scar running down a cheek of his weathered face. He held one arm in an awkward pose that made them sure he was concealing a pistol behind his back. Who the bullets in that pistol were meant for—himself or the Germans coming to arrest him—was better left a mystery.

Sylvie asked him, “How much is the price of milk today?”

“More than you can afford,” the man replied. “Would you prefer wine instead?”

“I never drink wine on an empty stomach.”

The password ritual completed, he swung the door open and beckoned the three women to come inside as he tucked the pistol—an ungainly Walther *broom-handle* no doubt taken from a dead German—into his waistband. “I am Pierre,” the man said with an air of great authority. “I am your *capitaine* now.” He directed the women to seats around a large, bare table.

Pierre launched into what the Brits and Americans called a *pep talk*. “You’ve been chosen because you are all thought to be reliable—”

Sylvie interrupted, “And all the *maquisards* in your unit have gotten themselves foolishly killed one way or another. Spare us the words of praise and encouragement. They aren’t necessary. Just tell us what we are to do.”

The other women smirked and nodded in agreement. They were no more willing than Sylvie to be patronized. They’d been through too much to put up with that.

“Very well,” Pierre said, his tone now dispassionate but no less commanding. He unfolded a map. “We are to sabotage the rail line here”—his fingertip traced a pronounced curve in the tracks halfway between Vimoutiers and Orville—“at the foot of this downhill bend. The Allies try to bomb the tracks in daylight but have yet to cause any serious damage. At least nothing the *Boche* can’t quickly repair. As a result, far too many of them are reaching the fighting each night, when the troop and supply trains move without fear of attack from the airplanes."

Eva, the oldest of the three women at 32—and the coarsest and most cynical by far—asked, "And you need three *vagin* from Alençon to do this for you? Are you afraid of loud noises, scarface?"

"No, madame, I certainly am not. But no matter—the only loud noise you will hear is the crash of a train derailing."

The three women looked at each other quizzically. Surely he'd meant they were to blow up the tracks with dynamite, as they'd done a few times before. And those times, each step of the process—from detonation to derailment—had been plenty loud.

"Ahh, I see you don't understand," Pierre said. He grabbed a satchel from beneath the table, lifted it with a mighty grunt, and placed it before them. "You will not use explosives. You will use these instead."

He turned the satchel over, spilling its contents. An assortment of long, stout wrenches clattered out and came to rest on the tabletop. He watched as recognition of their meaning quickly lit the women's faces.

"We've found this to be a much more effective method," Pierre said. "We remove key bolts holding the track sections together. When the locomotive hits those sections…*voila*. The track separates and the train runs off the rails to ruin."

Sylvie asked, "And you will show us where these *key bolts* are?"

"Yes. It will take two of us to remove the bolts while the other two act as lookouts."

"So there will be *Boche* guards?"

"Occasionally. That's why we need lookouts. But lately, the *Boche* don't seem to be able to spare the manpower to guard miles and miles of track. The speed of the train becomes its primary defense…and our greatest ally."

The old grandfather clock in the next room chimed *three.*

"When will this operation take place?" Sylvie asked.

"Immediately," he replied. "The bend is only two miles from here, as you can see. That give us plenty of time to cycle there and do our dirty work under cover of darkness. Are you all armed?"

Sylvie replied, "With pistols, yes. But perhaps you can supply submachine guns for us?"

"Of course," Pierre replied as he loaded the wrenches back into the satchel. "Follow me, *vagins.*"

★★★★

They were at the tracks in less than half an hour. Stashing their bicycles among the trees lining the tracks, they walked to midpoint of the curve. Pierre pointed out the bolts on four rails—32 bolts in all—that were to be removed. "Get them all off and we'll have maximum results," he said.

At the women's insistence, they drew sticks for who would be the lookouts. Eva and Pierre drew the short ones and trudged off to stand guard from the woods near the top of the curve. Sylvie began to work on the tracks with Dominique, a quiet woman of 26. It took a few minutes to find the correctly sized wrenches and figure out how to exert the necessary torque without the cantankerous tools slipping off the bolt heads and nuts.

They quickly realized their arms lacked the strength for the job, but the solid push of a foot, with one's entire body weight behind it, succeeded in breaking the first bolt free. "Thirty-one more to go," Sylvie muttered. "The rest will be much easier, now that we know how."

She was mostly right. Ten minutes plus several bruised knees and knuckles later, they had 12 of the bolts removed. As they moved on to the 13th bolt, Dominique startled Sylvie by asking, "So your marriage to Bernard is finished?"

"*Merde!* Is that common knowledge already?"

Dominique nodded and then added, "And so is your American lover, that flyer."

Merde, Sylvie repeated to herself. *In a world where keeping secrets means staying alive, how could these secrets of mine be shattered so easily?* Then she laughed at herself, for on one count, the blame was solely hers. *At least as far as Tommy Moon is concerned, I should have expected as much, bringing him to Papa's House like I did. But how did she know about Bernard and me, unless…*

"Dominique, are you sleeping with Bernard, too?"

Her silence provided the answer.

"Does your husband know?" Her words were sisterly, not harsh.

"I don't think so," Dominique replied, more in hope than conviction.

Either the bolts were getting tighter or the two women were tiring faster than they realized. Each stomp on the wrenches was now accompanied by a loud grunt and followed by the need to catch their breath.

As the 16th bolt broke free, Sylvie said, "Don't worry, Dominique. Your secret is safe with me, at least."

They loosened two more. Dominique, who was kneeling with one knee against a rail, suddenly stood up, ramrod straight. "The track," she said. "It's shaking. Feel it."

Sylvie laid her hand on the rail, feeling the faint but steady vibration, like a mild electric shock running up her arm. She strained to hear the metallic *clacking* of the approaching train, but only the constant murmur of big guns miles to the west rode the night breeze.

"We must work faster," Sylvie said.

"I don't think that's possible," Dominique replied, struggling against the dead weight of the wrench to engage the next bolt. With all the exhausting effort, their tools now felt like they weighed a hundred pounds each. "We'll never get all four sections loose."

"But we can finish three, I'm sure," Sylvie replied.

"Is that enough?"

"It'll have to be."

Three sections, Sylvie told herself. *That's twenty-four bolts. Only five more to go.*

Adrenaline had kicked in, giving both women strength they hadn't realized they possessed. They'd loosened three more bolts when Eva came running from the trees, waving her arms in warning. "It's coming," she said. "We can see the glow of its headlight down the straightaway."

Sylvie asked, "How far?"

"A mile. Maybe a little more."

Dominique dropped her wrench into the satchel. "Wait," Sylvie told her, "We've got at least two minutes before it gets here. And we only need a minute to get away into the woods."

"It's too dangerous."

"If you're not going to help me, at least leave me your fucking wrench."

Dominique was about to do just that: drop the tool at Sylvie's feet and run off. But she hesitated and then changed her mind. She returned to their work, her wrench once again in concert with Sylvie's. Together, they quickly broke another one free.

"Last one," Sylvie said as they moved to the final bolt. But it wouldn't budge.

The sections they'd already loosened weren't just vibrating anymore; they were rattling loudly as the train, still invisible somewhere beyond the curve, grew closer.

Eva was pacing frantically in place, casting nervous glances up the track. "Come on, you stupid cows! Run! There's no need to die for that shithead Pierre!"

The rattling of the loosened sections grew louder, more urgent, like the angry drone of a buzzer announcing *time's up*.

"SHUT YOUR BIG MOUTH AND HELP US, EVA," Sylvie said, straining as their feet pushed against the unyielding wrenches.

For a moment, they thought Eva would simply abandon them and seek the safety of the woods. But to their surprise, she suddenly lunged at Dominique's wrench, hurling her body weight full against it. The collision sent all three women sprawling.

But it did the trick: Sylvie spun the loosened nut off the bolt. When it came free, it dropped to the track bed and began bouncing about like dice in a shaken cup. It wasn't just the loose track sections rattling anymore; the ground was trembling beneath their feet.

They could hear the screech and growl of steel against steel now, but the wooded curve prevented them from seeing the locomotive. "Go! Go!" Sylvie said, scooping up the two wrenches as if they were suddenly feather-light. On the dead run, she was the last to make it to the cover of the trees, getting there just as the train entered the curve.

It popped into view like a one-eyed phantom, its headlight piercing the night, the dark outlines of the locomotive and cars creating an ominous sense of invincible power. It seemed to be hurtling much too fast, closing the distance to the loosened track sections in the blink of an eye.

When it reached those sections, there was no discernible change in the locomotive's momentum; the only sign something might be awry was a brief shower of sparks from beneath the drive wheels. It kept plowing forward as if the sabotaged rails were nothing more than a mere inconvenience.

But then, as the three women looked on in wide-eyed amazement, the silhouette of the locomotive began to shift, growing inexplicably shorter until they realized what was happening: the locomotive was heeling over like a sailboat in a strong wind. It hung in that angular limbo for a moment that seemed like an eternity, and then it crashed on its side to the earth beside the track, sliding along like a felled behemoth on ice, tearing down sturdy trees in its way as if they were matchsticks. If it was slowing, the women couldn't tell.

The cars behind the locomotive fared no better. Following the locomotive's ruinous course, the first few in trail were dragged from the tracks, the wooden superstructure of the cars shredding themselves to the timbers from which they were built as they toppled. The rest of the train uncoupled from the forward contingent and, as they reached the sabotaged rails, each car derailed in turn. They piled into the accumulating wreckage at trackside and flew apart, disassembled by violent forces of impact they were never intended to withstand. To Sylvie, the *hiss* of escaping steam and the *crunch* of the cars' sequential disintegration sounded just like the ancient thresher on her uncle's farm as it slashed through the wheat—only a thousand times louder.

Pierre joined the women midway through the train's orgy of destruction. Once the entire train had left the tracks, he asked, "How many cars?"

Sylvie replied, "Who knows? Fifteen? Twenty? All we know is they are all destroyed."

"I guess three sections of track were enough," Dominique said.

"Three was all you women could manage?" Pierre said, as if scolding children.

"Yes," Sylvie replied, her tone defiant. "Is there some problem with that?"

"No, there's no problem because you were very lucky, *madame*. Very lucky, indeed."

"Luck had nothing to do with it," she replied. "It was simple physics."

They lingered for a few minutes to see if any survivors emerged from the rubble. If there were, though, the darkness was protecting them. The symphony of demolition which had filled the air as the train wrecked itself was reduced to nothing more than a one-note postscript: the *shiiissshhh* of steam escaping from the mortally wounded locomotive. "Let's take our victory and get out of here," Pierre said.

Back at the safe house in Orville, Pierre said, "Try and get some sleep, ladies. There'll be much more for you to do in the coming days."

"Good idea," Sylvie replied. "Where should we sleep?"

"There are mattresses in the basement for—"

"No, absolutely not," she replied. "Basements are traps if the *Boche* come. We'll sleep on the main floor."

Eva and Dominique stepped behind her, the three forming a phalanx of defiance.

Pierre adopted a defiant pose of his own. "Are you women always so impertinent to your *capitaine*?"

"It's not a question of impertinence," Sylvie replied. "It's one of experience. We *women* have been killing the *Boche* for four years now, and we're all still alive. That's more than we can say for the *men* of your unit, I believe."

Eva added, "And Sylvie has given more of herself for France than any man ever could, scarface. Unless, of course, you like the *Boche* up your—"

Sylvie cut her off. "That's enough, Eva. Let's not spit on the *capitaine's* hospitality before we've had a chance to enjoy it."

Pierre began to worry he'd need to sleep with one eye open. He'd been expecting novices, women who wore the black beret and but did little more than clean up after the maquis men. These women, however, possessed the poise, confidence, and knowledge of experienced fighters. And they appeared to have no qualms at all about killing; they'd been baptized in blood long ago. They'd be just as adept at knifing him in his sleep as killing the *Boche.* Perhaps the question of sleeping quarters wasn't so important, after all.

“Fine,” he said. “Sleep wherever you like, *mesdames*.”

Chapter Forty

The dawn was breaking, allowing Sean Moon the first real look at the place he had decided to lay up his tanks for the night. He was shocked to find the trees he'd considered good concealment in the darkness of night were little more than ornamental. Both of his tanks were in plain view from all directions, including the sky. They were much too close to the highway, as well.

This whole damn thing looks like some rookie mistake, he told himself. But he couldn't beat himself up too badly; lots of experienced troopers had made breathtakingly bad errors in the dark: *Like that artillery battery on the Cotentin that had one gun laid backward from the other five. Damn thing had to fire a round for them to realize their mistake...and that round landed right in the middle of our bivouac. We were damn lucky nobody bought it.*

"Drop the cocks and grab the socks, boys," he said as he roused those crewmen whose turn it had been to sleep and one whose turn it hadn't been, his assistant driver, Linz.

"Welcome to Sergeant Moon's shit list, Linz," Sean said as he shook the man awake.

"Gee, Sarge…I must've just dozed off. Really, I—"

"Save it, Linz," Sean replied. There were so many more threatening things he could say right now about the punishments for sleeping on guard duty, but they all seemed to pale in comparison to the danger they were in. He was sure every man in his crew—himself included—would rather be in the stockade than where they were at the moment, alone in this no man's land.

And there was the sound of more vehicles coming up the road. "We gotta get the hell outta here, Sean," Iggy Sposato yelled. "We're wide open to get creamed."

"Calm down, Iggy. Just listen."

There was something about the sound of the engines. They weren't German.

"Sounds like Dodge deuce-and-a-halves to me," Sean said.

"Are you sure?"

"Let's fucking hope so."

Sean climbed onto his tank's turret. "Hogan," he said to his driver, "pull her onto the road, with her right side facing that oncoming traffic."

"Are you sure, Sarge?" Hogan replied. "You want to show 'em our flank? Friendly or not, they could put a round right through us that way."

"I want 'em to see that big white star on her side. Now get moving."

Hogan did as he was told, but his fears made it far from easy. He ground her gears badly before *Eclipse* started to move. Once he stopped her in the middle of the road as Sean had ordered, he slid down in his seat and pulled his hatch closed, putting as much steel as he could between himself and the mayhem he expected any second.

Linz, manning the machine gun across from the driver, asked, "What are you doing, Charlie? They ain't gonna shoot. They're waving like they're real happy to see us, for cryin' out loud."

An American captain came bounding from the column to the tank. "Sure am glad to see you, Sergeant," he yelled up to Sean in the turret. "You must be from the tank support we're to meet up the road."

Sean eased himself through the hatch and onto the deck. "You're the second officer who's told me that since yesterday, sir. But I'm here to tell you the answer's still no. We ain't those guys."

Sean couldn't decide if the captain was annoyed or confused. As if unsure what to say or do next, he glanced back at his trucks stopped on the road. They were just a long line of soft targets, full of infantrymen and supplies, vulnerable to just about everything. Thirty-caliber machine guns were their heaviest weapons. A few panzers could decimate them.

"Maybe you could come along and help us out, anyway, Sergeant." It was spoken as a statement, not a question.

"No can do, sir. We're a recon team, and we were supposed to be back with our unit hours ago. Love to help you out, but—"

"Hang on just a damn minute, Sergeant. If you're recon, what can you tell me about the road ahead to Vimoutiers?"

"I can tell you it's crawling with Kraut armor, sir. Couple of battalions passed this way during the night."

The captain unfurled his map against *Eclipse's* sloping front armor, using his fingers as a ruler, sliding them from the scale in the corner to a point on a road. Looking over his shoulder, Sean knew it was the wrong road. He leaned in and planted the tip of his forefinger on their actual location.

"This ain't the Gacé-Vimoutiers highway, sir. You're way the hell over here."

Now the captain really looked confused. "That can't be, Sergeant."

"Afraid it is, sir. You missed a turn back there somewhere."

The captain puzzled over the map for a few moments, and then said, "But this road goes to Vimoutiers, too. How many tanks have you got?"

"Just two, sir, and like I said, we've gotta get—"

"Never mind that, Sergeant. Put your tanks at the front of my column and lead us up the road."

"Sir, I just told you this road's crawling with Kraut tanks. Two li'l ol' *Zippos* ain't gonna help you a damn bit."

"I'm giving you a direct order, Sergeant."

Sean climbed onto *Eclipse's* deck. "Ain't gonna happen, sir."

"Goddammit, Sergeant, I said I just gave you a direct order!"

Sliding into his turret hatch, Sean replied, "Then I guess I'm giving you a direct refusal, Captain."

"What's your name, Sergeant? I'm going to have your ass court-martialed."

"The name's *Mouse*, sir. Michael. No middle name."

"Spell that, Sergeant."

"Standard spelling, sir. *M-O-U-S-E.*"

The captain had written down the first few letters in his little notebook before he realized just how hard his leg was being pulled: *Michael NMN Mouse. Mickey Mouse.*

Eclipse was already backing away, the captain chasing after her, yelling over the roar of her engine, "WHO IS YOUR COMMANDING OFFICER, YOU INSUBORDINATE SON OF A BITCH?"

"SAME AS YOURS, SIR," Sean yelled back. "FRANKLIN DELANO ROOSEVELT."

In the light of day, Sean quickly found the trail that had eluded him in darkness, the one that would lead them back to 4th Armored. He told his crew, "Now we're *cooking with gas*. We'll be home before you know it, boys."

He expected an enthusiastic response from his crew but got none. For a moment, he wondered why. And then it hit him: *Maybe my choice of words wasn't that great. A Zippo can turn into an oven in a heartbeat. Nobody who rides around in one wants to think about cooking or gas...or any of that burning shit.*

★★★★

At 4th Armored's HQ, General Wood looked up at the sky with a growing uneasiness. The heavy bombers of the 8th Air Force were coming—they should be overhead any minute—and the low cumulus clouds which hung overhead would be anything but conducive to accurate, high-altitude bombing. The general thought those clouds resembled broad, flat swaths of cotton bandage roughly torn from a roll, leaving them with jagged holes in many places. Maybe those holes would be enough for the bombardiers above those clouds to see the ground clearly and drop their bombs on target.

Or maybe not.

He turned to Colonel Abrams and said, "I hear tell Monty asked to have this bombing raid called off because of the cloud cover. Ike gave him a flat out *no*. Said his Brits would actually have to be close enough to be in danger from an off-target drop…and they certainly aren't close. The *Supreme Commander* got that one dead on the mark."

His head bowed as if at a funeral, Wood paused before adding, "But those poor Polish bastards…they're certainly close enough. Hell, they're right in the damn middle of it all."

Abrams replied, "We might be, too, sir, depending on how bad their aim is."

★★★★

Sean figured they were halfway to 4th Armored when the sky began to darken. It wasn't due to the weather; there seemed to be an armada of aircraft—an *aluminum overcast*—above the layer of patchy clouds. He couldn't hear the low-pitched hum of their engines over the noises of his tank. But he could see them—a big B-17 here, a few more there—through the gaps in the cloud deck. Some of those planes would pass right overhead.

"They're our guys," he told his crew. There were cheers in response.

They were still cheering when Sean saw the first sticks of bombs plummeting downward. It was too late to do anything but button up the tanks. There was nowhere to run, nowhere to hide.

Each collision of bomb with earth felt like the tank was being struck by a giant mallet. Shrapnel bounced off her hull, sounding like driven rain on a tin roof to the tankers inside. They clamped their hands against the earphones of their helmets to keep the pressure surge of the blasts from rupturing their eardrums. They wished they had third hands to clamp over their crotches, because it felt like they were being kicked in the testicles by a mule. Squeezing their thighs together would have to suffice.

It all lasted less than a minute. The blasts became distant; a drumbeat of death by steel marching quickly away. Sean popped open his turret hatch to have a look outside.

Eclipse looked like she'd been sandblasted, the surfaces of her turret and hull scored deeply in countless places. Some of the track sections they'd hung on her front and sides—both as spare parts and a little extra steel between themselves and enemy fire—were either badly mangled or gone completely, having sacrificed themselves to save the hull beneath.

But when he turned rearward to check on Sposato's tank, his stomach gave a sickening lurch. *Anytime, Baby*—or what was left of her—was stopped dead about 100 yards behind. Her scorched turret lay nearby, upside down like an overturned turtle. The foredeck of her hull looked like it had been cleaved open by an ax. Flames roared from that rupture and the big, empty ring where her turret had once been attached. Every few seconds, the flames would yield to a fireball which shot dense gray smoke and sizzling metal fragments skyward as more of her ammunition cooked off in the blaze.

Sean knew what had happened to her: *Some fucking bombardier got himself a direct hit. A one-in-a-million shot, but on the wrong damn target. What the Brits call an "own goal." They'll probably give that fucking bomber jockey a medal for it, too.*

As *Eclipse* plowed onward toward her unit and Hill 262, Sean fought back his tears. A bitter voice in his head said, *Like it ain't hard enough just fighting the fucking Krauts…*

But what's the damn difference? It's just a matter of time.

The heavy bombers had done their worst and were headed back to England. Now it was time for the fighters to reclaim the sky over Hill 262. Tommy Moon slid into *Eclipse of the Hun's* cockpit as Sergeant McNulty completed the last of the preflight checks.

"Okay, sir," McNulty said, leaning into the cockpit. "You're good to go." He thrummed his fingers against the top of the windshield frame, where the rear view mirror Tommy had insisted he remove used to be. "Keep an eye on your *six*," he added. "With that mirror gone, you're gonna have to do a whole lotta head swiveling. And you'd better, too, because I'd like all that hard work me and my boys put in on this bird to last a while."

"As do I, Sergeant. As do I. Who's going to ride the wing for taxi-out?"

"I thought I'd do it myself today, if that's okay with you, sir."

"It'd be my pleasure to have you along," Tommy replied.

The safety man gave the *clear to start* signal as McNulty lay prone on the wing, his head over the leading edge. Tommy completed the pre-start checklist and engaged the starter. The big radial chugged to life with the usual cloud of bluish smoke. Chocks were pulled from the wheels, the throttle bumped up, and she began her slow roll. With a sharp left turn on McNulty's hand signal, *Eclipse* took her place in line on the taxiway.

It had been SOP for quite some time to have a guide ride the wing while taxiing. The pilot of a P-47 couldn't see a blessed thing over the ship's nose with the tail wheel sitting on the ground. Once some speed was gained on the takeoff role and the tail came up, he could finally see straight ahead. But a man on the wingtip during taxi always had an unobstructed view forward. Using hand signals, he'd guide the pilot to the runway threshold, then drop off and join the other ships' guides in the truck that shuttled them back to the ramp.

Before they began using the wingtip guides for taxi, the old procedure had been for the ship to *s-turn* back and forth across the taxiway as she moved forward. It afforded some semblance of a forward view at the 10 o'clock and 2 o'clock positions. But even then, there were big blind spots. Occasionally, a pilot got his rudder slashed to ribbons by the now-mangled prop of the plane behind, scrubbing both ships from the mission. Even more pilots put a wheel off the taxiway while zigzagging and got stuck in the soft mud, holding up the *conga line* of trailing ships as grumbling ground crews dug the mired plane out. And all that weaving back and forth wasted a lot of precious aviation gasoline. Tommy's squadron—the 301st—hadn't used the *s-turn* procedure since their first months in England.

Eclipse was at the runway threshold now, the next to take off. Tommy braked *Eclipse* to a stop so his wing rider could hop off. Rather than give the customary salute before leaving, though, McNulty offered what seemed a melancholy wave goodbye, as if he wasn't expecting to see Tommy for a long time. Or ever again.

At first, Tommy was amused, as if it was all some act the ground crewmen had cooked up. *What's Sarge playing at?* he asked himself.

All of a sudden, it wasn't funny at all. A little unnerved, Tommy asked himself another question: *What does that son of a bitch know that I don't?*

But there was no time to ponder unanswerable questions. He steered *Eclipse* onto the runway, locked the tailwheel, opened the throttle, and began the mad dash to get his heavily laden ship airborne.

Chapter Forty-One

10, Downing Street,
Whitehall.

August 18, 1944

MOST SECRET

My Dear Montgomery,

I feel the need to supplement our telephone conversation of August 16 with a few heartfelt thoughts that I am sure are in the best interests of this critical allied endeavour in which we are all so deeply involved. As I stated at that time, your opinions of General Eisenhower's abilities as Supreme Commander are well noted. But I must remind you once again of the significance of the word "supreme." Your statement that Eisenhower's "ignorance on how to run a war is absolute and complete" is far too easy to discount and does our collective cause no favours.

I urge you, dear fellow, to take whatever pains necessary to appreciate that there are often higher priorities than the ones in which we toil day to day. In those higher priorities, we often find political factors that are every bit as important as those of pure military consequence.

Field Marshall Brooke shares my opinion that in the campaign you are currently waging the initiative has passed from your command to the forces of our American allies. While we may not always agree with the direction our American friends take, and we may occasionally have no choice but to reward their failures, we must never be seen as trying to punish their successes.

Therefore, your request to initiate a review of the Supreme Commander's stewardship at the highest levels of state will not be pursued by His Majesty's government. But take heart, Monty, and remember that while all good things come to those who wait, your wait may not be as long as you fear.

Winston S. Churchill

Chapter Forty-Two

The clouds that had hindered the 8th Air Force heavy bombers just an hour earlier were breaking up now, their remnants pushed eastward toward Germany by the steady prevailing wind. The pilots of *Blue Flight* had a far better view of the ground—and the fleeing Germans—than the bombardiers who came before them had experienced.

The eager rookie flying *Blue Three*—Lieutenant Bobby Sample—could barely contain his excitement at the spectacle unfolding below. "Look at those Krauts!" he blurted into his microphone. "It's like a traffic jam down there! You won't even have to aim. You're bound to hit something. That briefing officer wasn't kidding when he called it *the triangle of death*."

That name was proving quite appropriate. The triangle was 10 square miles bounded by two towns—Trun and Chambois—and Hill 262. Within that three-sided hell, the fleeing Germans seemed bumper to bumper, shoulder to shoulder. Their exodus looked like a river of *feldgrau* surging eastward, being decimated by Allied artillery and then slamming against the dam of ever-strengthening American forces and the battered Poles still clinging to the hill.

"Knock off the chatter, *Three*," Tommy scolded, "and don't get any ideas about shooting them up, either. They're the artillery's job, not ours. Stay well clear of the triangle unless you want to get knocked down by our own guns. Those shells won't care what they hit. We've got other fish to fry, anyway."

Other fish to fry: protecting Patton's wide open right flank. His headlong advance to close the Falaise Gap had turned 3rd Army into a narrow salient over 10 miles long, curving north toward the British lines still miles away. The left flank of that salient faced the fleeing and panic-stricken former defenders of Normandy. They were still a formidable fighting force, just like any cornered creature, but they were quickly running out of ammunition and hope.

The Germans the 3rd Army faced on their right flank, where Colonel Abrams' 37th Tank Battalion was one of the units holding the line, were a different story entirely. Heavy in armor, well supplied and with room to maneuver, they were determined to slice through the American offensive and allow the breakout of their trapped comrades. Only the fighters of XIX Tactical Air Command were available to cover Patton's right flank. The four P-47s of Tommy Moon's *Blue Flight* were just a small part of that covering force.

The radio was alive with the familiar voices of 301st Fighter Squadron pilots serving as ASOs. Herb Clinchmore was one of them. He would've been flying *Blue Four* right now had not his loudly expressed lack of empathy for the ground troops singled him out for some on-the-job training. *I don't care if he was drunk when he said it,* Tommy told himself. *He had it coming...and it'll do him good.*

It sounded like Clinchmore's education was progressing nicely; he was already hard at work directing air support for 5th Infantry Division, guiding jugs from another squadron to attacks on the highway junctions south of Survie.

Charlie Webster was on the air, too. The sound of his voice sent a chill down Tommy's spine: *Where Webster is, so's my brother. And voices don't lie...when the pitch goes up an octave, they're in one hell of a fight.*

"Roger, *Halfback*," Tommy transmitted, "copy your coordinates, target concentrated vehicles with armor. Can you mark me a target line?"

"Negative, negative on the line, *Gadget Blue.* Things are a little crazy right now. Point marking only, yellow smoke. Come in top to bottom, okay?"

Top to bottom: attack out of the north. Less chance of hitting the GIs to the west that way.

With one terse transmission, Tommy organized *Blue Flight* for the attack run. Samples, the rookie flying *Blue Three*, would stay on his wing. Jimmy Tuttle, in *Blue Two*, would lead the other rookie in *Blue Four*, Lieutenant Ray Esposito.

Tommy and his rookie flew one high orbit over the target area to get oriented. Tuttle led Esposito around a wider orbit to buy time and distance behind *Blue Leader's* run. But Tommy's view of the melee below was troubling. Every tank and truck—American or German—looked alike from the air. And Webster's target marking wasn't helping distinguish them: *Yellow smoke, my ass. The only smoke I see is gray or black. I wish to hell they had the spare guns to give me a line in the sky.*

"*Halfback,* this is *Blue Leader*. I need more smoke, and with a *splash* this time. Can't tell you guys down there apart."

"Roger, coming right up. Stand by."

Tommy banked *Eclipse* hard for a wider view of the ground. *Any second now...*

It took almost another full orbit before Webster reported, *"Splash, over."*

One one thousand, two one thousand, three—

There it was, a tiny puff of smoke barely distinguishable as yellow.

If I take my eyes off it, I'm going to lose it.

"*Blue Three* from *Leader*. Stay with me, Bobby. We're going in. Pickle 'em all at once on my mark."

"Roger."

Tommy nosed her over into a descent for glide bombing, a brisk enough downhill ride but not as breathtaking as the screaming plummet of dive-bombing, where the pointers of the altimeter seemed to be spinning right off the post. He figured it would be a safer initiation for a rookie: *I shouldn't have to worry about him getting so target fixated he doesn't remember to pull out until it's too late.*

Passing through 3000 feet, the sunlight began to play off the battlefield smoke, turning it a satiny gray that masked the yellow marker and obscured Tommy's view of the ground. He could still make out the shapes of vehicles—but they could be anyone's vehicles now. *I think I've got a good enough reference point for the drop, though. And Webster says we're right on the target line...so even if I miss, I won't kill anyone I'm not supposed to.*

That last thought echoed in his head, a troubling question now instead of a statement: *I won't kill anyone I'm not supposed to?*

But there was no time for questions like that, only decisiveness. "On my mark, Bobby...three, two, one, RELEASE."

He pushed the button on the control stick that salvoed her bombs—the *pickle switch. Eclipse* lurched upward, suddenly 1500 pounds lighter as her three bombs fell away.

Climbing out, Tommy asked, "You still with me, *Three*?"

A breathless voice replied, "Roger, still here."

Tommy looked over his right shoulder, where Sample was supposed to be. But he saw no one.

"Where exactly are you, Bobby?"

"I'm back here on your *six.*"

"Get up on my right wingtip, where you belong, dammit. We ain't playing *follow the leader*."

A few seconds later, Sample's voice went from breathless to terrified. "OH MY GOD, THEY'RE EVERYWHERE! SHIT! SHIT! GET 'EM OFF ME!"

Then it was Tuttle's voice in Tommy's earphones, agitated but at least not panicking. "We've got bandits, Tommy. *FWs* are all over the place."

His head swiveled from side to side but he couldn't see anything behind him, not a jug, not a *Focke-Wulf 190*, either. He instinctively glanced up to where the mirror used to be, forgetting for a moment he'd ordered it removed. Then he cursed it and himself: "Fucking thing would've been fogged up, anyway."

Getting caught in a climb was the last place he wanted to be. He reminded himself that *jugs better be able to dive because they certainly won't climb*.

And his out-of-position wingman had put himself in a trap from which neither he nor Tommy could provide easy relief.

"Bobby, are you still climbing?"

In the high-pitched shriek of a frightened child, Sample replied, "Yeah, yeah, I am."

"Do a *split-s* out of there right fucking now."

Tommy put *Eclipse* into a diving right turn, hoping for a better view and a chance to help his hapless wingman. He never picked up Sample's diving plane, but he didn't have to look very hard for the *Focke-Wulf.* It sped right over his canopy, apparently trying to match *Eclipse's* turn but going too fast to achieve it.

That put Tommy right on his tail, but only for a second. The German kicked his rudder left and right a few times, fish-tailing his ship in an attempt to create confusion which direction he'd turn. Then he broke hard right.

This guy's no rookie. But I think I can keep up with him.

"*Blue Three* from *Blue Leader*, what's your status?"

There was no response.

"*Blue Two* from *Blue Leader*, are you guys okay, Jimmy?"

"Affirmative," Tuttle replied. "I think we scared a couple of 'em away."

"Any sign of Sample?"

"Negative. You need help?"

"Could sure use some, but find Sample first."

"Roger. Where are you, Tommy?"

"I'm not sure. East of you, I think, at *angels six*. Working my ass off trying to get a bead on this guy."

"Don't see you. You going up or down?"

"Up, at the moment."

Up took Tommy and the *Focke-Wulf* into a lingering deck of patchy clouds. The German plane could outclimb a P-47, but this pilot seemed reluctant to try, instead leading his pursuer on a twisting, turning rollercoaster ride across the sky.

Maybe he's their leader, and he's afraid to get too far from his rookies and leave them to the wolves. Good thing these clouds aren't too thick or I'd lose him for sure.

So far, Tommy had squeezed off three short bursts, to no apparent effect. *Wasted rounds, dammit. I'm not close enough.*

The *Focke-Wulf* broke left. It only took a second for Tommy to realize why: there was a bank of cumulus building in that direction, fluffing higher and wider by the minute. Once a stalked plane vanished into those clouds, its pursuer would have no idea where it might come out.

Gotta cut off his turn.

He pushed her throttle to the stop. Then he gingerly grabbed the supercharger lever.

I know I'm not supposed to do this, but...

He inched the lever up, watching the supercharger and prop rpm gauges climb to their red lines.

The roar of her engine took on a frightening, higher-pitched tone Tommy had never heard before. *Eclipse* leaped ahead like a scalded cat, closing the distance on the German in seconds.

Tommy fired another burst. He could see the flashes of bullet strikes on the *Focke-Wulf's* aft fuselage. She didn't falter, just reversed direction rapidly and headed up toward the peaks of the clouds.

It was all stick-and-rudder instinct from that point on. The two planes twisted and turned, vanishing for a second in downy puffs of cumulus, only to reappear and the dizzy dance continue.

The German kept going higher. *I guess he's finally trying to outclimb me*, Tommy thought. He fingered the supercharger lever again: *Do I dare?*

They must have been climbing almost straight up. There was no reference to judge the aircraft's attitude, and the airspeed was bleeding off rapidly. The clouds had erased the Earth's horizon; the artificial horizon in *Eclipse's* cockpit was pegged uselessly against its stops.

The only thing that matters now is I get a good shot at this Kraut before we both stall.

Eclipse's controls were getting mushy, making it almost impossible to line up the German in his gunsight. He'd never seen an airspeed indicator read that low on an aircraft that was still—technically—flying. But she wouldn't be flying much longer; the pre-stall buffeting had begun.

Just give me one damn shot!

He thought he had it. The *Focke-Wulf* slid into the gunsight's reticle. Before Tommy could squeeze the trigger, his prey suddenly went *straight up* and out of view.

UP? What the fuck is going—

And then the answer struck him like a brick between the eyes:

We're inverted. The Kraut stalled first. He didn't fall up. *He fell* down...*just like I'm about to do if I don't get this nose level and roll upright.*

By the time Tommy recovered his plane and broke out below the cloud deck, he was alone in the sky. The *Focke-Wulf* was gone.

"*Blue Two* from *Blue Leader*, you guys okay?"

"We're good. We got Sample back in the fold, too. Did you score?"

"Negative," Tommy replied. "You still in the target box?"

"Affirmative. Where are you?"

That was a good question. He'd been trying to figure that one out since the ground came back into view. But at least now he could see the smoke from the battle around Hill 262. "Looks like I'm about ten miles east. I'll be with you in a couple of minutes. How'd we do with the bombing? I haven't been paying attention."

"We did outstanding work," Tuttle replied. "The dogfaces will be buying our beer tonight, that's for damn sure. Got any rounds left?"

"About half a load."

"Good. There's still a little mopping up to do. Hurry on back…and watch your *six*, Tommy."

★★★★

The tankers of 37th Battalion quickly exploited the successes of the P-47s. By 1000 hours, they had pushed the few miles to the southern and eastern base of Hill 262. They left a killing field of dead soldiers and shattered vehicles from both sides. Once the GIs secured the north side of the hill, the Poles who'd survived the carnage would be rescued and the enemy's escape route to the east would be sealed. The Germans still fighting to keep that route open were being dealt the full wrath of the American fighter support.

Now that his tank had returned—alone—to Baker Company, Sean Moon found himself leading a different unit. Captain Newcomb told him, "With the Second and Third Platoons wiped out, we're down to two. Smitty will take the Second, you take the Fourth."

"No lieutenants in charge, sir?"

"Nope. They're all gone," Newcomb replied. "Simpson's still alive but his war's over. He's burned real bad. It's down to you four-stripers now. By the way, neither one of you has all his tanks, either. The B-17s knocked out three of our Shermans, counting Sposato's. The Krauts got the rest. But what the bomber jockeys did manage to actually drop on the enemy did a pretty good job. Of course, most of their fucking bombs didn't hit a damn thing, but that's par for the course, I guess."

"That's for damn sure, sir," Sean replied.

"But the P-47s put those eggs right where we needed them. Tell your brother thanks for me when you see him again. Opened up the playing field like a crowbar."

"My brother? You know he was flying one of those jugs?"

"No, I have no idea. Just guilt by association, I guess. Maybe Lieutenant Webster can tell you for sure."

"Do you know where the lieutenant is, sir?"

"Yeah. He and some of the artillery FOs are headed up Hill Two-Six-Two for a better view. You've got some work to do, though, don't you?"

★★★★

"Where the hell are we going now?" Fabiano asked Sean as *Eclipse* led the two other tanks in Fourth Platoon along a ridgeline road. "Ain't we done enough for one fucking day?"

"Apparently not, pal," Sean replied. "The colonel wants that road junction at the northeast corner behind *Two-Six-Two* sealed up. He don't want no surprises when the whole damn division moves up this way. There's already a couple of infantry companies holding it down, but they're gonna need some *Zippo* support if any panzers show their faces."

Fabiano shook his head in disgust. "I'll bet you volunteered us for this shit detail," he said.

"I don't volunteer for nothing, fuckhead. But you and that big mouth of yours just did." He called to his driver. "Hogan, stop the vehicle."

Eclipse clanked to a halt near three abandoned German tanks.

"Now, Fab," Sean said, "take a bucketful of them thermite grenades and roast all them tanks the Krauts were so thoughtful to leave unattended."

Fabiano didn't like the sound of that one bit. "I ain't getting out of this tank. We're in fucking Indian country. No place to be strolling around with my dick in my hand."

"You got a real taste for shit, Fab. Here's the deal: you can do it the easy way...or you're gonna do it with my size twelve up your ass. Your choice."

Fabiano's defiant expression and body language would indicate he had no intention of complying. Yet, he was already climbing out of the turret, mumbling, "This is bullshit, Sarge."

"Everything we do is bullshit, Fab. You oughta be used to it by now. Now hurry the fuck up. We ain't got all day."

Fabiano opened the case of thermite grenades tied to the aft deck. "And ain't it unsafe to have these fucking things sitting on the hull like this?"

"Would you rather have them inside with us? So they can roast our asses before we even have a chance to get out? Keep thinking like that and you ain't never gonna get your own tank."

"I don't want my own fucking tank, Sarge."

"I can live with that, too, Fab. No sweat off my nose."

Fabiano walked toward the nearest panzer, his Thompson strapped over his shoulder, his arms laden with grenades.

"Uh uh, Fab," Sean called out. "Not that one. Start with the farthest and work your way back, so you don't have to walk through a firestorm on the return trip. Let's use a little common sense here."

Sean couldn't hear what Fabiano mumbled in reply over the *thrum* of *Eclipse's* engine, but he imagined it was something like, *If you had any common sense, we wouldn't be doing this shit in the first fucking place.*

Sean called out, "Fabiano, you just volunteered again, didn't you?"

Hogan stood up in the driver's hatch, turned to Sean, and asked, "These Kraut tanks ain't even damaged. Why the hell'd they just leave them here?"

"It's the latest thing, Private," Sean replied. "They see fighter planes coming, they jump out and take a powder. They're scared shitless of them planes. Not sure why, though. To hear my brother talk, them flyboys only score hits on stuff by accident."

Hogan replied, "I wish they'd take a powder when they see us coming."

"Me, too, Hogie. Me, too."

Chapter Forty-Three

General Patton seemed more fired up than usual. Enthusiastically slapping General Wood on the back, he said, "I'll be a son of a bitch, John. Once again, your Fourth Armored has done one hell of a job."

Glad for the praise but in no mood to celebrate quite yet, Wood replied, "Thank you, sir, but we haven't turned the north corner of *Two-Six-Two* yet…and we've gotten the shit kicked out of us just getting to where we are."

He might as well have been barking at the moon. Patton's enthusiasm was undamped as he spread a map across the hood of his jeep. "Ah, but you will, John…and very soon. And when you do, that German exodus is going to turn north like diverting a great river, straight toward Monty. It's got nowhere else to go. We've got them blocked, Bradley's kicking them in the ass…and Monty's taking his sweet fucking time joining the fight, as always. Hell, I wouldn't be surprised if he started backing up when the Germans start coming at him. It'd be just like him."

Wood replied, "You really think that would happen, sir?"

"Hell, yes, I do. That little Limey clerk doesn't know a damn thing about pursuit. Hell, Ike doesn't, either, but at least he's learning. But Monty's so convinced the sun rises out of his asshole, he'll never learn a damn thing."

"Couldn't agree with you more on that score, sir," Wood said.

"Now listen up, John. You'll be taking more prisoners than you ever dreamed possible. We're setting up POW camps outside every town along the Argentan-Gacé highway. The one we set up at Nonant-le-Pin is already full to the gills. Over fifteen thousand of Hitler's finest in that camp alone. It's the same story at the camps First Army set up, too. Our engineers are doing nothing but building corrals for them right now."

"How many POWs are we expecting, sir?"

"At least one hundred thousand, John, when all is said and done. Maybe a whole lot more. Hell, we're talking about a whole Kraut army here…and maybe more. I'm hearing rumors we may bag some of Fifth Panzer Army, too."

Wood blew a whistle of surprise, like the sound of a bomb falling.

"Just keep those POWs out of your way, John, and don't slow down for anything. Use every admin trooper you got to play prison guard. Don't you dare take one man off your front line to babysit prisoners, you hear me?"

"Yes, sir. I understand," Wood replied.

Blue Flight was on their third sortie of the day. Their mission remained the same: protect the right flank of 3rd Army. Despite the abundance of targets on their first two sorties, they'd been lazily orbiting their area of responsibility for 30 minutes with no calls from the ASOs and no Germans in sight.

"Maybe the war ended and they forgot to tell us," Jimmy Tuttle offered.

Their headsets spit the reply, "In your dreams, *Blue Flight*." It was the voice of Charlie Webster with 37th Tank. He read off a string of coordinates and then added, "Something strange going on over that way. How about doing a little recon for us…and whatever else you feel is righteous?"

Two minutes later, *Blue Flight* was over the area Webster identified. At first, Tommy and his pilots saw nothing out of the ordinary, just another patch of hilly French farmland crisscrossed by a few narrow roads that were little more than trails. As Tommy dropped *Eclipse* lower for a better look, he told his pilots, "Don't forget—if we get jumped again, pickle those bombs before you try to tangle with them."

Despite the tinny, filtered audio quality of their aircraft radios, the tone of an indifferent adolescent came through loud and clear in Tuttle's voice: "Yes, mother. You really don't need to tell us that, you know."

Descending below a thousand feet, something began to look very strange to Tommy: a mass of gray was flooding over one of the roads, surging to the south like spilled oil.

At 500 feet there was no doubt what that mass was: German soldiers, hundreds of them, walking slowly—reluctantly—as if on some forced march. Their faces were looking up at Tommy. Some waved their arms. Others waved white flags of surrender.

"You aren't going to believe this, guys," he said, "but there are a bunch of Krauts surrendering to us."

"You're right," Tuttle replied, "I think you're pulling my leg. Gotta be some kind of Kraut trick."

"I don't think so, Jimmy. They look pretty keen on surrendering. I'm going to try and wrangle them south.

Once they hit the highway, there's bound to be an American unit to reel them in."

"How the hell are you going to *wrangle* them?"

"Just watch me."

Tommy brought *Eclipse* around in a full circle that encompassed the Germans. Then, heading south, he flew low over their heads straight down the road, waggling his wings the entire pass as if he was waving back. "There," he said, "complete with a gesture of good will. Let's see if they got the message."

They did. The Germans trudged off toward the highway, white flags flying. When Tommy advised Charlie Webster of what was coming down the road toward the GIs, the ASO thought his leg was being pulled, too.

Fifteen minutes later, *Blue Flight* was back on station with 37th Tank, dropping their bombs on Germans who were definitely *not* surrendering. In the middle of it all, Webster relayed a message from General Wood: *Congratulations! Before today, I'd never seen with my own eyes a case of ground troops surrendering to aircraft. It's a sure sign we've got them beat. Well done!*

The trip would take all afternoon, they were sure. The four *maquis*—Pierre, Sylvie, Eva, and Dominique—were bicycling from Orville to Vimoutiers. Not that the distance was great—it was just a little over six miles, a trivial stretch to people who pedaled everywhere—but the *Boche* had the highway totally clogged with men and vehicles in both directions, often forcing them to walk their bikes along the rough shoulder rather than ride. Fresh troops and tanks were trundling toward the fighting just a few miles west, what the Americans were calling the fight for Hill 262. Haggard, exhausted soldiers—the once-proud defenders of Normandy—staggered in the opposite direction, grateful for a moment to have escaped what they, too, had termed the *triangle of death*. But they knew their salvation would be a short one, for they'd be reorganized into surviving units and thrown back into battle against the Allies somewhere else.

"Look at them," Eva said of the escapees, "they're nothing but tired old men and terrified little boys." To the annoyance of the other *maquis*, she hadn't bother to keep her voice down.

"Are you trying to get us all killed, woman?" Pierre whispered angrily in her ear.

"No, I believe that's your job, *monsieur*," she replied, without a hint of the respect the term usually implied.

"Both of you, be quiet," Sylvie said. "Why don't we rest in the shade of those trees over there for a little while?"

Eva and Dominique liked that idea very much. They were already pushing their bikes that way when Pierre protested, "We cannot stop. We're already late."

Sylvie faced the highway and spread her arms wide, a gesture meant to take in the scope and impassibility of the traffic snarl before them. "There is nothing we can do about being *late*," she said. "If they can't wait for us, let them do whatever they have in mind without us." She looked up at the gathering clouds and said, "I'm a bit surprised the American planes haven't attacked. Once it gets overcast, they'll have missed their chance. Such a shame…the *Boche* look like such easy targets on this road."

Finding a shady spot to her liking, Eva parked her bike against a tree and lay down in the grass, luxuriating in the refreshing coolness. Sylvie and Dominique quickly joined her. Pierre remained standing, nervously smoking a cigarette. He cast an eye skyward and warned, "Sylvie is right about one thing—the weather will change very soon. You know how summer afternoons can be."

"So what? We've been wet before," Eva replied, cackling at her double entendre.

Sylvie and Dominique couldn't help but smile.

"You're disgusting," Sylvie said, pretending to scold but failing miserably to sound serious.

Eva suddenly stopped laughing. Her head reared back like a snake about to strike. "Is that so?" she snarled. "That's a very interesting comment from someone who whored for the *Boche*."

Dominique slid between them. "That's not true, Eva. You know she was—"

"Shut up, Dominique," Sylvie interrupted. "I can fight my own battles."

"Pretty young thing," Eva taunted. "Those *Boche* couldn't keep themselves from planting their filthy pricks between your legs, could they?"

"I played the part I was told to play. Nobody was at greater risk than me. And you're all still alive because I played the part so well."

Eva spit on the ground in disgust. "Such *merde*. You loved every minute of it."

"I hated every minute of it, Eva."

"Rubbish. Your *connard* of a husband loved every minute of it, too, I'll bet."

Sylvie thought that one over for a few moments. Then, without a hint of anger, she replied, "You're probably right on that score, Eva."

They realized Pierre was looking on, his mouth agape, his face a ghostly shade of white. He'd overheard the entire exchange. He looked so shocked, so scandalized, so ridiculous, that they couldn't help themselves. The women collapsed flat on the ground, laughing hysterically.

Once she could catch her breath, Sylvie said to him, "War is hell, no? Or didn't you realize?"

Pierre had no reply. He just walked away into the woods, hoping, perhaps, not to hear any more.

Eva asked, "So tell me, Sylvie, with all that fucking, did you ever get pregnant?"

"No, not once."

"You must have used some very good *prophylactiques*, then. Certainly not those *Boche* or French abominations that feel like barbed wire scraping out your *vagin*."

With an air of embarrassment, Dominique asked, "What's wrong with French *prophylactiques*?"

Sylvie snapped her reply: "Oh, is that what my husband used with you?" She watched the look of alarm spread across Dominique's face, letting the thunderous silence grow for a moment before adding, with an apologetic smile, "I'm only joking with you, Dominique." She leaned over and gave the trembling woman a hug. "No hard feelings, please?"

"Only men get *hard* feelings," Eva chimed in, reveling in the double entendre once again, "and the bastards get them all the fucking time. But you never answered my question about the *prophylactiques*, Sylvie."

"There is no answer. I didn't use any. It wasn't necessary. Not for me."

The silence loomed between the women once again until Eva took Sylvie in her motherly arms. "Oh, I'm so sorry, *mon amie*. Are you positive you can't conceive?"

"Three doctors say so."

On the verge of tears, Dominique whispered, "That is so sad."

"No, it really isn't," Sylvie replied. "For now, it's been a blessing. But I don't know how I'll feel about it later, though, when everything is different."

★★★★

Blue Flight wouldn't get to fly a fourth sortie that day. Thunderstorms were sweeping across Hill 262 and the battlegrounds surrounding it. All the squadrons supporting 3rd Army were grounded until they passed and the skies cleared.

"It's a damn shame," Colonel Pruitt told his pilots. "Patton had his sights set on securing Hill Two-Six-Two before sunset today. But since the weather's preventing us from flying *maximum effort* in support, that one final push is going to have to wait until tomorrow. Be ready for *wheels up* at sunrise. Have a good night, gentlemen."

"Ain't that great news?" Jimmy Tuttle said. "We've got plenty of time to go have supper and a few beers in Alençon and still grab a couple of hours' sleep before breaking ground again. The hell with the officers' mess."

"Yeah," Tommy replied, "sounds like a great idea. I'll catch up with you guys in a bit. I want to check a couple of things over with Sergeant McNulty first."

He found the crew chief at the supply shed, rummaging through stacks of sheet metal. "Your Lieutenant Sample is a lucky man," McNulty said. "There are exactly seventeen holes in his aft fuselage. It's a fucking miracle nothing important got hit. It's all just tin damage. I trust you gave him a right earful, sir?"

"Yeah, I don't think he'll be leaving our ass end uncovered like that again. Not if he can help it, anyway."

McNulty was holding out something in his hand. Tommy didn't recognize it for a few moments. Then it hit him: *It's my rearview mirror.*

"You sure you don't want me to stick this back on, sir?"

"No, Sarge. I'm fine without it. Really."

McNulty tossed the mirror back onto a shelf. "As you wish, sir. You still happy with the extra bomb instead of the rockets, too?"

"Blissfully happy, Sarge. They actually land pretty damn close to where you're aiming."

"You know, Lieutenant, I saw the tech specs for the new five-inch rocket *insulations* coming down the pipe."

"You mean *installations*, right?"

"Yeah, that's what I said. I'm telling you, sir…they look slicker than snot. Got the *imprint* of a one-oh-five cannon, too."

I'm sure he means impact*…but I'll let it go.*

"That may be, Sarge, but can you actually hit what you're aiming at? Do the tech specs say anything about that?"

McNulty just shrugged. Then he asked, "You see your gun camera film yet? Did you hit that Kraut bastard?"

"Yeah, it looks like I did. But he must've been lucky like Sample. My rounds hit *nothing important*, apparently. The son of a bitch flew away."

"Maybe you can claim a probable?"

Tommy laughed. "I don't think so, Sarge. He's got to actually go down. *Close* only counts in horseshoes and hand grenades."

"I don't know, Lieutenant…if you can get a credit, I say take it. Don't cut off your nose *despite* your face."

★★★★

Jimmy Tuttle was looking for a good meal. He led the two rookies of *Blue Flight*—Sample and Esposito—to his favorite *bistro* on Alençon's *grand-rue.* Tommy Moon was looking for something else, though.

"Where's the boss going?" Esposito asked as Tommy hurried away toward *Café Madeleine.*

Tuttle replied, "He's looking for a little *horizontal refreshment*, Espo."

"You mean he's going to that whorehouse? They told us that place was off limits. We'd get court-martialed if we got caught there."

"Kid, if they did that, every swinging dick in Third Army—and the Nineteenth Tac Fighter Command—would be in the stockade. They'd have to call off the war, and that's certainly not going to happen. No, laddie…our fearless leader's got himself a much sweeter deal than what you buy in a cathouse."

Sample asked, "You mean he found himself a *hershey bar*?"

Tuttle shook his head, like a schoolmaster disappointed with his naive pupil. "No, son. *Hershey bars* are so desperate they'll do it for candy. Maybe even cigarettes. Nothing desperate about the lady Tommy's shacked up with, believe you me."

★★★★

From his station behind the bar, Sylvie's uncle Honoré had been on the lookout for Tommy the past four nights. He had no trouble picking out the diminutive man wearing pilot's wings from the sea of Americans flooding *Café Madeleine.* Catching his eye, he motioned for Tommy to come to the bar.

Without saying a word or offering a smile, the uncle poured Tommy a beer and set it in front of him. Next to the glass, he placed an envelope. "This has been waiting for you, Lieutenant," he said in French, and then walked away to tend to some other GIs crowding the bar rail.

He didn't want to open it at first. *It's a goodbye letter. She's going to say how sweet and tender it was, how she'll never forget me, blah blah blah...but the bottom line's going to be she really can't, she really shouldn't...*

So fuck off.

But he opened it anyway. In English, she'd written:

My dear sweet Tommy,

I'm counting on you to destroy this note as soon as you've read it.

I've been called away. I don't know what I'll be doing or for how long. I couldn't tell you even if I did know. You understand why.

I hope with all my heart you'll still be at the airfield at Alençon when I'm able to return. In the meantime, I beg you not to worry about me. Let it be enough for us that I worry constantly about you.

It's only been a few hours but already I miss you terribly. Until we meet again,

Love,
S

Beneath her name was the lipstick impression where she'd kissed the paper.

His elation only lasted a few seconds, pushed aside by the dread of whatever unknown jeopardy she was in right now. He had to flee the café; he was in no mood to be surrounded by boisterous GIs, celebrating that, for at least this one night, no one was telling them to kill or be killed.

But somewhere—probably not too far away, either—he was sure someone was telling that very thing to the woman he loved. And all the begging she could muster couldn't stop him from being worried out of his mind.

Chapter Forty-Four

Sean had thought about it all night, and now that the sun was coming up, he was more convinced than ever: *We're screwed. When our guys try to round the north end of Two-Six-Two, this road we're sitting on is the one the Krauts are gonna come barreling down to stop them. And all we've got to hold them off is three Zippos and what's left of two infantry companies.*

This terrain ain't even good tank country...too hilly, too wooded, narrow roads running through valleys, trees cutting visibility in every direction. Our tanks are just fixed guns in steel tubs, with nowhere to maneuver. At least if we gotta go head to head with the Kraut armor, it'll be at real short range, so we might have a chance of a first-round kill. But if we miss, they'll turn us inside out. And with high ground all around us like this, these radios don't work for shit. Our only commo with the outside world is a relay through the artillery FO on that ridge behind us. Something happens to him, it's all over.

Kowalski, the loader and backup gunner, was the only man in *Eclipse's* crew who'd managed a nap during the night. Everybody else passed up their turn. They were too keyed up to sleep. "Hey, Sarge," Kowalski said, "now that the sun's coming up, how about I go outside, start a little fire and heat up this coffee?"

"No, *Ski*. No one's getting out of the fucking tank."

"What if I gotta take a leak?"

"Piss out the escape hatch on the bottom like everyone else."

"Ah, come on, Sarge. Just for a couple of minutes. I need my *joe*."

"I said *negative*, Private. For all we know, there are Krauts fifty fucking feet away in those woods. They had all night to sneak up here."

★★★★

Sylvie slid the baker's peel into the stone oven, slipping it beneath the big round loaves of bread called *boules*. With a smooth motion, she pulled the peel from the oven and deposited the boules on a waiting cart. The bakery's owner, a woman in her fifties named Angelique, nodded her approval. "You're getting the hang of this, young lady," Angelique said. "*Très bon.*"

The owner cast a wary eye to the old German sergeant lounging in a corner. He was a mess steward by trade, detailed by the local Wehrmacht commander to ensure maximum output and no trickery from this commandeered bakery at Vimoutiers. He'd found the duty most pleasing, since all the bakers were women. With the exception of that crone Angelique, most weren't too bad looking, either, in his estimation. Especially those three new ones who'd joined the staff just this morning, signing on to help keep the Wehrmacht fed. He'd written down their names to help him remember: *Eva, Dominique, and Sylvie.*

There were other benefits of this posting, as well. His supervisory duties weren't very taxing; the women required little oversight, since they'd worked as bakers even before the occupation. Free from the prying eyes of the officers, the sergeant could take a nip of schnapps whenever he wanted. Much more than just a nip, usually.

Once he got to feeling really *happy*, he found it great sport to stroll among the women as they toiled, pretending to take interest in what they were doing so he could rub against them, sneaking peeks down the front of their work dresses, unbuttoned to their brassieres in the sultry heat of the bakery. He found the rivulets of sweat running down between a woman's breasts to be a thing of fascinating beauty. Once he'd downed half a bottle, he'd be concocting schemes to convince one of the women to let him lick that sweat off. He didn't care who, just so it was anyone younger than *that old cow Angelique.*

Sylvie was pushing another cart of bread onto the delivery van when she saw Pierre standing across the alley behind the bakery. He wore a white flower in the lapel of his worn suit jacket. "That's the signal," Sylvie told Angelique. "The *plastique* has arrived. *Opération Pain Chaude* happens tomorrow."

When she walked back inside the bakery, Sylvie nodded to Eva and Dominique. Each woman grabbed a full cart and pushed it out to the delivery van. The German sergeant didn't notice; the bottle of schnapps was nearly half empty. Very soon, he'd be in his *happy* frame of mind.

"We'll need to distract that old *Boche* bastard when the time comes," Eva said.

Sylvie replied, "That shouldn't be too difficult."

Eva gave her a leering look. "Oh, I see. Your specialty, is it not?"

Before Sylvie could say a word, Dominique spoke up: "No. I'll do it. You two are better with the explosives, anyway."

"Fine," Sylvie said, pulling Angelique into their circle. "Now remember," she told the old woman, "none of the other women—and I mean absolutely *no one*—must know what we're doing. We can't trust any of them to keep their mouths shut, especially if they're interrogated by the *Boche*. Is that clear?"

"Yes," Angelique replied. "Quite clear."

Sean's tankers had been hearing the distant rumble of engines since dawn, but not one vehicle had challenged them. From *Eclipse's* turret, Sean could only see about a quarter of a mile ahead, to the bend in the road. He'd asked the captain commanding the infantry to put an observation post at the bend or even beyond, to give at least a few extra moment's warning of the Germans' approach. But the captain had refused, claiming he didn't have enough field telephones or working radios to stay in touch with an OP. "Besides," the captain had said, "that's what the FO on the ridge behind us is for."

Sean protested; he'd already talked with the FO and knew that from his position he couldn't see the road beyond the bend, either, just the tops of trees flanking it. "Maybe he'll see the smoke from their exhausts, sir," he'd told the captain, "but that's about all."

"That'll have to be enough, then, Sergeant," the captain had replied.

It wasn't enough. The first panzer—a Panther—rounded the bend unannounced. They'd heard her coming, but judging distance and direction as the sound echoed around the hills and valleys proved impossible. It was like watching a bad dream unfold as the muzzle of her main gun appeared first, quickly followed by the ominous gray bulk of her hull.

"You got him, Fab?" Sean asked, practically breathing down his gunner's neck.

"Yeah," Fabiano replied, his finger on the firing button. "On the way."

Eclipse rocked with the recoil of her own shot.

The round hit the Panther squarely on the split line between hull and turret. Her commander, standing in his turret hatch, was launched high into the air like human fireworks. She came to an abrupt stop, her main gun slightly off-center but not traversing, its tube sagging below the horizontal.

"Crank the engine, Hogan," Sean said. "Fight's on."

An infantry lieutenant was running toward *Eclipse*. From the corner of his eye, Sean saw him coming and watched as the bullet struck him in the chest, knocking him backward off his feet. He couldn't hear a sound over the roar of *Eclipse's* engine coming to life, but he felt that sickening *phftt-splat* of the round streaking to and hitting its target all the same.

Shit! They really do have snipers in the woods.

Sean felt sure he knew what the lieutenant was planning to tell him: *It's too hot! We're pulling back!*

He told his crew, "I think our infantry's gonna pull out, if they haven't already. Kowalski, get on the horn and tell the other two *Zippos* to *circle the wagons* and button up. We've got snipers out there somewhere. Then get the FO to relay to Lieutenant Webster so he can call in the jugs. Hogan, pull up behind that Panther we just knocked out."

Eclipse lurched forward as Hogan asked, "You really sure we knocked it out, Sarge?"

Thick smoke was starting to waft from the Panther's hatches and vents. The commander who'd been launched from his turret had been the only man seen to leave the tank.

"Yeah, Hogan, I'm pretty damn sure. Get us there, right fucking now."

"Hey, Sarge," Kowalski said, "the FO said he'd relay the message, but he's pulling out, too."

Sean replied, "Well, ain't that just fucking ducky? You'd think these guys have never been in contact with the enemy before."

Hesitantly, Fabiano joined the discussion. "If everybody else is leaving, maybe we should be pulling back, too, Sarge?"

"Bullshit. We don't take orders from some scared-shitless infantry captain. The colonel wants us to hold this road, and that's what we're gonna do."

Eclipse lumbered ahead. When it reached the dead Panther, Sean told his driver, "Okay, turn into her so the main gun's over her foredeck. Yeah, that's good. Just like that."

"You don't want me to push her out of the way, do you, Sarge? I don't think we can."

"Fuck no. We're gonna use her for cover. If their armor's so damn good, let's take advantage of it. Any Kraut coming up the road'll have to shoot through her to get to us."

"But she's already burning, Sarge. What if she blows up?"

"We're in a tank, numbnuts. Who gives a shit?"

Sean poked his head out of his hatch to check the positioning of the other two Shermans. They'd *circled the wagons* like he'd commanded, forming a close, three-pointed star with their aft ends facing each other and all their firepower facing outward. "Good job, guys," he said over the radio. "If our own infantry won't keep the Kraut infantry off our backs, we'll do it ourselves."

He didn't bother adding, *Of course, if we get smacked by aircraft while we're bunched up like this, we're fucked. But we ain't seen much of the Luftwaffe since hitting France, anyway, so what the hell?*

A second Panther rolled into view around the far bend, climbing the road toward her shattered sister. Watching the approaching tank, Fabiano asked, "She don't look too concerned. I can count their heads. All the hatches are still wide open."

Sean replied, "I don't think they can even see us, unless they got some clown up a tree somewhere. With this dead panzer in front of us and all the smoke she's making, we might as well be invisible."

"When do you want me to plug her, Sarge?"

"Take her at three hundred yards, Fab."

"That's cutting it awful close, ain't it?"

"Just want to be dead sure we kill her with one shot."

At 300 yards, that's exactly what Fabiano did, forsaking the thick frontal armor to knock another turret askew. "That's two," he muttered, as he watched the enemy tank brew up through his gunsight.

By the time the third Panther appeared, the German tankers had figured out the game. She was still nearly a thousand yards away when she stopped and fired. The round struck the dead Panther right in front of *Eclipse*, showering her harmlessly with sparks and metal fragments. The concussion made Sean's crew feel like they'd been hit in the balls with a hammer. But that was the extent of the damage.

"Should I take the shot?" Fabiano asked.

"Don't waste it. Let her get closer."

"Maybe she's not gonna, Sarge. Maybe she'll just sit there and lob rounds our way until this carcass in front of us blows itself apart."

"And when that happens, Fab, it'll be our cue to scram."

Blue Flight didn't recognize the voice of the ASO giving them the mission. It wasn't Charlie Webster or Herb Clinchmore; they were sure of that. But the authorization was per the code list, so they proceeded to the coordinates a few miles to the northeast of Hill 262. The target, they were told, was a column of German armor threatening this crucial pivot point in the push to surround and secure the hill.

Tommy wasn't happy the ASO didn't have eyes on the target. Even worse, there would be no smoke marking by artillery. *Blue Flight* would have to locate the target, identify it, and then attack it. That would be no easy task in the uneven terrain below, where an object might only be in plain sight for a brief moment in the constantly shifting view of a low-level pilot. In the next moment, that object could very easily have vanished into the shadows of a defile or the cover of trees.

I hate this shit, Tommy told himself. *This is how mistakes get made.*

He caught a hint of smoke rising from a road winding through the hills.

Exhaust smoke? Or a burning vehicle?

A hard bank, a quick change of direction to keep the smoke in view.

Holy cow...there's a shit-load of tanks down there on that road. But whose are they? The road runs north-south. Anybody could be coming from either direction.

Wait...there are some trucks way back in the column that don't look anything like GI deuce-and-a halves. And something small that looks like a jeep...but it's too angular. Probably one of those kübelwagen things.

These got to be the Krauts.

"Blue Flight from *Leader.* Target identified. Let's get 'em."

****

The third panther hadn't moved an inch from where it had fired its first shot. It had just put its fourth round into the carcass of her sister, *Eclipse's* first victim, now serving as her shield. "C'mon, Sarge," Fabiano pleaded, "let me take a shot at that bastard."

"No," Sean replied. "Bouncing one off her ain't gonna change a damn thing. Just hold your water a little longer."

There was a call on the radio from one of the other Shermans: "Hey, looks like the jugs are here, at your three o'clock. Keep your head down, though…that fucking sniper just *dinged* one off my turret."

Sean spun around for a better look through his open hatch. Sure enough, four aircraft began to orbit high overhead. He couldn't pick up a definitive silhouette as they banked steeply in the circle, showing only side views. But he told himself, *They sure look like jugs. Too bad I can't talk to them and tell them what's going on, because they'll never be able to figure out who's who in this little standoff we've got going on here. They need to be looking for Krauts farther up the road, anyway.*

One plane broke the circle, rolling hard on her back and plummeting almost straight down toward him.

Holy shit...it looks like she's attacking. What the fuck would a jug be doing that for?

Showing only her front profile, the plane seemed almost stationary in the dive for interminable seconds—until she pulled out. Then Sean could see the planform of her wings clearly for just a moment before she streaked past.

Ain't that shape all wrong for a jug? The wings should look like butter knives. That plane's are kinda squared off...

Maybe she's British?

Nah. There'd be invasion stripes on those wings if she was, just like every other Allied plane's got. And I sure as hell didn't see any.

Or maybe I did?

The aircraft had left a reminder of its dive behind: a small, almost invisible dot at first, growing larger with each rapid heartbeat as it fell straight toward him like a fly ball to a perfectly positioned center fielder.

Like Coach used to say, it's got my name on it.

But there was something Sean used to say, too, and he spoke it out loud in those last seconds when everything that's ever happened before was replayed and then erased forever:

"Just a matter of time."

Chapter Forty-Five

Blue Flight left the column of vehicles they'd bombed and strafed ablaze and battered. Circling so the other three jugs could form back up on him, Tommy felt the elation of the successful strike quickly draining away. It was being replaced by a vague dread: *If anyone asked me right now what kind of vehicles we just attacked, all I could answer is "German." And I wouldn't even be certain of that.*

We won't know what we hit until the intel guys see the gun camera footage later...and maybe not even then. I'm not looking forward to that debrief. Not one bit.

Sample had just tucked up on Tommy's left wingtip. For a split second, Tommy thought he could see Tuttle and Esposito climbing out after their final pass—but then he realized it couldn't possibly be them. There were more than two planes closing on him...*Three. No, four.* And though he could only see them head-on, there was no mistaking them for P-47s, Tempests, Typhoons, Mustangs, or any other single-engined fighter in the Allied inventories: *They're Focke-Wulfs. FW-190s.*

He didn't recognize his own shrill voice as he said, "SAMPLE, BREAK LEFT NOW. BREAK, BREAK."

Sure the Germans would overshoot, Tommy banked and pulled *Eclipse* hard to try and come around on their tails. He was relieved to see Sample doing the same, holding a perfect wingman's station off his leader's wingtip.

What he didn't see, though, was the trailing two *FWs* had pulled straight up, trading speed for altitude and advantage. Pulling hard over the top, they swooped down onto the Americans' tails. Two quick bursts sent Sample's plane tumbling down. If there was a parachute, Tommy never saw it.

But he couldn't help but see the flashes of bullet strikes on the top of his own wing, their sound like marbles being dropped on a hard floor.

He called to Tuttle, "Sample's down. Can you get this guy off my tail, Jimmy?

"Love to, Half. As soon as I get these two off mine."

Tommy's head swiveled rapidly, one side to the other and back again, trying to put eyes on his attacker. But he saw nothing but the sky swirling behind him.

He looked up to where the rear view mirror used to be. Whether it would have done him any good didn't matter now. All he knew was that it wasn't there, and he wished it was.

The Kraut must be underneath me now. I'll have to—

It was all happening too fast. Before his brain could tell his hands and feet what to do, bullets announced themselves with a rapid *thunk-thunk-thunk* as they punched holes in the aluminum of the fuselage. Those bullets had done their job: finding the range for the cannon shells which followed in the blink of an eye. Their much louder *POOM-POOM-POOM* sounded like death breaking down your door.

Eclipse's engine began to sputter as flames licked from beneath the cowl flaps. The control stick in Tommy's hand didn't seem to be controlling very much of anything anymore. She'd begun a slow roll that no amount of aileron input corrected. Her nose was dropping steadily. Her rudder pedals had gone limp against his feet.

He was already pulling the emergency release on the canopy. It was time to get out.

★★★★

Just before noon, the lead elements of 4th Armored fought their way to the north side of Hill 262, pivoted west, and sealed the Falaise Gap. The rest of Patton's 3rd Army began to push in behind them, forcing the German counter-attackers away. The hundred thousand or more German soldiers now completely surrounded had three choices: surrender immediately to the Americans west, south, and east of them; stagger north until they met the British, whose lines were still some five miles away; or fight to the death.

Very few elected the final choice. But a surprisingly large number turned north, toward the British.

Colonel Abrams pondered a possible reason: "Maybe they think they still have a chance for a breakout through Monty's boys?"

"That'd be my guess," General Wood replied, "although it'd be just wishful thinking at this point. But I'm guessing ol' Georgie Patton is enjoying the hell out of this. He did say that if Montgomery wouldn't come to the Germans, he'd push the Germans to him. And that's exactly what's happening."

Wood turned serious as he asked, "Your boys did a real fine job turning that corner, Creighton, but I know it was a hell of a rough ride. In your estimation, is your 37th Tank Battalion a viable combat unit at this time?"

"Negative, sir. We're little more than a glorified company now. I've got more dead and wounded than I've got able-bodied troopers."

It was difficult for him to speak that last sentence. Colonel Abrams turned away so the general might not see the tears welling up in his eyes. Softly, he said, "I just hope to God we bagged enough of those bastards to make this all worth it."

★★★★

The door to the cellar slammed open, startling Lieutenant Peterson awake. Another American officer—a pilot—was being pushed down the stairs at gunpoint by his German guard. The pilot's arm was in a sling. He looked like he'd been through hell.

The guard departed, slamming the cellar door behind him. Peterson heard the sliding bolt on the upstairs side of the door *clank* into place. The pilot, his slight frame now slumped into a corner, forced a smile and said, "My name's Tommy Moon, Three-oh-First Fighter Squadron. What are you in for?"

Peterson found himself smiling, too. *This poor bastard looks like he's had the shit beat out of him, and yet he can still manage to crack wise. Gotta respect that.*

"I'm John Peterson," he replied, "I'm a rifle company commander with Fifth Infantry Division…or at least I used to be. Moon, you say your name is? You wouldn't happen to have a brother who's a tanker, would you?"

Tommy sat straight up, as if the pain of his injuries had been suddenly overridden by a far more important consideration. "Yeah, I do. His name's Sean. He's with the—"

"That's the guy I'm talking about. Staff Sergeant Sean Moon."

"Have you seen him lately?"

"As a matter of fact, I ran into him two nights ago in the village of Survie. We were both part of a clever little plan to hit Second SS Panzer's HQ in Champosoult, which is exactly where we are right now. He was supposed to come back with a whole damn armored command—*CC Baker*, they called it—but they never showed. Now I ain't blaming your brother—I know a staff sergeant doesn't run this damn war—but those tankers left me and my guys high and dry."

Peterson's head dropped back against the wall, and he stared at the wood-beamed ceiling, bracing himself for the pain that would accompany the words coming next.

"I can only pray some of my guys got away," he whispered.

"What the hell happened, John?"

"We got cut to ribbons in a night fight. My own goddamn fault. I walked us right into a trap. At least twenty of my men were captured, though, along with me. The Krauts marched them off to someplace else. Can't put the officers and enlisted men together, you know." He raised his hand in a mock toast before adding, "So welcome to the officers' quarters, Tommy Moon." He shook the *slop jar* that served as a toilet. "Real deluxe accommodations."

"But Sean was okay when you last saw him?"

"Yeah. Fit as a fiddle. He's a tough cookie, your brother."

Tommy rolled his eyes. "Yeah, I know he is. So we're in Champosoult? At a panzer division HQ?"

"That's right. Second SS Panzer. I keep expecting to get hustled off any minute to Germany and some POW camp, but the Krauts seem to be pretty busy with other matters at the moment. Can't see a damn thing from down in this cellar, but I can hear them upstairs yelling orders all hours of the day and night. And about every ten minutes, this whole building shakes when some tanks roll by. I guess you got shot down?"

"Yeah, this morning. I think I broke my arm bailing out. Must've hit the stabilizer or something. Hurts like a son of a bitch. And let me tell you, it's pretty hard operating a parachute with only one good arm. Ended up in a damn tree. By the time I got myself down on the ground—and that was no small feat, either—they were all over me. I know my wingman got shot down, too. Don't know how the other two guys in my flight made out." It was Tommy's turn to forlornly contemplate the rafters in the ceiling as he added, "And I'm not real sure what the hell we were attacking."

"But are we winning, Tommy? Do we have those Krauts in the *Gap* trapped yet?"

"As of a couple of hours ago…no, I don't think we do."

"Shit. Another golden opportunity slipping through our fingers. It's all that slowpoke Montgomery's fault. That man's going to be late to his own funeral."

★★★★

Lieutenant Jimmy Tuttle walked across the ramp at A-14, trying to ignore the two empty parking spots where Tommy's and Sample's planes should've been parked. The mission debrief had been torture; he hadn't known the answers to so many of the intelligence officer's probing questions. Everything had happened much too fast, and there was so little of which to be certain.

To a debriefing officer, uncertainty smelled like negligence, carelessness—even guilt. He harped on the fact that *Blue Flight* had initiated an attack without positive identification of its target. "You do understand, Lieutenant, that there are procedures in place to prevent *friendly fire* incidents, and from what you're telling me, your flight didn't comply with any of them."

"Of course I understand that, sir," Tuttle had replied, "but they don't call it the *fog of war* for nothing, you know. How it was today is what it's like a good part of the time. We did the best we could with the little info we got."

Tuttle desperately needed the vindication of the gun camera footage. He swore the evaluation of that footage had never taken so long. When he saw Colonel Pruitt heading his way, he braced himself for the verdict.

"You took out a whole column of Tiger tanks and Ferdinand assault guns," the colonel said. "Excellent results. The intel boys are giving *Blue Flight* credit for seven armored vehicles destroyed outright and at least half a dozen more damaged and out of action."

Pruitt cast a solemn glance to the empty parking spots. "Hell of a price, though."

Across the ramp, Sergeant McNulty was searching for something in the parts shed. His eyes fell on the rear view mirror he'd removed from Tommy's plane. Reverently, he removed it from the shelf and placed it on the workbench. Then he picked up a heavy crescent wrench and began beating it into oblivion.

He'd struck the mirror a dozen blows already—the glass was long shattered, the fairing mangled almost beyond recognition—before Colonel Pruitt appeared in the shed's doorway.

"AT EASE, SERGEANT," the colonel said.

McNulty turned to him, arms outstretched, a teary-eyed child in a man's body.

"Do you realize the penalty for willfully destroying government property, Sergeant?"

McNulty laid the wrench down. Lowering his head, he clasped his hands before him in an act of contrition. "I'm well aware, sir. I'm ready to take my medicine."

"Very well. Come with me, Sergeant."

They walked in silence to the officers' mess. The colonel directed McNulty to take a seat on a bench outside. "I'll be right back," Pruitt said. "Stay put."

When he returned, he took a seat on the bench, produced a flask from his pocket, and placed it in the startled sergeant's hand.

"This is the only medicine I know for times like this," the colonel said. "Bottoms up, Sergeant. And when you're done, pass that thing back."

Chapter Forty-Six

21ST ARMY GROUP COMMUNIQUE

FROM: MONTGOMERY—COMMANDER, 21ST ARMY GROUP

DATE-TIME OF ORIGIN 19 AUG 44 2130 HRS

TO: EISENHOWER—SUPREME COMMANDER, SHAEF

COPY (FOR INFO): BRADLEY—12TH ARMY GROUP; HODGES—US 1ST ARMY; PATTON—US 3RD ARMY; DEMPSEY—2ND BRITISH ARMY; CRERAR—1ST CANADIAN ARMY; CONINGHAM—RAF 2ND TAF; QUESADA—IX TAC; WEYLAND—XIX TAC; BRERETON—9TH AIR FORCE

I AM PLEASED YOU HAVE SELECTED ME TO RECEIVE THE SURRENDER OF THE GERMAN FORCES NOW SURROUNDED IN THE FALAISE-ARGENTAN POCKET. THIS IS ONLY FITTING, SINCE IT IS UNITS UNDER MY COMMAND THAT HAVE FOUGHT OUR ENEMY TO A STANDSTILL AND BROUGHT THIS EXODUS TO A STOP.

BE ADVISED THIS SURRENDER WILL TAKE PLACE TOMORROW, 20 AUG 44, 0730 HRS, IN THE VILLAGE OF HORDOUSEAUX.

BE FURTHER ADVISED THAT ALL POW COLLECTION RESPONSIBILITIES SHOULD REST WITH BRADLEY'S 12TH ARMY GROUP, AS THIS COMMAND WILL BE IMMEDIATELY ADVANCING TO SECURE THE VIMOUTIERS-LISIEUX HIGHWAY. THERE IS NO NEED TO REMIND YOU, I AM SURE, THAT SPEED IS OF THE ESSENCE IF WE ARE GOING TO PREVENT A FORMIDABLE GERMAN DEFENCE AT THE SEINE.

SIGNED,
MONTGOMERY

Chapter Forty-Seven

His staff had seen plenty of Patton's fits of rage, but this one was setting a new standard. He'd begun to boil over at the very first line of Montgomery's communique, and it was all downhill after that:

"That little son of a bitch. Ike *selected* him to receive the surrender? *Selected*? I'm not sure what's crazier, gentlemen…that the Limey procrastinator might actually believe it's true he was selected, or that Ike is so much more a kisser of British ass than we all realized—and it actually *is* true. *I* closed the Falaise Gap—me and my men did. Not some fucking little English clerk. And he can't be bothered collecting POWs because he's too busy rushing off to do battle with the Germans at the Seine? What balls, gentlemen…what balls. Bernard Law Montgomery has never *rushed off* anywhere in his life. He doesn't know how."

He stepped over to the map on the wall. "Where the hell is this *Hordouseaux*, anyway?"

When his G3 pointed the village out, Patton said, "Really? Monty himself couldn't possibly be that far south yet, unless he's playing point man for his whole fucking Army group. I've got a good mind to beat him there, just like at Messina."

"I'm not so sure about that, sir," the operations officer replied. "You'd either have to trust your security to Monty's forces or cause a major flap by having a unit of ours crossing army group boundaries. Again."

"I don't give a good goddamn what kind of flap I cause, Colonel. I will not let Montgomery claim honor and glory that rightfully belongs to my men…and those Polish troops of his he sacrificed on that hill."

"And we'd have to do it in the dark, too," the G3 added. "That could easily lead to confusion and friendly fire incidents. Hell, we might not even find the place. We don't know the roads north of here."

That seemed to take some of the wind out of Patton's sails. "I see your point, Colonel. But I don't like this. Not one little bit. And I won't forget about it, either. No matter how Ike tries to smooth over the fact that he's knelt down to his British pals once again."

★★★★

Dawn was still an hour away. The first *boules* were already coming out of the oven at the Vimoutiers bakery. Angelique's staff had baked them in the extra-large style the Germans demanded; the domed, round loaves were each big enough to feed a dozen men. They were also big enough to bisect through their circumference, hollow out, and place *plastique* explosive inside.

As Dominique went looking for the German mess sergeant, Sylvie and Eva rigged the bread bombs for *Opération Pain Chaude*—Operation Hot Bread in English—in the corner of the bakery behind the storage shelves. "Ten pounds of *plastique*, a dozen timers, each with a small battery, and four cartons of nails," Sylvie said as she inventoried the crate Pierre had delivered in the dead of night. "These bombs should clean out the *Boche* headquarters mess at Champosoult very nicely."

Eva checked the clock on the wall. "We need to hurry, Sylvie. If the van arrives late, the mess may be empty."

"Don't rush me while I'm wiring explosives, Eva. We've got plenty of time."

"Speaking of time," Eva said, "are you sure it's a good idea to set the timers to just a few minutes and wait until we're almost there to start them running?"

"Yes, I'm very sure. If we got delayed on the road for any reason, we'd have to rip the *boules* open and set the timers all over again. Then we'd have to paste them back together again, and there wouldn't be enough time for it to dry. The tops could fall off the loaves as we're pushing the cart inside the headquarters, and the whole world would see our handiwork…and we'd be dead. You remember how rough the walkways are there?"

"I suppose you're right. But that means you'll have to ride in the back with the bread."

Sylvie smiled. "That would be wonderful. I'm feeling very hungry this morning. I can munch on bread while I twist together these little wires sticking out of the *boules*."

"Actually, what would be wonderful is if your American boyfriend and his pilot buddies just bombed the fucking place. Then we wouldn't have to be doing this at all."

"I'm sure the people of Champosoult don't agree, Eva. Bombs don't seem to be very discriminating who they kill."

Angelique tiptoed into the space behind the shelves, checking nervously over her shoulder. "I don't know where Dominique or the *Boche* sergeant are. I'm very nervous about the other women, too. They're growing suspicious—I hear them whispering you're up to something."

Sylvie replied, "Of course they are. That's why once the van has left for Champosoult, you're all going to vanish and not come back until the Americans are here. It should only be a matter of a few days."

"But that will make them all the more suspicious."

Sylvie pulled a fat envelope from the crate, stuffed full of 10-franc notes. "Here," she said as she placed the money in Angelique's hands. "The amount we agreed to is all there, with our thanks. Spread the rest around among the ladies. That should keep them quiet."

Angelique replied, "You think of everything, don't you?"

"Let's hope so."

It hadn't taken much for Dominique to lure the old mess sergeant to the basement. A quick flash of breast and a beckoning finger had him flying down the steps. But he posed a bigger challenge than she'd imagined; his resistance to the choral hydrate—*knockout drops*—she'd slipped into the bottle of schnapps seemed extraordinary.

There was enough in there to put a horse to sleep! He must've eaten an enormous breakfast, and that's delaying the process. Maybe that will help him sleep longer once the drug takes effect.

Worse, he kept offering her the bottle. To forestall taking that drink, she'd sat him in a chair and begun dancing a seductive striptease around him, humming the music she'd heard spilling from the cabarets of *Quartier Pigalle* in Paris for musical accompaniment. It would take considerable skill—and a bit of luck—to avoid ending up naked in short order, since her simple work uniform consisted of very few garments, with no garters, jewelry save her wedding ring, or other accessories to dawdle over as a true *folies* girl would. She labored to come up with lengthy, theatrical ways to drag out the shedding of head scarf, shoes, and socks. Each of the nine buttons down the front of her dress was worth several verses of a tune before it managed to become undone.

But good entertainment is infectious. Eventually the sergeant was humming along, sloppily out of tune like a drunk, as he drifted ever so slowly into unconsciousness. She breathed a sigh of relief when, down to just her panties, his head finally slumped forward against his chest. In seconds, she put her clothes back on and was bounding up the stairs, leaving the sergeant to his slumber.

When Dominique finally rejoined Sylvie and Eva, they were nearly finished loading the bread—most of the *boules* edible, but 12 deadly—into the delivery van. "We thought we'd have to come rescue you," Sylvie said. "You didn't have to...?" Her eyes widened as her voice tapered off, leaving the unfinished question hanging in the air.

Dominique asked, "Do you mean fuck him or kill him?"

"Either one."

"No, *neither* one," Dominique replied. "It just seemed to take forever for him to pass out. But he should sleep soundly enough for everyone in this place to be long gone by the time he wakes. Are we ready to go?"

"Yes," Sylvie replied. "Ride in the back with me and watch for planes out the rear windows."

★★★★

The guard roused Tommy Moon and John Peterson from sleep earlier than usual. There was an officer with him this morning, a Wehrmacht *leutnant*, who informed the American captives they would be transported to camps in Germany immediately after the morning ration. Peterson's destination would be an *oflag*, where ground forces officers were held. Tommy, as a flyer, was being sent to a *stalag luft*.

The morning ration was the usual offering: a slab of round bread—*quite fresh and delicious, actually*—washed down with horrible ersatz coffee that tasted like it was brewed from the sweepings off a workshop floor. Perhaps as a going-away present, there was a special treat: each man received an apple. "Good for your teeth," the *leutnant* said as he climbed the stairs. "Have a pleasant journey." The door at the top of the stairs slammed closed behind him.

They hadn't finished wolfing down their food when a rapid series of explosions from the floor above knocked them to the floor and instantly filled the cellar with a thick cloud of dust. One final blast splintered the door at the top of the stairs and propelled the *leutnant* down into the cellar. His body lay motionless on the floor like a charred and broken toy soldier. If the blast hadn't already killed him, the plummet certainly had. Through the doorway above, the morning sun blazed down like a beacon.

Tommy and Peterson looked at each other in amazement. "What do you think?" Tommy asked. "Sign from God?"

"Only one way to find out."

They climbed the stairs. When they stepped out into the sunlight at the top, they saw the entire front wall of the building was blown out. The only Germans inside were lying dead in the debris.

Peterson asked, "I say we make a break for it. You with me?"

"Absolutely," Tommy replied. "Let's go."

When they got to the rubble-strewn street, the only Germans they saw were a few soldiers, dazed and bloody from the blast, who didn't seem to notice the Americans stealing away right before their eyes.
"We've got to go southwest," Tommy said. "That should be the most direct route back to our lines. They couldn't be more than a couple of miles away unless something went really *fubar* during the night. C'mon…let's cut down this alley."

They'd barely made the turn when the strangest contraption on four wheels they'd ever seen came barreling down on them. It was a boxy delivery van, at one time conventionally powered by gasoline, no doubt, but its nose had been extensively modified. Mounted alongside the engine bonnet were two cylinders, one much taller and wider than the other, resembling upright boilers with a maze of interconnecting plumbing. All together, it made the van look like a locomotive.

If they hadn't jumped aside quickly, it would have run over them.

They expected to see German soldiers in the cab. Instead, there were two women, one behind the wheel, the other looking at them with a startled look of recognition. She screamed something to the driver, and the ungainly vehicle rattled to a halt.

"TOMMY," Sylvie cried as she jumped from the cab to the ground. There was no time for a kiss, an embrace, or questions. She swung open the van's rear doors and said, "Get in. Hurry!"

They scuttled into the back of the van, joining another woman who seemed even more surprised than Sylvie had been when first laying eyes on the Americans. "We'll talk once we're clear of here, Tommy," she said. Then, switching to French, she told Dominique, "This is a total surprise, but they can be trusted." Sylvie slammed the doors closed. In a few seconds, the van was moving again.

Speaking French, Tommy introduced himself and Peterson to Dominique. He explained to her how they'd come to be prisoners at the German headquarters. She explained how they'd just blown up the place.

"Holy shit," Tommy said. "You blew the Krauts to kingdom come with *bread*?"

"*Pain Chaude*," she replied, with the coy wink of an eye. "*Hot* bread. We had no idea we'd be freeing *Ami* prisoners as well." Then she explained what her job was now: to be the rear lookout for the American aircraft that tended to strafe anything that moved on French roads. He didn't miss her sneer at the pilot wings on his jacket as she said it.

Speaking little French, Peterson was getting more confused by the minute. "Am I getting this right? You mean *they're* the ones who blew the place up? And where the hell are they taking us?"

"Hang on, John. I was just about to ask that."

They were both thrilled by her answer: "We're going to the American lines."

"Great," Peterson said. "Why walk when you can ride?"

They were well clear of the town when the van came to a halt on the narrow road. The rear doors flew open again as Sylvie climbed in. "Switch with me," she said to Dominique, "so I can talk with our American friends."

With a shrewd smile, Dominique pointed to Peterson and asked, "Would you like me to take him, too, so you and your pilot can be alone?"

"Don't be such a pain in my ass," Sylvie replied. "We're not in the clear yet. Get up front with Eva and be her lookout."

"*Mais oui, mon général*," Dominique said, and even Peterson understood enough to catch the snarkiness in her compliance. They heard the cab door slam, and then they were moving again.

"Your arm…is it broken?" Sylvie asked.

"Yeah, I think so."

"Does it hurt very much?"

"Only when I laugh…or move…or breathe."

"Well," she said, "the important thing is you'll be safe soon. We'll all be safe soon."

Peterson chimed in, "I sure hope you're right about that."

"You know, Tommy," she said, "I was just thinking how coincidental this all is."

"Coincidental? What do you mean?"

"When I was being held prisoner by the Gestapo in Gacé, your bomb rescued me without you even realizing you were doing it. Now, I've returned the favor…in exactly the same manner. That's a coincidence, isn't it?"

The van gave a shudder and began to slow down.

"Something wrong?" Tommy asked. "This thing runs on wood gas, right?"

"Yes, and we may be pushing its fuel supply a bit too much. This van only gets about thirty kilometers to a tank…and that's about how far we've driven since we last stoked the gas generator. It would be so much easier if we just had some petrol."

The van lurched a few times as its engine sputtered. Then it fell silent, and they rolled to an unceremonious stop in the middle of the road.

"*Merde*," Sylvie said, "I guess we'll be walking after all."

"And we'd better walk pretty damn fast, too," Peterson said, his face drawn, his voice agitated. "We've got some jugs circling overhead like vultures." He jumped out and ran to the cab to warn Eva and Dominique. Soon all five of them were on the run, looking to put as much distance between themselves and the van as possible.

With the pain of his broken arm, Tommy found it impossible to keep up. He dropped to his knees, hoping the blinding pain would subside just enough to let him continue. But he knew he was still much too close to the van—and he could hear the rasp of a jug's prop as it began its attack dive.

"NO! KEEP GOING," Tommy called to the three women as they raced back to him. "DON'T WAIT FOR ME."

They didn't listen. "Sorry, Tommy," Sylvie said, "if it's going to hurt either way, let it be this way."

The women picked him up and started jogging toward Peterson, who was watching them, stationary and dumbstruck. “You could help, you know,” Sylvie told him as they passed.

He knew he *should* be helping. The three women never stopped running with their wounded cargo.

But the jug was *so* close. The roar of her engine blotted out everything but the instinct to survive. Peterson threw himself on the ground, hoping any rock, any blade of grass might save him.

And then .50-caliber bullets ripped their world to shreds.

★★★★

At 0725, the German staff car pulled into the cobblestoned village square of Hordouseaux, white flags of truce flying from its front fenders. When it rolled to a stop, the ranking general of the vanquished German forces, *General der Panzertruppe* Heinrich Eberbach, climbed from its back seat. He found no Allied officer waiting to take his surrender.

“We are five minutes early,” the general fumed to the aide standing beside him. “You would think they’d be just as eager as we are to get this business over with as soon as possible.”

“*Jawohl, Herr General*,” his aide replied. “One would think.”

But they had to wait four more minutes until a small convoy of light armored vehicles rolled into the square, forming a cordon around his staff car. They were obviously British. General Eberbach was expecting Yanks.

An American jeep with British markings rolled into the square and came to a stop nose to nose with the

German vehicle. A slight, wiry man stepped from its passenger's seat. Eberbach had seen enough pictures to instantly recognize him as Bernard Law Montgomery.

"What is your name and title?" Montgomery asked.

"I am Eberbach, commander of *Panzer Group Eberbach*, representing all forces currently contained in the Falaise-Argentan encirclement."

"Very well, I am—"

"I know who you are," the German interrupted, and then turned to his aide and said, loud enough for everyone in the square to hear, "I will not surrender to this *spectator*."

Switching to German, he told his aide, "Tell this man I will only tender our surrender to a man who actually defeated us."

Chapter Forty-Eight

Lieutenant General Walter "Beetle" Smith, Eisenhower's chief of staff, found the situation in SHAEF's London headquarters that morning quite frustrating: *Things around here weren't this screwed up when disasters were going on. Now we've got a victory on our hands, and we're all running around like chickens without heads.*

Yelling into the telephone carrying his call to General Bradley in France, Smith said, "We can't *order* a German general to surrender to Montgomery, Brad. If he wants an American, we'll give him an American. Who's closest—you, Hodges, or Patton?"

"None of us," Bradley replied. "The only American general in the area is John Wood, Fourth Armored commander."

"No good," Smith said. "Only two stars. This Eberbach guy is equivalent to three, right?"

"That's what I understand, Beetle. But Monty's got four and he wouldn't surrender to him."

"A different kettle of fish entirely, Brad. Monty could have ten stars and it wouldn't make any difference now. Let's not fuck up something as momentous as this by insulting this Kraut twice in the same day. It's got to be you, Hodges, or Patton—and it's got to be quick."

There was silence on the line for a few long moments, so long that Smith thought the connection might have been broken. "Brad, are you still there?"

"Yes, I'm still here, Beetle. My people are checking the latest command post reports."

"Come on, Brad, we don't have all fucking day. Ike's breathing down my neck. Who's going to take this surrender?"

Bradley sighed, loud enough to be heard through the telephone line. Then he said, "If we need it done fast, we'd better give it to Georgie."

Bradley's instincts were correct: Patton had hit the road as soon as he caught wind of Montgomery's humiliation. He was only a few miles from Hordouseaux when Bradley's call was patched to his jeep's radio directing him to take Eberbach's surrender. It put a smile on his face that lasted all the way to the village outskirts. Now it was time to get serious. A major event in history was about to take place in this village, and no one felt more entitled to play the starring role in that event than George Patton.

I took the gamble, when everyone else was cowering in caution, held back by imaginary lines. Don't those fools know that good things never come to those who wait?

I risked everything...

And now my brave men and I will be forever known as the ones who brought down that paper-hanging son of a bitch Hitler once and for all.

He found Heinrich Eberbach waiting in the tiny café on the village square. The German rose and offered a slight bow as he asked, "Ah, you are Patton, are you not?"

"Yes, General, I am. Am I correct that it's *general* and not *field marshal*?"

With an amused smile, the German replied, "Are you referring to Paulus at Stalingrad, General?"

"Yes, I am. We understood it was Hitler's standard procedure to promote a general who was about to surrender."

"Apparently, *Der Führer* is no longer enamored with the practice, since it didn't yield the desired result at Stalingrad. You understand the point of such a promotion, don't you, General?"

Patton understood fully: *No German field marshal had ever surrendered, so in Hitler's mind, promoting a general intent on surrendering to field marshal was a mandate for that man to commit suicide.*

There was no point saying that out loud, though. Instead, he said, "I understand, General. Completely."

"Good," Eberbach replied. "Then let me make it clear: this surrender will feature no promotion. And no suicide."

Patton looked around the establishment and asked, "Has Montgomery decided not to join us?"

A British major replied, "No, sir, the general has other business to attend to." Placing a document of several pages on the table, he added, "These have been left for you."

"What a pity he can't be here," Patton replied, a smirk on his face as he riffled through the pages. "But we've never gotten his help before. We certainly don't need it now. Would you like to look these papers over before you sign, General Eberbach?"

"No need. I've had ample time to read them pending your arrival. But before I sign, I must remind you, General Patton, that the document indicates my men will be afforded the full protection of prisoners of war as provided by the Geneva Convention. The barbaric reprisals your troops and airmen have been committing against my men are to cease immediately."

Patton's face hardened into a narrow-eyed glare. "What *reprisals* are you referring to, General?"

"I refer to the wanton slaughter you've been inflicting on troops that are no longer a threat to you. Again, I use the term *barbaric* to describe the Allied behavior."

Patton leaned back in his chair and shook his head. "General, I can assure you that surrendering troops have been treated with all due military courtesy and will continue to be treated as such. I further assure you that troops who resist, however—and there have been vast numbers of them right up to this moment, based on my casualty reports—will be neutralized by all means possible."

"And I can assure you, General Patton, that all troops within the encirclement have ceased resistance. The troops to the east, however, beyond the encirclement, are not under my control and are not surrendering. You do understand this, do you not?"

"Yes, General, I do. But I'm sure once your surrender is complete, the capitulation of the remaining elements of Germany's forces will follow in short order. There will simply be too few of you left to stop us from celebrating Christmas in Berlin."

Now it was Eberbach doing the head-shaking. "Talk like that is delusional coming from a general who has not yet reached Paris, let alone Berlin. I must be sure you understand the scope of this surrender document before I sign."

“Oh, I understand fully, General. But allow me to remain convinced your signing marks the imminent end to this war.”

Eberbach laughed dismissively as he put pen to paper. “I suppose, General Patton, that will depend on your definition of *imminent*.”

Chapter Forty-Nine

I need this place like I need a hole in the head. All I've got is a broken arm and the holes left by a bunch of wood splinters the size of pencils in my ass. But that damn doc won't release me...got to hold me a few days more to make sure there's no infection. Hell, aren't the three days I've already been here enough for that?

Haven't slept much in all that time, either. Maybe that's why I'm getting so cranky. Can't sit down or lie on my back because my ass hurts. Can't lie on my stomach or my side because of this damn cast on my arm. So I'm wandering around this hospital like some sort of zombie. Sure, I can't fly for a while—not with one arm, anyway. But there must be some way I can be of use back at the squadron.

Half the GIs in this place aren't even wounded...they've got VD. "Whores de combat," the nurses call them. With smirking delight, I might add.

Speaking of nurses, here comes one now. She looks all cranked up about something, too. Probably just can't wait to tell me I've wandered out of bounds again.

Nearly breathless from running, the nurse said, "Lieutenant Moon, there's someone back at the ward waiting to see you."

Who the hell could it be this time? Another personnel officer, trying to figure out if I actually qualified as a POW or not?

But the nurse shook her head when he asked. Then she replied, "No, Lieutenant. It's another patient. He says he's your brother."

There was no pain that could keep him from running back to his ward. Sure enough, Sean was parked next to his bed in a wheelchair, thumbing through the months-old copy of *Life* magazine that had been Tommy's only reading material the past three days.

When his brother rushed in, Sean smiled as best he could with a head swathed in bandages and said, "So what's all this shit about you kicking my ass all the way back to Canarsie?"

Despite the hindrance of their wounds, they managed some semblance of an embrace. That done, Sean said, "Have a seat, little brother. Let's talk a while."

"Mind if I stand?" He explained about the splinters in his ass and how they'd gotten there.

"You got strafed by your own guys, Half?"

"Some jug outfit did it, that's for sure."

"Maybe we've got something in common then, little brother."

If it hadn't been for Colonel Pruitt's visit yesterday, Tommy might have died a little right then and there. But what Pruitt had told him left no doubt he wasn't the one who'd nearly killed his brother.

Sean told his story, or at least as much as he could remember. When he got to the part of watching the bomb coming down, he said, "It got like slow motion, you know? And then…well, you remember being in the movies when the film gets jammed? It got kinda like that—like watching that real bright light burn that film up from the inside out, real quick. I don't remember nothing after that. I come to find out my *Zippo* got flipped upside down."

As his eyes began to glaze with tears, he continued, "Two of my guys bought it—my driver and bow gunner. The rest of us up in the turret got our brains beat in bouncing around inside." After a deep sigh, he added, "Hey, at least we didn't fucking burn."

Tommy let his brother compose himself before asking, "You think it was a jug that hit you?"

"Half, I ain't fucking sure of nothing. Maybe it was a Kraut. I don't know. But it wasn't you, right?"

Tommy took the copy of the after-action report Colonel Pruitt had given him from under his pillow. Like the piece of evidence that sets the defendant free, he held it up for his brother to see. "I got it in writing, Sean. It wasn't me."

"Well, ain't that good news?" Sean replied. "And those French skirts…they're all right?"

"Yeah. They got a little scratched up, but nothing serious. I was glad to see the Army treated them like the heroines they are. Gave them a limo ride back to Alençon and everything."

"Great," Sean said, "but I still feel kinda bad about that Lieutenant Peterson, the way he got left out on a limb that night. But hey…it wasn't my call. At least he's all right. Too damn bad about the rest of his company, though."

"Yeah, he feels the same way, believe me."

Sean leaned closer to read the writing on Tommy's cast. It seemed every nurse in the ward had signed it. But standing out prominently was a message in French. It was signed, simply, *Sylvie*.

"What'd she write, Half?"

"It says *you're a real swell guy and I wish you luck*."

"Bullshit. That ain't it. Tell me what it really means."

"Nope."

"C'mon, you little asshole. Tell me."

"That's *lieutenant asshole* to you, Sergeant. And the answer's still *nope*."

"Okay, suit yourself, *sir*. But it ain't gonna matter a rat's ass because this is all gonna be over before you know it. It's just a matter of time, Half. Just a matter of fucking time."

When Tommy had first heard his brother speak those words two weeks ago—*Has it really only been two weeks? It feels like a lifetime*—they'd sounded like a death sentence.

"It's good to hear you say it like that, Sean."

"Damn straight," Sean replied. "This war's as good as over, Tommy. Everybody knows it."

Chapter Fifty

10, Downing Street,
Whitehall.

August 25, 1944

<u>MOST SECRET</u>

My Dear General Eisenhower,

I was aghast to learn that word of Montgomery's promotion had somehow come to be known to the press before I was able to inform you personally. We in His Majesty's service fully understand the rumours and suppositions which could come to life if such information was not dispensed within the proper protocols. Unfortunately, and as you are well aware, those rumours and suppositions have indeed come to life with a tenor and ferocity that have astounded even those of us accustomed to being under the scrutiny of the fourth estate every second of our lives. For this accidental but inexcusable breach, I offer my most sincere apologies.

Please read nothing into the fact that Montgomery, now a field marshal, technically outranks you. I can assure you that I, as well as every last man in His Majesty's government, continue to look to you as the Supreme Commander of our allied effort in Western Europe, just as we always have. Montgomery remains your superbly experienced subordinate in all matters tactical and strategic. He understands his position completely, as I know you do yours. He looks forward to providing his wise counsel in the same manner you have always enjoyed.

The decision to promote did not come easily, I can assure you. But I beg you to remember you are not the only one expected to perform a delicate ballet to keep all aspects of the Allied effort moving forward in concert. You must understand the position I am in as the elected leader of the British people, who have suffered far greater hardships in this conflict than our American cousins across the sea, and for far longer. For the sake of morale, they need to be reassured from time to time that all is going according to plan, effort is being rewarded, and the end of this terrible ordeal is in sight. Would it not be unfair to deny them some token of this final victory, inevitable but not quite upon us yet, which we all so desperately crave? That token is what we have provided with Montgomery's promotion. As to the ravings of the press as to what it all actually means to the running of the war, I will do everything in my power, as will every member of His Majesty's government, to keep speculation in check and expectations realistic.

Of course, it is the nature of things that none of this will happen overnight, so I beg you, dear Eisenhower, to face this unfortunate episode with the wisdom, patience, and fortitude you have never failed to show in the past.

With an undying commitment to our collaboration, I remain,

Winston S. Churchill

****

Kay Summersby couldn't pretend to be asleep any longer. The American general in bed beside her—*the* American general in the war for Europe—was so agitated by what he was reading their entire bed seemed to be trembling. When the aide had delivered the envelope to the cottage on the Thames late that evening, she had hoped the general wouldn't bother to open it until morning. But she knew better. He'd promptly switched on the reading light clamped to the bed's headboard and unfolded what looked like a typewritten letter.

Now that he'd read it, over and over again, she knew that whatever it said, it wouldn't do a bloody thing to calm the tensions that had gripped SHAEF Headquarters since the *Daily Mail's* morning delivery.

"What bullshit," Eisenhower said, addressing not her but the author of the letter in his hand. "You actually had the balls to write, *Somehow come to be known to the press. Somehow,* my ass. That was no accident. You deliberately leaked it."

She was sure his blood pressure must be through the roof. Pretty dangerous for a man who hadn't had a normal reading in months. Even with his head in shadow, she could see the blood vessels at his temple pulsing their rapid cadence. Gently, she touched his shoulder and asked, "Maybe I should call for the doctor, Dwight?"

He snarled his reply: "That's the last person I need to see right now, Kay."

She hated this position, the one she'd been thrust into all too often: the *de facto* shield between the *Supreme Commander* and a stroke.

But it's all part of the job, she supposed, *right in there with driver, secretary, confidante, companion...*

"You know, Dwight, maybe this is a good thing. Now they'll have to promote you, too."

"You know that's impossible. There's no general rank above four-star in the US Army. This is just the clever little British way of pissing in my face all over again."

"Then maybe your army should create such a rank."

"That's not the point, Kay. Bad enough I have to put up with that pompous little ass Monty, but your Prime Minister is a duplicitous son of a bitch."

That made Kay Summersby laugh. "Darling, all you brass hats are sons of bitches. That's how you came to be brass hats in the first place, isn't it?"

Whether it was the Irish lilt of her laughter or the words she'd spoken, it didn't matter. The desired effect was achieved. She could feel the tension drain from his body.

"You're probably right…on both counts," he said. "Maybe this is just the incentive the War Department needs to slip a five-star authorization bill through Congress. We can't have our allies one-upping us now, can we?"

"Now you're talking, Dwight. With clever thinking like that, you might want to consider going into politics when this is all over."

Chapter Fifty-One

The atmosphere in the Paris café was surprisingly subdued, considering it was full of GIs on leave and a week before Christmas 1944. Each man's disappointment centered on one shattered dream: the holidays were here, but they were in Paris. Not Berlin like their leaders had promised. Not Chicago or Wichita or Boston, either—or any other place a GI might call home.

And the war was nowhere near over. Four months after crushing the Germans in the Falaise pocket, no Allied army had so much as a toe-hold across the Rhine.

Tommy and Sean Moon shared a table in a dark corner of the café, nursing the bottle of whiskey between them. It was Sean who finally broke the dispirited silence.

"What the hell happened, Tommy? We had it knocked…and our generals threw it all away."

"You're preaching to the choir, Sean."

"Yeah, I know. But it just pisses me off so damn much. After we sewed up *The Gap* at Hill Two-Six-Two, we could've pushed them right back across the Rhine…"

"Easy does it, Sean. We had to push them across a bunch of other rivers first."

"But you and I were *there*, Tommy. We both saw it. You up high, me down low. The Krauts were ready to throw in the towel. And we let them get back on their feet."

"*There*? What do you mean by *there*? I was shot down and a prisoner *there*. And you, well—"

"Hey, I did my fucking job. Not one of them Kraut bastards got past me. Not then, not ever."

Tommy raised his whiskey in a toast. "All right, then—to my brother, and a job well done."

They clinked glasses and drank them dry.

Sean wasn't finished spewing his displeasure, though. "But really, Half, ever since—when we should have been steamrolling straight to Berlin—we've been fucking up left and right. Up north, that stupid Montgomery tries to push a bunch of divisions up *one fucking road* in Holland, gets a lot of guys killed to accomplish exactly nothing. *One fucking road* for a column thousands of vehicles long—and this guy's supposed to be some kind of tactical genius? Any fucking traffic cop in Brooklyn could tell you that was never going to work. In the middle, First Army got tired of looting and catching *the clap* in France, so now they're doing the same damn shit in Belgium and Luxembourg."

"And what about Patton?" Tommy asked. "That obsession with taking Metz didn't make any sense. Why were we wasting time attacking old forts like it was the Middle Ages? He got a lot of GIs killed for nothing."

"Now *you're* preaching to the choir, brother," Sean replied. "So here we sit, still in France, almost out of gasoline again and freezing our asses off without proper winter uniforms."

"And no Christmas presents from home, either," Tommy added, "since the brass figured we wouldn't still be here come Christmas."

"I coulda really used those socks Mom sends me, too," Sean said.

"You get socks? You lucky son of a bitch! Hell, all I get are books. And soap."

Sean laughed. "I guess she knows her boys pretty well then, eh?"

The waiter brought another bottle.

As Sean poured, he said, "But you know, Half, I ain't understanding why the hell you're still here. Ain't it a rule that an escaped POW pilot gets shipped home?"

"Not home, Sean. He gets shipped to the Pacific. Or at least he used to, because he supposedly knew too much about the *maquis* who helped him escape, and if he got shot down again and broke under interrogation, that knowledge could put them in danger."

"So? Ain't that exactly what happened to you? You were a POW, your *maquis* girlfriend saved your ass, right?"

"True, but the *maquis* is pretty much out of business now, so by the time my arm was healed and my paperwork got to the adjutant general's desk, there wasn't much reason to ship guys like me out anymore. Most of the *maquis* men are in the French Army now, and the women, well…they just went home. Besides, I was never technically declared a POW."

"Speaking of the women, Half, when is Sylvie supposed to show up, anyway?"

"Later tonight."

"She ain't riding her bicycle all the way from Alençon, is she?"

"No, she's coming on a bus, I think."

"And you're gonna make that long trip worth her while, right?"

"Hope so. Got a cozy little garret reserved at the hotel. Cost me a bundle."

"You pay for it one way or another, brother. But you're an officer. You can afford it."

There was a commotion by the door. Several MPs entered the café, a lieutenant in the lead.

"ALL PERSONNEL ARE ORDERED TO RETURN TO THEIR UNITS AT ONCE," the lieutenant said. "ALL LEAVES ARE HEREBY CANCELED, BY ORDER OF SUPREME COMMANDER, SHAEF. PROCEED TO YOUR DESIGNATED TRANSPORT POINT IMMEDIATELY."

A voice called out from the throng, "What happens if we don't, Lieutenant?"

"THEN YOU'LL BE ROUNDED UP AND CHARGED WITH DESERTION IN THE FACE OF THE ENEMY."

Desertion in the face of the enemy: a guilty verdict could get you a firing squad.

Sean walked up to one of the enlisted MPs and asked, "What the hell's going on, buddy?"

"Krauts got a breakthrough going on in the Ardennes Forest, Sarge," the MP drawled. "I hear tell they just about wiped out the Twenty-Eight Division, and there ain't no stopping them, neither."

Tommy was already standing on unsteady legs when Sean returned to the table. "I got to stop by the hotel," he said, "and leave a note for Sylvie."

"I'm real sorry this little *rendezvous* is all going to shit for you, brother."

"Not as sorry as I am, Sean."

They tried to shake hands, but halfway through that awkward gesture, it collapsed into a long hug as they sought refuge—even just for a moment—from the torrent of emotions neither of them could verbally express.

As they broke apart, Tommy offered the words that had always been Sean's to say, at first as a somber *fait accompli* and later as a triumphant certainty. Now those words would be only a wish for a brighter tomorrow, where joyful plans could be made and kept, where the odds this wasn't your last goodbye would be a bet anyone would take:

"Just a matter of time, Sean," Tommy said. "Just a matter of time."

* * *

More Novels by William Peter Grasso

Operation Fishwrapper
Book 5
Jock Miles WW2 Adventure Series

June 1944: A recon flight is shot down over the Japanese-held island of Biak, soon to be the next jump in MacArthur's leapfrogging across New Guinea. Major Jock Miles, US Army—the crashed plane's intelligence officer—must lead the handful of survivors to safety. It's a tall order for a man barely recovered from a near-crippling leg wound. Gaining the grudging help of a Dutch planter who has evaded the Japanese since the war began, Jock discovers just how little MacArthur's staff knows about the terrain and defenses of the island they're about to invade.

The American invasion of Biak promptly bogs down, and the GIs rename the debacle *Operation Fishwrapper*, a joking reference to their worthless maps. The infantry battalion Jock once led quickly suffers the back-to-back deaths of two commanders, so he steps into the job once again, ignoring the growing difficulties with his leg. When his Aussie wife Jillian tracks down the refugee mapmaker who can refine those *fishwrappers* into something of military value, the tide of battle finally turns in favor of the Americans. But for Jock, the victory imparts a life-changing blow.

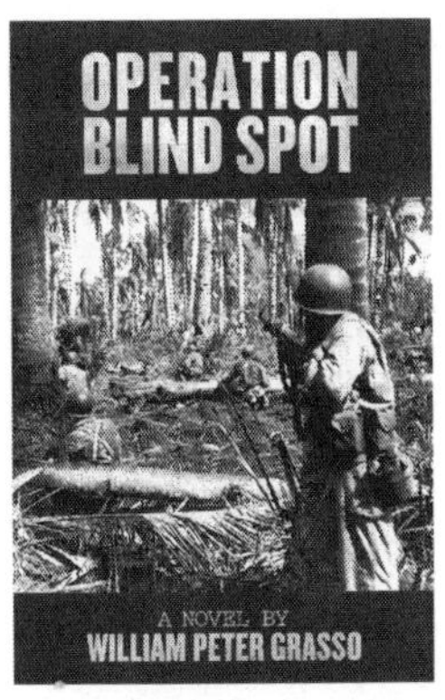

Operation Blind Spot
Book 4
Jock Miles WW2 Adventure Series

After surviving a deadly plane crash, Jock Miles is handed a new mission: neutralize a mountaintop observation post on Japanese-held Manus Island so MacArthur's invasion fleet en route to Hollandia, New Guinea, can arrive undetected. Jock's team seizes and holds the observation post with the help of a clever deception. But when they learn of a POW camp deep in the island's treacherous jungle, it opens old wounds for Jock and his men: the disappearance—and presumed death—of Jillian Forbes at Buna a year before. There's only one risky way to find out if she's a prisoner there…and doing so puts their entire mission in serious jeopardy.

Operation Easy Street
Book 3
Jock Miles WW2 Adventure Series

Port Moresby was bad. Buna was worse.

The WW2 alternative history adventure of Jock Miles continues as MacArthur orders American and Australian forces to seize Buna in Papua New Guinea. Once again, the Allied high command underestimates the Japanese defenders, plunging Jock and his men into a battle they're not equipped to win. Worse, jungle diseases, treacherous terrain, and the tactical fantasies of deluded generals become adversaries every bit as deadly as the Japanese. Sick, exhausted, and outgunned, Jock's battalion is ordered to spearhead an amphibious assault against the well-entrenched enemy. It's a suicide mission—but with ingenious help from an unexpected source, there might be a way to avoid the certain slaughter and take Buna. For Jock, though, victory comes at a dreadful price.

Operation Long Jump
Book 2
Jock Miles WW2 Adventure Series

Alternative history takes center stage as Operation Long Jump, the second book in the Jock Miles World War 2 adventure series, plunges us into the horrors of combat in the rainforests of Papua New Guinea. As a prelude to the Allied invasion, Jock Miles and his men seize the Japanese observation post on the mountain overlooking Port Moresby. The main invasion that follows quickly degenerates to a bloody stalemate, as the inexperienced, demoralized, and poorly led GIs struggle against the stubborn enemy.

Seeking a way to crack the impenetrable Japanese defenses, infantry officer Jock finds himself in a new role— aerial observer. He's teamed with rookie pilot John Worth, in a prequel to his role as hero of Grasso's East Wind Returns. Together, they struggle to expose the Japanese defenses—while highly exposed themselves—in their slow and vulnerable spotter plane.

The enemy is not the only thing troubling Jock: his Australian lover, Jillian Forbes, has found a new and dangerous way to contribute to the war effort.

Long Walk to the Sun
Book 1
Jock Miles WW2 Adventure Series

In this alternate history adventure set in WW2's early days, a crippled US military struggles to defend vulnerable Australia against the unstoppable Japanese forces. When a Japanese regiment lands on Australia's desolate and undefended Cape York Peninsula, Jock Miles, a US Army captain disgraced despite heroic actions at Pearl Harbor, is ordered to locate the enemy's elusive command post.

Conceived in politics rather than sound tactics, the futile mission is a "show of faith" by the American war leaders meant to do little more than bolster their flagging Australian ally. For Jock Miles and the men of his patrol, it's a death sentence: their enemy is superior in men, material, firepower, and combat experience. Even if the Japanese don't kill them, the vast distances they must cover on foot in the treacherous natural realm of Cape York just might. When Jock joins forces with Jillian

Forbes, an indomitable woman with her own checkered past who refused to evacuate in the face of the Japanese threat, the dim prospects of the Allied war effort begin to brighten in surprising ways.

Unpunished

Congressman. Presidental candidate. Murderer. Leonard Pilcher is all of these things.

As an American pilot interned in Sweden during WWII, he kills one of his own crewmen and gets away with it. Two people have witnessed the murder—American airman Joe Gelardi and his secret Swedish lover, Pola Nilsson-MacLeish—but they cannot speak out without paying a devastating price. Tormented by their guilt and separated by a vast ocean after the war, Joe and Pola maintain the silence that haunts them both...until 1960, when Congressman Pilcher's campaign for his party's nomination for president gains momentum. As he dons the guise of war hero, one female reporter, anxious to break into the "boy's club" of TV news, fights to uncover the truth against the far-reaching power of the Pilcher family's wealth, power that can do any wrong it chooses—even kill—and remain unpunished. Just as the nomination seems within Pilcher's grasp, Pola reappears to enlist Joe's help in finally exposing Pilcher for the criminal he really is. As the passion of their wartime romance rekindles, they must struggle to bring Pilcher down before becoming his next victims.

East Wind Returns

A young but veteran photo recon pilot in WWII finds the fate of the greatest invasion in history--and the life of the nurse he loves--resting perilously on his shoulders.

“East Wind Returns” is a story of World War II set in July-November 1945 which explores a very different road to that conflict's historic conclusion. The American war leaders grapple with a crippling setback: Their secret atomic bomb does not work. The invasion of Japan seems the only option to bring the war to a close. When those leaders suppress intelligence of a Japanese atomic weapon poised against the invasion forces, it falls to photo reconnaissance pilot John Worth to find the Japanese device. Political intrigue is mixed with passionate romance and exciting aerial action--the terror of enemy fighters, anti-aircraft fire, mechanical malfunctions, deadly weather, and the Kamikaze. When shot down by friendly fire over southern Japan during the American invasion, Worth leads the desperate mission that seeks to deactivate the device.

17540605R00228

Printed in Great Britain
by Amazon